ELF KING

ELF KING

AN ELVEN ALLIANCE COMPANION COLLECTION

TARA GRAYCE

ELF KING

An Elven Alliance Companion Collection

Elven Alliance Book 9

Copyright © 2023 by Tara Grayce

Taragrayce.com

Published by Sword & Cross Publishing

Grand Rapids, MI

Cover Illustration by Sara Morello

www.deviantart.com/samo-art

Iron Heart artwork also by Sara Morello

Typography by Deranged Doctor Designs

Derangeddoctordesign.com

Map by Savannah Jezowski of Dragonpen Designs

Dragonpenpress.com

To God, my King and Father. Soli Deo Gloria

LCCN: 2023906662

ISBN: 978-1-943442-43-0

AUTHOR'S NOTE

Since this book covers hundreds of years, there are a lot of time skips. I soon realized I would need some kind of numbering system to keep track of everything, both for myself and for readers.

While I could have created a convention for in-story years (such as 1000 years after the fall of the Elven Empire), that is something usually seen in epic fantasy rather than light romantic fantasy. Besides, such a thing would just mean more math and confusion for all involved.

Instead, I simply labeled each scene by how it is related to *Fierce Heart*. For these characters, *Fierce Heart* is the pivotal moment when their world changes. To keep this even more simple, "Before *Fierce Heart*" is shortened to "BFH."

It might be slightly unrealistic, but most of the main events happen in increments of five or ten years. The math was easier. You're welcome.

Also, since this book deals with backstory, I'm stuck with the tragic deaths and heartache that I already wrote into the story. For that reason, this book has a slightly darker, sadder tone than the rest of the series. There is still a lot of hope. A lot of joy. But a lot more people die in this book rather than just get really, really hurt.

Fair warning: I didn't cry while writing the Elven Alliance series. Not even during *Death Wind* or *Troll Queen*. But I bawled while writing chapter ten of *Iron Heart*. Then I sobbed again while editing it. So you have been warned. Keep tissues and chocolate on hand for that chapter.

IRON HEART

CHAPTER
ONE

650 YEARS BFH

L eyleira clasped her hands demurely in front of her as she sat next to her father and mother across the table from King Illythor and his son Prince Ellarin. Several pieces of paper—the details of the arrangement, the statement of health provided by a healer after examining Leyleira, and the genealogy of her family —lay on the table between them as her father and King Illythor discussed the details with cold efficiency.

Why should they be anything but cold? There had been no warmth in any part of this process. Just logic.

Across the table, King Illythor's deep voice rang as he explained his demands. His hawkish nose was set in a hard face, framed by his golden hair and topped by the glittering crown he wore, an ornate one of silver leaves and set with both diamonds and emeralds, likely chosen to remind those sitting across from him that he was the elf king with all of the power and authority that came with that title.

Beside him, Prince Ellarin sat straight and tall in his seat with his long golden-blond hair flowing down his back. A much simpler circlet formed of silver branches and intertwining maple and oak leaves rested on his hair while his light blue tunic brought out the sky blue of his eyes. While his expression remained as blank as his father's, there was something softer about the set of his mouth and the light in his eyes.

Or perhaps she was imagining the look there, and this prince was as cold as his father. She had never spoken with him. She had seen him at a distance before now, of course. Her family was noble enough that they had traveled to Estyra before. Once or twice.

But they did not have the connections of many of the elven noble families, nor was her father on the king's council. Their home lay deep in the forests of Tarenhiel, and it was a long ride to Estyra. Not that any of them had a great longing to make the ride often. They preferred their quiet life in the solitude of their small treetop estate.

For that reason, her dacha did not have the power to refuse when he had received the official communication from the king, offering an arranged marriage between his son Prince Ellarin and Leyleira.

When the elf king made such an offer to a family like theirs, one did not say no.

Such arrangements were not unheard of, and they were becoming more common. The elves did not arrange marriages for alliances with other kingdoms, the way the human kingdoms often did, but the elves were not above making arrangements among themselves.

As surreptitiously as she could, Leyleira smoothed the deep burgundy of her dress, a color chosen to set off her black hair and dark eyes well. She forced herself to keep her chin raised in a regal posture, as befitted the future queen of Tarenhiel.

Across the table, Prince Ellarin's gaze came to rest on her, and she refused to look away. While she was willing to agree to an arranged marriage, she was not going to be a simpering, delicate flower to bend to his every demand and whim.

At least she could hold on to her dignity where she could, even if she was powerless to truly fight King Illythor's demands or Prince Ellarin's, if he should make them.

"This is all acceptable." King Illythor finished his perusal of the papers. He drew the official marriage agreement toward him and reached for his pen and ink. "I see no reason why we cannot sign now and begin planning the wedding."

A wedding that would take place only a week from now. It seemed that the king, now that he had decided that she was an acceptable match for his son, wanted to waste no time.

Her dacha shot her a glance, his eyes pained and searching. He would refuse King Illythor if she asked, no matter the consequences King Illythor could place on their family and the tiny town they oversaw.

Her happiness was too ephemeral a thing for which to risk her parents and their people.

She tipped her head in the slightest of nods. She was prepared to do her duty for her family and her kingdom. She was nearly two hundred years old. She did not have anyone else waiting for her back home who had claimed her heart. This marriage to the future king was a far better prospect than anything else she would receive.

If this arrangement was to be all cold logic, then that was what she would be. Logical.

Dacha faced the king once again. "We are in agreement and are prepared to sign."

As King Illythor reached for the pen, Prince Ellarin's hand shot out, stopping the king. "Before we sign, I would like to speak with Lady Leyleira privately."

"No." King Illythor glowered at the prince, the hard lines etching deeper into his face. "You will have plenty of time to speak with her once you are wed."

"Damasha, I will not sign until I have spoken with her." Prince Ellarin glared right back.

Leyleira worked to keep her expression blank. Something strange was going on. The king seemed overly insistent that they wed without so much as speaking to each other. And Prince Ellarin had called his father the far more formal *damasha* instead of the more common and intimate *dacha*. That spoke of tension between father and son.

King Illythor's jaw worked but he finally nodded.

Prince Ellarin pushed to his feet and turned to Leyleira. "Would you please grant me a few moments of your time, Lady Leyleira?"

He was polite, at least. And of course she wanted to know why the prince wanted to speak to her so badly before the official paperwork was signed—and why his father was so reluctant to let him.

Leyleira glided to her feet, all grace and dignity. "Of course, amir."

With the king staring after them with heavy disapproval tugging at his brows, Prince Ellarin opened the door for Leyleira, then shut it quietly after her once she stepped onto the porch. The prince offered her his arm, and she lightly rested her hand on it.

They did not speak as they strolled along the branches of the elven palace of Ellonahshinel. Servants halted and bowed as they passed. Likely, news of their betrothal would be all over Ellonahshinel—and Estyra—before the ink even dried on the official paperwork.

Finally, Prince Ellarin led the way to a gazebo set far onto a branch. Benches ran along either side of the space, padded with cushions to provide a comfortable place to read or talk or simply enjoy the birds and the trees. No benches blocked the railing at the far end, where the gazebo overlooked an open, empty stretch of the forest.

Prince Ellarin halted before the railing, dropped her arm, and gripped his hands behind his back. Something in him went even more stiff and controlled than before as he stared into the forest rather than at her.

Leyleira clasped her hands in front of her and waited, alternating between taking in the forest and studying this prince who would soon be her husband.

Prince Ellarin's shoulders rose and fell before he spoke in a level, almost detached tone. "I have been diagnosed with a degenerative disease. While my healer believes he can slow its progression, there is no cure, even with healing magic. Sooner or later, it will kill me."

Leyleira released a slow breath, absorbing that news. It explained so much. The king's rush to arrange a marriage. His insistence on having a healer examine Leyleira. The genealogy, which proved that not only had her family never intermarried with the royal family before, but they were also known for strong magic and a lack of hereditary diseases. Yes, their magic ran toward the common plant growing magic, but that was likely the only failing in her pedigree.

She had been carefully selected, much like breeding stock, for what genetics she would bring to the marriage and pass to the future heir.

Not only would she be expected to do her duty when

it came to producing the next heir of Tarenhiel, she would be expected to do it soon. There could be no delay, if the health of Prince Ellarin was uncertain. He was King Illythor's only child, and the king's only sibling had died long ago without ever having children.

Leyleira's tone came out as flat and logical as his. "I see."

This news was concerning, to be sure. But she would not let it discompose her. Of course King Illythor had some agenda in choosing her as his son's bride. In some ways, it helped, having the reason set in front of her so openly.

She would do her duty. She would marry the prince, bear his children, and that would be her life. She was not the type to get all emotional over such things. Perhaps a lack of emotion would be best, given the circumstances.

Prince Ellarin still did not look at her. He raised one of his hands in front of him, letting wisps of crackling blue magic play over his fingers. "My father might be disappointed with this diagnosis, but I still have the magic of the ancient kings that I can pass to my children. My magic is not nearly as strong as my uncle's was—something the healers now hypothesize is caused by this disease—but my father believes that failing can be corrected with the strong magic found in your family."

So he, too, was being considered as breeding stock for this match. Should she find that as comforting as she did? She probably should have been more disturbed by how coldly the king was arranging this, even when it came to his son.

But it was entirely logical. King Illythor had the future of the kingdom to consider. That was paramount. The happiness of his son was a distant second. And her happiness? Well, that did not even rate a drop of consideration.

Prince Ellarin closed his fist, snuffing out his magic. "I know what my father expects of me. Of us."

Marry and produce an heir as soon as possible to ensure that the elven royal line would not die out with Prince Ellarin.

Leyleira lifted her chin, her back straight. "I am prepared to do my duty."

For the first time, Prince Ellarin turned to her. Some of the hardness faded, leaving pain and desperation twisting his features and glinting in his eyes. "I promise that I will never pressure you. My father might have his expectations, but this marriage will be ours. Only the two of us—together—will determine our future. We have time. I will not live to an old age, but Taranath—my healer—assures me that I have time enough."

His assurances were sweet. Really, they were.

But she was not going to fool herself. It was easy to say that they had time, but the reality was that they did not. They would be foolhardy to risk the kingdom's future on niceties like taking the time to fall in love.

Yet his sincerity gave her some hope. Not for love, exactly. She was too practical to dream for that in such an arrangement. But fondness seemed an achievable hope.

"Linshi, Ellarin Amirisheni." Leyleira met his gaze with all the dignity she could muster. She might have been chosen for her genetics, but she would not give the king or the prince any reason to doubt that she could exude all the regal qualities of a queen. "I appreciate your honesty in this matter. Now, I do not believe we should keep our fathers waiting to sign the paperwork any longer."

Prince Ellarin's eyes darted over her face. Searching for what, she did not know. But after a moment, he gave a slight nod and held out his arm to her again.

ELLARIN FOLLOWED his father's instructions to create the eshinelt, the tingling in his fingertips only partially caused by his disease.

This felt so wrong. He never should have agreed to this arranged marriage. Sure, his father had not given him much of a choice. King Illythor had already started the process of narrowing down the prospects before he told Ellarin of his intentions to arrange a marriage for him. He had given Ellarin three options for his bride and told him to pick one. And so Ellarin had.

Ellarin could have fought harder. He could have dug in his heels and protested more. There was not much his father could have done if he had simply refused to entertain the idea.

Yet he had still been reeling from the news that he was dying. He might live for a paltry few hundred years yet, if he was fortunate and if the healer Taranath could slow the progression of the disease as much as he hoped. Ellarin had not had the energy to fight his father on top of trying to process the utter upending of his life and dreams.

"Now stir in your magic, and your part of the eshinelt will be complete." His father's voice rang with the same cold efficiency he used for every facet of his life.

Perhaps his father had once been softer, kinder. But that would have been long before Ellarin was born. Maybe King Illythor had lost the last sense of kindness when his father had been killed fighting the trolls and his brother had died creating the Gulmorth Gorge. He certainly had been all hard logic by the time Ellarin's mother had died over a hundred years ago.

Ellarin stared down at the silver bowl in front of him,

filled with the green paint used in the marriage ceremony. "This is not right."

"The eshinelt is correct." His father scowled, his tone deepening.

Ellarin shook his head. "Not the eshinelt. This wedding. It is wrong to force Lady Leyleira into an arrangement like this. She deserves the chance to find love and happiness."

Lady Leyleira. She was quite the enigma. She had not so much as blinked when he had told her about his disease. He had seen the way she had processed the news, its implications, and absorbed it with a quiet dignity.

"Love." His father snorted and gestured at Ellarin. "Look at what it got me."

Ellarin gritted his teeth and refused to flinch. Him. The disease that was slowly eating away at him and made him an unworthy heir. That was what love had gotten his father.

Ellarin's mother had come from a good family, but their family line had developed a hereditary disease over the millennia. Back then, Illythor had not cared about such things, and he had married Ellarin's mother anyway.

She had died young. And now Ellarin, too, would die young.

"You know your duty, Ellarin." King Illythor waved his hand in a sharp, final motion toward the silver bowl. "You *will* marry Lady Leyleira today. You will ensure the continuation of our family line before…"

For the first time, King Illythor's voice choked off. The only hint of emotion about Ellarin's impending death.

"Before I die. Just say it, Damasha. It is the reason we

are here today." Ellarin did not try to minimize the bite to his words, even as his father flinched.

Ellarin was dying. Slowly, but ever so surely.

He had the magic of the ancient kings running in his veins, but he would never join the ranks of the great kings and warriors of legend who had wielded this magic before him.

In all likelihood, Ellarin would never be king. His father would outlive him, passing the crown directly to Ellarin's son or daughter.

The only thing left to Ellarin was to produce the next king or queen. That was all. Once that was done, there would be nothing left for him but to wait to die.

How could he ask Leyleira to marry him, knowing that this would be her future? It was not fair to her.

But he had to marry and have an heir, the sooner the better. He had no choice in that.

His only choice had been in whom to marry, and his father had given him only the three options. Ellarin had chosen Leyleira.

She was practical. From what he had seen, she was nearly as coldly logical as his father. She had taken all of this with far more composure than he had. If anyone could take the burden of this arrangement, she could.

King Illythor drew in a breath with the faintest of shudders before his expression closed once again. "Now put your magic into the eshinelt so we can get this done."

Ellarin called up his magic, the bolts weaker than they should have been, and did as he was told.

TWO

Leyleira rested her hand on Ellarin's arm as they
left the noise and the music of the great hall and
stepped into the quiet night that shrouded
Ellonahshinel. Leyleira's silver dress swished around her
while the breeze brushed against her bare shoulders,
making her all too aware of the drying eshinelt on her
forehead, cheek, and upper chest above the line of her
dress.

Beside her, Ellarin wore a light blue tunic edged in
silver embroidery that glinted along with the silver crown
of intertwining maple and oak leaves that graced his
golden hair. The eshinelt she had painted on him during
the wedding ceremony earlier that evening glinted
slightly in the moonlight. Looking at him now, strolling at
her side so strong and tall, she would never have guessed
that he was dying.

She did not attempt conversation as they navigated
the branches of Ellonahshinel. Heading for the royal
branch. Heading for his room.

The silence stretched, uncomfortable and strangely

soothing at the same time. Ellarin was not pressuring her, not even for conversation.

Perhaps it was that knowledge—and his promise from a week ago—that kept her knees from wobbling and her stomach from churning. All right, so her chest was a bit tight, and she hoped beyond hope that he did not notice the slightest tremble to the fingers she rested on his arm.

But she would never admit to such things if he asked. No one would ever be able to say that she had faced her duty with any less bravery than the great elven warriors of old.

They arrived at the broad branch that contained the royal suites of rooms and immediately turned to the left to the rooms set across from the king's. Within moments, they stepped inside, the room so bathed in moonlight that there was no need to whisper the words that would brighten the elven lights overhead.

The darkness would make this easier. Hopefully.

Ellarin halted them before the four doors at the far side. One of the doors belonged to Ellarin. The others would be for their children someday. That was the expectation, anyway. The duty which she had been carefully selected to perform.

"Leyleira." Ellarin gently turned her to face him, his eyes soft in the moonlight. Slowly, giving her plenty of time to pull away, he brushed his fingers against her cheek.

She held her breath, expecting to have to force herself to stay where she was.

Yet instead of the urge to pull away, a shivery tingle swept through her, causing her breath to catch in her chest.

Ellarin held her gaze, the look in his eyes as gentle as his touch on her cheek. "Forget my father. Forget the pressure. The kingdom. I have no expectations for tonight. The second bedchamber is yours if you wish."

She refused to release the breath of relief that built in her chest. A week had been little time to get to know Ellarin, but he was proving to be as courteous when they were alone as he had been when they had been in public. "Where are my things?"

Ellarin hesitated, his gaze dropping from hers though his hand remained cradling her face. "My father oversaw the transfer of your things."

"Ah." In other words, it was highly likely the king had ordered them placed in Ellarin's room. A clear statement of the king's expectations tonight and going forward.

A slight quirk twisted Ellarin's mouth. "But that does not mean we cannot move your things ourselves to whatever room you wish. It is not like my father can forbid such a thing."

No, but he could make his disapproval quite clear. With the king's rooms directly across the branch from their own, there would be some privacy, thanks to the magic covering the windows, but not much. The king would likely be able to see if they slept in separate rooms, given the open staircases they would have to traverse. He might not be able to make demands on their marriage, but he could certainly pressure both her and Ellarin.

There was only one option, in the end.

Leyleira drew in a deep breath, forced herself to step away from Ellarin's comforting touch, and faced the doors. "We might as well begin as we mean to continue. Which room is ours?"

Ellarin's hand dropped, even as his gaze snapped back to hers. For a moment, he gave her that searching look, the one that attempted to peel back the layers of duty to see her heart beneath. Then he gave that small nod of his and reached for the door closest to them. "This one."

He lifted the latch and held the door open for her.

Leyleira gripped her skirt, strode through the door, and up the short length of stairs that had been grown into the branch. The bedchamber above was ringed with a lovely porch, a bench to one side underneath one of the windows where it would be out of sight of the main royal branch. A screen of broad leaves offered some privacy, though it was still far closer to the other rooms than she was used to back home in her family's small treetop home overlooking a lake.

Ellarin padded up the stairs behind her, his footsteps nearly silent.

Leyleira hoped he could not see the way her fingers trembled as she opened the door to the bedchamber and swept inside.

A large bed was grown into the wall to her left, framed by gauzy curtains. To her right, much of the room was blocked by a large folding screen, the type found in a seamstress's shop.

The screen seemed out of place. Why would a prince need a screen for changing? Unless...but surely not. She glanced over her shoulder, not sure how to go about asking.

Ellarin closed the door behind her with a soft click, though he did not take another step into the room as if he did not want to crowd her. He tipped a nod toward the screen. "I am a prince. I made a few requests of my own when the servants were preparing this room for you."

"Then you knew we would have no other option." She clasped her hands in front of her, not quite sure what she was feeling. The gesture was just as sweet and thoughtful as she had come to expect from him. And she did appreciate it. Of course she did.

But there was also disappointment, knowing that Ellarin always intended to cave to his father's demands, even in this. Yes, that was exactly what she was doing. But it seemed more disappointing, coming from Ellarin. Perhaps because, of the two of them, he was the only one with any real power to stand up to his father.

"The second bedchamber was prepared for you as well. I was not lying when I offered it to you. You can still stay there, if you wish." Ellarin eased a step forward, though he did not touch her, not even to trail that gentle, tingle-inducing caress across her cheek. "But in the past week, I have observed that you are incredibly practical. I guessed this would be your choice. I asked for a screen to be brought in to accommodate your choice, not because of any thought of what my father would wish."

So he had been standing up to his father after all. A seemingly small gesture, yet with it, Ellarin was shielding her. From pressure. From expectation. From discomfort.

She found herself wanting to reach for Ellarin to steady herself, her knees feeling a bit wobbly. She had thought herself prepared for tonight. Yet as the burden of duty lifted from her shoulders, all she felt was a relief so intense that she had to swallow back the lump in her throat.

But she gathered herself before she did more than sway in his direction. It was far too soon to be reaching to him for steadiness and comfort. Better she found such things in herself, especially given how short this marriage might be. "Linshi."

Ellarin huffed a breath, his shoulders sagging, as if he had been holding his breath while he waited for her answer. "Go ahead and take your time."

Leyleira tore her gaze away from him and hurried behind the screen. Once she was out of his sight, she just stood there for a moment, feeling like she could finally breathe for the first time that day.

Two windows let in the moonlight, though she could tell the magic had already been set so that it would appear opaque from the outside for privacy. One set of shelves held her familiar dresses, shirts, trousers, and other items of clothing, which she had packed a mere three weeks ago when her family had received word of the arrangement and been summoned to Estyra.

In front of her, a pitcher and basin sat on a shelf beneath the window. She crossed the space and touched the water inside the pitcher. Still warm and smelling faintly of lavender, so a servant must have brought it, preparing the space for their return.

Several towels lay folded next to the basin. Also likely the work of a servant.

But beside the pitcher of water, set where she could not help but see it, was a white porcelain vase with a single red rose.

Her throat closed, and she had to blink several times as she reached out and traced a finger over the petals. Perhaps a servant had left this as well, but she did not think so. This rose was another sweet gesture on Ellarin's part.

He deserved so much more. He should have had the time to properly court a lady who shared his same sweet nature. He should have had the chance to give this thoughtful heart of his to someone who would truly appreciate it.

Instead, he got this. A marriage arranged in a cold, calculating manner by his father to a woman who was too practical to let herself fall in love with a dying man. All to make sure the royal line continued in a genetically healthy manner, hopefully breeding out the disease Ellarin had inherited and passing along the best of their magics.

Leyleira shook herself. As Ellarin had noted, she was practical. Because she was practical, she knew better than to linger over romantic gestures, no matter how meaningful or thoughtful.

She changed into her favorite sleeping shirt and trousers. They were thick and soft and comfortable. She poured some of the water into the basin, leaving enough that Ellarin could wash up after she was done. It only took a moment to scrub away the eshinelt from her skin, though the reality of her marriage was not so easily set aside.

She dried her face, and her gaze caught on the rose once again. She hesitated for a moment longer before she picked up the vase. Straightening her back, she strode around the screen, holding the vase in front of her. A shield. A peace offering. She did not know.

Ellarin was perched on a plush chair beside a window, the book in his hands tilted to catch the moonlight. As she stepped into view, he glanced up, then closed the book. He glided to his feet, a hint of a smile on his face as he took in her and the rose she held.

"I…" Her voice failed her, squeaking past the lump in her throat. She should not be this moved by something as simple as a rose. "Linshi."

His smile widened, and he nodded in an acknowledgement of her thanks. But he did not speak as he walked past her, disappearing behind the screen.

Leyleira forced herself to walk across the room and climb onto the large bed. Ellarin would claim the side closest to the door, most likely. So she crawled to the side of the window, carefully so she did not spill the water in the vase, and set the rose and vase on the windowsill.

She might be incredibly practical, but perhaps even she could be just a little bit sentimental.

ELLARIN TOOK his time changing and washing up, hoping to give Leyleira the space she needed to become comfortable.

But when he stepped around the screen, the tense way Leyleira lay on her side, her back to him, told him that she was still very much awake.

He eased himself onto the bed, leaving plenty of space between them so that he did not so much as accidentally brush her when he slid beneath the blankets. He lay on his back and stared at the ceiling for a long moment.

Earlier, when they had walked from the feast to his room, he had sensed that silence would be more appreciated than conversation.

But this moment felt like one that needed conversation to break the tension. They had so little time to talk in the past week. Honestly, they had shared only that one frank discussion. It would be hard, talking about this. It was far too personal for such a brief acquaintance, yet Leyleira was now his wife. She needed to know, and perhaps it would help her relax if she heard him vulnerable.

"It started about a hundred years ago when I was coming into my magic." Ellarin stared at the ceiling, thankful for the darkness broken only by the shafts of moonlight streaming between the leaves outside and through the windows. "It was just little things, at first. My magic did not seem as strong as it should have been.

Perhaps not unusual for a son to be less powerful than the previous generation, except that I have the magic of the ancient kings. By its very nature, it is incredibly powerful."

Leyleira remained absolutely still next to him, her back a stiff wall between them.

"Then there was the numbness that would come and go in my fingers, which started escalating into pain, especially when using my magic. The best healers in Estyra could not figure out exactly what was going on, except to confirm that something was not right." Ellarin smoothed his hand over the blanket, the movement sending painful tingles through his fingers. He needed his rest after the long, exhausting day.

He shoved aside the memories of the constant healing consultations. The pitying looks of the healers. The uncertainty of knowing something was wrong and yet never getting confirmation of what it was.

Was that a slight shift to her back? The barest softening to the set of her shoulder blades?

"Then one of the healers told my father about Taranath, a young healer barely past his years of training. He has great finesse with his healing magic. He can go deeper and heal at the chemical level in a way most healers cannot." Ellarin clenched his fingers in the blanket, fighting to keep his thoughts and his voice steady. "Taranath was able to confirm what the other healers could not. My magic and my body are fighting, consuming and destroying instead of working together as they should. Coming into my magic triggered the disease. With his magic, Taranath believes he can slow the progression, even if he cannot fully heal it."

This was the reality he was facing. What she was facing too, now that she had married him.

Perhaps it was a relief to her, knowing that this arranged marriage was only temporary.

Leyleira remained quiet for another moment before she shifted slightly. "That must have been difficult."

"It was." Still was. How did he go on living, knowing he was dying? Especially when his father got that darkly disappointed scowl every time he looked at Ellarin. As if it was Ellarin's fault that he had inherited something like this from his mother.

Ellarin let the silence fall between them again and stared at the ceiling with all its familiar twisting lines of branches.

He did not want to say the next part. But he needed to give her this. A piece of his heart, even if he would never ask her for anything she did not want to give.

"Ever since I was diagnosed, I have had this…fear that I will suddenly take a turn for the worse during the night when I am all alone. It is irrational, I know. Taranath has assured me that the slow progression of the disease will give me plenty of warning before…" Here, in the night, he could not bring himself to say it out loud. It was harder to be blunt when such things were so raw and real in the darkness. He swallowed and forced himself to continue. "Thank you for choosing to stay here. With me. It helps, knowing that I am not alone."

For another long moment, the silence stretched between them, heavy with his words.

Then she rolled to her back as well and tilted her head to face him. "A week ago, you promised that you would never pressure me. Well, this is my promise in return. You will not be alone. Not tonight. Not…not in the end."

She had no reason to give him this promise. Yes, they were married. But it was a union without love or emotion. Yet a pledge like this would demand much of her. It would not be easy, especially toward the end when...

He could not think of it. He was not brave enough for that.

He pushed himself onto an elbow so that he could better see her face. "Linshi, shynafera."

Her eyes widened at the endearment. Perhaps it was presumptuous when they had only known each other a week. And perhaps someone other than Leyleira would find being called *iron heart* more offensive than endearing.

But hopefully she could hear the care behind his name for her. Even the endearment felt too small for what she had given him in that promise.

He met her gaze, the moonlight glimmering in the dark brown depths of her eyes, and gently reached out a hand. When she did not flinch, though something in her gaze shuttered, he eased his fingers through a few strands of her hair where it spread across her pillow. "May I kiss you?"

This close, he could watch the thoughts flick through her eyes. The calculations of risks and pressures and duty until she shoved it all behind that iron composure of hers and nodded.

She was saying yes, but the emptiness in her eyes, the stiffness to her body, said no.

The sweetness of her promise a moment before died in a bitter churn in his chest. She did not trust him enough yet to tell him the truth. Instead, she was telling him what she thought she should because it was her duty. And perhaps, given the stubborn set of her jaw, she thought saying no would be taking the coward's way out.

A kiss should not be a question of courage or cowardice, but an expression of love.

Ellarin leaned forward and brushed a light kiss to

Leyleira's forehead rather than her lips. "Goodnight, Leyleira."

In that moment before he turned his back to her and lay down, he thought he caught the flash of relief in her eyes.

He had made the right choice, then. The forehead kiss had not been unwanted, as the kiss to her lips would have been. She might be aloof, but she seemed to appreciate when he showed her that he cared.

If she was too practical, too cold, to ever fully fall in love with him, that was just as well. He would not want to risk forming an elishina, something that would risk her life and hurt her more when his time came. It would be best, after all, if her heart remained as untouched as possible so that she could move on more easily once he was gone.

But if he did not have to worry about an elishina, then he was free to love and cherish her with his whole heart, even if he knew she would never love him the same way in return. While he might not be her one and only, she would be his.

He did not have much time, but he had enough. He could afford to be patient and build this relationship the right way.

Leyleira was his wife. He would love her. Cherish her. Perhaps, someday, she would grow to feel enough fondness for him that his kiss would not be unwanted. Only then would he consider the question of an heir, no matter what kind of pressure his father would place on them in the meantime.

After all, Ellarin was dying. There was not much his father could do to him at this point.

CHAPTER

THREE

640 YEARS BFH

Leyleira woke when Ellarin rolled out of their bed as the first gray blush of dawn filtered through the broad leaves of Ellonahshinel.

As had become their routine when the days dragged into weeks, weeks into months, months into years, Ellarin disappeared behind the screen and into the water closet. Moments later, the faint sounds of water running through the tree branches in magically protected pathways to prevent rotting the tree joined the twittering of the birds.

Leyleira rolled out of bed, shrugged into her dressing gown, and perched on the window seat, the pillows already arranged just how she preferred. She picked up her book from its place on the windowsill, cracked it open, and had the time to read exactly twenty pages while Ellarin showered and dressed for the day.

When he stepped around the screen, she set her book aside, glided to her feet, and brushed past him without a word.

Today, she found a white lily in the vase next to the basin. Even after ten years, she was not quite sure how Ellarin sneaked in these little gifts for her nearly every morning. Perhaps he left them the night before, since he was usually the last one in here before they retired.

Often she would find a flower. Sometimes it would be a small, sweet note. Other times, it would be something larger, like a necklace or a jeweled pin for her hair.

Such adorable gestures. And yet, this was all their relationship was. Thoughtful. Vaguely pleasant. But surface level. They had become very good at living side-by-side without ever truly living together.

Leyleira showered and dressed in a deep purple dress with gold embroidery at the neckline and hems.

When she entered the main room below, Ellarin had already set out the bread and cheese for their breakfast. A servant had already delivered the tea tray, and as she sat in her chair at the table, Ellarin set her teacup in front of her. Her morning green tea with spearmint, steeped for exactly seven minutes, as she preferred.

They ate breakfast in silence. What was there to talk about? She had her weekly tea luncheon with the ladies of the court, as he well knew. He had his weekly healing session with Taranath, as she knew, though she also knew he would not tell her about it except to say that the healings were working as hoped and that she should not worry.

But did he actually discuss his health with her? No. Nor did he encourage her to join him in his consultations with Taranath. Besides a few whispered admissions in the darkness—when night seemed to give him the courage to share his heart—he was as closed off with her as she was with him.

Once they finished breakfast, Ellarin pushed to his

feet, collected the dishes onto the tray for the servants, and brushed a light kiss to her forehead—always that infernal forehead kiss and never anything more.

She appreciated his thoughtfulness. She truly did. But sometimes, she just wished he would stop being so frustratingly noble and get it over with. The need for an heir hung over them like a sword dangling by a thread. Always there. Always sharp and glinting.

Ellarin might deny that it was there. He might placate her with assurances that he had plenty of time yet.

But the word *dying* lingered like a specter around him.

Someday, the pressure would become too much. The thread would snap. The sword would fall. And the fall would be all the worse for the delay.

But she never said it. Never acknowledged the growing pressure.

Once she had finished her tea and the breakfast dishes were cleared, each of them left, going their separate ways for the rest of the day, until they saw each other again that evening.

Since the king had no queen, Leyleira had already assumed many of the duties of the queen in the court, even though she was merely a princess. Yes, she was married to the heir, but there were many—likely even King Illythor—who believed Ellarin would not live long enough to become king and make her a queen.

But Leyleira was all they had, so the duties were hers.

Perhaps she was not accomplishing her first and most important duty—providing an heir—but no one had any complaints about her handling of the rest of her duties.

For most of the morning, she sorted through the paperwork of those asking the crown for aid of some kind. She made notes about which organizations and people she would need to meet in person to follow up before she approved their applications.

There was also the stack of requests for her presence at various events, from the opening of a new housing tree at the outskirts of Estyra to a luncheon hosted by one of the members of the king's council, and she needed to write out her replies, mostly acceptances. She had no reason to say no. It was not as if she had anything better to do, and she might as well be the painting-perfect crown princess, since she could not accomplish the one reason she had become a princess in the first place, thanks to Ellarin's frustrating integrity.

Late in the morning, she left the small office room she had been given down the branch from the king's study and made her way along the branches to the large meeting room where she was hosting the tea.

As she passed the king's study, she held her breath, her chin raised, and resisted the urge to glance through the doorway, lest she catch the king's eyes. Her days were usually better when she avoided the king's glower, as if the lack of heir was all her fault.

Thankfully, she made it past the king's study without him calling out to her.

When she stepped into the meeting room, servants still glided about, laying out the place settings and arranging the vases of flowers on each of the tables.

Leyleira meandered around the room, nudging a fork slightly straighter here, adjusting the flowers in a vase there.

The head servant strode to Leyleira and bobbed a bow. "Is there anything else you need, amirah?"

Leyleira swept a critical eye over the room. Everything was perfect, down to the deep purple hyacinths that were the exact same shade as Leyleira's dress. "No, linshi. You and the staff have done exceptional work this morning. Please inform the kitchen staff that they can send up the tea and luncheon in twenty minutes."

"Yes, amirah." The servant bowed again and hurried off.

After a few minutes, the staff cleared out, leaving Leyleira alone in the meeting room for a few precious minutes to gather herself before the ladies of the court descended.

She took stock of herself. Her head was held high at the correct angle to be both regal and composed without being arrogant. Her shoulders were straight, as was her back, in perfect posture. Her dress draped around her flawlessly. Not one strand of her black hair straggled out of place. Nothing for anyone to tear apart.

They would find something. They always did. Especially the young ladies or their mothers who felt they had been passed over in favor of Leyleira for the arranged marriage with the prince.

Well, they were not missing much. Though she would never breathe a word of that to them.

At noon on the dot, a light rap signaled the arrival of the first of her guests.

Leyleira stepped away from the wall, placing herself before the door, as a servant opened the door and admitted the guests.

With a practiced smile, Leyleira greeted each one and directed them to their designated table. The tea trays arrived on the heels of the guests, and the servants distributed the trays between the tables. The variety of sandwiches provided something for everyone while the water in the teapots was the right temperature for pouring over whatever tea the guests selected.

Leyleira prepared her cup of black tea and set it aside

to steep for exactly five minutes. While she waited, she kept up the polite, empty conversation with those at her table.

After ten minutes with this table, she politely bowed out of the conversation, stood, and glided to the next table to spend ten minutes with the ladies there. As the luncheon progressed, she moved from table to table, mentally making note of all the little things to remember for next time. Which elf maiden was courting which elf lord. The gossip of who was currently snubbing whom. Which floral scent was currently the most popular for shampoos and conditioners.

As she neared the next table, the soft tones alerted her first. The way the ladies at the table leaned forward.

"Ten whole years. And no heir yet." One of the ladies clucked her tongue. "We all know an heir was the only reason our dying prince married her."

"Which one of them is incapable, do you think? The dying prince or the ice princess?"

"It is no wonder there is no heir yet. She is so cold that she makes our king appear warm." This last was said with a giggle.

Leyleira let out a breath, refusing to bend beneath their scathing words. It was nothing that she had not heard before, whispered in corners when the ladies thought she would not overhear. Or when they simply did not care if she did.

Her composure in place, she slid into the open seat at the table and reached for what would be her third cup of tea that luncheon. "I thank you for the compliment."

The ladies either started, snapped their mouths shut, or—if they were particularly brazen—simply blinked back at her, not a flicker of guilt for their words in their eyes.

Leyleira dredged up a smile, though it was sharp-edged rather than warm.

Ellarin had put this off for ten years due to his stubborn honor, but the sword was dropping. She could feel its icy edge at the back of her neck. Why put it off any longer? It was what the king wanted. What the kingdom wanted. Why did it matter if it was not what she or Ellarin wanted?

No one had cared that they had not wanted their wedding. Why would anyone care if they wanted this?

It was simply duty. That was all there was to it.

She was prepared to do her duty. But was Ellarin?

ELLARIN KNOCKED on the door to Taranath's suite of rooms. While there was a set of rooms dedicated for the use of the royal healer, Ellarin had his appointments directly with Taranath in his own healing room. Perhaps it was because King Illythor wanted to keep the news about Ellarin's disease as quiet as possible, even if everyone in the entire kingdom already knew about it. Or perhaps the official royal healer had not wanted to share his space with a young upstart healer like Taranath.

Either way, Ellarin appreciated it. At least here, in the privacy of this quiet branch at the far side of Ellonahshinel, he did not feel so much like a prince with the eyes of the kingdom scrutinizing even this most personal aspect of his life. Here, he could just be a man. Scared. Struggling with the reality he was facing. Searching for any help he could grasp.

"Come in." Taranath's voice came from inside.

Ellarin lifted the latch and stepped inside. Instead of the normal kitchen and sitting room layout, this room was filled with shelves upon shelves of jars, powders, and dried herbs. One side of the room held two padded benches. A single wooden table filled the center of the room.

Taranath was bent over an open notebook lying on the workbench beneath a section of shelves. Taranath's long brown hair was braided at each side over his ears to keep it out of his way, while his soft green tunic and trousers were clean, though there was the hint of something vaguely disheveled about him.

He glanced up, then gestured toward the table. "Ah, Prince Ellarin. My favorite patient."

Ellarin huffed something almost like a laugh as he tugged his tunic over his head. "Am I your favorite because I am an interesting specimen to study or because my father has ordered you to consider me your favorite?"

"The former, I assure you." Taranath flipped to a fresh page in the notebook, his pen nearby, ready to jot down his notes from this session.

"Is it strange that I find that comforting?" Ellarin dropped his tunic onto one of the benches, then his shirt.

"I have met your father. I see nothing strange in preferring to be a scientific experiment." Taranath turned to him, his expression all somber professionalism.

"You should be careful. Someone might consider such talk treason." Ellarin sat on the examination table.

"I am the healer keeping his only son and heir alive. I am fairly sure I could say a great deal of treasonous things before the king would take issue with it." Taranath shrugged and pressed a hand to Ellarin's chest. His brown eyes went slightly unfocused as green magic swirled around his fingers and sank into Ellarin.

Ellarin tried to hold still, breathing normally. He knew the drill, after over ten years of weekly appointments.

After several long moments, Taranath nodded and wandered back to the worktable, his eyes still slightly unfocused. Utterly distracted by whatever his magic was telling him about Ellarin's body.

Taranath jotted a few notes. "How has the numbness and tingling in your fingers been?"

"The same. It is always there, though it sometimes gets worse at the end of the day." Ellarin stared down at his hands, rubbing his thumb against his palm, sending that tingling feeling through his senses. It was not painful, exactly. But it was not normal, even if it was his normal.

"Hmm." Taranath did not look up as he scribbled a few more notes.

"I had one of those bouts of pain two days ago." Ellarin swung his legs, watching the movement and thankful when it did not cause any pain. "Shafts of pain running down my arms and my legs, like before."

"And you did not summon me?" This time, Taranath glanced up, giving him a raised eyebrow look that was far more effective than his father's glowers at making him squirm.

"I was in a meeting with my father." Ellarin shrugged. Not that it did him any good to attempt to hide any progression in his disease from his father, but the last thing he wanted to do was admit to weakness caused by it in front of him.

"You still should have called me afterwards." Taranath fully turned to him and crossed his arms. "I could have made the recovery easier."

Yes, he could have. But that would have meant telling Leyleira that the healer's presence that evening was necessary and breaking their normal routine. That routine was the only thing they had managed to build when it came to a relationship.

"It was not necessary." Ellarin gripped the edge of the table until a glimmer of that same pain lanced through his hands. It had taken everything in him to grit his teeth through the soreness and pretend everything was all right so that Leyleira would not realize he was in pain.

It was foolish, perhaps. But the longer he was married to her, the less he wanted to admit his weakness to her. It had been easier to tell her the truth when they had been complete strangers.

Now...now he wished he could be far more than what he was in her eyes. Perhaps then she would actually soften to him instead of maintaining that iron wall around her heart that refused to budge an inch.

"Summon me next time. The quicker I can heal you during or after a bout, the less damage it will cause." Taranath turned back to his book and flipped back through the pages. "It has been nearly four months since your last bout like that, correct?"

"Yes." Ellarin forced himself to release his grip on the table.

Taranath flipped back and forth in the book, that distracted look returning to his gaze. While jotting a few more notes, Taranath made a vague motion at Ellarin.

At this point, Ellarin had no trouble interpreting Taranath. He lay down on the table on his stomach, crossing his arms in front of him and resting his chin on his arms.

After another moment, Taranath strode to the table and rested his hand on the back of Ellarin's neck, right over his spine. When Taranath's magic flooded into Ellarin, it swirled along his nerves and into his fingers and toes, the sensation somewhere between pleasant and painful.

Ellarin's magic stirred in his chest, and he clamped down on it before it lashed out to stop the pain on instinct. A side effect of the magic of the ancient kings, that it came to the surface at any hint of threat, even if that "threat" was a healer who was doing nothing but helping.

The minutes ticked by as Taranath slowly, methodically, healed Ellarin's body as much as was possible.

Finally, Taranath lifted his hand and stepped back, a weariness in his posture and on his face. Eyes unfocused, he stumbled to the work table and started scribbling once again in the notebook.

Ellarin swung upright, watching Taranath for a few moments before shrugging. There would be no interrupting him for several more minutes.

After hopping off the table, Ellarin shrugged back into his shirt and tunic. By the time he finished, Taranath was still writing, pausing to flip through the book, then writing some more. He made a vague flapping motion in Ellarin's direction. "You are free to go. Continue to rest when needed and avoid using your magic in large quantities."

Ellarin straightened his collar. This was the moment when he normally left. He usually avoided asking questions as if, by avoidance, he would not receive the answers he was dreading.

But just because he had been putting off asking, did not mean the answers were not there, breathing cold and clammy down his neck.

Instead of heading for the door, Ellarin crossed the room and braced himself against the table behind him, facing Taranath. Over the past ten years, Taranath had become a friend. He was probably the only person in all of Tarenhiel who would tell him the truth. "You have been healing me for ten years now. What is my prognosis?"

Taranath paused, blinked, then he slowly set down his pen. He leaned against the wooden countertop behind him and met Ellarin's gaze. "I have been able to slow the progression to a minimum. Frankly, I am more optimistic than I was ten years ago when I first started healing you. I have become more familiar with your condition, and I have been able to implement what I have learned. I still cannot cure you. The minimal progression will eventually add up, and you will continue to experience slow degeneration. But you likely have hundreds of years yet before you."

Ellarin huffed out a breath. "I might be dying more slowly, but I am still dying."

Taranath snorted and waved. "We are all dying. Yes, you are dying slightly faster than an elf without your condition. But you are dying far more slowly than a perfectly healthy human."

"That is hardly a fair comparison. Humans are lucky if they live a mere ninety years." Ellarin was not one of those who dismissed humans as inferior because of their few years. Instead, he pitied them. So few years. How did they even figure out how to live life in that short amount of time?

Perhaps many of them did not. His father gave him the reports on the human kingdoms to read. Busywork for the unworthy heir. At least, that was how his father saw it.

"My point still remains." Taranath waved again, his deep brown eyes filled with some kind of mix of sympathy and humor. "And, honestly, given the tendency of kings in your family line to charge into battle and get themselves killed off, you might actually enjoy a far longer life than many of them."

"Because I am too weak to send into battle." Ellarin crossed his arms, hunching his shoulders under the weight of his reality.

"We are at peace. There is no need to send you into battle, even if you were healthy and had the full use of your magic." Taranath shrugged and braced his hands on the countertop on either side of him. "Besides, I do not think battle is all that it is made out to be. You are better off avoiding it."

Ellarin clenched and unclenched his fists against his arms, feeling that ever-present hint of numbness in his fingertips. Perhaps he should be comforted. This was good news. Taranath's healing magic was working. Ellarin had hundreds of years before him yet.

But nothing Taranath said or did could erase the fact that Ellarin was dying, and he would feel that he was dying every day of the hundreds of years he might or might not live.

"Perhaps it is time you focused less on the fact that you are dying and more on simply *living*." Taranath stepped forward and rested a hand on Ellarin's shoulder, giving him a small shake. "If your time is shorter than most, then so be it. Make the most of the time you have. It is all any of us can do, no matter how long or short we have."

Ellarin released another long, slow breath and let Taranath's words settle into his soul. *Dying.* It had become the defining thing about him. No one spoke about him without adding that little word *dying* somewhere in there. Somewhere along the way, he had come to think of himself in that way as well. As if he had been reduced to merely that one descriptor.

He could not wallow like this any longer. It was time to start living again for whatever time he had.

Finally, he relaxed his stance. "When did you become so wise? You are barely older than I am."

"I am three hundred and ten years young." Taranath grinned, though the expression faded seconds later. "I am a healer. While we elves enjoy long lives and great magic, life is still filled with frailties, maladies, and death, and as a healer, I am acquainted with all of them. It is the burden I bear, much as you carry the burden of the crown."

"As my father never fails to remind me." Ellarin shook his head, huffing out a harsh breath.

"Speaking of your father, I might as well write up the report and have you deliver it to him directly. Since you have waited around this long." Taranath turned back to his work space and drew out a fresh sheet of paper from a drawer. "I will make sure to stress my belief that your situation is not as imminently dire as first believed."

"I am not sure it will help, but I do appreciate the effort." Ellarin squeezed his eyes shut and simply breathed, listening to the scratching of Taranath's pen.

When was the last time he had truly *lived*? For the past decade—perhaps even before that—he had just been going through the motions, waiting for death. But that was not how life was supposed to be. He should not be wallowing in despair, but living the time he had been given before stepping into the hope of the life beyond death.

Even with Leyleira, he went through the motions of caring for her, but when was the last time he had put any heart behind the general kindness? Had he ever?

40

It was time he changed that. If only he could figure out how.

"Here."

Ellarin blinked and found Taranath standing in front of him, holding out the written report. Medical confidentiality was paramount—except when it came to King Illythor. He had argued that since Ellarin was heir to the throne, his condition was a matter of national importance.

Ellarin took the paper and nodded to Taranath. "Linshi, Taranath. For everything. Healing me. The advice. For being a friend."

Taranath shrugged and turned back to his notebook. "You need a friend."

That he did. If being a prince had not been bad enough for forming friendships, adding that little word *dying* made forming friendships that much harder.

Not dying. Living.

But first, he needed to face down his father.

CHAPTER
FOUR

Ellarin strode along the branch and entered the king's study without bothering to knock.

King Illythor glanced up, that frown already etched onto his face. When his gaze landed on Ellarin, the scowl deepened, but he motioned to the clerks. "Leave us. I would like to speak with my son alone."

Once all the clerks had left, the last one closing the door behind him on his way out, King Illythor held out a hand. "Is that Taranath's report?"

"It is." Ellarin handed the paper over, then clasped his hands behind his back. "His magic has been quite effective. So effective, in fact, that he believes my prognosis is not as dire as he initially thought ten years ago."

"Hmm." The king perused the report, that frown never softening. After another moment, he set the report aside and lifted his gaze to Ellarin. "Perhaps he is correct. But even his magic cannot stop your disease from taking a sudden turn for the worse. I would not take this minor reprieve as an excuse to delay producing an heir."

Perhaps Ellarin should simply lie and tell his father

42

that he and Leyleira were trying. But he bristled at having to broach even that much with his father.

King Illythor had been three hundred when he had Ellarin, nearly a hundred years older than Ellarin was now. It was not as if King Illythor, after watching his father and brother both die young, would assume he had years to waste either. As Taranath had pointed out, elven kings tended to die young in battle. Yet King Illythor had not had an heir for a hundred and fifty years after he had become king and last of his line.

Instead of mentioning any of that, Ellarin clenched his hands tighter behind his back, fighting to keep his tone level. "It is none of your business when such a thing should occur."

King Illythor planted his hands on the desk and shoved to his feet, glowering. "I am the king and you are my heir. That means everything about you, from your marriage to your health to your children, is my concern. Therefore, it is within my purview to order you to give me an heir before this disease renders you incapable of doing so."

Ellarin gritted his teeth. In his father's mind, Ellarin was already written out of the picture. As far as King Illythor was concerned, the crown would jump directly from him to Ellarin's son or daughter.

Well, Ellarin was not dead yet, and he had no intention of allowing desperation to cause him to throw away his integrity. "Perhaps you should have thought of that before you ordered me to marry a stranger."

"You went along willingly enough at the time," King Illythor shot back.

Yes, he had. But he had still been reeling from the news he had been given, and an arranged marriage had seemed prudent at the time.

Yet now that ten years had passed and he had taken the time to truly ponder this decision, he doubted things should have been as rushed as they had been. He might be dying mildly faster than most elves, but he still had time. He could have taken the time to properly court Leyleira—or someone else of his choosing—rather than forcing both of them into something they had not wanted.

"Be that as it may, you cannot force me to cross lines that should not be crossed." Ellarin held his father's glower without flinching. "There are things I am unwilling to sacrifice."

"Sacrifice. You do not know the meaning of the word." King Illythor stalked around the desk, halting face-to-face with Ellarin. "I held my father as he bled out on the stones of the north, having driven the accursed trolls from our homeland. I watched helplessly as my brother gave his last breath to rend the earth and pour his magic into the ground so that his protections keep us safe from the trolls to this day. I became king when I was a mere one hundred and fifty years old because every last member of my family was dead on the field of battle."

Ellarin opened his mouth. He knew all this. He did not need his father to remind him of their family's history.

His father kept right on, his voice rising. "Thanks to their sacrifice, you have had the luxury to grow up in a peace and safety that previous generations have not enjoyed. If not for them, you would have been sent into battle, regardless of the fact that using your magic in large amounts would kill you all the faster. So do not whine to me about sacrifice."

"This is different." Forget about keeping his tone calm and level. Ellarin glared right back. "You are ordering me to violate the sacred bond of marriage by forcing what should not be forced."

"She knew her duty when she married you." King Illythor waved, as if that objection was of no concern.

"As I know my duty. To love and cherish her." Ellarin spun on his heel and marched toward the door. He was done with this conversation.

As his hand landed on the latch, King Illythor's voice rang hard and sharp behind him. "Your first duty is to your kingdom. Do not forget it."

Ellarin flung open the door and stomped out, not bothering to reply.

WHEN ELLARIN STEPPED into their suite of rooms, he knew they were in for trouble the moment he caught sight of Leyleira's face.

She sat at their table, her back far too straight, her expression too blank. But her eyes were flashing as she turned to him. "Kiss me."

"Pardon?" Ellarin halted just inside the room.

Leyleira rose to her feet and stalked toward him. "Kiss me. Just get it over with. You know it is what your father, the kingdom, everyone wants."

"It is not what you want." Ellarin resisted the urge to clench his fists.

"That does not matter." Leyleira's voice rose in a way he had never heard from her before. "This is our duty."

"Yes, it does matter." Ellarin eased a step closer, not sure if she was going to flinch, flee, or lash out if he moved too quickly. "And, frankly, I am concerned that you do not have more of a problem with this."

"Because I am not supposed to have a problem with it!

I am supposed to do my duty. That was the agreement. That is the only reason we married, after all." Leyleira spun away from him, digging her hands into her hair. "I am just sick of the waiting. Of always having this hanging over my head, knowing the sword is going to have to drop someday, and I would just rather get it over with. I am sick of the stares. The whispers. The pressure."

"Leyleira…" Ellarin took another step toward her, not sure what to say to that. He should have seen how much these past ten years had been breaking her.

She whirled back to him. "Is it because I am cold? Because you do not want me? Is that the reason?"

"No." He reached out, though he stopped short of gripping her shoulders. "It is because you do not love me."

"I am…fond of you." She halted, some of the fire quenching in her eyes. Her gaze dipped away from his, her posture returning to iron.

Perhaps his anger had already been roused, thanks to his *discussion* with his father. But her words—and that shift to her gaze that said she was lying—heated his blood.

"Are you fond of me because of *me*?" Ellarin jabbed his thumb toward his own chest. "Or because I am dying and that makes me easy to pity?"

"I…" Leyleira trailed off, her mouth working as if she could not come up with something to say.

"That is what I thought." Ellarin clenched his fists, the heat of ten years of the stares, the pressure, the whispers building in his chest. His voice rose with each word, and he was not sure who he was angry at. Leyleira. His father. The kingdom. "That is all I am to anyone anymore. Simply *dying*. Oh, and if I could just kindly leave behind an heir before I go, that would be much appreciated. But I am still a person. I am more than this disease. I am more than dying."

"I know that." Leyleira, too, clenched her fists as she faced him.

He spun away from her, unable to meet her gaze any longer. "Do you? Does anyone? The kingdom certainly does not. My father does not. He only gives me paperwork to keep me busy, but he is not training me to take the crown someday. According to my father and the kingdom, I will never be king. I am just dying."

"The only way to end the pressure and the whispers is to do the one thing you refuse to do." That bite returned to Leyleira's voice. She stalked into his line of sight and spread her hands, as if to indicate herself. "What do you want from me? Do you want me to love you? What if I cannot? As you have said, I am practical. What if I am too practical for love? What then? Will you refuse the kingdom an heir because I am incapable of love?"

He whirled to her, trying to put the jumble in his head into words. "You love your parents. You love the kingdom. You can love."

"This is different, and you know it." She gestured between them.

He huffed a breath. "I do not want you to fall in love with me. Not fully, anyways. I would rather you were not put in danger by forming an elishina with a dying man. I do not need you to love me. But I want you to choose me."

"Like you chose me?" Leyleira stepped closer, tapped his temple, then jabbed her finger into his chest. "Perhaps you chose me with your head, but you have chosen me with your heart no more than I have you. You have become very good at going through the motions, but you put very little heart behind it."

He opened his mouth to refute her claim, but what could he say? She was right. He had realized the same thing just that morning when talking with Taranath.

He claimed he had chosen her, but had he? Yes, he had chosen her out of the three options his father had given him. But that choice was not because of her, but because she was the only one whose family was not grasping for power. Nothing but logic went into that choice.

Resting his hands on the back of one of the chairs by the table, he released a long breath, his anger evaporating with it. His next breath came out on something almost like a laugh. "I do believe that is the most emotion we have ever demonstrated to each other."

"Yes." Leyleira clasped her hands in front of her, a hint of a smile on her face. "At least we know we are capable of passionate anger."

"I would take that over the placid emptiness we have had so far." Ellarin tightened his grip on the back of the chair, the tips of his fingers tingling.

"Me too." She stood there for a moment, the tension still lingering between them. After a moment, her voice softened into barely above a whisper. "Where does that leave us?"

Where did it leave them?

In some ways, nothing had changed. They still had duty hanging over their heads. His father was not going to stop pressuring them. Ellarin's illness was not going away.

Yet everything had changed. Ellarin did not want to go back to the way they had been. He wanted to *live*. And part of living was moving forward with Leyleira.

Not because he needed an heir, but because he wanted a wife. His wife. Leyleira.

He pushed away from the chair and faced her. "You have not been home in ten years, have you?"

"No." She lengthened the word, blinking at him. Probably wondering why he was asking when he well knew that she had not. Her parents had visited a few times over the years, but she had not left Estyra.

Well, it was about time to remedy that. Ellarin stepped forward and gripped her shoulders. "We will visit your parents. The whole summer, if they will let us."

"They will." Her smile grew, lighting her deep brown eyes in a way he had so rarely seen over the past ten years. "My parents are very practical. They will welcome us, then go about their business and barely take notice of us."

"Perfect. We can get away from my father, the court, the pressure, and just be *us*." He pulled her a little closer, daring to brush the backs of his fingers over her cheek. "Perhaps we can start over? You can be the retiring country girl, and I will be the charming prince, overwhelmed by your wit, practicality, and beauty."

"I would like that." Leyleira met his gaze, her deep brown eyes far more open than they had been in a long time. Though, within another blink, the iron dropped down over her gaze. "Will your father let us leave?"

"If he thinks this will secure him that heir he keeps going on about, then of course he will." At the way the light in her eyes further died, he squeezed her shoulders again. "That is the excuse for my father. I want to go for *us* and wherever we go from here. No pressure. No thought of duty. Just us."

Leyleira breathed out a long breath, and the hint of a smile returned. "In that case, when do we leave?"

"As soon as possible." Was it too late to arrange to leave today? If they sent a message through the root system, her parents would still have enough warning before their arrival, since the ride to her family's home would take a week.

The sooner he and Leyleira could get out of Ellonahshinel and away from his father, the better.

FIVE

L eyleira resisted the urge to nudge her horse into a gallop. She knew each tree, each twist in this trail, from her childhood.

The farther they had ridden from Ellonahshinel, the more it felt like she could finally breathe. That sword of duty was still there, but it was distant now, the thread more a solid rope holding it far away from her.

Last night in Arorien, she had barely been able to sleep, knowing she would arrive home late the next morning.

The trail bent one last time, then opened into a sunlit space filled by a sparkling lake spreading out from the base of a trailing willow tree.

Lethorel.

Home.

She glanced at Ellarin, riding next to her on a large white horse befitting his station as prince.

He smiled and nodded. "Do not hold back on my account. Go on. Gallop the last stretch."

Here, she did not have to be the perfect queen-to-be.

There was no one to judge or criticize.

Nudging her heels into her horse's sides, she urged her mare into a gallop. Within a few strides, the mare bolted from a walk into a run.

Leyleira laughed, the wind tearing at her hair. This was the freedom she had been craving for a decade.

The mare's hooves pounded on the grassy soil, then on the stretch of sand.

Leyleira reined in at the base of the tree, swinging from the horse's back before the mare had fully halted.

Her macha and dacha were already there, stepping off the broad stairs that wound up into the willow tree's branches.

"Macha! Dacha!" Leyleira gripped their shoulders in turn, as they gripped hers back.

"Welcome, sena." Dacha's voice remained the same grave monotone. Only the crinkles at the corners of his eyes betrayed his happiness that she was here. An expression Leyleira knew well.

"It is so good that you were able to come." Macha squeezed Leyleira's shoulders. "Are you truly able to stay the whole summer?"

"Yes." Leyleira glanced over her shoulder as Ellarin, Taranath, and the small squad of guards reined in their horses.

As Ellarin had predicted, his father had been more than happy to let them leave, believing that it would be a great way to inspire them to start thinking about that heir.

Perhaps it would. There was something idyllic about Lethorel. If she and Ellarin could not fall in love here—or at least develop enough fondness for a decently happy marriage—then their relationship was well and truly doomed to be miserable.

As Ellarin dismounted, her dacha and macha bowed.

The crinkles disappeared around Dacha's eyes as he spoke in that same grave tone. "Welcome to Lethorel, amir."

"Linshi. I am grateful that you are willing to host us for the summer." Ellarin nodded in return, just as grave and formal.

At least this summer would give Ellarin the chance to see where Leyleira had gotten her practical and unemotional temperament.

Ellarin gestured to Taranath. "This is my personal healer, Taranath Sillavan."

"He is, of course, welcome as well." Dacha gave a smaller bow toward the healer.

Macha gestured toward a table that had been placed overlooking the lake, a white tablecloth covering the wood and place settings for all of them already laid out. "Luncheon is nearly ready. Your dacha caught several perch this morning, along with a bass."

And just like that, it was as if Leyleira had never left. She shared a smile first with her macha, then her dacha. "I have missed Dacha's fresh fish."

Dacha's eyes crinkled again with his pleasure.

Macha flapped her hand toward the stairs upward into Lethorel. "Your rooms have been prepared. I am sure you would like to wash up after your journey."

"Linshi." Ellarin held out an arm to Leyleira. "We will return shortly."

Ellarin started up the stairs, and Leyleira kept pace with him as they climbed. When they were almost to the top, Ellarin sucked in a breath and stumbled.

"Ellarin?" Leyleira turned to him, gripping his arm to steady him. "What is wrong?"

Taranath's footsteps hurried up the steps behind them, and he appeared at Ellarin's other side. He took Ellarin's arm over his shoulders. "As I feared. You have overdone it on the ride here."

"I rested every evening as instructed." Ellarin focused on the steps, not looking at Leyleira as she and Taranath helped him up the last of the steps.

At the top of the stairs, the large main room filled the space where the branches spread out from the main trunk. Leyleira steered Ellarin and Taranath toward one of the branches.

"It was a week-long ride. That is tiring for anyone." Taranath shook his head, but he pressed his mouth shut, as if refraining from pointing out that such a ride would be far more taxing for Ellarin.

Perhaps they should not have come. But Ellarin had never mentioned that Taranath was worried the ride would be too difficult for him.

Leyleira directed them to one of the suites of rooms grown into the branches, made private by the thick, trailing leaves of the willow tree around them. Unlike their suite of rooms at Ellonahshinel, which were spread across several branches, here at Lethorel the main room, two bedrooms, and water closet were all one building grown out of the branch.

It was far cozier than Ellonahshinel, but Leyleira did not even hesitate as she helped Ellarin through the door into her childhood bedroom.

Nothing had changed in the ten years since she had left. The shelves were empty of her clothing, since it had all been moved to Ellonahshinel. But the light pink blankets on the bed were the same, though they had been freshly laundered. A few of her childhood knickknacks, such as a bird's nest she had found and the child-sized fishing rod her dacha had given her, sat on the high shelves above the windows.

Ellarin released a breath as he eased down onto the bed, briefly closing his eyes as if gathering himself.

Leyleira remained near the door. Should she make some excuse to leave? Ellarin had never shared the details of his healing sessions with Taranath with her, much less asked her to go along.

Not that she necessarily had to go along. She certainly did not expect him to come along every time she saw a healer for a checkup. But this was something far different than a simple check to make sure someone was in good health. Yet she did not want to push him, if he was uncomfortable having her there. Would he want her to leave?

"I should..." She edged toward the door.

Ellarin's gaze snapped to her, and he struggled a bit more upright. He held out a hand to her. "No, please stay."

Leyleira glanced from him to Taranath and back. "Are you sure?"

Ellarin nodded, his light blue eyes meeting hers, though his posture and expression remained tight. With pain or discomfort or both, she could not tell. "Yes."

Something shifted between them. A frisson that had her crossing the room and crawling around him to claim her spot between him and the window before she had really thought much about it.

Taranath was glancing between them with an eyebrow raised. "If I may?"

"Yes, please." Ellarin leaned forward, drawing up his knees and resting one arm on them.

Only then did Leyleira realize she was gripping his other hand between both of hers. She did not even remember claiming it, yet his hand felt so natural there, in hers.

Taranath rested his hand on the back of Ellarin's neck, his fingers glowing green. "How is the pain?"

"Stabbing up my arms and down my legs." Ellarin's tight expression eased, and he tipped his head to face Leyleira. "Taranath finds it easiest to heal me starting at the back of my neck. He can tap into the nerve in my spine and go from there."

"Ah." Leyleira squeezed his hand. Ellarin was being so frank with her at the moment, in a way he had not been for most of the past ten years.

After long moments, Taranath withdrew his hand. "That should do it. But you still should remain in bed for the rest of today. Healer's orders."

Ellarin opened his mouth to argue, then sighed and sank back onto the pillows. "Leyleira, could you please give my regrets to your parents?"

"Taranath can give our regrets. I will stay with you." Leyleira had not yet released Ellarin's hand.

Ellarin smiled and patted her fingers with his free hand. "Enjoy luncheon with your parents. I am going to ask Taranath for a little magic to send me right to sleep. There is no reason for you to stay here watching me sleep when you can instead spend time with your parents."

"All right." Leyleira forced herself to let go of his hand, then eased off the bed. She was probably going to be terribly distracted all through the luncheon. But she had been looking forward to that fish Dacha had caught. "Perhaps we can eat supper in bed, once you wake."

"That sounds terribly messy." Ellarin smiled at her, but the smile turned into a wince as he attempted to sit upright again, reaching for his boots.

"Let me." Leyleira set to work on the laces.

Ellarin sagged onto the pillows, lines of weariness etched into his face. "Taranath, you do not have to stay.

Once I am asleep, feel free to ride back to Arorien to continue flirting with the healer's pretty daughter."

Taranath gave a little cough, the tips of his ears going red. "Perhaps I will ride into Arorien tomorrow. But it would be wise if I remained on hand tonight."

Ellarin's sigh was so soft Leyleira barely heard it. "I thank you for your dedication."

Hopefully the rest would be enough, and no more of Taranath's help would be needed tonight. Perhaps tomorrow or the day after, she would help Ellarin in convincing Taranath to ride back to Arorien. She had noticed how taken Taranath had been with the healer's daughter, who was a healer in her own right.

Perhaps Leyleira and Ellarin would not be the only ones to find a little bit of romance this summer.

Taranath brushed magic-laced fingers over Ellarin's forehead. "Rest well, amir." He nodded to Leyleira. "I will let your parents know that you will be down shortly."

"Linshi." Leyleira returned Taranath's smile. As the healer quietly ducked out of the room, closing the door softly behind him, she pulled off Ellarin's boot. By the time she unlaced and tugged off the second one, Ellarin's eyes had closed, his body relaxing.

She tugged the blankets over him, then paused. She had seen him asleep before, his long blond hair pooled around him and his face smoothed from the burdens of living as the dying prince.

Every night of their marriage, Ellarin had given her a kiss on the forehead and wished her goodnight. It had become such a habit that she hardly thought about it anymore. It just was.

Should she? It seemed wrong just to turn and walk away.

Leaning down, she pressed a quick kiss to his forehead, though he likely was too deeply asleep to even notice. "Sleep well."

When she straightened, a faint smile twitched his mouth.

LEYLEIRA EASED the door to her room open slowly, not wanting to wake Ellarin if he was still sleeping. She had lingered long over lunch, chatting with her parents. They had caught her up on all the news of Arorien, and she could not help but note that Taranath acted far too casual every time Neia, the healer's daughter, was mentioned.

When the door swung open, it revealed Ellarin, sitting up on the bed, a book propped on his knees. He glanced up, smiling. "No need for sneaking. I am awake."

She closed the door and crossed the room. "The rest seems to have helped."

"It did. That, and Taranath's magic." Ellarin rubbed his fingers over the blanket. "I have been getting bouts like that every few months."

"Why did you not tell me?" Leyleira clasped her hands in front of her, stepping closer.

Ellarin sighed, his gaze dropping to his book. "Pride, I suppose. In the eyes of the entire kingdom, I am nothing but the dying prince. I guess I wanted you to see me as something more. I did not want to admit to weakness." He shook his head, staring at his hand as he flexed his fingers. "A futile attempt. The reality is that you will see me weak. It is inevitable."

"I do not think you are weak." Leyleira eased another step forward, halting next to the bed. She waited until he finally looked up at her, his blue eyes deep with pain and resignation. Feeling daring, she rested a hand on his shoulder. "I think you are one of the strongest people I know."

"I am glad someone thinks so." Ellarin shook his head, as if shrugging away the gloomy mood. When he glanced up at her, his smile was back, though it was edged with weariness once again. "How was your luncheon with your parents?"

"Enjoyable." Leyleira dropped her hand from his shoulder and crossed the room to where her packs had been set on the floor. She dug out one of the books she had brought along, then faced the bed again.

Ellarin had gone back to his own book. Or making a pretense of reading, anyway.

She could curl up on the window seat and read there. It was what she would have done, even a week ago before they had left Ellonahshinel.

But here in Lethorel, she could finally breathe and think and feel in a way she could not while under the king's glower and the court's pressure.

Choose him. It was all he wanted from her. And, perhaps, all she wanted from him was that he would choose her in return—not because she was simply the best option of the three his father had given him but because he was choosing her for her.

That would take both of them bending and giving. He had given much in arranging for this summer at Lethorel, including risking his fragile health.

It was time she made a move of her own.

She crossed the room, climbed onto the bed, then leaned not against the pillows on her side of the bed but against Ellarin's chest.

His breath caught, his muscles stiffening. "Leyleira?"

She tipped her head so that she could look up at him. "Is this all right?"

"I...yes...of course. I just..." Ellarin swallowed, holding his one hand in the air as if he was not sure what to do with his arm. "I do not mind at all."

"Good." She shifted, trying to get a bit more comfortable. This would be a lot better if Ellarin would just put his arm around her properly.

But he was still frozen. Apparently she had shocked him beyond coherent thought.

With a huff, she reached up, grabbed his wrist, leaned forward just enough so that she could tug his arm around her before she leaned back again. There. Much better. Especially when she tucked her hand over his on her waist.

That sword she so feared...it had never been Ellarin. Every time she had stiffened or flinched away from him, it had never been because of *him*. No, it had always been the pressure. The duty forcing her beyond what she was ready to give. King Illythor's glower.

But never Ellarin. He had never forced her. Never demanded. Never pushed her even when she was pushing herself beyond her own comfort. Instead, he had always been her shield.

Here in Lethorel with the sword removed, she could finally relax. Finally let herself fall for this prince she had married.

Ellarin still had not moved. She was not sure he had even breathed.

She laced her fingers with his. "You are supposed to be reading."

He made a noise in the back of his throat, then his breath stirred her hair. "And here I thought you would take my idea to start over to heart and make me sleep in the next room so I could court you properly."

It was a bit of a struggle to open her book with only

one hand, but it was worth it to avoid letting go of Ellarin's hand. "You are welcome to sleep in the other room if you wish."

"I have strict instructions from Taranath not to leave this bed." Paper rustled as Ellarin turned a page in his book, though she did not think he had registered what he was reading.

"Well, this is my bed, and I have no intention of giving it up." Leyleira pretended to read, though she did not take in any of the words on the page. How could she, when Ellarin's chest was warm against her back and his hand rested lightly on her waist? She worked to keep her tone that same sharply practical one that disguised any hint of her true emotions. "We shall just have to continue sharing. I am rather used to it, after ten years."

Besides, she had promised him on their wedding night that he would never be alone. She was not about to break that promise now.

But she was not going to bring that up now. She did not want to break this lighthearted moment between them.

"Is that how it is?" Ellarin's chuckle rumbled deep in his chest.

"Yes. And do not sound so amused by it." Leyleira kept her focus on her book, though she had read the last paragraph three times at this point, and she had yet to actually take in a word of it. "Now read your book."

He laughed again, his breath stirring her hair. "Very well, shynafera."

Iron heart. He had called her that many times over the years. But here in Lethorel, snuggled on her bed and reading—or pretending to read—as the peace and quiet of the place wrapped around them, she actually believed he meant it.

CHAPTER
SIX

D ressed in a lightweight shirt and trousers, her feet bare, Leyleira dove from one of the lower branches of Lethorel's willow tree. After a heartbeat of soaring through the air, she plunged into the water, her hands leading the way into the dark, frigid depths. The refreshingly cold water washed over her skin, sweeping away everything but that moment. She did not have to think. She did not have to feel. She could just *be*.

She swept her arms and kicked with her legs, propelling herself back to the surface. As her head broke into the warmth of the late summer day, she shook her head, swiping the water from her eyes. Her hair stuck to the back of her neck and her shoulders.

She glanced up just in time to catch sight of Ellarin diving off the same branch. She stayed where she was, treading water, to best appreciate his strong, graceful arc before he hit the water with minimal splash.

The water of the lake was clear enough that she caught a glimpse of his golden hair in the depths before he swam upward, breaking the surface within arm's reach of her.

Wet as it was, his blond hair appeared darker, framing his face. His white shirt plastered to his shoulders. Yet it was the bright flash of his smile—wide, unshadowed by the specter of death or duty—that sent a flutter through her. Had she ever seen Ellarin as happy and unburdened as he had been these past months here at Lethorel?

She kept treading water, facing him. "That was an impressive dive, amirami."

Her prince. The endearment felt natural after these past few months.

Ellarin's grin quirked as mischief glinted in his blue eyes. He flicked his fingers across the surface of the lake, sending droplets of water in her direction. "Not bad yourself."

"Not bad?" She flicked water back at him. "I will have you know that I have been diving from that branch since I was old enough to walk."

He swam closer and looped one of his arms around her waist, tugging her closer while treading water with his other arm. "I am sure you looked adorable back then."

He was so close, looking all handsomely water-slicked. His hand warmed against her waist, a contrast to the numbing water. Her breath caught in her chest, and it took all her concentration to keep treading water.

Time to turn things back to light and joking.

"Only back then?" Leyleira splashed him again, this time catching him full in the face.

Ellarin sputtered, releasing her as he lurched away. He swiped the water from his face, grinned, then sent a wave of water back at her.

She laughed and swam a little farther away before she turned and shoved more water at him.

With more laughter, they swam and splashed each other, the sunlight gleaming on the droplets.

Her parents sat on a bench at the base of Lethorel, sipping tea and placidly reading their books. Unlike Ellarin's father, they were perfectly content to stay out of Ellarin and Leyleira's business. The only comment either of them might make would be her dacha observing that they had scared away all the fish.

With a final splash in Ellarin's direction, Leyleira made a break for the shore. She staggered out of the water, then collapsed on a grassy patch mostly in the sun, still laughing and trying to catch her breath.

Ellarin scrambled out of the water after her, sprawling next to her. His shirt stuck to his chest while his blond hair straggled around his face and onto the grass around him. Right now, he did not look like he was dying. No, he looked very much whole and alive.

He swiped some of the hair from his face and glanced at her. "I do not think I ever heard you laugh before this summer."

Probably not. The oppressive weight always on her shoulders at Ellonahshinel was not conducive to laughter.

Feeling bold, she reached out and clasped his two fingers, the backs of their hands pressed together. "I do not think I heard you laugh either."

"No. I do not think you did." Ellarin stared upward, his face dappled with the shadows of the leaves overhead. "I am not the type to laugh in the face of death. With my father and the kingdom forever throwing that reality in my face, it makes for a somber mood."

That it did. As Ellarin's wife, she was subject to the same reality.

Leyleira took in the deep greens of the trees, the shimmering reflections on the lake, the arch of the pure blue sky above. She hardly dared admit it out loud, but she knew he would understand. "I do not want to go back."

"Me neither." Ellarin heaved a sigh, the last of the light disappearing from his eyes. "Here at Lethorel, I have felt more alive than I have in years. Yet when we go back, my father will be back to his glowering self. He is going to go back to pushing you for an heir and shunting me off to meaningless work when I know I can do so much more for our kingdom. I do not have to sit around twiddling my thumbs waiting to die. I want to actually *live*."

"Then live." Leyleira turned her head to face him again. "What duties would you like to take on, if you were given a choice?"

For a long moment, Ellarin continued to stare at the sky. Then he faced her, shifting just enough so that their shoulders brushed. "I would like to take over the weekly court sessions where the king meets with petitioners. As we both well know, my father is hardly the most sympathetic of kings. I could actually hear our people in a way he cannot. Then there is you."

"You would want me to sit in court with you?" Leyleira held her breath, her heart pounding harder.

It was traditional that the queen sat in court with the king. She was the assurance to the female petitioners that their needs would be heard and understood.

Right now, King Illythor had no queen. Nor was the queen mother alive to take the queen's place. In the ten years since Leyleira had married Ellarin, King Illythor had yet to ask her to sit in court in the queen's stead. Perhaps he merely had not thought of it, since he had been sitting court alone for so long. Or maybe he did not think of it since he assumed Leyleira would never be queen because Ellarin would never be king.

Not that Leyleira was about to approach King Illythor

to ask. She did not want to sit in court at King Illythor's side.

But at Ellarin's side? That was a different matter entirely.

"If you would like to do so." Ellarin raised their linked hands, then pressed a light kiss to her fingertips. "I want you at my side in all things."

"I would like that." She tightened her grip on his fingers. "I think we can do much for our people, if we are given the chance."

"So do I." Ellarin held her gaze. "I do not want to go back to the way things were when we return to Ellonahshinel. Not just when it comes to my father, but also when it comes to us. We have found something together, here at Lethorel. I do not want to lose that."

"I do not want to lose this either." Leyleira searched the depths of his blue eyes, finding the same hopeful desperation mirrored there that welled in her own chest.

They had come so far over the summer. For the first time, what they had actually felt like a marriage instead of two strangers living next to each other.

But would this tenuous relationship be enough to withstand the pressure of his father and the court once they returned? Or would it snap?

If it did, their relationship would be in tatters, worse even than the cold indifference of before.

ELLARIN HELD LEYLEIRA'S HAND, savoring this moment with her. This summer at Lethorel had been even better than he imagined.

Except for that scare the first day, all the relaxation had seemed to help his illness. So much so that, while

Taranath checked in every other day, he spent most of the summer in Arorien courting the healer's daughter Neia.

Leyleira's parents were everything his father was not. They ate meals together. Her dacha invited him to go fishing in the mornings at least once a week.

Yet for all their warmth, they did not ask awkward questions. They kept to their own business and stayed out of Ellarin and Leyleira's. Even now, they were sipping their tea and very pointedly looking everywhere but at where Ellarin and Leyleira lay on the grass partway around the lake from Lethorel's huge willow.

He did not want to lose what he had found with Leyleira here. Nor did he want to return to the person he had become at Ellonahshinel. He wanted to smile. Laugh. Live.

Ellarin rested their clasped hands on his chest. "We have been learning how to choose each other here at Lethorel. As long as we continue to choose each other when we return to Ellonahshinel, then we will be strong enough to withstand whatever we face there."

He had to believe that. He could not lose her, now that he had found out just how much she meant to him.

"I hope so." Her voice held a doubtful note, and she turned her face away to stare at the sky instead of looking at him. That iron composure was tightening her features again.

Perhaps she was right to doubt. Would one summer really be enough to undo the habits of ten years of yielding to the pressures?

On their own, they had broken beneath the burdens. But if they actually faced the challenges together? That would make all the difference. He had to believe that.

Yet the thought of going back to Ellonahshinel and all its suffocating pressures after the freedom to breathe here at Lethorel tightened his throat, as if the weight was already crushing his lungs. What if they went back to the way they were? What if…

He would not let it happen. He would choose Leyleira. And when everything got too much, they could always come back here.

Actually…

He rolled onto an elbow and braced himself so that he was looking down into Leyleira's face. "We can come back here to Lethorel every summer."

She blinked up at him, her eyes widening. "Every summer?"

"Yes. Every summer." He grinned at his own brilliance. This was the perfect solution. As long as they never went more than a year without a trip to Lethorel, the weight of the court and the kingdom would not have a chance to crush them like it had before.

Leyleira gave a small snort, though her eyes held a glint of something that might have been hope. "It took ten years to get away the first time."

"My mistake for not thinking of this sooner." Ellarin held her gaze, their faces only inches apart. "It might not be for the whole summer, like this year, but for at least a week or two every summer."

Leyleira let go of his hand so that she could press both of her palms to his chest, over his heart. "And what about your health? The trip this time was difficult for you."

He refused to flinch at the implication. If the ride had been difficult this year, it would only grow more so as his illness became worse.

"Then we will drag Taranath along. I do not believe he will mind." Ellarin gently eased strands of her damp hair from her face. "This is important enough to risk a little discomfort on my part. I want to choose us, and if that takes a trip to Lethorel every summer, then that is what we will do."

Her brown eyes had gone deep and luminescent as she blinked up at him, her lips parting slightly. When she spoke, his name came out breathy. "Ellarin…"

He gathered her closer, leaning over her as he cradled her face with his hand. "Shynafera."

She fisted her hands in his damp shirt, as if prepared to tug him down to force him to cross the last few inches of space between them. "Kiss me."

"For duty? Or…" He traced his thumb over her cheek.

"Because I choose you." Her whisper was a breath of warmth between them.

He leaned closer and murmured into her ear, "And I choose you."

Her fingers tightened still further in his shirt. "Kiss me already. And it had better not be one of your chaste little forehead kisses."

"I thought you liked my forehead kisses." He brushed a kiss to her jaw below her ear.

"I do, but not when I have been waiting years for a proper kiss."

He trailed gentle, light kisses from her jaw to her cheek. "So demanding."

"Ellarin." A hint of a growl joined the frustration in her voice.

He kissed her nose, then her other cheek. Anywhere but her mouth.

"Ellarin." That growl deepened, her grip on his shirt so tight it was clear she was about to take matters into her own hands if he did not finally kiss her.

Well, he would not keep the lady waiting any longer. He dug his fingers into Leyleira's hair and kissed her as he had wanted to do for the past ten years.

CHAPTER
SEVEN

620 YEARS BFH

Ellarin lay on his stomach on the table in Taranath's healing room, clenching his fists and holding back his magic.

Taranath's magic spread through him, somehow scouring and soothing all at once.

Ellarin tipped his head and peered past Taranath to the benches along the far wall. Taranath's wife Neia and Leyleira sat side-by-side, laughing and talking softly enough that Ellarin could not hear what they were saying.

The sight brought a smile to Ellarin's face, despite the discomfort of Taranath's healing magic. The summers in Lethorel had not only brought Ellarin and Leyleira a deepening of their love, but Taranath had found love as well. After years of visiting, he had finally worked up the courage to court Neia properly. Ten years ago, they had finally married.

Ellarin glanced up at Taranath. "Linshi, Taranath. For giving me as much time as possible with her."

Taranath's smile tilted, both warm and sad all at once. "I only wish I could do more."

"You have done enough. Far more than anyone else has or could have." Ellarin shifted his gaze from Taranath back to Leyleira.

Her brown eyes danced with laughter as she and Neia talked. That smile, reserved but bright, curved her mouth in a way that was growing increasingly familiar to Ellarin.

A companionable silence fell once again before Taranath lifted his hand, his magic snuffing out. "All finished for this week."

Ellarin pushed upright and swung his legs over the edge of the table. He straightened his shirt and reached for the tunic he had set aside.

As he shrugged into it, Leyleira and Neia stood. The two of them shared one last smile—this one seeming to hold something unspoken between them that glinted in gleeful smiles in their eyes—before Leyleira swept across the room. When Ellarin held out a hand, she gripped it, holding it between both of hers. Both of them turned to Taranath.

Taranath gave a slight shrug. "Same as each week. The degeneration remains minimal, and I have healed as much of the damage as I can."

Ellarin gave a nod. It was as he expected. Yes, he was still dying. But Taranath was slowing it as much as possible. He could not halt it entirely, but Ellarin could tell the difference. He had far less progression in the past thirty years since Taranath had started healing him than in the years before Ellarin had found out exactly what was going on.

Ellarin hopped from the table, thankful when no pain lanced from his feet at the jolt against the floor. How he loved healing days. He always felt so much better afterwards.

Leyleira clasped two fingers with his, the backs of their hands pressed together. "Linshi, Taranath."

Taranath nodded to her, then reached a hand to Neia as she stepped to his side. "Are you still planning on tea tomorrow?"

"Yes." Leyleira smiled, then started for the door.

Ellarin hurried to fall into step with her before he was forced to let go of her hand. In the years since Taranath had married Neia, the four of them had begun to take tea together once a week. It was nice to socialize as friends in a setting other than one that centered around healing. It almost made him feel normal.

Leyleira set a brisk pace. Even quicker than her normal, graceful strides.

Ellarin swung their linked hands, taking in the quirk to her smile, as if she knew something he did not. "What has you grinning?"

"Not here." She glanced around, her smile fading into calm composure as a servant hurried in their direction. "I will tell you in our rooms."

Ellarin quickened his pace still further. If that was the case, then there was no reason to dawdle.

They had to slow once they reached the center of Ellonahshinel. The bustle on the branches made haste too difficult. Nor did they want to start rumors by hurrying.

They did, however, take the long way around to avoid going past the king's study. The last thing Ellarin wanted was to get cornered by his father and be forced to give the weekly report on his health. Whatever Leyleira wanted to tell him was far more important.

Finally, they reached the royal branch. Ellarin tugged Leyleira into their main room and kicked the door shut with his foot so that he could rest his hands on Leyleira's waist and tug her close. "We are alone now. What is it that you needed to tell me?"

He had a suspicion, but he hardly dared let himself even think it, much less voice the hope out loud.

Leyleira met his gaze, her smile returning, her eyes filled with a light he had never seen before. "I asked Neia to confirm my suspicions. I am expecting."

Expecting. He was going to be a father. They were going to be parents.

Ellarin buried his fingers in her hair and kissed her. When they were both breathless, his senses reeling, he pulled back enough to hold Leyleira close and press a softer kiss to her forehead. "I love you, shynafera."

"And I love you." Leyleira rested her head against his shoulder. After a moment, her arms tightened around his waist. "Do you think we can avoid telling your father until we have to?"

Ellarin could not help but chuckle. "Absolutely. Though, I am going to be hard-pressed to keep this a secret."

"In that case, could we perhaps leave for Lethorel as soon as possible?" The warmth in Leyleira's voice disappeared. "I would rather savor this between the two of us rather than spend the next few months under the scrutiny of the entire court and kingdom as they anticipate their long-awaited heir."

"That sounds like an excellent plan to me. I will see what I can do." Ellarin pressed a light kiss to her hair.

The entire kingdom would celebrate their child as the heir they needed to replace their dying prince. King Illythor would gloat that he had finally gotten exactly what he wanted.

Only Ellarin and Leyleira knew that they, too, wanted

this child. Not because they had to have a child for the sake of the kingdom, but because they wanted to be parents. Wanted a child of their own to raise. Wanted to build a family.

"I suppose we will have to return to Ellonahshinel before the baby is born." Leyleira sighed, her breath stirring against his neck. "Though it is rather tempting to just stay at Lethorel until after the baby is born."

He laughed against her hair, though the chuckle lacked true warmth. "My father would be apoplectic."

"All the more reason to do it."

If only he dared. His father might become so enraged that he would doubt the baby was even theirs. Yes, Taranath would be able to verify paternity with his magic, and Neia as Leyleira's midwife could attest to the truth. But King Illythor would never treat their child the same. Not that he was ever going to be a kindly dachasheni, but he could make their baby's childhood quite awful if he wished.

He would still be angry enough once they returned from Lethorel and he noticed the pregnancy. He would be able to add up the dates. He would know that they had known before they left for Lethorel, and they had not told him. Yet the anger would not last long. King Illythor was, after all, getting the heir for which he had so carefully arranged.

Leyleira cradled her newborn son in her arms, marveling at his small weight and perfectly tiny fingers. Tufts of black hair covered his head while his tiny lips pursed in sleep.

Ellarin sat on the bed next to her, his gaze fixed on

their son as well. Almost tentatively, he reached out and smoothed a hand over the fluff of Lorsan's hair. "He is perfect."

"Yes." Leyleira snuggled the baby close. Their son. So small. So innocent. So unaware of the burdens that already rested on his tiny shoulders.

Ellarin pressed a kiss to her temple. "And you are amazing."

She opened her mouth to reply but froze as footsteps scuffed on the stairs to their room a moment before someone pounded loudly on the wood. She suppressed a sigh. Only one person would have the audacity to demand entry and intrude on such a moment.

Ellarin heaved a sigh, rolled to his feet, and opened the door. "Daresheni."

King Illythor swept past him with barely a glance. He halted next to the bed, his glower barely wavering as he stared down at Lorsan in her arms.

Leyleira cradled Lorsan closer, fighting the instinct to jump from the bed and run from the room to protect her son from King Illythor.

It was one thing for King Illythor to manipulate and pressure her and Ellarin. But she would not allow him to do the same to her son.

"You have done well, finally producing my heir." King Illythor's gaze never left Lorsan to indicate if he was addressing Leyleira, Ellarin, or the two of them. "Though it would be best if you produced a spare or two. We will not know if this heir is viable or if he inherited his father's malady until he comes into his magic."

That was it. Holding her son in one arm, Leyleira slapped her other hand to the wall beside her and shoved her magic into it.

Branches lashed out of the wall, though she halted

them just short of touching King Illythor. She was angry but not enough to risk being accused of treason.

Not yet, anyway.

She met King Illythor's gaze with all the iron and anger welling inside her. "Get out. We have done as you demanded. But Lorsan is *our* son. You will leave him alone."

King Illythor clenched his fists, green magic winking around his fingers as if he was prepared to fight her, magic-for-magic. "He is *my* heir. He will need to be raised to know his duty."

"We will raise him as we see fit. You will *not* interfere." Leyleira's fingers shook as she barely restrained her magic from lashing out at the king. She had put up with his harassment for thirty years. But she refused to let him harm her son.

Ellarin stepped forward, placing himself between Leyleira and King Illythor. Bolts of blue magic crackled over his fingers. "Lorsan is *my* heir, not yours. As long as I live and breathe, *I* am your heir. And I have no intention of dying anytime soon."

For the first time, King Illythor's expression wavered, cracking with something almost like concern. Or, at least, as much concern as someone as hardened as him could manage. "Ellarin, your magic..."

"I will use however much of my magic as it takes to protect my son." Blue bolts grew up Ellarin's arm, crackling with far more power than Leyleira had ever seen him use.

Her skin prickled with the power filling the room, the taste of it coating her tongue. In her arms, Lorsan shifted and gave a whimper.

King Illythor took a step back, his eyes widening. He might be able to fight Leyleira, if it came down to it. But no one could stand before Ellarin if he ever used his magic, even if his magic was weaker due to his disease. King Illythor's throat bobbed with his swallow. "I would never harm your son."

"You have harmed the two of us plenty with your words. I do not trust that you will not do the same with my son." Ellarin stalked forward, his blue eyes blazing, his hair lifting as if on a breeze thanks to the electric power of his magic. "My wife asked you to leave. Now."

King Illythor darted a glance between Ellarin and Leyleira before he spun on his heel and marched from the room, as if he was hurrying but trying to appear that he was not. He slammed the door behind him.

Leyleira exhaled and released her magic, dropping her hand from the wall to cradle Lorsan in both arms once again. She rocked Lorsan slightly to soothe him.

Ellarin turned to her, his magic still shivering around him, his eyes still blazing.

He had been amazing. So fierce. So strong. So much an elven warrior of old. He had defended her and their child, risking his own life by using his magic even knowing doing so would trigger his disease.

She loved him. Utterly, wholeheartedly, in a way she had never imagined herself capable of loving anyone.

Something shifted, deepened, inside her chest. And she felt *him*. His pain. His roiling emotions. The essence of him lodging in her chest as she was hidden in his.

An elishina. It had to be. She had suspected one was forming, though it had remained so mild it had been hard to pin down.

But this was the deep elishina. The kind found in stories of old.

LEYLEIRA HAD BEEN AMAZING. The way she had stood up to his father, her eyes blazing, her magic flooding the walls of their bedchamber, protectively cradling their son to her side...he would have kissed her then and there if his father had not been there.

That confrontation had been long in coming and, together, they had forced his father to back off. He drew in a deep breath, and it felt like the first breath of freedom he had tasted outside of those summers in Lethorel.

He turned to Leyleira and held her gaze, a crackle not caused by his magic shivering between them.

He loved her. So much more than he had ever imagined loving anyone.

Something jolted, deep inside his chest. So strong and fierce that he caught his breath and dropped his magic.

An elishina.

He savored the sense of her as it washed through him. Soothing. Comforting. Composed yet fierce.

Wait. No. No, they could not form an elishina. He loved her, but he did not want this. An elishina was too dangerous for her.

"No, no." Ellarin spun away from her, trying to stuff down the panic that sparked his magic once again. "This was not the plan. We were not supposed to form an elishina."

"We have been choosing each other for years. What did you think love was, except choosing each other each and every day?" Leyleira's voice held a hint of a laugh.

"Yes, yes. I know. And I love you. I just did not want an elishina." Ellarin dug his fingers into his hair as pain lanced down his arms. This could not be happening. It was bad enough that he had to suffer—that he was dying. But he could not let Leyleira be put in danger because of this disease. He just could not.

"Well, we have. You cannot take it back now." Leyleira's voice cut stern and matter-of-fact. A hint cool, even.

When he glanced over his shoulder at her, her expression had shuttered into that composed look he knew all too well. He had angered her with his reaction to this.

He dropped to his knees beside the bed and took her hand, peering up into her eyes. "I love you. If I was not dying, then I would be thrilled to form such a deep elishina with you. But I *am* dying, and an elishina like this will put you at risk."

Her gaze softened. "What if this is for the best? What if I can keep you alive, like the stories of old?"

Panic surged through him, far more powerful than the pain stabbing through his body after using his magic. "No. No, please, do not. I will not be Daesyn to your Inara. Our situation is not like theirs. My injury is not a temporary one that can be fully healed if you just hold on a little longer. It *will* kill me, and it will kill you too if you try to halt it."

"But what if I can give you some of my years? What if I can buy us more time?"

"No. Such a thing usually happens between an elf and a human. I do not know if it will work between two elves." He squeezed her hand between both of his, despite the agony the movement sent up his arms. "If you tried such a thing, you might feel what I feel. And I will not inflict my pain on you, not even to give me a handful more years. I could not bear it if I had to watch you suffer for hundreds of years, knowing that I was the source of that pain. Please, do not ask that of me."

Leyleira blinked, her eyes wet. "But that is exactly what you are asking of me. If an elishina could give me more time with you..."

"I know." He lifted her hand and pressed a light kiss to her knuckles. "But I am thinking of more than just us. Our kingdom—our son—will need you when I am gone. If we were both to die, that would leave the kingdom and our son solely in the hands of my father."

Leyleira gave a slight shudder and glanced down at their newborn son, cradled in her arm. A single tear trickled down her cheek. "I do not want to watch you die, Ellarin."

He reached up and cradled her face, swiping the tear away with his thumb. "I know. I do not want to die. I do not want to leave you and Lorsan. But it will come eventually, though I will likely have hundreds of years yet before it does."

She drew in a shuddering breath, leaning into his hand.

He started to push himself upright, but a fresh wave of pain sent him back onto his knees. He dropped his hand from Leyleira's face as his fingers spasmed with agony. He could not help his gasp of pain as he gritted his teeth, struggling to breathe through it.

"Ellarin!" Leyleira bolted straighter, reaching for him. "Do I need to send for Taranath? Is this because you used your magic? Here, get on the bed. You need to rest."

He all but collapsed beside her on the bed. He sank onto the pillows, trying to fight the waves of pain. "Yes."

As he squeezed his eyes shut, he could sense when Leyleira accessed her magic. She must be using it to send a summons through Ellonahshinel itself.

After a few moments, Leyleira's fingers gently brushed hair from his face. "Is there anything I can do?"

"No." He cracked his eyes open. "This is why I do not want you to try to use the elishina to prolong my life. You can feel my pain, can you not?"

She gave a slight nod, as if she did not want to admit the truth.

He fumbled for her hand, finding it and squeezing her fingers as much as he could. "Promise me, Leyleira, that when the time comes, you will let me go. Please. Do not try to fight my death with the elishina. It is a fight you cannot win."

For a long moment, she stared down at their newborn son, as if taking in the reason why she needed to make this promise. Then she met Ellarin's gaze and gripped his hand. "I promise. But I also promise that I will be here as you fight this."

"Linshi." Ellarin let his eyes drift closed again. "And I promise that I will fight for every day, every breath, every moment I am given with you."

If she said something, he missed hearing it. He drifted in a haze of pain until the vague sound of voices came from above him moments before Taranath's familiar, soothing magic washed through him. As the magic banished the pain, he sank into sleep.

CHAPTER
EIGHT

600 YEARS BFH

"Linshi, amir. Amirah." Smiling, the petitioner bowed, then exited the great hall, escorted by a clerk.

Moments later, Ellarin's personal clerk stepped into the hall. "That was the last petitioner for today. Amirisheni."

"Linshi." Ellarin rose, straightening his formal robes around him, then extended an arm to Leyleira. "Please see that action is taken as per my decrees today."

Leyleira rested her hand on his arm and gracefully rose to her feet, meeting his gaze with a hint of a smile playing around her mouth.

The clerk bobbed a bow. "Yes, sire. I will see that it is done." He turned on his heel and hurried from the great hall.

He was an efficient clerk, and he would see that the promises Ellarin and Leyleira made to the various petitioners were carried out. If he needed to follow up with Ellarin, he would.

In the years since Ellarin and Leyleira had taken over meeting with petitioners in King Illythor's stead, the number of petitioners had risen. It seemed that many had been reluctant to bring their problems to King Illythor, but they found a much more sympathetic ear in Ellarin and Leyleira.

Ellarin enjoyed it. This was what it meant to be king. Not manipulating or bullying, but caring for the people, down to the individuals who came seeking help.

Would Ellarin ever become king for real? Or would he die before he had a chance to do more than take whatever scraps of responsibility his father would give him?

He and Leyleira made their way across the branches of Ellonahshinel, their formal attire rustling, heavy and hot, in the summer heat, despite the coolness provided by the thick foliage overhead. Without discussing it, they took the long route, in spite of the heat, to avoid going past the king's study.

Finally, they reached their suite of rooms. As soon as Ellarin opened the door, Lorsan bounded across the main room and flung himself at them. "Dacha! Macha!"

Ellarin caught Lorsan, patting his back. "Sason."

Leyleira smiled and gripped Lorsan's shoulders. "Were you good for Neia?"

Lorsan nodded, his eyes wide and innocent. "Uh-huh."

Across the room, Neia unfolded herself from the floor and stood. She stepped around the scattered toy animals on the floor. "Of course he was good. He is a dear."

Ellarin smiled and shared a look with Leyleira. Of course Lorsan was good for Neia. He saved all his tantrums and rebellion for them.

While Leyleira spoke to Neia, Ellarin hurried up the stairs into their bedchamber and changed out of his heavy robes for something less formal and more comfortable.

When he returned to the main room, Neia had left and Leyleira was on the floor with Lorsan. He was playing with his toys, and there seemed to be some kind of crisis among the woodland realm.

Ellarin pressed a kiss to Leyleira's temple, then ruffled Lorsan's black hair. "I will be back shortly."

Leyleira nodded, though her smile faded. She did not say anything out loud in front of Lorsan, but her concern was there in the pained glimmer in her eyes.

He would be fine. Things with his father had been cold and formal since their showdown over Lorsan. But in a strange way, that was better than before. King Illythor had refrained from bullying them, and he had stayed away from Lorsan beyond a few glowers now and then.

Ellarin ached, wishing his father could be a true dachasheni to his son. The only true grandparents Lorsan had were Leyleira's parents during their visits to Lethorel each summer.

Ellarin had never had a dachasheni since both of his had died several hundred years before he had been born. Would his own grandchildren also lack a dachasheni? Would Ellarin at least live long enough to meet them?

He shook himself, forcing himself to leave his little family behind to face his father. He strode along the branches, then halted outside of the king's study.

The door stood open, his father's voice all but shouting inside. A clerk cringed in front of the king's desk.

King Illythor pounded the oak with his fist. "Those upstart humans! Who do they think they are, to harass our ships?"

Ellarin stepped into the room. "The human pirates are still harassing our fishing vessels?"

"They killed an elf and sank a ship this time." King Illythor shoved to his feet. "Inferior ants. They are a nuisance, but they have crossed a line. It is time they were dealt with."

"Yes, sire." Ellarin clasped his hands behind his back. What else could he say? If not for this illness, he would have been sent to deal with such things.

His father regarded him for a moment, as if thinking that same thing. Then he pushed away from the desk. "I am going to the border to deal with this myself. Ellarin, you will be in charge here until I return. Do not fail me."

Ellarin gritted his teeth. His disease did not affect his mind. He was perfectly capable of handling paperwork and making decisions for the kingdom. "I will see to the kingdom while you are away."

"Good. I will leave in the morning." King Illythor swung his gaze to the clerk. "Send word to my warriors. I want four squads waiting for me at the outskirts of Estyra in the morning. We ride at dawn."

ELLARIN HANDED the stack of paperwork to the waiting clerk. The clerk bowed, then hurried from the room.

One stack down, several more to go.

As Ellarin tugged the next stack of paperwork closer, another clerk hurried into the room. Ellarin took the first paper from the stack, no more than flicking a glance at the clerk. "I am not yet finished with the aspen blight reports yet."

"S-sire. I am not here for the reports. I have a message for you." The elf shifted from foot to foot, his face pale.

Ellarin set the paper aside and faced the elf. Only then did he realize this elf was not a clerk. He wore travel-stained clothes, his hair hanging limp and grungy down his back. "What is the message?"

The elf swallowed, then bowed fully from the waist as he would to his king instead of his prince. "Daresheni, I regret to inform you that your father has been killed."

Ellarin froze, a faint buzzing starting in his ears. He could not so much as blink, much less breathe, as he gaped at the messenger.

"His ship was attacked by the pirates." The messenger swallowed, as if he feared Ellarin's reaction to this news. "The pirates had weapons that fired with the human invention of gunpowder, and they were able to stand off far enough that your father and his warriors could not use their magic. Your father's ship was sunk and one of the other ships was severely damaged."

Ellarin drew in a breath, trying to sort through the roil inside him. What should he feel at this news? Grief, yes. Yet the grief was more a sorrow over the lack of relationship with his father than his father's death.

Mostly, there was just…relief. And guilt, for feeling so relieved.

Ellarin forced himself to meet the messenger's gaze, his voice strangely calm in his ears. "And they are sure my father is dead?"

"His body was retrieved from the water after the pirates left. The warriors are transporting his body back to Estyra for burial as we speak."

His father was dead.

Ellarin was king.

ELLARIN KEPT his head high as he strode down the center aisle of the great hall of Ellonahshinel. Leyleira's hand rested on his arm as she kept pace with him. His dark green robe trailed behind him, blending with her silver one. His silver tunic hung heavy with intricate embroidery in patterns of trees and leaves, but it left a section of his chest visible.

Leyleira's deep green dress was shoulderless, though gauzy sleeves trailed from her upper arms down to her elbows.

To either side of them, benches were lined up in rows and packed with elves from all over the kingdom, both noble and common. In the front row, Leyleira's parents sat tall, honoring their daughter by making the trip to Ellonahshinel to witness her coronation.

In one corner, musicians played a regal, swelling tune on pipes, giving Ellarin a beat for his measured pace.

At the front of the room, a male elf stood, dressed in a light green tunic only barely less ornate than Ellarin's. He had been elected by the elven council to perform this duty today, thereby representing all of Tarenhiel. In his hands, he cradled a silver bowl filled with an amber viscous liquid. Sap from the heart of Ellonahshinel itself.

When they reached the front, Ellarin knelt, and Leyleira knelt next to him.

The elf presented Ellarin with the bowl. Ellarin dipped his finger into the sap, then traced a rune onto his own forehead. It was more difficult doing it on himself than it had been tracing the rune on Leyleira's forehead at their wedding. But the sap would be far less noticeable to others if he messed it up too badly.

Once he was finished with the rune on his forehead, he dipped his finger into the sap again and traced a rune on his right cheek. Then he moved to draw a rune on his chest. As he finished this rune, he spoke in a voice that he hoped would carry throughout the room. "I vow to dedicate my mind, my thoughts, my words, my body, and my heart for the good of my kingdom and my people."

The elf took one step to the side and presented the bowl to Leyleira. She repeated his movements, drawing the runes on herself with the sap, then repeating the vow.

Once she was done, the elf set the bowl aside and picked up the ornate silver crown of the elf king. It was shaped like twining branches of an oak tree rising in spires and was set with a few winking, green gems. The elf stepped forward and placed the crown on Ellarin's head. "With this crown, you take on the duties of the throne. May you reign as a servant to your people and a guardian of the trees of Tarenhiel."

Ellarin closed his eyes, taking in the weight of the crown resting on his head.

The elf picked up a second crown, a smaller version of his but set with diamonds. He repeated the declaration as he placed the crown on Leyleira's head.

As he did, Leyleira's fingers tightened on Ellarin's arm. But it was the only sign she gave of how seriously she took this moment.

The elf straightened and faced the two of them. "Rise, Ellarin Daresheni, Leyleira Maresheni. May your reigns be long, peaceful, and prosperous."

Ellarin stood, Leyleira at his side. Together, they faced their people.

In the front row, Leyleira's macha smiled and joined in the gentle cheers that filled the room. At her side, Leyleira's dacha gave what was the closest thing to a smile Ellarin had ever seen on the grave elf. In his seat between his grandparents and Neia, Lorsan glanced around, more puzzled than excited by what was happening. Neia was beaming and Taranath was cheering the loudest of anyone in the room.

Ellarin was never supposed to be king. He was supposed to die, the forgotten prince who never wore the crown.

Instead, here he stood. King of Tarenhiel. With Leyleira, his heart-bonded wife as queen at his side.

Ellarin was not sure he could be a better king than his father was—for all his faults, King Illythor had ruled Tarenhiel well enough—but he was determined to be a better father, even if it meant sacrificing his kingdom. Perhaps that made him a bad king. But he would not place the burdens on Lorsan that his father had on him.

CHAPTER
NINE

"Dacha! Macha!"

The panic in Lorsan's voice froze Ellarin's blood. He bolted from the desk in the main room at Lethorel, where he had been poring over paperwork. He dashed down the stairs, catching sight of Leyleira as she raced past, her book abandoned on the bench beneath the shade of the willow tree.

Had Lorsan hurt himself? Been attacked by a rabid animal? Tarenhiel was not at war. Even the human pirates were not the concern they had once been. Ellarin had reached out to the humans and through emissaries he had negotiated a semblance of cooperation for patrolling the Hydalla River and ocean coasts.

Ellarin reached the ground and raced in Leyleira's footsteps to where Lorsan stood at the edge of the lake.

As he neared, Ellarin nearly tripped over the roots that were bursting from the ground. Green magic poured from

Lorsan's hands, and all the underbrush around him grew inches in mere seconds.

"It is all right, sason." Leyleira touched their son's shoulder. Her magic flooded over Lorsan's, calming the plants before the trees got out of hand. "Magic can be a bit unruly the first time it manifests. Just take calming breaths and concentrate on the feel of the magic inside you."

Ellarin halted a few yards away. There was nothing he could do to help since Lorsan had inherited Leyleira's plant growing magic instead of the magic of the ancient kings.

Ellarin could not help but feel relieved, though he likely should not harbor such thoughts. The kingdom might not feel the same way. Many had been hoping that Ellarin and Leyleira's heir would inherit his magic and become the warrior that Ellarin could not be.

But that magic might come with the greater chance that Lorsan would inherit Ellarin's disease as well.

Leyleira managed to get Lorsan's magic under control. But Lorsan's eyes remained wide, and he glanced from his hands up to Ellarin. "Does this mean...will I..."

Ellarin crossed the distance between them and gripped Lorsan's shoulders. "We cannot know. But Taranath can examine you once he and Neia return from Arorien this evening."

Lorsan nodded, but his gaze dropped to the ground rather than focusing on Ellarin or Leyleira.

Ellarin had to swallow back a lump in his throat. His son was growing up so fast. He stood nearly as tall as Ellarin now, though he was still skinny and gangly with youth. And now he had come into his magic, a sign that he was truly on his way to adulthood and leaving childhood behind.

Ellarin and Leyleira had always been honest with Lorsan about Ellarin's condition and the fact that Lorsan could inherit the disease.

Now the possibilities could be a reality. They would likely know for sure tonight once Taranath returned.

It was bad enough facing this disease himself. How could he handle it if he had to watch the same fear, the same pain, flash in his son's eyes?

He would tell him that he was still valuable. That he might be dying, but he could still live a long and full life. That this disease was not the end.

But he would rather not have to face that conversation.

LEYLEIRA PACED across the main room, trying to still the roil inside her chest before her own magic broke loose and tore through Lethorel.

Their son had come into his magic. Would the signs be noticeable enough that Taranath could tell if the magic had triggered the same disease that Ellarin had? How could she bear it if she had to watch her son slowly die in the same way that she had watched her husband deal with the pain and weakness for the past hundred and ten years of marriage?

The door opened, and Taranath and Ellarin stepped inside, followed by Lorsan.

Leyleira glanced from Ellarin to Lorsan to Taranath, searching their faces for any sign of the result. They were all somber, but not as defeated as she might have expected, had the news been bad. She faced Ellarin. "Is he..."

Ellarin gripped her shoulders. "Our son is fine."

"I could not find any sign of the disease, and I am very familiar with it after all these years." Taranath shrugged, the only one of them with anything resembling a smile. "I would like to examine him once a year for the next decade or so as he continues to come into his magic, just to make sure, but I do not think there is any cause for concern."

"Linshi, Taranath." Leyleira released a long breath. Their son was fine. He was not dying the way Ellarin was. He was healthy and strong. She then reached a hand to Lorsan.

Lorsan stepped forward, and she gripped his shoulder. He gave her a hint of a smile, though he still seemed burdened.

"What is wrong, sason?" Leyleira squeezed her son's shoulder, but he stared at the floor rather than meeting her gaze.

"Nothing."

"Sason." She dragged out the word, her tone brooking no argument.

Lorsan sighed and peered first at her, then at Ellarin. "I am relieved, but I feel guilty for being so relieved. It feels wrong to celebrate when Dacha still...you are still..."

Ellarin rested a hand on Lorsan's other shoulder, but he shared a look with Leyleira before he turned to their son. "As a parent, all I want for you is that you are thriving in the life you are given. I am thankful that you will not have to face what I do. You do not have to be ashamed by your relief. This disease is terrible. Yes, I have come to terms with it, and I have a good life. But that does not mean I am not angry or frustrated or that I do not struggle with the realities of it. I would not wish that for you."

Lorsan nodded, but the hunch to his shoulders remained. "Why does life have to be so hard sometimes?"

Leyleira swallowed. She had asked that same question many a time. Especially in the long, dark nights when Ellarin was curled on the bed, wracked with pain from his latest bout as the disease ravaged his body, doing his best to block her in their elishina so that she did not feel what he did.

Ellarin released a long breath, his gaze shifting to stare into space rather than look at any of them. "This world is broken. It is slowly dying, much the way I am. The reality of life is that you will face hardships and suffering. Perhaps that hardship will not be this particular disease, but there will be other things you will have to face. Yet you cannot let the hardships break you or harden you. Instead, the hardships will teach you compassion for others, a depth of love for those around you, and an unshakable hope in the things worth believing."

Lorsan swallowed and nodded.

Leyleira drew both him and Ellarin closer. "Your dacha is right. We are a family. We will be here for each other no matter what comes."

430 Years BFH

Ellarin set the satchel filled with supplies on the table in Lorsan's suite of rooms. A silver bowl already rested on the table. "Are you ready to begin?"

Across the table from him, Lorsan rocked back and forth on his feet as if he was still a little elfling instead of a grown elf about to be married. He was beaming from ear to ear. "Yes, Dacha."

Ellarin could not help but smile in return. His son was

so happy on this, his wedding day. So different from the way Ellarin had felt on his own wedding day.

Not that Ellarin would ever regret the decision to marry Leyleira. She was his heart. They had found their way, despite his father's best efforts.

Ellarin unpacked the items needed for the eshinelt, speaking as he did so. "This eshinelt is a symbol of the vow you will make today. While the magic the two of you place in the eshinelt is believed to bind you, the true binding is in your hearts."

Lorsan nodded, his attempt at a solemn expression unable to hide his eagerness. "I understand, Dacha."

He did not. Not truly. But he would. Today, he and Vianola were young and in love. Everything was easy, life spreading golden and lovely before them.

Their love would deepen during the first argument. The first hardship. The shared trials. The shared joys. The decades of laughter and smiles.

Ellarin placed the last item on the table and met Lorsan's gaze. "Love is hard. There will be days when you do not feel like loving Vianola, as unimaginable as that is today. You will need to choose to love her anyway, no matter what you might be feeling."

For the first time, Lorsan's sober expression matched the solemness in his eyes. He took in Ellarin before he looked away, staring down at the items laid out for the eshinelt. His repeated answer came out softer. "I understand."

Perhaps, this time, he did.

Ellarin did not need to belabor the point. Lorsan had grown up with the reality of Ellarin's illness. He had watched his parents deal with the difficulties that came with such a disease. Hopefully Ellarin and Leyleira had provided a good example for him.

They were at least a better example than Ellarin's father had been. Not a high tree branch to get over, granted.

Ellarin gestured to the herbs and dried flowers he had brought. "Let us begin."

Lorsan reached for the bowl, then halted and met Ellarin's gaze. "I am glad you are here today, Dacha."

Ellarin had to swallow back the sudden lump in his throat. He cleared his throat, reached out, and gripped Lorsan's shoulder. "So am I."

As unlikely as it had seemed, Ellarin was still here, still alive. Yes, he grew tired faster than he used to. Tonight, he would likely be wracked with pain after the busyness of the day.

But he was alive and standing. He had lived long enough to teach his son to make the eshinelt and he would watch his son marry in a few short hours.

He did not take this day for granted, and he intended to savor every moment.

LEYLEIRA SAT NEXT to Ellarin behind the table on the raised dais. Before them, tables ringed the edges of the great hall while graceful dancers swayed to the lilting of the flutes.

In the center of the hall, Lorsan held his new bride Vianola as they glided through the dance steps. His black hair flowed down his back, a match to Vianola's dark brown hair that paired well with her warm brown eyes and the silver dress she wore. The two of them stared into each other's eyes as if they found their whole world there.

Her son was happy and married. Her husband was still alive to witness this day, though by the lines etched into Ellarin's face and the dark circles under his eyes, he was exhausted.

She clasped his hand beneath the table, holding his fingers lightly to avoid paining him. She leaned closer, whispering into his ear. "I do not think anyone would notice if we left."

Everyone was enjoying the feasting and dancing. Vianola's parents, who had traveled all the way from their home in the north of Tarenhiel near the Gulmorth Gorge, were too busy mingling with the other nobility to notice if Ellarin and Leyleira left.

Ellarin sighed, staring at the whirling dancers before them as if he did not want to admit just how weak he was.

But he could not lie to her, even if he wished to try. She could feel his stabbing pain and dragging exhaustion through their elishina.

Ellarin dipped his head in a reluctant nod. "Yes. I need the rest."

Leyleira glided to her feet, then turned to Ellarin. He stood, though he used his grip on her hand to steady himself. She ached to see Ellarin struggling, but she kept her expression smooth.

Hand in hand, they made their way around the edge of the room, headed for the nearest door.

As they passed, Taranath and Neia got up from their table and followed them out.

Once they were on the quiet, deserted branch outside, Ellarin halted and pressed a hand to the wall of the great hall.

Leyleira stepped closer and wrapped her arm around his waist to steady him. He had given so much to be there for their son today. But now he needed rest.

Taranath joined them and rested a hand on the back of

Ellarin's neck. As soon as he did, a frown added lines to Taranath's face. "You are exhausted, Daresheni."

Ellarin gave a tired huff of a laugh. "It could not be helped today."

"I advise at least a day of bed rest, if not two." Taranath withdrew his hand. "I will be by in the morning to check how you are faring."

"I will be fine." Ellarin pushed away from the wall, only to stagger.

Leyleira hurried to prop him up. "I will see that he rests."

It would not be easy. Ellarin could be awfully stubborn when he set his mind to it, especially when he became frustrated by his body's limits.

Perhaps she would declare a "work on paperwork in bed" day for both of them.

"Do not hesitate to send word tonight if needed." Taranath met Leyleira's gaze.

She gave a slight nod. They all knew that she would be the one making the call that Ellarin needed another healing. "Linshi, Taranath. Now, I need to get him to bed."

"I am not a child to be sent off to bed." Ellarin's voice held a hint of a growl. But he draped his arm over Leyleira's shoulders, leaning a bit more of his weight on her.

"No. Perhaps I should have said that *we* need to get to bed." Leyleira shifted to better brace herself under his weight.

Taranath nodded, sent one more glance over Ellarin as if to make sure he would be all right, and returned to Neia's side.

Neia sent Leyleira a smile, but an edge of sadness remained in her eyes. Today must have been hard for her.

She and Taranath had been married for over two hundred years, but they had yet to have a child. Over the years, Neia and Taranath had always willingly watched Lorsan, treating him as a nephew. But that relationship was not the same as having a child of their own.

Leyleira was not quite sure what to say to Neia, especially today. She could not fully understand that ache. She had a son. Today, she had watched him marry the love of his life. She did not experience the same empty ache that Neia did.

Taranath and Neia headed one way along the branch while Leyleira and Ellarin went the other way.

Leyleira set a slow pace that Ellarin could manage without having to lean on her too heavily. Thankfully, their rooms were only one level and one branch away from the great hall. The hardest part was the stairs that led from their main room to their bedchamber. They were both breathing heavily by the time Leyleira pushed open the door to their room.

She settled Ellarin on their bed, and he sighed as he collapsed onto the pillows. She sat on the end of the bed and pulled one of his feet onto her lap and started to unlace his boots. He must have been tired because he did not protest her help as she took off one boot, then the other.

Once she had dumped both of the boots to the side, she climbed onto the bed—awkward in the flowing skirt and slight train from her formal attire—and took one of his hands. She gently massaged his fingers, working her way up each finger, then his palm before she moved to his arm.

He heaved another sigh, his eyes closed. "That feels good. Linshi, shynafera."

"Should I send for Taranath?" Leyleira set down his

arm and reached for his other hand.

"I am fine. I just need rest." Ellarin cracked his eyes open, giving her a slight smile as he gently brushed his fingers over her cheek. "I am alive today. I saw our son get married. A little pain was worth it."

"I wish…" Her words were choked off by the lump in her throat.

Ellarin tugged her down, and she settled in next to him, her head on his shoulder. He wrapped his arms around her, then pressed a kiss to her hair. "I know. But wishing cannot change our reality. Right now, I am simply going to be thankful for the time I am given and enjoy the life I have instead of wishing for the impossible."

Wise. But it did not make the difficult moments any easier.

Leyleira held him and told herself that she was not going to cry. Not today. Their son had just gotten married. Today was a day of celebration.

The past few years, the degeneration of Ellarin's disease had gotten noticeably worse. The two of them had been given far more time than anyone had expected. Yet it was not enough. She was not ready to lose him, even as that day marched inevitably closer with each passing day.

"Shh, shynafera." Ellarin rubbed her arm and pressed a kiss to her forehead. "Do not go there. You have not lost me yet."

She did not have to ask how he knew what she had been thinking. He would be able to guess, based on the emotions coming from her through the elishina.

He had a point. As hard as it was to shove the morbid thoughts away, she should not taint the time they had with the pain that was coming. When that day came, then she would face the pain and deal with it.

Until then, she would savor each moment she had with Ellarin.

370 BFH

Ellarin held Leyleira's hand, their fingers clasped in a way that put their palms together. It was different than how most elves held hands, but the traditional two-finger clasp put too much strain on his fingers. This way was more comfortable for him.

Together, they strolled across the royal branch from their suite of rooms to Lorsan and Vianola's across the way. He knocked on the door, then shared a smile with Leyleira.

The door swung open, revealing Lorsan standing there. His grin was wide, his dark eyes beaming. He stepped aside, waving them inside. "Come in."

Vianola lounged on one of the cushioned benches grown into the side of the room. She cradled a bundle wrapped in a dark green blanket. A fuzz of black hair was just visible above the blanket.

Leyleira's pace quickened, off-rhythm as if she wanted to hurry across the room but did not want to set a pace faster than Ellarin could manage.

As they neared, Vianola shifted the baby in her arms. "Meet Weylind, your sasonsheni."

Weylind was a tiny bundle with his eyes closed in sleep and his face scrunched. His head was covered in a fuzz of hair as black as Lorsan's and Leyleira's.

Lorsan halted next to Ellarin, and Ellarin reached out and clasped his son's shoulder. "Congratulations, sason, sena."

"He is adorable." Leyleira let go of Ellarin's hand and sat next to Vianola.

Vianola held the baby out to Leyleira. "Would you like to hold him?"

Leyleira's nod was quick, and she was already reaching for Weylind before she finished saying, "Yes!"

Vianola passed Weylind over, and Leyleira cradled the babe, smiling down at him.

Ellarin smiled, a warm contentment momentarily banishing the ever-present ache in his body. He was a dachasheni. He had not been sure if he would live to see this day.

After another moment, he squeezed onto the bench beside Leyleira and wrapped an arm around her waist, holding her as, together, they took in the sight of their sleeping grandson.

320 Years BFH

Leyleira took a seat next to Neia and smiled down at the babe in Neia's arms. "She is beautiful."

"The most beautiful baby in the whole world." Taranath leaned close and touched Rheva's tiny hand, as if he could not quite believe she was real. "No offense to Lorsan or Weylind, of course."

Leyleira laughed and shook her head. She would not begrudge Taranath and Neia their utter joy at the birth of their daughter. Not to mention that Rheva was an especially adorable baby with perfect pink cheeks and soft brown hair. "None taken. Rheva is quite perfect."

"Congratulations." Ellarin clasped Taranath's shoulder, his other hand resting on Leyleira's shoulder. Ellarin had refused a seat, but he was now leaning on Leyleira in a way that told her he was trying not to sway on his feet.

She would have to convince him to sit down sooner rather than later.

But until then, they would enjoy this moment of happiness with their friends.

290 YEARS BFH

Ellarin started to struggle to his feet at the knock on the door, but Leyleira waved for him to remain where he was.

He sank back against the cushion, stifling a hiss of pain at the flare that shot through his legs. He could barely feel the cover of his book as he closed it and set it aside.

Leyleira opened the door to reveal Lorsan standing on their porch, the evening dark and chilly around him. She stepped aside, motioning Lorsan inside. "Is everything all right, sason?"

"Everything is fine." Lorsan glanced from Leyleira to where Ellarin still sat across the room. "I just wanted to let you know. Weylind came into his magic today."

Ellarin braced himself against the wall, ignoring the flare of pain up his arm. "And?"

If his grandson had inherited his malady...if he was responsible for inflicting this slow death on Weylind, even if he had no control over which traits were inherited by each generation...

"Taranath assures me that he is fine." Lorsan smiled, though there was a hint of sadness there as well. "He would like to keep an eye on him, as he did with me, but he is optimistic that Weylind did not inherit this disease."

Ellarin exhaled and sagged even more fully against the wall behind him. Weylind was fine. He was not slowly dying the way Ellarin was.

280 Years BFH

"Your senasheni Melantha."

Ellarin reached for the child, hoping Lorsan and Vianola would not notice the way his hands were trembling. He remained where he was, sitting comfortably on one of the cushioned benches in his and Leyleira's main room. His feet were propped up on a footstool to try to ease some of the pain in his joints.

Lorsan smiled as he eased the newborn into Ellarin's arms. "She takes after Macha a great deal. Do you not think so?"

Ellarin nodded, taking in Melantha's fuzzy black hair, round face, and dark eyes blinking up at him far too seriously for a newborn.

Leyleira perched on the bench next to him, lightly resting her hand on his shoulder. "I do not see it. But she is lovely, Lorsan, Vianola."

That she was. Ellarin touched Melantha's tiny hand, marveling at the way her tiny fingers closed around his.

Though he could barely feel her fingers past the ever-present ache in his hands. Already, Melantha's slight weight ached in his arms. Each day, he could feel death coming for him, ever closer, ever more real.

But he was holding his granddaughter in his arms. A precious granddaughter as well as a grandson. Death might be coming—and soon—but Ellarin could not imagine being more blessed.

CHAPTER
TEN

270 YEARS BFH

Ellarin held Leyleira in his arms, the night dark around them. Even the softness of his pillow and mattress beneath him sent spikes of pain through him.

Leyleira touched his cheek. "Do I need to fetch Taranath?"

He shook his head, then leaned his face into the top of her head. "He will not be able to help."

The pain was so constant now that even Taranath's healing magic could not fully stave it off. It could provide Ellarin with a measure of relief, but that was all. In the past year, Ellarin had lost weight, and in the past months he had become all but bedridden. At times, his mind grew fuzzy, and he struggled to talk.

Ellarin pressed a kiss into Leyleira's hair, murmuring, "It will not be long now."

"I know." Leyleira's arms tightened around him as she shifted closer.

He could feel death breathing down his neck. The specter that had been lingering at his shoulder for hundreds of years was poised to snatch him away very soon.

He was ready. He was ready to cross into the life beyond, to shed the constant pain and weakness.

He had lived a good life. Looking back, he had no regrets, except perhaps for those first ten years of marriage. But they had needed the time to grow into the people they had become. In spite of the way they had begun, he would not change a thing.

Ellarin had reigned over Tarenhiel for over three hundred years. In that time, Tarenhiel had experienced peace and prosperity. He had witnessed his son's wedding. He had held his grandchildren. When he looked back, he did not see death. No, he saw a life that was *lived*.

He had no regrets for himself.

But it ached, knowing he would be leaving Leyleira alone. She would likely have a long life without him.

"Years ago, you did not want me using the elishina to help you." Leyleira pushed up onto an elbow. "But our son is grown. He is married. He has children. What if I…"

"No, shynafera." Ellarin reached up a trembling hand and smoothed her hair from her face, hating the way tears glimmered in her eyes in the moonlight. "You cannot stop this, no matter how determined your heart. Trying would just condemn you to sharing my pain and early death. Please. I cannot die, knowing I would be killing you too."

"I do not want to watch you die." Leyleira's whispered words tore through the space between them.

He drew her down and held her as close as he could manage with the pain and weakness. "I am sorry. But I am at peace with dying. It is my time to pass to the life beyond. It is not something to grieve. Not for me."

She gave a slight nod, but the way her body shook against him gave away her silent tears.

Perhaps he should ask for her promise that she would be open to love again. But he knew his Leyleira. It had taken her decades to fully fall in love with him. She would not easily open her heart again, if she ever did. If he made her promise, then she would force herself, and he never wanted her forced into love ever again.

Even if she never loved romantically again, she would be surrounded by the love of family and friends. All he wanted for her was that she would continue to live her life fully without holding herself back from those who mattered most.

"I am at peace, knowing you will be there for our family when I no longer can." It hurt, saying the words. Yes, he was at peace. But he still mourned the milestones he would miss. The ache he knew his passing would cause for his family. "Lorsan has Vianola, but you know the burden of the crown better than anyone. Be there for him so that the burdens do not break him."

While Ellarin's reign had been marked by peace, Ellarin did not think his son would experience the same. The magical protection placed on the border with the trolls by Ellarin's uncle was fading, and it would soon disappear altogether in a few years since there was no elf with the magic of the ancient kings to renew it. Even if Ellarin wanted to try, he did not have enough magical strength to reinforce the border.

As soon as the protections fully faded, the trolls would attack. The human kingdoms to the south were rising in power and they, too, would soon eye Tarenhiel to the north, coveting its rich forests.

His son would need wisdom to lead Tarenhiel into this new age. Ellarin could not be there for him, but Leyleira could.

Leyleira gave another nod, but this time she could not fully stifle her sob.

He rubbed her shoulder, ignoring the way the movement sent shafts of pain into his hand and up his arm. A little bit of pain did not matter. "I know I cannot ask you not to mourn for me. But please, shynafera, do not forget to live."

"I will try. But I do not…" Her voice choked off.

"Shynafera." He pressed a kiss to her forehead. He needed to bring a bit of lightness to the night. "Do you know what I realized the other day?"

Leyleira sniffed, swiping at her face. "What?"

"For all his harping about my impending death, I have actually lived longer than my father did." Ellarin felt a hint of a smile tug at his mouth. Even smiling hurt. "Sure, I have only lived thirty years longer than he did, but it still counts."

Leyleira's laugh came out short and teary. "Yes, it does."

Taranath had been right, all those years ago. Ellarin had experienced a longer life—and in many ways a better life—than many of his recent ancestors. He had enjoyed peace, raised his family, and cared for his people, untouched by war. Perhaps dying young and in his sleep was not the worst end.

That end was coming soon. He might only have hours. Or perhaps he would linger for a few more months yet. Either way, he did not have long.

He shifted as much as he could, stifling his moan of pain. He would get very little sleep tonight, wracked with too much pain.

But he did not want sleep, no matter how tired he was at the moment. All he wanted to do was hold his wife and savor what might be his last few precious moments with her.

He pressed a kiss to her temple, then whispered into her ear, "Kiss me. And I do not mean just a little forehead kiss."

She pushed onto an elbow, her face shining with tears in the moonlight. But a slight smile broke through as she brushed strands of his hair from his face. "I thought you liked forehead kisses."

"I do, but not when I want a real kiss." Ellarin worked to keep his tone light as he lifted a shaking hand to trail his knuckles across Leyleira's cheek, his fingers coming away damp with her tears.

"So demanding." She trailed light kisses across his cheek, then his nose, whispering, "I choose you."

Then she kissed him, and he held her, kissing her as passionately as he could past the pain and weakness. He murmured against her mouth, "And I choose you."

For however long he had left, he would tell her those words often, so that once he was gone she would never forget how much she had been loved.

LEYLEIRA SQUEEZED HER EYES SHUT, Ellarin's limp hand gripped in both of hers.

Taranath's voice came from the other side of Ellarin. "He is gone."

She did not need Taranath to tell her that. She could feel the gaping emptiness in her heart where her elishina with Ellarin had been. Now there was just pain and aching loneliness.

Tonight, she had kept two promises. When the time had come, she had let Ellarin go. And he had not died alone.

"Macha." Lorsan's hand rested on her shoulder, pulling her back from the edge of the dark emptiness of that hole inside her. His voice was rough but steady, as if he was already the king he had become the moment Ellarin had died. "Come. Vianola can get you settled in the other room. Taranath and I can prepare Dacha's body for lying in state."

"I can use my magic to help you sleep." Taranath's voice was far too quiet. Too compassionate.

Leyleira shook her head. She did not want to leave him. Or sleep. She did not want any of this.

She wanted to cry. To scream. To break. Ellarin was gone, and she was alone. So very alone.

Lorsan gently gripped her shoulders and tugged her to her feet. "Please, Macha. Vianola is waiting outside."

Leyleira turned back to the bed, reaching for Ellarin as his fingers slipped from her hand, dropping limp onto the bed. "The formal robes for lying in state. They are on the shelf. I need—"

"We can take care of it. There is nothing more you can do, Macha." Lorsan gently steered her to the door, where he passed her to Vianola.

Leyleira did not resist as Vianola took her arm and drew her down the stairs. She was far too numb to care where she was or listen to the vague, soothing words Vianola was speaking.

Ellarin was gone. Leyleira was now alone.

Leyleira strode at a methodical, ceremonial pace as the procession wound through the trees from Ellonahshinel to the section of woods known as the Forest of Resting Souls. Birds chattered overhead while the slight breeze blew her dark green dress and tossed her hair, the joyful forest a sharp contrast to the ache inside her.

For the past week, Ellarin's body had lain in the great hall, dressed in the formal green and silver robes of a king with his crown on his head and the sword he had never raised in battle resting at his side.

Now Ellarin lay on a stretcher, carried at shoulder height by Weylind and Lorsan in front and two warriors at the back.

Leyleira halted, numbly staring at the tree where Ellarin would be laid to rest.

Lorsan, Weylind, and the two warriors laid Ellarin down at the base of the tree, then stepped back. Weylind swiped at his face, his face twisting as he stared down at his dachasheni.

Vianola joined Lorsan and Weylind, though Melantha was not there, too young to bring to a burial. Taranath and Neia, too, stood off to the side, with their young daughter Rheva at their side.

Lorsan met Leyleira's gaze. "Macha, if you would like me to…"

She shook her head, swallowing. "No. This is something I need to do myself."

One last way she could care for the husband she had loved for nearly four hundred years.

Leyleira knelt, taking in her husband's face one last time. Instead of the formal attire from lying in state, now Ellarin had been dressed in a simple light green shirt and trousers, appearing more her beloved Ellarin rather than the king for all of Tarenhiel to mourn. He was so still, so devoid of life. Framed by his golden hair, his face was so pale and tinged slightly green with the healing magic that was preserving his body while he lay in state.

Drawing in a deep breath, Leyleira pressed a hand to the tree beside her, flooding it with her magic. "Ellarin Luirlan, I dedicate your body to the care of the trees until the end of time."

He had always feared he would be known as Ellarin Muirtin—the Dying One—but instead he had earned the title of Luirlan. Peace of the Land.

Roots burst from the ground on either side of Ellarin's body, interlacing until they formed a network over and around Ellarin.

She had one last glimpse of his face, then the roots closed around him, fully encasing his body. With one last burst of her magic, the roots sank back into the ground, taking Ellarin's body with them to rest in the cradling arms of the trees for all time.

CHAPTER
ELEVEN

180 YEARS BFH

Leyleira numbly knocked on the door to Lorsan and Vianola's rooms.

The door swung open, revealing Lorsan standing there, a barely suppressed smile beaming in his eyes and twitching his mouth. "Come in, Macha. Come meet your newest senasheni."

A part of her did not want to step into that room. She and Ellarin had another granddaughter—and Ellarin was not here to meet her. It did not feel right, marking this moment without him.

But life moved forward as inevitably as his death had been. While she had lived the past hundred years in a numb fog, going through the motions, everyone else had gone on living.

She forced herself to step into the room. To smile at Lorsan and Vianola. To voice the expected congratulations.

Almost without knowing how, she found herself perched on the bench, and Vianola was passing over the tiny bundle of baby. It was all déjà vu from holding Weylind and Melantha the first time, except that the baby in her arms now had fluffy brown hair like Vianola's and there was no Ellarin beaming down at their grandchild.

No Ellarin. For a moment Leyleira hunched over the child in her arms, struggling to breathe through the pain of the empty place in her chest where her elishina had once been.

She blinked down at the baby in her arms, and it took a moment to clear the blur so that she could actually see the baby's tiny, round face.

Weylind and Melantha had greatly resembled Lorsan and Leyleira. But the baby in Leyleira's arms had Vianola's hair, nose, and chin. She was so perfectly adorable. Petite and delicate, even as a baby.

Leyleira gently touched the baby's cheek, something shifting in her chest, filling some of the yawning emptiness inside her. "What is her name?"

"Jalissa." Vianola glanced from the baby to Leyleira, compassion deepening her brown eyes, as if she could see how hard this was for Leyleira.

Jalissa. A beautiful name for a lovely little baby.

Leyleira drew in what felt like her first real breath in far too long. Ellarin would not have wanted her to live this empty half-life. It was the last request he had ever asked of her.

It was time she pulled herself together and started truly living again. Ellarin could not be there for their son, his wife, their grandchildren. But Leyleira could.

"You do not have to leave, Macha. This is your home."

Leyleira placed another stack of her clothes into the bag. She could ask a servant to pack her things for the short walk down the royal branch to the new set of rooms Leyleira had chosen, but there was something soothing about doing this herself. "It is time, Lorsan."

She could not find a new life while lingering in the rooms where she had shared so many years with Ellarin. His presence was everywhere she looked. From the screen they had eventually folded and leaned against a wall but had never bothered to have hauled away to the vase he had used so often to leave her flowers in the morning. Many of his things remained on the shelves since she had yet to sort through them and pack them away.

"Are you sure?" Lorsan stood in the center of the room, as if he was not sure if he should help or leave her in peace.

"I thank you for your concern, but as I said, it is time." Leyleira faced her son. She was thankful that he cared, but she was set in this decision. "Weylind will propose to Rheva sooner or later, and he will need these rooms."

Ellarin would have loved to see that romance unfold. Their grandson and the daughter of their dearest friends. Taranath and Neia were already like family, and if all went well in the next few years, Leyleira looked forward to claiming their daughter as a granddaughter.

"Perhaps, but that does not mean you have to move right now." Lorsan shifted, gesturing at the room.

It was traditional that the first two rooms on the royal branch were reserved for the king on one side, and his heir on the other. Well, Weylind was the heir. These rooms really should have been his for the past hundred years already.

Leyleira had chosen rooms at the far end of the branch. The rooms had quite a spacious living area, perfect for having tea with her family, yet it had only a single bedchamber. It was meant for visitors or as a home for the dowager queen.

Well, she was the dowager queen. It was time she stepped aside and figured out what new life that meant for her.

"I am ready, Lorsan. There is no reason to drag it out." Leyleira added one last shirt, then buttoned the bag and set it next to the others to be carried to her new rooms. "I am rather looking forward to making a new space my own. I cannot do that here, knowing that these rooms will be Weylind's before long. If I move now, he will have time to make the space his own before he marries. Though, I would think he would get Rheva's advice on any changes."

Lorsan released a long breath, then nodded. "I just needed to be sure that you were all right with this. Is there anything I can help with?"

"Yes, you can help me carry the first load to my new rooms." Leyleira hefted several of the canvas bags onto her shoulders. She still had more things to pack, and she would have to go through Ellarin's things to decide what she wanted to keep and what should be given away.

But she would need an afternoon to herself for that task. There would be tears, and she refused to shed them in front of her son.

Lorsan hurried forward and took several of the bags from her. "Of course, Macha."

Together, she and Lorsan strolled from the rooms she had shared with Ellarin, down the length of the royal branch, and finally into the room tucked away at nearly the end of the branch.

Leyleira drew in a deep breath and set down her bags on one of the chairs at the plain table. The benches along the wall lacked cushions while the windows were bare. An empty space that she could decorate to her heart's content.

Perhaps she would order custom, dark green drapes and matching cushions for the benches. With her magic, she could update the table herself, adding a few ornate touches.

Through the side window, she could just make out the gazebo tucked at the far end of the branch. The same gazebo where Ellarin had first spoken with her. The gazebo where they had spent many a quiet evening, looking for some peace and quiet here at Ellonahshinel in between their trips to Lethorel.

For the first time in years, she could look at that gazebo and smile at the memories, even through the pain aching in her chest.

This room would do quite nicely. Quite nicely indeed.

Lorsan set the bags he had carried next to hers. "Is there anything else you need? Would you like servants to help you pack?"

"No, I would prefer to do this myself. I am in no rush." She glanced around the room. "Though, I will need to request a few amenities if I wish to sleep here tonight."

Lorsan opened his mouth, probably to offer to contact the servants for her.

Leyleira held up her hand. "I was queen for years, Lorsan. I am perfectly capable of making requests of the servants."

Lorsan shifted, a hint of a sheepish smile on his face. "Of course, Macha. I just wish to help."

"I know. And I do thank you for your care, sason." Leyleira stepped closer and clasped her son's shoulders.

She had to reach up to do so. Her son had grown tall and strong, far more muscular than his dacha had ever been, with long black hair, a hawkish nose, and a sharp chin in a masculine version of her features. But he had his dacha's thoughtful personality without the iron she wrapped around herself.

In the years since Ellarin had died, Leyleira had found herself resorting to that iron more often than not. She was once again more the hard composure than the softness she had learned as Ellarin's wife.

Lorsan squeezed her shoulders in return. "Whatever you need, Macha. Vianola and I are here for you."

This was what she needed. To move on and create a new life for herself.

It would not be easy, and the aching emptiness from her broken elishina still remained. But she had promised Ellarin that she would keep living. And she would keep that promise, no matter how much it hurt.

"Linshi." Leyleira drew in a breath, hating the way she shuddered a bit. She was stronger than this. Stronger than the grieving woman she had been for the past hundred years. Stepping out of Lorsan's grip, she drew on her composure and faced him. "There is one more thing I wanted to talk to you about."

Lorsan raised his eyebrows. "This sounds serious."

Leyleira gave a small shrug, not wanting to show her son just how close to her heart this was. "Now that my parents are gone, Lethorel has become mine."

She refused to let her voice shake at that. Both of her parents had passed three decades ago within a few weeks of each other. They had gone as they had lived: quietly, without any fuss.

Lorsan gave a small nod, as if he was not sure where she was going with this.

"I would like to give Lethorel to the royal family." Leyleira kept her tone clipped, matter-of-fact. No quaver to give away her emotions.

Lorsan's gaze snapped to her, searching her face. "Are you sure, Macha? Lethorel is yours to do what you want with it."

It was. She could keep it for herself. She could even move there permanently. Though, as much as she loved Lethorel, living there by herself sounded lonely. She had promised Ellarin that she would be there for their family, and she could not do that if she left for Lethorel.

Perhaps she should deed it to one of her grandchildren. While Weylind was the heir and would someday become king, Melantha and Jalissa did not have such established futures. Perhaps one of them would need an estate of her own.

But there was every chance that they would marry elven nobility and inherit estates of their own. Not to mention that, as princesses of the kingdom, they would always be welcome in the royal palace of Ellonahshinel.

"I know the weight of the crown." Leyleira faced Lorsan without flinching away from his scrutinizing gaze. "Lethorel was always a welcome retreat for me and your dacha. I would like it to remain so for future generations of the royal family."

It was not as if she would lose access to Lethorel due to this decision. It would still always be there for her to visit. Lorsan had continued the tradition of spending a few weeks at Lethorel each summer.

After a moment, Lorsan nodded. "As you wish, Macha. Lethorel will always be treasured."

Perhaps that would be her and Ellarin's legacy for the royal family as well as the kingdom. Ellarin's reign had been marked as a golden age of peace, and now her family's estate would be a sanctuary for the royal family to find their own moments of peace.

CHAPTER
TWELVE

106 YEARS BFH

"You need to pull yourself together, Lorsan." Leyleira faced her son in his study, the door firmly closed so that they would not be interrupted by any clerks or nobles seeking an audience with the king.

Sweet, gentle Vianola. She had been as a daughter to Leyleira. She had not deserved to die so brutally.

Over four years ago, Vianola, her parents, and her extended family had been killed by a sudden, unprovoked attack by the trolls. The first troll attack in nearly a thousand years. Lorsan had planned to join her in a few days. Instead, he had only been able to helplessly cling to her in their elishina until death tore her away.

Perhaps Leyleira should be more sympathetic. She knew the pain of a shattered elishina better than anyone. She had taken nearly a hundred years to start living again.

But Lorsan had a family and a kingdom depending on him the way Leyleira had not back then.

The kingdom was all but at war with the trolls. Both sides were conducting small raids across the border, but it was only a matter of time before the tension escalated to a full-scale mobilization and war.

Weylind had taken on the burden of ruling the kingdom, even though he was not yet king, due to Lorsan being all but crippled by his grief.

Melantha was currently in what was clearly an unhealthy relationship. Every time Leyleira saw Melantha with Hatharal, her shoulders were more slumped, the light in her eyes fading. She was slowly being controlled, yet she refused to admit what was happening, claiming that she and Hatharal were in love.

Then there was Jalissa. She had just come into her magic, and she needed her dacha to be there, teaching her how to use it.

Leyleira tried to help where she could, but she was their machasheni. She was not their dacha.

"I know, I know." Lorsan dug his fingers into his hair, slumped in his chair behind his desk. "I just...I need time. Space."

"Your kingdom and family need you." Leyleira gestured toward the door, as if to encompass all the problems demanding Lorsan's attention. He needed to drag himself out of this dark spiral that had started from the moment Vianola had been killed. "Pull yourself together and be the king and father I raised you to be."

Lorsan sighed, his dark brown eyes bleak as he peered up at her. "I will. Just...I will take this one last trip to clear my head."

"To Lethorel?"

Lorsan shook his head. "Not Lethorel. Too many memories. Just...away."

He was running with no plan and no way to truly find the peace he was looking for. It was hardly a healthy way to handle his grief.

But he refused to listen to Leyleira. She had done all she could for him. At this point, he would need to navigate this grief on his own.

95 YEARS *BFH*

Leyleira perched on the bench beneath Lethorel. She could see why her parents had always claimed this particular spot. From here, she had the perfect view of the entire lake, including the grassy meadow to the one side.

She sipped her tea, her book neglected on her lap, as she watched her family enjoy a relaxing retreat at Lethorel. Behind her, she could hear Melantha and Jalissa laughing as they practiced archery in the range on the far side of Lethorel. Weylind and Rheva strolled along the lake's edge, their hands clasped.

In the meadow, Lorsan stood to one side, keeping a careful eye on Farrendel. The little boy darted from flower to flower, plucking each one and clutching the wildflowers in a haphazard fashion in his tiny fist.

Once he had quite the handful, Farrendel darted from the meadow, dashing past Lorsan and racing up to Leyleira, his silver-blond hair flying around him. He skidded to a halt in front of her and presented the bouquet of wilting flowers to her, his silver-blue eyes wide and innocent. "For you, Machasheni."

Leyleira gently took the bouquet from him, then sniffed it. Most of the wildflowers had only a faint scent, but it was sweet and green. "These are lovely. Linshi, sasonsheni."

Farrendel grinned and bounced on his toes as if he could not manage to stand still.

Lorsan finally joined them, strolling at a leisurely pace. If he raced around after Farrendel all day, he would collapse in an exhausted heap by mid-morning. It was wise to pace himself.

"Those are pretty flowers, sason." Lorsan held out an arm, and Farrendel's grin widened. Farrendel latched on to Lorsan's arm, then giggled as he swung his feet up, hanging from Lorsan's arm by both his arms and his feet. Farrendel's giggles only increased as he let go with his hands and swung himself upside down. Lorsan gripped Farrendel's ankles, making sure he did not slip and fall onto his head.

Not that Farrendel seemed to care. He enjoyed hanging upside down.

After a few seconds, Farrendel swung up, grabbed Lorsan's arm again, then wiggled free to land lightly on the ground. He bounded over to the bench and hopped up next to Leyleira.

Lorsan took the opportunity to slide into the seat on the far side of Leyleira, his sigh so muffled Leyleira barely heard it.

Farrendel swung his feet, fidgeting for several seconds, before he leaned closer to her and pointed at her book. "What are you reading?"

Leyleira showed him the cover. "It is a history of the rise and fall of the elven empire."

"Huh." Farrendel's brow furrowed as he studied the book rather intently for several seconds. "Sounds boring."

"For a ten-year-old, it would be, I am afraid. But I find it fascinating." Leyleira reached for a bookmark, stuck it between the pages, and closed the book. "It is filled with stories of noble warrior-kings, who wielded amazing magic and fought great battles."

"That does not sound boring." Farrendel glanced from the book to her.

"No, you are correct. The book does not sound boring when put that way." Leyleira smoothed her hand over the leather cover. Perhaps it was foolish, but reading about the kings of old with their magic like Ellarin's—though far stronger than his had been—made her feel closer to him, even as her empty elishina ached for him.

Farrendel nodded, then returned to swinging his feet and fidgeting. After a few more minutes, he craned his neck and peered over the back of the bench to watch Jalissa and Melantha as they practiced their archery. He climbed onto his knees to watch them better.

After a few minutes of watching, he plopped back onto his rear end, then hopped to his feet. "I should pick flowers for Melantha and Jalissa too."

Then he was off, racing toward the meadow.

Lorsan groaned and pushed to his feet. "I do not remember the others being quite this exhausting."

"He does seem to possess an overabundance of energy." Leyleira studied Farrendel as he dashed around the meadow, gathering another handful of flowers.

Boundless energy. It reminded her of something she had read in this history book. Those with the magic of the ancient kings tended to be overactive children, with so much energy bottled inside them and no outlet until they came into their magic in their late adolescent years.

But surely it could not be. None of Lorsan's other children had inherited Ellarin's magic. And even in Ellarin's case, his magic was far from the great power described in the books and legends. Was that only because of his disease? Or because the magic of the ancient kings was dying out forever?

In the centuries of peace under Ellarin's reign, it had seemed a little thing if the magic of the ancient kings died with him. Such magic was a thing of the past.

But as war loomed again, people were talking of warriors and magic and how much Tarenhiel needed a warrior of old.

Perhaps Tarenhiel did. But she would rather that warrior was not her grandson.

20 YEARS BFH

At the knock on her door, Leyleira set her book aside, pushed to her feet from where she had been curled in her reading nook, and swung the shawl over her shoulders. Who could be knocking on her door at this hour?

When she opened the door, a cool evening breeze washing over her, she found Lorsan standing there, his face etched with a weariness that did not seem entirely due to the late hour of the evening. "Lorsan, sason. I did not think you were due to arrive until tomorrow."

"We rode late and arrived an hour ago." Lorsan gave a slight shrug. "May I come in?"

"Yes, of course." Leyleira stepped aside. When Lorsan brushed past her, she shut the door behind him. "It is good to have you and Farrendel back at Ellonahshinel."

Leyleira had not been in favor of Lorsan's plan to retreat to Lethorel to raise Farrendel. While Lethorel was a retreat, it was not intended to be a place to hide from the world forever. She could see the damage Lorsan's retreat had done to the rest of the family. Weylind had become more burdened and grim. Melantha had been left parentless in the wake of the breakup of her unhealthy relationship, becoming bitter and withdrawn. Jalissa had harbored the pain of always missing part of her family—either Weylind and Melantha when she was at Lethorel or Lorsan and Farrendel when she was at Ellonahshinel.

Then there was Farrendel himself, who had been deprived of growing up in Ellonahshinel with his siblings.

Leyleira had done everything she could to mitigate the damage, but there was only so much she could do. At times, it seemed all she could do was watch helplessly as her and Ellarin's family slowly fell apart.

Anytime she tried to bring it up with Lorsan, he argued that Farrendel needed to be protected from the court. Perhaps he had a good point, and he had valid reasons. Maybe there truly was no other way to raise Farrendel away from the court that was so prejudiced against his illegitimate birth.

"It is good to be back." Lorsan clasped his hands behind his back in a gesture so like Ellarin, pacing back and forth across her main room.

There was something agitated in Lorsan's pacing, a grave look etched across his face.

Leyleira studied him. "Is everything all right, sason?"

"Yes, yes." Lorsan halted his stilted pacing, spinning to face her. "Farrendel has come into his magic. He has the magic of the ancient kings."

Ellarin's magic. Leyleira felt herself swaying, and she pressed a hand to the wall to steady herself.

If Farrendel had Ellarin's magic, did that mean he also had Ellarin's disease? It had been bad enough watching Ellarin slowly die, but if she had to watch her grandson suffer the same, she was not sure how she would survive it.

She loved all her grandchildren. Each one—from Weylind and Melantha who had inherited so much of her own looks and sharp, iron personality to Jalissa who was so much her macha's daughter with her dark brown hair and gentleness—was precious.

But Farrendel was so much Ellarin's grandson. His blond hair and blue eyes were both lighter than Ellarin's. His face shape was a bit more refined, taking after that mother of his.

Yet his smile and his thoughtfulness were all so much like Ellarin.

If only Ellarin could have met Farrendel. He would have loved him as much as Leyleira did.

"And he...does he..." She could not bring herself to say the words out loud.

"Taranath is going to examine him in the morning. But Farrendel has not mentioned any numbness or pain when using his magic." Lorsan took a step closer to her, something in his eyes grave but also strangely awed. "He is powerful, Macha. Far more powerful than Dacha ever was."

More powerful than Ellarin. That was not saying much, considering that Ellarin had never been able to use his magic beyond small amounts.

But the one time he had...the crackling power had taken Leyleira's breath away.

"Are you sure? You never saw your dacha wield magic." Leyleira studied Lorsan's face.

"I am sure." Lorsan tugged on his sleeve, as if trying to hide something.

Leyleira stepped closer, then pointed at his wrist, giving Lorsan that no-nonsense stare that never failed to make him squirm even now.

Lorsan sighed and lifted his sleeve, showing the scattering of burn marks that seared his arm. "As I said, Farrendel is powerful. It is all I can do to contain his magic when it lashes out of his control."

Leyleira blinked, taking in the burns on Lorsan's arm to the look in his eyes. Lorsan was powerful. More powerful than Leyleira herself. If he struggled to contain Farrendel's magic when it was in its infancy, then Farrendel must be powerful indeed.

Pain throbbed in her chest in that empty place where her elishina had been. Ellarin had never had a chance to use his magic at full power. From the moment he had come into his magic, it had been slowly killing him.

It was almost as if the magic of the ancient kings also carried a curse. Those who had it rarely lived a happy, long life. Ellarin's uncle had died creating the Gulmorth Gorge. Ellarin had died of a disease tied to his magic.

Would Farrendel suffer the same because of his magic? Either a death in the war that was coming or a debilitating illness?

LEYLEIRA PERCHED on the bench outside of Taranath's healing room, sipping the cup of black tea Neia had given her before Lorsan and Farrendel had arrived.

Leyleira resisted the urge to glance over her shoulder at the window behind her. It would do little good. The magic was tinted so that those outside could not see inside, protecting the privacy of Taranath's patients.

How long would it take for Taranath to examine Farrendel? Surely it would not take as long as one of Ellarin's long ago healing sessions.

She measured the minutes with sips of tea, a book open on her lap in the semblance of reading.

Finally the door opened, and Farrendel stepped out, alone. His silver-blond hair flowed over his back while his eyes flicked from her to the floor of the porch.

Lorsan must have remained inside to quietly ask Taranath to heal the burns on his arms.

Leyleira smiled and patted the open space next to her. "Sit, sasonsheni."

Farrendel hurriedly sat on the bench, his shoulders slightly hunched. Even sitting, he was never fully still, his feet swinging, his hands fidgeting. In the years he had been at Lethorel, he had grown into a gangly young elf only a few years from adulthood. "Dacha said to tell you that I am fine."

Leyleira released a long breath and set aside her empty teacup. Her grandson was fine. He had not been condemned to a slow, inevitable death. "Good. Did your dacha tell you why he was worried?"

"He said Dachasheni died from a disease that manifested when he came into his magic." Farrendel's knees bounced as he stared at the large leaves and broad branches before them.

"He did. But Taranath verified that you do not have it, so there is no cause for concern." Leyleira closed her book and set it on the windowsill next to her teacup. "Did your dacha also tell you that Dachasheni Ellarin had magic like yours?"

Farrendel nodded, his bouncing knees and fidgeting fingers growing more pronounced, as if he was struggling to sit still this long. "Yes." A pause. More fidgeting. Then Farrendel's silver-blue eyes turned to her, wide and almost desperately. "What was he like?"

"I am afraid he did not use his magic often, due to his illness." Leyleira hoped Farrendel could not hear the slightly rough note to her voice. "Instead, he found a way to be a great king and father essentially without magic. In the end, he proved that having a great heart mattered far more than great magic."

"Oh." Farrendel slouched slightly more, his gaze dropping to the floor again.

Poor Farrendel. He must feel so alone. The only one with magic like his. The first with full use of his magic since his great-great-uncle died nearly a thousand years ago.

What would happen to her innocent sasonsheni in the coming war? With the magic of the ancient kings, he would be expected to take his place as a warrior, like all the warrior kings and princes of old. Never mind that he was far too young.

Had Ellarin been spared such a fate because of his illness? What would Illythor have done, if Ellarin had full use of his magic? Would Illythor have crossed the Gulmorth Gorge, attacked the trolls, and resumed the war with the intent to conquer the trolls once and for all, with his warrior son at his side?

Instead of war, Ellarin had lived in peace. He might have been dying, but his life had been full and happy.

She did not think Farrendel would be given the same chance for peace.

Farrendel was still sitting there, fidgeting and poised to jump to his feet at the first chance. She needed to tell him something to give him a connection to Ellarin and their similar magic.

"There was one time I saw your dachasheni Ellarin use his magic. It was the day your dacha was born." Leyleira felt a smile tug at her lips as Farrendel's gaze snapped back to hers. The empty place of her shattered elishina ached, but there was a sweetness to holding this memory close. "Your dachasheni's father was a good king, I suppose, but he was a rather hard father."

From behind Farrendel, Lorsan quietly opened the door and stepped onto the porch. Farrendel did not seem to notice, his gaze still fixed on Leyleira's face.

"Ellarin's father said a few things that made it clear that he was not someone we wanted near our son, your dacha." Leyleira refused to grimace. Even hundreds of years later, a hint of fury burned through her chest at the thought of Illythor. "Your dachasheni used his magic, even knowing that doing so would cause him pain, and all but threw his father from the room. It was magnificent, seeing his magic. Something I will never forget."

Lorsan pushed away from the door. "I have never heard that story."

Farrendel jumped and shot a glance at his father. He bolted partway to his feet before he dropped back to his seat.

"It was not a story I cared to tell before." She gave a slight shrug. There was healing, in finally being able to tell stories about Ellarin without the pain overwhelming her. "I did not want to taint any memories you might have of your Dachasheni Illythor."

"From the few memories I have of King Illythor, he was not much of a dachasheni." Lorsan rested a light hand on Farrendel's shoulder, the gesture stilling some of Farrendel's incessant movements. "Dacha was a much better dachasheni to Weylind and Melantha. I know he would have been the same for Jalissa and Farrendel, had he lived."

"Yes, he would have." Leyleira swallowed back the lump in her throat.

"I wish I could have met him." Farrendel flexed his fingers, then stiffened as sparks of magic appeared around his fingertips. He clenched his fists, but that did not fully halt the bolts of magic that fizzled around his fingers, growing stronger by the moment. "Dacha!"

Lorsan hurriedly knelt on one knee in front of Farrendel, gripping both of Farrendel's shoulders. "Breathe, sason. Reach into your chest and concentrate on the source of your magic."

Farrendel squeezed his eyes shut, but the blue magic kept growing, crackling with ever more power. "Dacha —" Panic turned Farrendel's voice tight and scratchy.

Leyleira caught her breath, tasting the power of the magic in the air. The last time she had felt this kind of power had been the day of Lorsan's birth when Ellarin had drawn on his magic in such quantities.

But there was a depth to this magic that she had never felt with Ellarin. He had never mentioned a struggle to control the magic. No, he had always mourned that his magic was weaker than it should have been, not to mention that he could not use his magic without causing progression in his disease.

This was what the magic of the ancient kings should have felt like. Raw. Powerful. Dangerous.

Deep green magic wrapped around Lorsan's fingers, traveled down Farrendel's arms, then formed a barrier around Farrendel's hands. "You can control your magic. Just breathe and concentrate on pulling your magic back."

Farrendel's magic surged, crackling against the barrier of Lorsan's magic.

Lorsan flinched, yet he poured more magic into his barrier.

Leyleira rested her hand on Lorsan's shoulder and added her own magic to the barrier. It was a rare gift to have plant growing magic so strong that they could create this barrier with their magic. Weylind, too, had inherited this strength of magic.

Even with their two barriers, Farrendel's magic strained against them, threatening to overwhelm their combined power.

Lorsan had not been exaggerating. Farrendel had power the likes of which Leyleira had never seen. This was the magic of ancient kings as spoken of in stories of old.

"Think about Lethorel, sason." Lorsan kept his tone calm, soothing. "Think about the peace of the trees. Swimming in the lake. Running along the branches."

Farrendel drew in a deep breath, which he released in a long, shuddering exhale. His magic surged, then burst into a flare of sparks, which dissipated against the barrier. Farrendel slumped against the back of the bench, hugging his arms to his stomach.

"Well done, sason." Lorsan, too, released a breath and his magical barrier.

From behind Lorsan, Leyleira spotted Taranath and Neia. They must have stepped outside at the commotion, though they had not interrupted.

Over the past hundred years, Taranath's brown hair had gone completely white while Neia's was streaked with gray. Leyleira's own hair now held a hint of gray among the black strands.

Taranath met Leyleira's gaze, his mouth quirked with a hint of a smile. "You can see why I am so confident that Farrendel has not inherited Ellarin's disease."

"Yes." Leyleira, too, withdrew her magic. Such strong magic would surely have caused quite noticeable deterioration, if Farrendel had the same illness as Ellarin.

Farrendel would need training beyond what she or

Lorsan could give him. But who was there to teach him? There was no one left with the same magic.

Even if Ellarin lived, would he have been able to teach Farrendel? Or would his illness have put too many limitations on him?

It was galling to have to admit that King Illythor, for all his faults, had succeeded in one thing. Ellarin's disease had not been inherited by future generations.

That was the only credit she would give him. Strangely enough, Illythor was becoming, in many ways, a forgotten king. His father and brother featured in many stories as the last true warrior king and prince who had banished the trolls from Tarenhiel.

Far from only being known as a dying king, Ellarin was revered for his peaceful, prosperous reign. Even the peace of the last few years of Illythor's reign was credited more to Ellarin, since Ellarin and Leyleira had ruled the people while Illythor had ruled the kingdom.

Not to mention that Illythor's ignoble death at the hands of mangy human pirates was not the thing of legends.

Leyleira rested a hand on Farrendel's shoulder again. "You, sasonsheni, have both great magic and a great heart. Because of that, you will do great things. I have no doubt."

10 YEARS BFH

Leyleira joined Taranath at the base of a tree in the Forest of Resting Souls. The other mourners had all left, including Rheva leaning against Weylind for strength.

Taranath rested a hand on the bark, staring down at the place where his wife Neia had been dedicated to the trees moments ago. When he finally raised his head and met Leyleira's gaze, his eyes held a bleak, empty expression that Leyleira knew all too well. "How do you move on when your heart is gone?"

Leyleira stared without seeing at the tree before them. "You do not. There is no moving on; you just keep moving. You never get over your grief; you just get through it."

She had to blink at the pain welling inside her, her words as much for herself as for Taranath. The emptiness of her broken elishina. Grief for her son Lorsan. Fresh grief at the loss of her dear friend Neia.

Lorsan. Her only child. Her oak since Ellarin's death. Five years ago, he had been killed rescuing Farrendel.

His death had left their family shattered. Weylind bore the full weight of the kingdom. Melantha was wallowing in bitterness. Jalissa was retreating into herself. And Farrendel...

Farrendel had been tortured and shattered, perhaps beyond repair.

With the loss of her son, Leyleira had nothing left to give to her grieving grandchildren.

Now Neia, her best friend, had passed away, though her death had been peaceful.

So much grief. Even as she counseled Taranath, she was not sure if she could survive walking through this dark tunnel another time.

Who was she to give advice on grieving? She had failed to help Lorsan in his grief. What made her think she could comfort Taranath now?

She wrapped her arms over her stomach. "Did I do enough, Taranath? If I had counseled Lorsan better, would there have been a way to avoid this?"

"You did all you could." Taranath's voice was soft,

understanding. "Lorsan made his own decisions. In the end, there was nothing else he could do but sacrifice himself for his son. It was what any father would do."

The grief hurt so badly she could barely breathe, but she was also so very proud of Lorsan. He had made mistakes in those final years, but he had continued Ellarin's legacy in loving as a father ought until the end.

Now Lorsan was reunited with his Vianola in the life beyond. They were with Ellarin, and there was comfort in holding to that hope.

She swiped at the single tear that trickled down her cheek. "I am sorry. Here I am supposed to be comforting you, but you are comforting me."

"You lost your son. I can only shudder to imagine the depth of that pain." Taranath released a shaky breath, his eyes wet as they had been all morning through the dedication. "There is a strange comfort in knowing that you have experienced the same pain I feel. You know the emptiness of a broken elishina."

"Yes." She nodded, blinked again. She refused to cry, even in front of Taranath. "Because I have been where you are, I know that the pain never truly goes away. But it does fade and become bearable. We are not without hope. We will see Ellarin and Neia again. Until then, you will find reasons to keep living. This is an end, but it is not the end of everything that makes life rich and meaningful. You still have your daughter Rheva. Your grandchildren Ryfon and Brina. They will need you to be there for them, especially now that Neia is not."

Taranath shuddered with his inhale, but his nod seemed steadier.

They lapsed into silence, both quietly grieving and drawing comfort from that shared grief.

THIRTEEN

FIERCE HEART

L eyleira hurried through the streets of Estyra as quickly as she could, pushing aside her weariness after traveling through the night.

At least the train made travel between Estyra and Lethorel much quicker and easier than it used to be. What had been a week-long ride was now a morning ride by horse to Arorien, then an easy day's trip by train.

Such an invention would have made Ellarin's last few summer trips so much easier. He had kept his promise, and they had visited Lethorel every summer of their marriage, even that last year where the trip had left him bedridden and in agony.

Leyleira shook herself and focused on not plowing into any of the elves milling about Estyra. Today was about Farrendel and his arranged marriage to a human princess.

What had Weylind been thinking, allowing such a thing? Had Leyleira not made it quite clear to Lorsan and to Weylind that arranged marriages were not to be countenanced? Marriage should not be forced. Yes, it had worked out for her and Ellarin, and she would not go back and change that.

But those first few years had been hard. She would not wish such a beginning on any of her grandchildren.

And yet here they were. She took a few weeks' holiday at Lethorel in quiet contemplation and memories, and Weylind went and made a muddle of things.

Well, she would just have to straighten this out as best she could.

When she reached Ellonahshinel, she climbed the stairs at a quick enough clip that she was breathing hard by the time she reached the top.

A frenzy met her as servants bustled about with flowers, garlands, and other decorations, darting in and out of the great hall where Melantha barked orders and arranged things with a critical eye. More servants hustled past her, carrying papers that were likely lists of instructions for the cooks in the kitchens at the base of the tree or invitations for the various nobility staying within Ellonahshinel or Estyra at the moment.

At least the wedding preparations seemed well in hand. If Farrendel was going to be married off in such a fashion, the elven royal family should make a good go of the wedding. Farrendel deserved nothing less than the full celebration due an elf prince.

Voices came from one of the rooms to the side and on a branch slightly above the great hall.

Leyleira made her way in that direction before she peeked into the room.

A red-headed girl perched on a stool in front of a mirror, her rounded ears showing that she was human. A light spattering of freckles dotted her nose while her smile was wide and open. She was chattering a mile a minute as Jalissa and several servants attempted to tame the red, wavy hair into some kind of elven style.

Leyleira remained frozen where she was as she took in the sight. The girl did not look scared. Not at all.

Instead, her expression was open. Beaming. Grinning, even.

Happy.

Leyleira released a breath and pushed away from the door before anyone inside spotted her.

There was hope for Farrendel yet, if this was the human princess he was marrying—was already married to, if the hasty message Leyleira had received was to be believed.

Well, this was a fine basket of acorns Weylind had gotten them all into. But there was hope. It would just take a little meddling on Leyleira's part.

Leyleira strode along the branches of Ellonahshinel until she reached Taranath's rooms and knocked on the door.

The door swung open after the first knock. Taranath smiled at her. "Ah, I was expecting I would see you this morning, Leyleira. I am glad you arrived back in time."

"Trains are wonderful inventions. I would not want to miss Farrendel's wedding." Leyleira pressed her mouth together before she blurted out her true thoughts on the matter. Now was not the time to discuss such things, even with a dear friend like Taranath. "I came to fetch the items for the eshinelt."

"Yes, I began collecting them once I received word about the wedding." Taranath stepped aside, waving her in. "Take a look and feel free to grab anything else you think you might need."

Leyleira crossed the room to the examination table,

which currently held a jumble of jars and clumps of dried herbs. Good, good. All of the basic ingredients for the eshinelt were here.

She wandered over to Taranath's supplies and plucked a few bundles of dried flowers from the shelves. Once she had gathered everything, she packed the items into the leather satchel Taranath handed to her.

She headed for the door but halted and turned back toward him before lifting the latch. "Linshi, Taranath."

He met her gaze, his eyes holding the knowledge of the memories that were too close to the surface. "You are welcome, Leyleira. You know that I am here if you ever need anything."

"I know." Leyleira managed to work up a twitch of a smile. Taranath was the only one who knew what this day would mean for her, the memories it would evoke.

Painful memories of Illythor and the pressure and the cold arrangement of her marriage.

Treasured memories of Ellarin's patient, thoughtful courtship that eventually softened her iron heart.

With one last nod, she gripped the satchel tighter and hurried out the door.

And nearly ran into Weylind as he was stepping onto Taranath's porch.

Weylind froze, one foot on the porch, one on the branch, and blinked at her. "Machasheni. What are you doing here?"

"Where else did you think I would be when I received news that Farrendel's wedding is today?" Leyleira eyed Weylind as she shut Taranath's door behind her.

Dark circles smudged under his eyes, which held a slightly wild, panicked look.

Perhaps she had been too hard on this, her oldest grandson. He, too, was a bit lost at the moment.

"Well, yes." Weylind gave a slight cough. "I am glad you arrived in time, Machasheni."

"As am I." She stared him down until he squirmed. "What were you thinking, sasonsheni? An arranged marriage?"

"The humans demanded it as part of the peace treaty. What was I supposed to do?" Weylind dragged a hand over his face. "At least she is human. This will only be temporary."

If that was Weylind's attitude on the whole ordeal, then this was more of a mess than she had realized.

"Weylind, sasonsheni, I know you were raised better than that." Leyleira added another level of iron sternness to her glare until Weylind was all but quailing like a child caught climbing out of bed in the middle of the night. "It is a marriage. There is nothing temporary about that."

"Well, yes. But the human is only going to live a few decades, then Farrendel will be free of her." Weylind gestured toward the main part of Ellonahshinel, speaking more rapidly than normal.

Leyleira clamped down on her exasperated breath. There was just so much wrong with that statement, but she did not have the time to deal with this now. She only had the energy to help one of her grandsons today, and right now Farrendel needed her more. "We will discuss this later. Until then, is Farrendel in his rooms?"

"Yes." Weylind gestured at the satchel. "I see you asked Taranath for the items for the eshinelt. I can take them from here."

"Actually, I believe I will teach Farrendel to make the eshinelt." Leyleira tightened her grip on the satchel's strap. There was no way she would let Weylind help with the eshinelt with that attitude.

Besides, if there was anyone who knew what Farrendel was going through at the moment, it was her.

Weylind's eyes widened as he gaped at her again. "I am his closest male relative. The duty falls to me."

"Traditionally, yes. But it is not unheard of for a mother or grandmother to perform the task." Leyleira kept her back straight, her tone firm.

Due to the years of war, there were far too many lost fathers, grandfathers, and brothers, leaving mothers, grandmothers, and sisters to take their place.

Farrendel still had a living brother, but that did not mean Leyleira could not take Weylind's place.

But such logic would likely not appeal to Weylind. It was time to formulate a different attack.

Leyleira softened her tone, resting a hand on Weylind's shoulder. "Sasonsheni, you have a great deal to accomplish today to organize a wedding fitting for our Farrendel. Let me take care of the eshinelt so that you can be the king your brother needs you to be today."

Weylind released a long breath, some of the panic fading from his eyes as he nodded. "You are correct as always, Machasheni. Very well. I will leave the eshinelt in your capable hands."

Leyleira brushed past Weylind and set off down the branch. "I suppose the court is playing its usual games of snobbery over this wedding."

Weylind fell into step with her, that weary, harried look returning to etch lines in his face. "Yes. This is a royal wedding sealing an alliance between kingdoms. We cannot allow the court to snub the wedding and risk offending the human princess. Even more importantly, Farrendel deserves to be honored as the prince he is."

Leyleira completely agreed, though she was perfectly happy to leave haranguing the court into behaving in

Weylind's hands. She had always hated dealing with the intrigue as queen.

When they reached the main part of Ellonahshinel, Leyleira left Weylind to handle the vagaries of the court while she kept on past the bustle until she reached the far branches of the treetop palace.

Farrendel's rooms were tucked away into a quiet section of Ellonahshinel, all empty branches, broad leaves, and birds singing in the trees.

Stepping onto Farrendel's porch, Leyleira knocked on his door.

Long moments ticked by before his door swung open, and Farrendel peeked out at her with such panic and desperation in his wide eyes.

She knew that panic. She had felt that desperation. She had tasted that same fear.

For a moment, it was all she could do to breathe. It had been six hundred and fifty years since her own wedding day in an arranged marriage, but the stab of emotions was just as palpable.

Farrendel ducked his head in the way he did when nervous. "Machasheni. What are you doing here?"

Again with the question. Was it so unbelievable that she had hopped on a horse yesterday and had been traveling ever since to make it here in time? "My grandson is getting married. Of course I came. I am only sorry I was unable to arrive in time to greet you and your bride with the others. Now, may I come in?"

Farrendel nodded and shuffled aside to let her in.

She swept by him and eased the door shut behind her. The way Farrendel was poised—every muscle tensed— any loud noise might startle him into flight.

She should tell him about her own arranged marriage. While her family knew about her and Ellarin's love, none of them knew about how they began. She had never felt the need to tell them.

If anyone should hear the tale, it was Farrendel. Especially today.

But when she opened her mouth, all that came out was a clipped question. "Now, Farrendel. What is this I hear about you getting married for an alliance with the humans?"

She had never realized just how much pain she carried from the coldness of her arranged marriage, even to this day. Even now, she could not bring herself to speak of it.

That day had been tough, but it had brought her Ellarin, the love of her life. Despite the trauma she had not even realized she had suffered, she would not regret that day.

Perhaps she would tell her family the full story someday. But not today. Today she would keep the focus on Farrendel and on his arranged marriage.

Farrendel shifted, his gaze focused on the floor rather than on her. "It was the condition the humans placed on the treaty. I was the most logical choice."

She raised her eyebrow at him, not saying anything. That answer was something she would have given. But Farrendel was not as coldly logical as she was. He would have a deeper, more emotional reason for making this choice.

"It was either marry her or risk more war and more killing." Farrendel gave a small shrug, yet he peeked up at her as if seeking her approval. "It seemed like the better option."

"The better option for you or the better option for your people?" She kept her voice level, not giving a hint of her own thoughts just yet. Probably because she was still formulating them.

Farrendel squirmed under her stare, giving her that same wide-eyed look that he had always given her as a child. "Both. I do not wish to shed more blood. Nor do I wish to see elves and humans slaughter each other so needlessly."

And there was the Farrendel she knew. The one who was both somehow innocent and yet haunted by the guilt of bloodshed. "You would spare both elf and human lives?"

Farrendel peeked at her, then his gaze dropped to the floor. "Yes."

She had her answer. Farrendel was desperate enough to avoid war and killing that he would marry a stranger to avoid it.

That was, perhaps, better than a cold "for the good of the kingdom" answer. But it still meant that he was running away from something rather than running to it.

But she could work with this. "And your human bride? Is she as willingly marrying you for the sake of her people as you are for the sake of yours?"

His answer was immediate. More confident than the answers about himself. "Yes."

That had been Leyleira's impression too, in the brief glimpse she had snatched of the human princess.

What would she have wanted to hear on her wedding day? What could someone have said that would have made it easier, better, than the cold terror that had caused her to retreat behind her iron walls?

What would Ellarin have said in this situation, if he was facing his grandson now? Ellarin had always been the heart of their relationship, while she had been the iron.

Leyleira touched Farrendel's cheek, encouraging him

to hold her gaze. "Then I wish you every happiness with your bride, sasonsheni."

Farrendel blinked at her, freezing in place for several heartbeats. Tentatively, he gripped her shoulders, as if reaching for any kind of steadiness and hope he could find on this day. "You believe happiness is possible."

How those words hurt for the hopeless edge that tore through Farrendel's voice.

It would be up to her to give him hope before he shattered further. Deep down, Farrendel wanted to make his marriage work. He believed in the love and commitment of marriage, and he was struggling to reconcile that belief with an arranged marriage to a soon-to-die human.

She forced a smile and patted his cheek before dropping her hand. "Of course. Surely two people so willing to sacrifice themselves for the sake of their peoples will find a way to turn such deep love and loyalty toward each other."

Surely if Leyleira and Ellarin could find their way to love, then Farrendel and his human princess could as well. The princess was going into this with a smile instead of iron while Farrendel had Ellarin's caring heart. They would be fine, if given the right nudge.

Farrendel stumbled back, releasing her shoulders, his eyes going wide once again. "First happiness, now love? You are not going to counsel me to avoid forming an attachment to the human?"

"Is that what your brother has been telling you? Pah." She snorted, waving his words away. "Do not listen to him. You would think he would give better advice after the counsel I gave him when he married his Rheva. But he is young. He is not as wise as he thinks he is."

She really needed to have a long talk with that boy

—Weylind, not Farrendel—once they had a moment. This was just the kind of thing Ellarin had feared would happen. The pressures of the court and the tragedies of recent years had gotten to Weylind. He might handle burdens the way she did, by locking his true emotions away behind a mask, but he was hurting just as much as Farrendel was.

Farrendel kept staring at her, as if he was not sure how to handle that statement. Finally, he made a slight noise in the back of his throat, sounding much like his older brother Weylind at that moment. "What is your advice?"

She did not even have to think about which advice to give him. It was exactly what Ellarin would have said, if he were here. He had said it often enough to her, in life. "Choose her. Do not hold back."

Farrendel did not have the luxury of decades to come to that conclusion himself the way she and Ellarin had. Farrendel could not risk taking thirty years to form an elishina with his bride.

While all the others would counsel against an elishina, Leyleira would not. No, an elishina was exactly what Farrendel and his new bride needed.

It would cost Farrendel hundreds of years of his life, and he would die at what other elves would consider young.

But Leyleira had seen firsthand how full a short life could be.

When she patted Farrendel's cheek again, she hoped he would not notice the way her fingers trembled. "For years, you used to pick me and your sisters bouquets of flowers every day when we were at Lethorel. If you show this human princess that sweet boy I know is still in there somewhere, she will not be able to help loving you."

Farrendel ducked his head, the tips of his ears turning pink.

Ah, yes. Farrendel would fall in love with his human princess. Leyleira had to believe that, even if no one else did at this moment. He was Ellarin's grandson, after all.

This was exactly why Ellarin had asked Leyleira to keep living for their family. He could not be here today for Farrendel, but she could. She would give him the wisdom she and Ellarin had learned through the difficulties of their own arranged marriage, and hopefully prevent Farrendel and his human princess from experiencing the years of floundering she and Ellarin had gone through.

As soon as she could, Leyleira would need to have Farrendel's bride over for tea and conversation. She needed to truly meet her new granddaughter.

If the princess was as sweet and joyful as she had seemed in the glimpse Leyleira had taken, then Leyleira would tell her the truth about Farrendel's illegitimate birth. No one else was likely to tell her.

Yes, Leyleira probably should leave such a thing for Farrendel to tell. It was his secret, and he should be the one to tell the princess.

But Farrendel would not. At least, not at first. He was too shy and too hurt by the pain he had suffered over the years because of his birth.

Like it or not, the issue would stand as a barrier between them, even if the princess did not know what wall she was facing.

For Farrendel's sake, Leyleira could not let the poor girl stumble around blindly. Such a thing would only hurt her and Farrendel's chances of finding love and forming an elishina.

Yes, Leyleira was meddling. Utterly, unashamedly meddling.

Their family was shattered, years of hurt piling

tragedy upon tragedy, and now an arranged marriage for her youngest grandchild.

Well, she was going to hold her and Ellarin's family together no matter how much advice and meddling it took.

CHAPTER
FOURTEEN

7 YEARS AFTER FH

L eyleira sat on the bench outside of Taranath's healing room, breathing in the crisp, morning air. Wisps of mist still drifted between the branches, the dew heavy on the leaves, though the walkways remained dry thanks to the protective magic that prevented dew or snow from making them slippery.

She had leaned her cane against the wall next to her. She would never admit it to Edmund—even if she was becoming quite fond of the young whippersnapper—but she found herself using the cane to steady herself far more often than she cared to admit.

The door opened, and Taranath stepped out, juggling two cups of tea. He nudged the door closed with his foot, then held out one of the cups to her.

"Linshi." She took the cup with a smile. Her morning green tea, steeped exactly seven minutes, with just a dash of honey. Just the way she preferred it.

"You are welcome." Taranath eased onto the bench

next to her with a slight groan, cradling his own cup of tea. "These old bones do not appreciate these damp mornings."

Leyleira took a sip of her tea to banish the lump in her throat. Taranath was over a hundred years older than her. Soon, he too would pass into the next life, and she would be left entirely alone. No husband. No son. No friends. No one else who would remember Ellarin the way she and Taranath did.

Taranath sipped his tea, glanced at her, then gave a soft chuckle. "Do not look at me like that."

"Like what?" Only Taranath would be able to hear the emotion beneath her clipped, iron-hard tone.

"Like you expect me to keel over where I sit at any moment." Taranath gave a slight shake of his head, his white hair flowing around the sensible brown tunic he wore. His smile remained bright, lighting his brown eyes with warmth. "I know I am rather ancient, but I do believe I have a few decades in me yet. Who knows? Perhaps I will see my thousandth birthday yet."

She forced a light laugh and took another sip of her tea. When would she learn not to borrow grief before it came? "No doubt you will."

"You will outlive all of us, I suspect." Taranath's smile remained in place as he sipped his tea.

She wished she did not have to. It was so lonely, watching everyone she loved die.

Yes, she treasured her grandchildren and great-grand-children. But they did not know her the way Taranath did. He had known Ellarin. He had been there for all the struggles, all the joys, all the healings and pain, beginnings and endings. He knew her the way her grandchildren could not.

She had seen the way her grandchildren shared looks

when they saw her and Taranath together, as if they suspected there was more going on.

There was not. Neither she nor Taranath was looking to fill the empty elishinas inside them.

No, what was between them was the platonic companionship of years of friendship. It was the folly of youth to discount the satisfaction found in such fellowship.

She rested her teacup in her lap, staring off into the mist and the leaves. "I still miss him. Every day."

"I know." Taranath's voice held a depth that said he knew exactly what she meant, since he felt the same ache for Neia. The pause lingered for a moment, before he gestured, as if to encompass the entire kingdom. "This alliance our kingdom now enjoys with Escarland and Kostaria...that is Ellarin's legacy."

"How so?" She swiveled to face Taranath more fully.

"Do you think a king like Illythor would have ever considered an alliance with the humans, much less the trolls?" Taranath raised his eyebrows before he took a sip of his tea.

Leyleira shook her head, not sure if the expression twisting her lips was a smile or a grimace. "No, he would not."

"No. He would have gladly conquered them, if he had a son with full use of the magic of the ancient kings." Taranath waved at the serene morning around them. "But Ellarin's illness made him a peacemaker rather than a warrior, and he passed that love of peace to his son and grandson. Even while Lorsan and Weylind fought wars, they always did it with the goal of peace, not conquest."

She drew in a deep breath, savoring the chill of the air, the scent of the tea wafting from her cup, the soothing balm of Taranath's words.

Ellarin's legacy was peace.

He would have loved to see the alliance, the current peace, and all his grandchildren happily married. Despite his short life, his stunted magic, and the weakness caused by his illness, Ellarin's life had been full, meaningful, and impactful. He had changed the direction of the kingdom and left a deeply held love for peace behind.

"Linshi, Taranath. For remembering him when few people still do." Leyleira stared off into the dissipating mists, not really seeing the forest before her.

"You are welcome." Taranath reached out and rested a hand on her shoulder. "And thank you, for being a machasheni for my grandchildren when Neia no longer can be."

"That is hardly a burden. They are my great-grand-children, after all." Leyleira let a small twist curve her mouth upward. She understood what he meant. Ellarin and Neia could not be there, but Leyleira and Taranath still were. They would fill the holes left behind by those who had passed on the best they could. "Ellarin and Neia would have loved to see where our families are now."

"Yes, they would have." Taranath shook his head. "Even if things were a bit touch and go for a while."

Leyleira tapped her fingers lightly against the warm porcelain of her teacup. "Yes."

Farrendel's arranged marriage. Melantha's betrayal, then her arranged marriage to Rharreth. Edmund and Jalissa's drama. It had taken all of Leyleira's years of experience to drop a few nudges here, drips of wisdom there, to attempt to set things right.

Not that she could take much of the credit. Her grand-children had sorted themselves out eventually.

"But now everything is back to peace and tranquility." Taranath shot her a glance, a quirk to his mouth. "Well, except for your great-grandchildren. They are downright chaotic. Unlike my grandchildren. They are perfectly composed."

Ryfon and Brina were, by far, the most well-behaved of all of Leyleira's great-grandchildren. Granted, they were the only ones who were older than six, so that could be part of the reason. "I cannot imagine where they get their poise. It certainly did not come from you."

Taranath laughed, resting his teacup on his knee, steadying it with a hand. "You are quite correct. I am far too quirky for most elves."

"It is why I enjoy our early mornings. I would become far too dour without your influence." Leyleira took another sip of her tea.

"Speaking of your great-grandchildren..." Taranath gestured at the branch before them. "It appears a few of them are headed this way."

Leyleira glanced up and set aside her nearly empty teacup as Farrendel and Elspetha strode through the mist toward them. Farrendel held six-year-old Fieran, who had his face pressed to Farrendel's shoulder. Elspetha carried two-year-old Adriana, the toddler clinging to Elspetha as if terrified.

As the little family stepped onto the porch, Fieran lifted his face from Farrendel's shoulder. The boy's face was a mask of blood from his forehead all the way down to his chin. Bloodstains dampened the front of Farrendel's shirt as well as the cloth that must have been pressed to Fieran's face, but now lay draped over Farrendel's shoulder.

Leyleira stilled and fumbled for her cane to push to her feet. "Oh my."

Elspetha adjusted Adriana on her shoulder. "Don't worry. It looks worse than it is."

Leyleira certainly hoped so, for the poor boy appeared quite the mess.

Taranath wobbled to his feet, stretched his back out with a groan, then reached for the door. "Come along, then. Let us get this young man all fixed up, shall we?"

Gripping her cane, Leyleira pushed to her feet and followed the others inside, closing the door after them. She took a seat next to Elspetha on the benches while Farrendel perched on the table, still holding Fieran.

Elspetha patted Adriana's back, and the girl gave a small whine, as if she was afraid her macha was going to set her down. Elspetha glanced at Leyleira, a wry twist to her mouth. "Adriana was a bit freaked out by all the blood. She was chasing Fieran when it happened. It was such a lovely morning that I left the door to the porch open to give the children a bit more space to run."

Leyleira nodded, not sure if she should smile or grimace at this story. Farrendel and Elspetha's rooms were draped in a protective net of roots to prevent either of the children from accidentally throwing themselves out of the tree. Rambunctious as they were, Fieran and Adriana just seemed to think the nets were all the better for climbing.

"Fieran was looking over his shoulder, sticking his tongue out at Adry, and wasn't looking where he was going. So instead of running through the open doorway, he smacked face-first into the edge of the door." Elspetha rubbed Adriana's back. "The latch put a nasty gash in his forehead, his nose was gushing blood, and he bit his tongue and that was bleeding. Let's just say it was a lot of blood, all before breakfast."

"Ah." Leyleira flexed her fingers on the head of her cane. "That does sound quite traumatic."

At the exam table, Taranath was keeping up a lighthearted stream of chatter as he dabbed away the blood from Fieran's face, then gently touched Fieran's forehead with magic-laced fingers. In moments, the gash smoothed away, not even leaving a scar.

"All set." Taranath straightened and gestured toward a glass jar on his work table. "Would you like a peppermint stick for being such a good boy?"

"Yes!" Fieran wiggled out of Farrendel's grip and launched himself from the table, landing on the floor lightly before bounding over to Taranath. Except for the blood still crusted on his face and staining his shirt, one would never guess that Fieran had been hurt.

Elspetha sighed and shook her head. "He never learns."

Farrendel and Taranath talked quietly for a few seconds before Taranath walked to the candy jar.

Farrendel crossed the room and perched on the bench on Leyleira's other side. He plucked at his bloody shirt, then drew in a breath and released the fabric as if deliberately trying to ignore the mess. "Was I this troublesome at Fieran's age? I do not remember quite so many trips to Taranath while I was growing up."

Leyleira patted his shoulder. "You were beyond energetic. Your dacha used to let you run in circles to attempt to tire you out. But you were a little less..."

"Accident prone?" Elspetha laughed. "You can say it. I know Fieran's propensity for getting hurt is likely his human side showing. But, Farrendel, you have to own that his recklessness is all you."

Farrendel opened his mouth, as if to refute Elspetha's claim, before snapping his mouth shut and giving a slight shrug.

"Machasheni! Machasheni!" Fieran raced across the room, then scrambled onto Leyleira's lap. He opened his fist, showing her the peppermint stick he had picked out. "I got a peppermint stick for being brave."

"Yes, you were very brave." Leyleira was not sure where to hold Fieran. He was still rather grubby and bloody.

"I ran into a door." Fieran made a motion with his hand, then added a smacking sound. While most of his sentence had been in elvish, he had used the Escarlish word for door.

"That is what your macha said." Leyleira finally settled on resting her hands on Fieran's waist.

Not that it mattered. Fieran stayed on her lap only a few seconds more before he squirmed free, sliding to the ground. He dashed across the room and started pointing at various jars and herbs, peppering Taranath with such rapid-fire questions that Taranath did not have time to answer one before Fieran was already spouting the next one.

Leyleira smiled. Even with his red hair and slightly rounder features, Fieran was very much his father's son.

Perhaps he would inherit the magic of the ancient kings, as they all suspected. His inexhaustible energy certainly pointed to that conclusion.

But he would have a father to teach him how to use his magic. He would be a warrior like his father but hopefully with a love of peace like his great-grandfather.

Likely, Leyleira would live long enough to see it. She still missed Ellarin each and every day. But she was content with the long years she had lived. She would be there for Ryfon, Brina, Fieran, Adriana, Rhohen, and any other great-grandchildren who had yet to be born.

And, once they were old enough to hear the story, she would tell them about their great-grandfather Ellarin.

ELF KING

CHAPTER
ONE

Weylind gripped the rope, then launched himself off the branch. The warm, summer heat blasted against him as he swung through the air, faster and faster, the exhilaration pounding through him. At the rope's apex, he let go, flipped, and dove, slicing into the sun-heated waters of the lake at the base of Lethorel. The deeper he glided, the colder the water grew.

As his momentum slowed, Weylind twisted and propelled himself toward the surface. His head broke into the sunshine, and he swiped water from his face. A reckless kind of energy still filled him, and he dove beneath the water again, staying below until his lungs burned.

He swam until he was pleasantly tired, then climbed from the water, his clothes wet and dripping, his black hair plastered to his back.

At the edge of the lake, his dachasheni Ellarin rested

among a mound of cushions and blankets, propped up on pillows at the base of a tree. He was so thin his skin stretched over his cheekbones and his blond hair was dull. Despite the heat, he had a blanket draped over him. But his smile was warm, his eyes sharp, as he patted the spot next to him. "Come, sit, sasonsheni."

When his dachasheni wished to speak, Weylind was not going to say no. None of them talked about it, but this was likely Dachasheni's last summer trip to Lethorel. He probably should not even have come this year. He could not sit to ride, and instead had made the trip on a litter harnessed between two steady horses.

But Dachasheni had been determined, so he had come.

Weylind flopped into the patch of sunlight next to Dachasheni, the sun quickly warming his sodden clothes. "Is there something I can get for you, Dachasheni?"

"No, just sit with me a moment." Dachasheni Ellarin flicked a glance to him, a hint of a smile creasing his wan face. "I know sitting still is rather difficult."

"I think I can manage to sit for a few minutes." Weylind could not help but grin. At one hundred years old, he was starting to get a handle on his magic. But the intense energy still surged through him, demanding that he move, run, dash about until it was exhausted.

Farther around the lake in a small meadow, Dacha and Macha chased ten-year-old Melantha around, trying to wear her out. On the bench beneath Lethorel, Machasheni Leyleira sat next to her parents, Weylind's great-grand-parents, and the three of them were talking quietly.

At the far side of the lake, the healer Taranath, his wife Neia, and their fifty-year-old daughter Rheva came into view, riding back to Lethorel after an overnight trip to Arorien to visit with Neia's parents.

"I have heard the talk in the court." Dachasheni

glanced at Weylind before his gaze focused out at the lake once again as if trying to store up the sight in his memory. "I know many were disappointed when you inherited your dacha's magic rather than mine."

Weylind grimaced and buried his fingers in the grass. His magic was strong, but he had inherited the perfectly mundane plant magic. He had not inherited the magic of the ancient kings, as many in the court had hoped.

There had never been more than a generation without a warrior king or prince with the magic of the ancient kings. Weylind's great-great-uncle had it, then his grandfather.

But his dacha had Machasheni Leyleira's plant magic, as did Weylind.

Would Melantha inherit the magic of the ancient kings? Or had the magic of the ancient kings faded from the royal line entirely? That was what the court was whispering.

Weylind pushed upright and rested his arms on his knees. "Do you think the magic of the ancient kings is fading?"

"Perhaps it is." Dachasheni Ellarin lifted his hand, only the faintest blue glow surrounding his fingers, as if that was all the magic he could call up. "Maybe it is just as well that I am the last with the magic of the ancient kings. Those who inherit it seem cursed to die young."

Weylind swallowed the lump in his throat. He could not imagine life without his dachasheni as king of Tarenhiel. But that day was coming all too swiftly

Dachasheni Ellarin gave a small shrug. "Perhaps we elves are fading. Our time of great empires and potent magic is long over. Many will wish to retreat, as if the way to deal with the changing times would be to quietly fade away and disappear entirely. Maybe it would be easier if we could just leave this world to the humans."

Weylind kept his mouth shut, not sure where his dachasheni was going with this.

"The human kingdoms are rising in power. I will not live to see it, but I fear our time of peace will soon be over." Dachasheni Ellarin gave a slight sigh, his blue eyes tinged with sorrow. "It will be up to your dacha—and to you—to lead our people into this age of human machines and inventions."

Tarenhiel had enjoyed over seven hundred years of peace, ever since Weylind's great-great-uncle had died creating the Gulmorth Gorge, filling the stone with so much magic that the trolls had been unable to cross the border.

But after so many centuries, the magic was fading away, and it would soon be gone entirely. Then there were the human kingdoms. The small, rural kingdoms had been steadily growing in power, and eventually they would get sick of fighting among themselves and would turn their sights on the rich forests of Tarenhiel to their north.

Dachasheni Ellarin reached out a trembling hand and lightly clasped Weylind's shoulder. "Ignore the naysayers, sasonsheni. I suspect Tarenhiel's future kings will need to be great diplomats rather than wield great power."

Weylind nodded, glancing to where his dacha and macha had corralled Melantha. Perhaps great power would not be necessary, but it probably would not hurt.

Machasheni Leyleira strode over to them and handed a cup of tea to Dachasheni. "Honey chamomile, as you prefer."

"Linshi, shynafera." Dachasheni smiled at her, brushing her hand as he claimed the teacup. He took a sip, then gestured to Weylind. "Go on. I can see you fidgeting. I have dampened this sunny day with enough of my musings."

Weylind clasped Dachasheni's shoulders, then hopped to his feet and gave Machasheni a quick shoulder-hug clasp before he raced off.

He grinned at Dacha and Macha, then swept up Melantha. She shrieked and laughed and kicked all at once, as if she could not decide if she found being swung about by her big brother fun or annoying.

Dachasheni Ellarin made some dire predictions for the future, but right now, Weylind did not care. He was young, with his whole life spreading rosy and open before him. Why should he worry about what would come?

Besides, he had a little sister to tease.

CHAPTER
TWO

185 YEARS BFH

"I cannot believe Dacha is having me escorted like a criminal."

Weylind shook his head as he strolled next to his sister Melantha. "You are the one who was caught skipping your healing lessons to watch the warriors train instead. Worse, you were copying their stances."

"Is that so wrong? You are training to be a warrior." Melantha waved her hand with a sharp, stabbing motion. Her black hair blew in the slight breeze, contrasted against the bold red dress she wore.

Melantha always tended to wear red, as if in perpetual protest. Even though she had a deep fire inside of her, she had come into healing magic, which precluded becoming a warrior.

"I am the heir, and I have the magic for it." Weylind refused to grimace. Yes, plant magic was perfectly boring, but it was also perfectly logical and acceptable. He had plant magic, like his father and grandmother. Perhaps he had not carried on the tradition of the magic of the ancient kings, but no one could complain about the strength of his magic, least of all him.

"I do not even like people." Melantha gestured with both hands now, her fingers curling with tension. "It is so unfair. Why can I not be a warrior with healing magic? It is just so stifling being the perfect, placid princess all the time. I cannot be all smiles and gentleness like the other healers. I just...I am so...argh."

Weylind was not sure what to tell Melantha. He felt for her. He did.

But she was a healer. And healers did not become warriors. That was that. "It is traditional."

"Just because it is traditional does not mean it should not be done." Melantha huffed and crossed her arms.

"It is traditional for a good reason." Weylind frowned. Those with healing magic wielded great power over the body. It was considered especially horrific if a healer killed with their magic. They were banned from training as warriors and swore solemn oaths to prevent them from turning their magic from healing to killing.

Not that they had needed warriors in many centuries. But with the protections at the border with the trolls failing, their dacha had begun strengthening their army in the case of a coming war.

Melantha spoke through another harsh sigh. "I suppose. It would be pretty awful killing someone with my magic. I would be able to feel their heart stop, their body shut down."

That did sound awful.

Weylind did not want to imagine killing anyone with his magic either. Honestly, this whole conversation was rather depressing. Time to change the subject. "At least you are training with the best."

Taranath and Neia were the royal healers and incredibly skilled.

While most elves were trained in their magic by their parents, healing magic was the one exception. An elf with healing magic trained with their parents—or their closest relative with healing magic—while they were coming into their magic. Once they had a certain level of control, they were taught by a fully trained healer for a hundred years before they took the healer's oath and became a healer in their own right.

Melantha had trained with their macha while she gained control over her magic. Now she would finish her training with Taranath and Neia, the royal healers and friends of the family.

"I suppose. And I will be spending time with Rheva." Melantha swatted at a leaf.

In the years since Dachasheni Ellarin had died, Taranath, Neia, and Rheva had not traveled to Lethorel with them as often. And when they did, they usually stayed in Arorien the entire time. Weylind could not even remember the last time he had seen Taranath and Neia's daughter Rheva. All he could think of was a gangly young girl, not the grown woman she would be now.

He shook himself and kept his smile in place. "Even if you hate healing, you do not have to practice it if you do not want to. Mother is a healer, but she does not act as a healer because she is too busy being queen."

"I think I would do very well as queen. I like bossing people around." Melantha grinned and nudged him with an elbow. "But that role is reserved for your wife, when you get around to finding yourself one."

"I am not even two hundred yet. I have time." Weylind scowled at Melantha. She was just teasing, but it was a sore spot. He could have married long before now

—if he had been willing to court one of the noble elf daughters who kept throwing themselves at him at every court event.

"Two hundred. So old." Melantha's grin took on an edge.

He nudged her with his own elbow. "You are a hundred and ten. You are rather young, but perhaps a long courtship..."

"Not a chance." Melantha shuddered. "I do not want to marry one of the stuffy noble sons."

"Is that really why you kept sneaking off to watch the warriors train?" Weylind raised an eyebrow at her in that way he knew always made Melantha squirm. He was rather proud of the fact that he could raise just one eyebrow. "Perhaps you should have used that as your excuse."

"The warriors *are* rather...uh...impressive." Melantha grinned, but the tips of her ears got a little red, proving that she had, indeed, noticed the young male warriors while they were training. "Everyone except you. You are just sweaty and gross."

"Very funny." Weylind tried to add an even more dour tilt to his frown. He was trying to perfect his kingly frown. Not that he planned to need it any time soon, but all kings needed a good, regal glower. "Not all of the nobles are stuffy. And as you said, you like bossing people around. You would do very well as the lady of an estate with a section of forest to oversee."

"Perhaps." Melantha sighed and swatted at another nearby twig. "I think I would rather marry a warrior. At least warriors do interesting stuff."

"So do nobles. Perhaps you could find one interested in becoming an ambassador and traveling to the distant dwarven mountains or across the sea or..." Weylind lowered his tone as if to impart a great secret. "Or even to one of the human kingdoms."

"Ew, no." Melantha gave a shudder that was more real than exaggerated. "Why are we even talking about this? I need to get through training first."

"You know, healing would be a rather handy skill to have for someone who wants to marry a warrior..." Weylind dodged out of the way as Melantha tried to elbow him in the ribs.

With a last huff and shake of her head, Melantha brushed past him and hurried ahead as they reached Taranath and Neia's healing room.

Melantha knocked, shifting from foot to foot.

When the door opened, it was not Taranath or Neia standing there, but a young elf female with big eyes and long hair the same rich brown of loamy earth after a rainstorm.

Rheva. And she had grown up. She had grown up very nicely.

Weylind swallowed, freezing where he stood with one foot on the porch, one foot on the branch.

Melantha said something that made Rheva smile and step aside, but he could not hear it past the rushing buzz filling his ears. Melantha flounced inside, and Rheva returned to the door.

It took him another moment to realize she had said something to him.

"I...uh...pardon?" Weylind blinked at her.

"Was there something you needed, amir?" Rheva looked at him with those big brown eyes set in a heart-shaped face.

"No, I...I was just here...Melantha..." He waved vaguely toward the door, his brain just a fizzling mess.

Rheva gave him a slight smile, still holding the door

and his gaze as if waiting for him to say something coherent.

"I hope you have a good day," Weylind blurted out, spun on his heel, and hurried away from the healing room before he said something silly. Well, more silly.

RHEVA SCRUBBED the wooden work surface, swiping away any hint of dust to keep the healing room as sterile as possible.

Footsteps scuffed on the porch outside, and she quickly stuffed the rag behind a jar, then smoothed the apron she wore. Should she ditch the apron too? How did her hair look? She really should have gone with the pink dress instead of the blue one. No, she loved this blue one.

Her dacha huffed and flapped a hand at her. "You look perfectly fine, sena. Now go open the door for your young man."

Her young man. Weylind was hardly that. He was the prince. The heir.

Not to mention that he had only been coming each day for the past few months to escort his sister Melantha and ensure she did not skip her healing lessons. Melantha had not shown any sign of bolting for a while now, but Weylind kept coming every single day.

Rheva hurried to the door, ignoring her dacha's waggling eyebrows and her macha's knowing smile.

When Rheva opened the door, Melantha smiled at her and brushed past her, leaving Weylind standing there on the porch. He shifted from foot to foot, his dark eyes flicking from the floor to her and back again.

Rheva caught herself giving him a love-loopy smile and struggled to rein in her emotions. "Elontiri, amir."

"Elontiri. I..." Weylind shifted again, made a noise in the back of his throat, then met her gaze. "Would you....would you walk with me? It does not have to be now. At your convenience. But if you want to go now, I would like that too, of course. Unless you are needed here. I..."

Weylind trailed off, his gaze dropping away from her again as the tips of his ears turned pink.

Rheva glanced over her shoulder. In the room, hidden from Weylind's view, Melantha had her arms crossed as she sighed. Dacha was making shooing motions, mouthing, "Say yes." Macha was smiling even more knowingly, and she gave an encouraging flick of her fingers.

Rheva quickly stepped all the way onto the porch, shutting the door behind her. "A walk sounds perfect. Let us go right now."

She was not needed for Melantha's training. While Rheva was not finished with her healing training, her parents could train her whenever they wished. And it had seemed like both of them were highly in favor of her accepting this walk.

Weylind blinked at her for a long moment, as if he could not believe she had actually said yes.

She gestured to him. "Are you going to offer me your arm?"

He cleared his throat, and his arm came up with a jerky, hurried motion. "Of course."

She rested her hand on his arm. His sleeve was warm beneath her hand, his forearm well-muscled in a way that sent little flutters through her chest.

It was like all her childhood infatuation was coming to reality, and she could not quite comprehend it.

Perhaps she should be more daunted, out on a walk with the future king of the elves.

But she had basically grown up at Lethorel, seeing her prince as just a boy. So much older than her at the time, but still young and foolish and someone she would tag along with since they were the only two children at Lethorel until Melantha came along.

"How has warrior training been?" She peeked at him as they walked.

The question helped, and they soon broke past the awkward silence into comfortable conversation. The first of many walks and conversations.

180 Years BFH

"She is adorable." Rheva cradled the newborn princess Jalissa in her arms. The little one had a fuzz of dark brown hair and the prettiest, round little face.

"We certainly think so." Queen Vianola was comfortably ensconced on one of the cushioned benches in the royal rooms. She smiled, first at the baby, then at King Lorsan, who stood next to her with a hand on her shoulder in a protective, proud kind of way.

It was a glimpse of what she and Weylind could have, if things continued as they were. They had been taking their time, courting for the past five years.

They had been taking it so slow to keep it out of the public eye as much as possible. Given that Taranath and Neia were longtime friends of the family, it was not too noteworthy that Weylind and Rheva had been spending time together, especially since Melantha was training with Rheva's parents.

Even now, Taranath and Neia had come as well to

meet the new princess. Anyone who saw Rheva here would dismiss her presence due to the family connection.

Rheva appreciated that she had been spared the court's scrutiny so far. But she would have to face them eventually, if she was serious about Weylind.

The court expected Weylind would marry someone noble. While Rheva's dacha and macha were respected—especially Dacha for the depth to his magic and the way he had kept Weylind's dachasheni alive for so long—Rheva was not nobility. She was still a common healer from a family of common healers.

When their courtship became public, the gossip would be brutal.

Could she handle it? Or would she break under it?

But what was her other option? She either faced it and survived or she walked away from Weylind now.

She could not do that to Weylind. She could not leave him to face the court alone. Who else would see the heart he had beneath the stoic exterior? She had loved him since they were both young. She knew Weylind as himself rather than just the elf prince everyone else saw.

Rheva glanced up. Weylind was leaning over her shoulder, peering at his baby sister. "Do you want to hold her?"

Weylind's face paled. "I...uh..."

Rheva raised her eyebrows at him and gave him that look that he could not seem to argue with. Then she tilted her head to indicate the seat next to her.

Weylind sat. "I do not need to..."

"Of course you do." Rheva gently handed Jalissa over to Weylind. "You held Melantha when she was a baby."

"That was a century ago. What if I have forgotten how to hold a baby properly?" Weylind might have protested, but he rather competently cradled Jalissa's head and body as Rheva handed the baby to him.

"See? You have not forgotten. How to properly hold a baby is not something you forget." Rheva's heart twisted at the sight of Weylind with a baby in his arms.

The young ladies of the court wanted Weylind because he was the prince—the future king. They wanted him for the power he would wield.

But she wanted him for the man he was. For the husband and father he would be someday.

"ARE YOUR EYES CLOSED?" Weylind steered Rheva through the twilight forest just out of sight of Ellonahshinel. They were on the far side of the palace, away from the subdued bustle of Estyra.

"Yes. Though I am beginning to wonder where you are taking me." Rheva laughed slightly, her shoulders lifting and falling beneath his grip.

"Nowhere sinister, I assure you." Weylind's excitement tightened his chest. Would Rheva like the surprise he had planned?

He needed her to like it. He had never felt like this about anyone before. They had grown up together, during those summers at Lethorel. She knew him better than anyone outside of his family, and yet she still wanted to spend time with him. Not because he was the prince but simply because she liked *him*.

And he adored her. Her quiet manner with a spark of humor. She was not afraid to tease him. When she put her mind to something, she did not back down.

Weylind halted Rheva. "All right. Open your eyes."

Rheva blinked, then gave a small laugh. "It is a tree."

Before them, a willow tree trailed thick branches all the way to the forest floor. A small creek wound through this part of the forest, disappearing between the branches of the willow.

"A tree I specifically grew just for us." Weylind stepped forward and drew aside a clump of branches.

Rheva shot him a look, then stepped into the little haven created by the branches.

He followed her inside, letting the branches fall into place behind them.

Fireflies glittered among the branches, providing a yellow glow along with the elven lights that he had grown into a few of the branches. A shield of his magic kept the fireflies from flying off while making sure no mosquitoes got inside. A blanket had been spread out on the thick grass beside the creek, and a picnic basket waited.

"A picnic?" Rheva laughed, then gracefully eased to a sitting position on the blanket beside the basket. "This is lovely. Did you catch all these fireflies yourself?"

"Yes." Weylind sprawled on the blanket across from her. Only with her would he admit just how long he had spent gathering up fireflies and stashing them in here for this moment.

"It is magical." Rheva leaned back on her hands, as if to better take in the glow in the branches above them. She turned her gaze back on him, a little twist to her mouth. "It makes me wonder what you are up to with such a private, romantic setting..."

He was not proposing. Not yet. Though this would have been a good setting for it.

"We have been courting for over five years now, and I would like..." Weylind's throat closed. He could not get all flustered and wordless now. He had practiced this speech long enough that surely he could get through it without too many stumbles. "I would like to take our relationship public. I love you. I do not want to keep hiding from the court. But I know doing so will put a great deal of the focus on you, and…"

Rheva leaned over the picnic basket and pressed a finger to his mouth. "I love you too. And I know that loving you means that I will have to face the court sooner or later. I am ready. I will face all the snide remarks to be with you."

He did not deserve Rheva. He really did not. She was making all the sacrifices here while he was bringing all the baggage.

Weylind took her hand, then pressed a kiss to her knuckles. He would just have to spend the rest of his life making sure that Rheva never regretted her choice to court him and—someday, when he asked—to become his queen.

CHAPTER
THREE

175 YEARS BFH

W eylind could not stop grinning as he paced, waiting for his dacha to arrive so they could make the eshinelt together.

He was getting married today. To Rheva.

It had been a long time in coming. Not that a ten-year courtship was unusual among elves. There was great wisdom in being deliberate when it came to relationships.

But he was more than ready to stop courting and start building a life together as husband and wife.

At the knock on his door, he all but yanked the door off its hinges flinging it open.

His dacha stood there, smiling and shaking his head. "Weylind, sason. The eshinelt will need steadiness, not haste."

Weylind shifted sheepishly and stepped aside to let his father enter. Making the eshinelt was a solemn moment, and he had to try to rein in his enthusiasm for a few minutes. He closed the door, then joined his dacha at the table. "What do we do first?"

"First, I give you the same talk your dachasheni gave me on my wedding day." Dacha leveled a steady look at him, complete with solemn dark eyes framed by his black hair, so like Weylind's.

Weylind nodded and waited.

Dacha set a silver bowl and a satchel on the table, then faced Weylind. "Today is the easy day. But marriage will not always be easy. You and Rheva have already faced difficult times, due to the backlash in the court."

"We have." Weylind nodded, gripping the back of a chair. The court's disapproval for Weylind's choice of bride had been quite fierce. Many of the ladies had actively snubbed Rheva—as much as they could, anyway. Once they realized that Rheva was going to be their future queen, whether they liked it or not, some of them had changed their tune and acted more civil, at least on the surface. They could not afford to find themselves snubbed in turn once Rheva rose in power.

"Then you have likely already figured out that when life is hard, you need to choose each other. Choose to love each other, even when you do not feel like doing so." Dacha met Weylind's gaze.

Weylind nodded, fighting to remain solemn.

But, really, he knew all this. He and Rheva would be fine. They loved each other, and that was not going to change.

RHEVA SMOOTHED her hand over the silver of her skirt, the silk edged in green embroidery dotted with tiny diamonds and emeralds. The bodice fit snugly enough to hold up the dress without the need for straps, leaving her shoulders bare. It was a dress fit for a future queen.

Future queen. Rheva swallowed, her fingers trembling at the shaft of tension that coursed through her.

She loved Weylind. But she did not love the thought of someday wearing the crown.

A light hand rested briefly on her shoulder, the touch warm against her skin. "It will be all right, sena."

Rheva glanced over her shoulder, meeting the gaze of Queen Vianola. "I know, it is just..." She did not want to voice her doubts, especially to Weylind's macha. Even if his macha had already embraced her as a daughter.

"It is daunting, marrying the future elf king." Queen Vianola's gaze remained warm, understanding.

Of course she understood. She had also been a gentle healer who had set that aside to become queen.

But unlike Rheva, Vianola came from a noble family. Yes, her family was not among the most wealthy or powerful, but they were well-respected and they had a history of great feats of bravery during the wars with the trolls nearly a thousand years ago, given the location of their estate along the Gulmorth Gorge in the north.

Rheva was common. Her parents were common. Yes, they had been raised in status due to her father's unusual healing magic and his long friendship with the late King Ellarin. But that was not enough in the eyes of the court. It never would be.

Queen Vianola was still holding her gaze. "You will find that you grow to fit the role, even as you make the role your own. You will be the balance for Weylind. Where he has a tendency toward logic, you will remind him of compassion. When he must be the hard, unyielding king, you will be gentle. So that, together, the two of you can effectively rule when that day comes."

Rheva released a long breath and nodded. Had she not seen that same thing in King Lorsan and Queen Vianola? By being what Weylind needed, she would be what the kingdom needed as well. Weylind would be the same for her.

Rheva started at a sudden, sharp tugging on her skirts. She glanced down to find the little princess Jalissa standing there, both fists gripping the silver silk.

Jalissa blinked up at Rheva with huge, dark eyes and gave a broad, child's grin. "Pre-ee! Pre-ee!"

"She thinks your dress is pretty." Vianola knelt, then gently extracted Rheva's skirt from Jalissa's fists. "No, sena. You need to leave the pretty dress alone."

Jalissa whined as her fingers were peeled off the silk. When Vianola picked her up, Jalissa squirmed and kicked, reaching again for the dress. Vianola sent another smile at Rheva, even as she headed for the door. "I should get her energy out before the ceremony starts."

When Vianola opened the door, she revealed Rheva's macha standing there, holding a silver bowl wrapped in one arm, her other hand raised to knock.

Macha nodded and stepped aside to let the queen exit before she entered the room, closing the door behind her.

Rheva pushed to her feet, that swooping feeling back in the pit of her stomach.

Macha set the bowl of eshinelt on a table, then crossed the room to Rheva. She gripped Rheva's shoulders, her eyes a hint teary. "You look so beautiful, sena. So grown up. I am not ready to lose you."

"You are not losing me, Macha." Rheva returned her macha's shoulder-grip hug. It probably felt that way, to her parents. They had waited so long to have a child, finally having Rheva when they were into their six hundreds. "You are gaining the son you never had."

Macha smiled, her eyes wet but her voice holding a trace of laughter. "I never expected that son would be the grandson of my dearest friends."

Their families had been close for centuries, and this marriage would only make it more official. Rheva was especially looking forward to claiming Melantha and Jalissa as sisters. In many ways, Melantha had already felt like the sister she had never had. Now Melantha would be her sister in truth.

Macha stepped back and waved toward the bowl. "Let us see to the eshinelt so that you can marry your prince."

Rheva smiled and crossed the room to the table, the clenching in her chest caused more by joyful anticipation than nerves.

No matter the court or the burdens, Weylind was her choice. She loved him, and he loved her. That would make everything else that came with the crown bearable.

RHEVA SHIVERED as Weylind traced the ancient runes on her forehead, cheek, and upper chest above the line of her dress and repeated the vows that bound them together. Was she shivering with the solemnity of the moment? The cold wet of the eshinelt on her skin? Or Weylind's gentle touch? Perhaps all of the above.

Then Weylind took the bowl of eshinelt from her, and it was her turn. She dipped her finger into the eshinelt, then lifted her finger, raising her head to meet Weylind's gaze.

His black hair lay sleek down his back and over his shoulders. The silver, sleeveless tunic he wore was edged with green and embroidered with the Tarenhieli tree emblem in a silver thread slightly darker than the tunic's silk. With the collar of the tunic so open, much of his chest was visible, making her ears burn and her stomach get all fluttery.

His dark brown eyes held her gaze, both warm with his love and filled with a steadiness that in turn steadied her. Even as she watched, that one eyebrow eased upward, as if asking her what she was waiting for, as just a hint of a smile curved his mouth.

That smile, that eyebrow, was exactly what she had needed to banish the weight of the stares, the buzzing nerves.

With a deep breath, she reached up and traced the first rune on his forehead. While everything in her wanted to whisper the vow, she dug deep and tried to speak loudly enough to be heard throughout the packed great hall of Ellonahshinel. "May our minds sharpen each other and may we always provide each other wise counsel."

She dipped her finger into the eshinelt again, then drew a rune on his cheek. "May our speech be filled with kindness, gentleness, and understanding."

Just one more, and she would be done. She refreshed the eshinelt on her finger one last time, then she made the last rune on his chest, the tips of her ears burning. "May our hearts be bound as one for all our days together."

She lifted her gaze to Weylind's again, that fluttery jolt making her heart beat harder once again. Weylind was now her husband, and she his wife.

No matter what came, they would face it together.

CHAPTER
FOUR

110 YEARS BFH

Macha gripped Jalissa's shoulders, smiling and saying something quietly. After the farewell with Jalissa, Macha spoke with Melantha, having to just about elbow Hatharal out of the way to do so.

Weylind resisted the urge to make a fist at the sight of Hatharal. The lordling was tall, with a slim, straight nose, dark brown hair, and eyes that never seemed to stray from Melantha. It might have been romantic, if not for the possessive gleam in his eyes and the way his hand dipped a bit lower on Melantha's back than it should for a couple that was not yet married. For any couple in public, really.

Hopefully they would never be married. Dacha, Macha, Machasheni, Weylind, and Rheva had all warned Melantha that they did not think her relationship with Hatharal was healthy.

But she would not listen, no matter what they said. Dacha and Macha were at their wits' end. Dacha had, in the end, agreed to the betrothal since Melantha seemed determined to marry Hatharal whether they gave approval or not.

How could his sister not see what Hatharal was doing to her? Even now, she stood with her shoulders hunched, as if trying to appear smaller. The spark that used to flare in Melantha's eyes was all but snuffed out. If she had thought herself stifled before, now she seemed all but smothered beneath Hatharal's control.

Macha glanced at Hatharal, but she gave him nothing more than a brief nod before moving on to Rheva. Treating Hatharal politely but not embracing him as a future son.

Macha gripped Weylind's shoulders, her smile returning. "Do not run yourself too ragged, sason."

"I will not let him." Rheva smiled up at him, her eyes glinting. She knew his tendency to take his job seriously, whether it was the role of the heir or temporary king while his macha and dacha enjoyed a much-needed holiday in the north.

Weylind gripped Macha's shoulders in return. "Enjoy your trip, Macha."

"It will be good to see my family again." Macha's smile widened, her eyes dancing a bit as she glanced past Weylind to Dacha. "Especially when your dacha arrives."

"I will leave as soon as I can." Dacha sighed and shook his head. "But I am afraid the yearly meeting of the King's Council cannot be moved."

It was the one thing Weylind could not cover for his dacha. The King's Council would not take him as a substitute.

But for everything else, Weylind would be in charge until his dacha returned from his and Macha's holiday in the north.

Surely he could handle this. It would be good, actually, to get some real practice at being king. Not that he would need to be king for years and years yet.

Macha gave Weylind's shoulders one last squeeze, then stepped back. "We will see everyone at Lethorel at the end of summer."

She and Dacha shared a look, then Macha took Dacha's hand and drew him behind one of the horses.

Jalissa giggled. "Do they really think we do not know what they are doing back there?"

"Disgraceful display," Hatharal muttered. As if he did not have Melantha tucked so close to his side that Melantha could barely move.

After a few more moments, Dacha lifted Macha onto her horse. They shared one last look, before Macha lifted a hand in a wave, smiling. Her guard fell into place around her.

Then the traveling party rode down the street of Estyra, all flapping flags, traveling cloaks, and weapons glinting in the sun, ready to lay down their lives to protect their queen.

Not that it would be necessary. Yes, there had been some minor incidents at the border recently with the trolls, but nothing serious. The warriors surrounding Macha were more for show than anything else.

THREE WEEKS LATER...

Dacha strapped his pack onto the back of his huge white horse. "I left a pile of the most important paperwork in the center of my desk. I have done my best to clear the most pressing items, but I could not complete everything."

"I can handle it, Dacha." Weylind held the reins to Dacha's horse. He had been training from the time he was little to take over as king.

"I know. If I did not thi—" Dacha's word cut off, his gaze going distant.

"Dacha?" Weylind reached for his father with his free hand.

Face twisting, Dacha crumpled to the ground with a cry, clutching at his chest.

"Dacha!" Weylind released the horse and dove for his father. He gripped his father's shoulders. What was happening?

He was vaguely aware of the guards clustering around him. Someone was calling for a healer.

In Weylind's grip, his dacha fought for breath, his eyes squeezed shut, his mouth moving though Weylind could not hear any words.

Taranath knelt next to Weylind, then pressed a hand to Dacha's forehead. After a moment, Taranath's eyes widened, then saddened as he lifted his head to meet Weylind's gaze. "Your dacha is fine."

"Then what is wrong with him?" Something was clearly wrong. In Weylind's grip, Dacha was shaking, sweating, curling in on himself.

"I suspect it is his elishina with your macha." Taranath's voice was soft. Sad.

If this was caused by the elishina between his dacha and macha, then Dacha was not the one in danger. Macha was.

And there was nothing any of them could do. While Taranath could tell it was the elishina, the magic of an elishina was something between the two people involved. Taranath could not touch it in order to attempt to heal Weylind's macha through Dacha.

Weylind gripped his dacha's shoulders, even as his utter helplessness churned through him. He could do nothing but hold his dacha and hope.

Dacha gave a wrenching cry and stilled in Weylind's arms, breathing heavily.

"Dacha?" Weylind was not sure what to ask. Did he want to know?

With a deep breath, Dacha pushed upright, but his head still hung. "Weylind, sason, your macha...your macha was killed."

The words sank, heavy and unreal amid the buzzing in Weylind's ears.

"I must..." Dacha staggered to his feet, then fumbled for his horse's reins. "I must go to her. We must turn the trolls back. We must retrieve..." He shook his head, hunching against his horse's flank for a moment as a shudder passed through him.

Then Dacha swung into the saddle, his expression blank and bleak. When he raised his voice, it rang cold in the morning air. "Warriors. The queen has been killed by trolls in the north. We ride to battle, to vengeance, to bring the queen's body home. To me!"

Without another glance at Weylind or back at Ellonahshinel, Dacha nudged his horse, urging it into a gallop on the path heading north.

After only a moment's hesitation, the warriors spurred their horses to follow at the king's heels.

Weylind stepped back out of the way. Taranath rested a hand on his shoulder, as if to offer comfort. But Weylind could not bring himself to look at Rheva's dacha, nor acknowledge the comfort, as an emptiness spread through him.

His macha was dead. It was too terrible. Too unreal. Surely it was not real.

And yet he had seen the look on his dacha's face. Heard his struggle as he fought to keep Macha alive.

Macha was gone, and Dacha had left, meaning that the burden to tell Rheva, Melantha, Jalissa, and Machasheni Leyleira rested on Weylind's shoulders.

Weylind drew in a shaking breath, trying to stuff down any hint of the grief that threatened to send him to his knees on the moss there before the steps of Ellonahshinel.

He should summon the warriors and send more north to reinforce Dacha. He would have to somehow find the words to tell his family. Then he would have to gather the King's Council and tell them.

The plan had always been for Weylind to act as king this summer. But no one had thought he would have to be king in quite this manner or carry this burden.

He was not strong enough. He just was not. He could not do this.

He needed Rheva. Now.

Spinning on his heel, Weylind marched up the stairs of Ellonahshinel.

The head clerk met him at the top. "Amirisheni, I have some reports that need you to—"

"Send for all the warriors here in Ellonahshinel. Tell them they must be ready to ride within an hour." Weylind brushed past the clerk, not waiting to see if he acknowledged the orders or not.

Weylind strode through Ellonahshinel at as quick a pace as he could manage without actually running.

He found Rheva in the queen's study, a smaller room tucked farther down the branch of his own study. A few clerks bustled in and out, but as soon as Rheva glanced up, her gaze resting on Weylind, her face paled and she gave quiet orders for the clerks to leave them.

As soon as the last one left, closing the door behind her, Weylind crossed the room and gathered Rheva into his arms, even as everything in him was breaking. "My macha...she...she..."

He could not manage any more words as his grief shook through him. He hardly felt it as the two of them slowly collapsed to their knees as he buried his face against Rheva and struggled not to give in to the tears that were shaking through him, threatening to pour out as if he were an elfling instead of a grown prince.

Rheva gently ran her fingers over his hair, murmuring soothing words.

Could she feel the utter devastation of his grief? Their elishina had never been strong, not like the elishina his parents shared—had shared. All he ever sensed through the elishina was the faintest flickers of emotions every once and a while, though he always had a steady sense of Rheva tucked deep inside his heart.

"She was killed. The trolls killed her." He gasped the words between choking breaths.

Rheva's arms tightened around him, and for long moments she simply held him.

WEYLIND WRAPPED one arm around Rheva's shoulders, the other around Jalissa's, as the procession wound through the streets of Estyra, coming toward them.

Dacha rode at the fore, his face etched in lines that made him appear far older than he had a mere few weeks ago when he had ridden away.

Behind Dacha, two horses, led by guards, bore a stretcher between them. A body lay on the litter, draped in a dark green sheet with only her pale face and dark hair visible.

Jalissa made a noise in the back of her throat and pressed her face against Weylind's shoulder.

This was real. For the past weeks, a part of Weylind had hoped that this was all some kind of nightmare and he would soon wake up.

This was a nightmare, but it was all too real.

Weylind steered Rheva and Jalissa into place behind the horses carrying Macha's body. Melantha and Hatharal fell into place behind them.

They walked through Estyra, silent crowds filling the streets to pay homage to their queen.

At the base of Ellonahshinel, four guards unharnessed the queen's litter, carrying it up the endless stairs to the great hall, where Queen Vianola would lie in state for a week before she was buried, dedicated to the trees.

As the acting king, Weylind had read the reports that Dacha and his warriors had sent back to Estyra.

It had been a massacre. His macha, her family, and all her guards had been attacked and killed. For the first time in nearly a thousand years, the trolls had raided into Tarenhiel.

Dacha and his warriors had followed the tracks and raided into Kostaria in return. Dacha had not described the battle in more than brief, stilted lines.

The trolls had paid for killing the elf queen.

For the first time in nearly a thousand years, Tarenhiel was at war.

CHAPTER
FIVE

105 YEARS BFH

Rheva smoothed her hands over her skirt, wishing her palms were not so clammy.

Today the king met with petitioners, as he did each week. King Lorsan currently sat on his throne in the great hall, listening to the petitioners one by one. Since he no longer had a queen to sit in state with him, Machasheni Leyleira was at his side.

Someday, that would be Rheva's role, when Weylind became king in the long distant future.

For now, she would start to familiarize herself with the role by speaking with those waiting to petition the king. She ensured that they had refreshments and anything else they needed while they waited.

Rheva drew in a deep breath, smiling at the first few in line before walking to talk to those in the back. Those in the beginning of line would be in to see the king shortly. It was those at the end of the line who had a long wait.

Most in line seemed to be on their own. There was one woman with a young child at her side. Rheva directed a servant to bring them refreshments. Likely a widow seeking aid from the king to help support herself and her child.

A wail shattered the stillness, causing everyone in line to subtly shift. A few more people down the line, a female with silver-blonde hair juggled an infant. The infant squirmed in her arms, wailing at a pitch to shatter eardrums and windows.

The poor thing sounded hungry. The mother was likely too embarrassed to feed her baby in public.

A shaft of pain stabbed Rheva's heart, as it always did at the sight of a baby. She and Weylind had been married for seventy years, and they had yet to have a child of their own.

Weylind's father did not pressure them, but the court was always ready to gossip. Especially when it came to Rheva. They had never forgotten that she was a commoner and thus not truly one of them.

Rheva shook herself. She had a duty to do here, taking care of these petitioners. Now was not the time to mull over her problems with the court.

Rheva hurried to the mother's side and lightly touched her arm. "Elontiri."

The woman jumped, her silver-blue eyes widening at the sight of Rheva. There was something hard about the woman's eyes and mouth, a weariness that made her appear older than she likely was.

In her arms, a tiny baby squirmed in a bundle of blankets. The baby had a shock of blond hair the same color as the mother's, and his face was screwed up and red as he screamed.

The woman patted the baby's back as she bobbed into something of a bow. "Amirah."

"If you would like, I can have a servant take you to somewhere private to feed your baby." Rheva gestured, and a maid stepped forward. "Your place in line will be held for you."

The woman looked down at the baby in her arms, and something that almost looked like disgust twisted her features. "There is no need. I have a bottle of goat's milk in my pack."

She twisted, struggling to get the bottle out of her bag with one hand while holding the baby in the other arm.

Rheva was not going to judge. There were those who could not feed their babies who needed to supplement for whatever reason. "I can get the bottle out for you, if you would like."

The woman stilled, sending a glance over Rheva before she nodded.

Rheva dug into the pack, then pulled out the bottle of milk. It was warm. Perhaps too warm. How long had this milk been in this bag? Had it been properly laced with healing magic to make it digestible for the little one?

The woman snatched the bottle from Rheva and shoved it at the baby in her arms before Rheva had a chance to protest.

The baby gulped at the milk, chugging it so fast that he gave a cough, spitting up some of the milk.

The mother gave another sigh and dabbed at the milk with a corner of the blanket.

Rheva lingered, though she was not sure what else she should do. Something seemed off, but she was not sure if she should intervene further.

The line moved, and the woman brushed past Rheva without any gratitude for her help.

Rheva moved to talk to the next person, though she kept the woman and her baby in the corner of her eye.

After a few more minutes, the woman and her baby were called into the great hall.

Rheva meandered in that direction and peeked through the doorway.

King Lorsan had partially risen to his feet, his face paling. After a moment, he waved to the guards. "Please leave us. I will be taking no more petitioners today."

Rheva ducked out of sight as the guards left the great hall, leaving the woman and her child alone with King Lorsan and Machasheni Leyleira. What was going on? What about that woman and her child had caught King Lorsan so by surprise?

The guards stepped onto the branch outside and closed the doors to the great hall. One of the guards stepped forward. "The king will be taking no more petitioners today."

As a few of those waiting grumbled—they had, after all, been waiting for hours for their chance to talk to the king—Rheva strode forward, motioning to a nearby clerk. "Please step forward and give your name to the clerk. We will make a note of your place in line, and you will be given the first spots in next week's line, if the king does not reach out to you sooner."

That settled the people down, and they each stepped forward, gave their names to the clerk, then left quietly.

As the last of the petitioners left, Rheva lingered on the branch outside. What was going on in the great hall? What did that woman want?

A few minutes later, the door finally opened, and the woman walked out, her arms empty.

What was going on? Where was the child?

The woman strode down the branch at a purposeful pace, her head high, her expression hard and set.

Yet as she passed Rheva, the woman halted and glanced over her shoulder, something almost like pain in her eyes, before she focused on Rheva. "Will you see that he is cared for?"

She must be talking about her baby. But why was she leaving him behind?

There was no time for questions. Rheva nodded. "Of course."

The woman held Rheva's gaze for another moment, something in her gaze broken. She glanced over her shoulder one last time, swaying backwards.

Then she straightened her shoulders, the look in her eyes going blank. She faced forward again and marched off without another look back. A guard fell into step behind her to escort her from Ellonahshinel.

Before Rheva had a chance to question what was going on, the door opened again and King Lorsan strode onto the branch, holding the squirming, fussing baby in his arms. He turned to Rheva, a weary look etched into his features. "Is your dacha in his healing rooms at the moment?"

"He should be." Rheva glanced from King Lorsan to the infant he held. What was he doing with the woman's child?

"Linshi." King Lorsan started to stride past her, but then he paused. "Could you please fetch Weylind? And the rest of the family? I would like to meet with everyone in my rooms in half an hour."

With that, the king strolled off, still holding the fussing baby in one arm.

Rheva remained rooted to the spot for a long moment, not sure what to do or say.

The doors opened behind her, then Machasheni Leyleira halted next to her.

Rheva glanced at her, searching her face. "What is going on?"

Machasheni Leyleira sighed, her face set into stoic lines that gave nothing away. "I am not at liberty to say. But I fear we are all in for a storm ahead. Be there for Weylind. He will need you more than ever."

With that, Leyleira swept off, as if her cryptic words did not make everything that much more confusing.

WEYLIND PACED BACK and forth across the main room in his father's suite.

To one side, Hatharal had Melantha tucked to his side so closely that one would need a lever to pry them apart.

Jalissa huddled in the corner, her arms wrapped over her stomach, her shoulders hunched as if trying to make herself smaller.

Only Machasheni Leyleira remained steady and stoic where she sat on one of the cushioned benches. Rheva perched beside her, glancing at Machasheni as if wondering if she should say something to the group.

She had told him about the strange happenings with the petitioner when she had told him about the meeting his dacha had called.

The door opened, and Dacha stepped inside, carrying a baby. He faced them, the infant quiet in his arms, his focus on the baby rather than on them for a long moment before he looked up. "He is my son. Taranath just confirmed with his magic that I am the babe's father."

Weylind froze, gaping at the baby in his father's arms. Surely not. The baby looked nothing like the rest of them, with such a light-colored fuzz of hair in sharp contrast to Dacha's black hair.

But Dacha would not say something like this if it was not true. Nor would Taranath—Rheva's dacha—make a mistake in something this important. If he said this child was Dacha's son, then it was true.

It meant that his dacha had...Weylind could just mutely shake his head. Surely his dacha would not have crossed such lines of morality. He had raised all of them knowing better than to step outside of the bounds of matrimony.

Yet here his father was, without a wife, claiming this son was his.

Jalissa was the first one to move, blinking with wide, disbelieving eyes. "Dacha?"

Melantha dug her fingers into Hatharal's arm, clinging to him as she wordlessly glared at the infant.

Machasheni Leyleira squeezed her eyes shut with a sigh. Her lack of reaction nailed the truth of Dacha's claim home far deeper than anything else could have.

"Nine months ago on that trip I took, I met Filauria. She made me *feel* for the first time since your macha died." Dacha stared down at the infant in his arms rather than facing them. "I knew it was wrong, yet...well, I do not need to explain when this is the result."

No, Dacha did not, and Weylind definitely did *not* want the details.

Weylind could not seem to do anything but stand there, gaping from his dacha to the baby in his arms. He could not process that his dacha—his pinnacle of integrity —had fallen in this manner.

Hatharal stepped forward, taking Melantha with him. "What is the child doing here? Where is the brat's mother?"

"Filauria came today. She does not wish to raise the boy."

Hatharal muttered under his breath, "Then perhaps she should have properly disposed of the brat before he became a problem."

Weylind clenched his fists, breathing deeply as he resisted the urge to unleash his magic on Hatharal. Sure, Weylind was not happy about this situation either, but he was not going to suggest that the baby in Dacha's arms should have been killed to make the problem go away. Or abandoned the baby to the streets. Or whatever else Hatharal might have been implying.

Dacha's eyes flashed, his jaw working. "She did the right thing and came to me. She knew I would raise him. He is my son."

Machasheni Leyleira snorted, her eyes turning a shade icier. "It is hardly the right thing if she used the child as leverage to extort money from you."

"A small price to pay." Dacha's sigh was sad, his eyes compassionate. "She has had a hard life. Perhaps she will take the opportunity to get out of the life she is living."

"Or she will fall deeper into it." Machasheni raised her eyebrow at Dacha.

"Perhaps. But I do not think a shred of compassion is amiss."

Weylind did not care what kind of life this Filauria was living. He did not care about Dacha's compassion or about the pain that had led him to do...this.

All he cared about was the way his view of his dacha —of their family—shifted and shattered inside him

He had thought their family could not get more broken after Macha died. But this...this was worse. Much worse.

"Well, it is clear what we must do." Hatharal gestured

to the baby, a sneer curling his mouth. "Send the child away to be raised by some family far from Ellonahshinel. Deny any knowledge of him. Keep him far from the public eye if you are forced to acknowledge him."

Weylind probably should not, but a part of him wanted to agree with Hatharal, little as he wanted to agree with him on anything. Just sending this child away and letting him quietly disappear sounded so much easier than the alternatives.

Dacha sent Hatharal a scathing look. "No. He is my son. I will raise him with no less love and care than I did any of the rest of my children."

Weylind's shoulders tensed. It was the right thing to do. Even if he hated to admit it.

This decision would not affect just Dacha and the baby. All of them would face the court's ire when news of this scandal reached them.

Hatharal gaped. "You cannot be serious. You cannot mean to raise your by-blow as if he were a real son."

"He is my real son, just as much as Weylind is," Dacha snapped back.

"This is absurd. We are leaving. I hope you come to your senses. This will taint your entire legacy." Hatharal marched toward the door, dragging Melantha with him. The door slammed behind them.

For a long moment, the rest of them all stood there, frozen in place. Still absorbing the shock. Still slowly shattering.

Rheva glided to her feet and clasped Weylind's hand before she faced Dacha. "What is the baby's name?"

Dacha blinked, then glanced down at the infant once again. "Farrendel. His name is Farrendel."

CHAPTER
SIX

The wailing pierced the night, ringing even through the layers of magical protections surrounding the rooms.

Weylind groaned, grabbed his pillow, and pulled it over his ear. The pillow did little good. The crying continued, loud and howling. "Why will he not stop crying?"

Next to him, Rheva pushed onto an elbow, reaching for the blankets. "Perhaps I should see if your dacha needs help. The baby should not be crying this much."

"He is Dacha's problem, not yours." Weylind flopped onto his back, lifting the pillow from his face.

"Something is wrong." Rheva rolled upright. "The poor thing is just a newborn."

Two weeks old, if Rheva's mother Neia was correct. And she likely was, as a healer and a midwife.

Weylind sighed and swung to his feet. "Fine."

As they stumbled down the stairs to their main room, the pitch of the crying changed, somehow getting even louder and piercing another octave higher.

Just before they reached their door, a knock sounded.

Weylind shared a look with Rheva, then swung the door open.

Dacha stood there, harried and covered in spit-up. He rocked the baby slightly, but the infant just squalled louder, his tiny back arching, his face red and twisted.

Dacha all but shoved past Weylind to hold the baby out to Rheva. "There is something wrong. He will not stop crying, and he cannot seem to keep any of the milk down."

"The poor thing." Rheva took the baby from Dacha and touched magic-laced fingers to his sweaty forehead. "His tummy hurts. The milk does not seem to be settling."

"I have been giving him the goat's milk with healing magic, as instructed." Dacha ran his fingers through his hair, tousling the black strands further. A few dried flakes of spit-up fluttered down.

"With his stomach this pained, he likely would not be able to keep anything down." Rheva put the babe to her shoulder and rubbed his back gently. "Daresheni, you need your rest. Weylind and I can look after Farrendel tonight."

Weylind started. "No. I am not going to give up more sleep for his..." Weylind gestured at Dacha, unwilling to say the word he was thinking out loud.

Rheva shot him a quelling look. "Yes, we will." She smiled at Dacha. "Go on and rest."

"Linshi, sena." Dacha nodded to Rheva, but any soft-ness vanished as he met Weylind's gaze.

Weylind followed Dacha to the door, then stepped outside with him and closed the door. He crossed his arms, the taste of all the anger that he could not put into words coating his tongue.

He did not know how to face his dacha—shattered image and all.

Dacha whirled on him, his face in hard lines. "I know I cannot demand your forgiveness for what I did. I cannot ask that you accept Farrendel as your brother. But he is just a child, Weylind. If you can find even a shred of compassion for anyone in this situation, then give it to him. He is innocent. He did not ask to be born like this. He has been ripped away from his mother—the only family he has ever known—and given to strangers."

"I know all that." Weylind slapped a hand to the wall.

He wanted to lash out with this anger boiling inside him. But who could he be angry at?

Not the baby currently in Rheva's arms, even though he was the visible reminder of the scandal embroiling their family.

Not at Dacha, though Dacha was the one who deserved his anger the most. But Weylind was not sure how he could live with the anger if he kept it festering.

Perhaps at this Filauria. She was the one who had abandoned her son and walked away.

But hating her did not make Weylind feel much better, any more than this anger at his dacha soothed the raw places inside him.

"Just think about it." Dacha jabbed a finger toward the door. "You have every right to be angry at this situation. You are just as innocent as he is. But you, at least, grew up in peace with both a dacha and macha. But Farrendel will grow up with looming war with only a dacha to raise him. Hate me, if you must. But pity him."

Dacha spun on his heel and strode along the branch, headed back for his own rooms.

Weylind drew in a deep breath of the cool night air. Then he stepped back into the main room.

Rheva rocked the infant. He had calmed to a light, shuddering fussing.

As Weylind approached, Rheva glanced up, her face still set into determined lines. Then she held out the infant. "Hold him. I need to fetch fresh milk."

Weylind stumbled back, holding his hands out. "I do not want—"

Rheva's eyes flared, and she all but shoved the baby at him. "He is your *brother*. You had better have gotten your mind straight about that by the time I get back."

Weylind wrapped his arms around the baby, holding him gently.

Rheva shot him one last glare before she stormed from the room, though she closed the door quietly behind her.

Weylind stared down at the baby in his arms.

The infant gave another shaky breath, his tiny body shuddering against Weylind's hands. The strands of his blond hair plastered against his sweaty face. When he blinked up at Weylind, his lashes were beaded with glistening tears.

Weylind sank onto the cushioned bench along one wall. He stared down at the tiny infant in his arms as he released a long, slow breath.

Farrendel. His little brother.

Something shifted inside his chest. Dacha was right. Rheva was right.

Farrendel was innocent in all of this. So were Weylind, Melantha, and Jalissa. But they were at least grown—or mostly so, in Jalissa's case. They had memories of a happy childhood to lean on.

But Farrendel would have none of that. He was a helpless infant who would bear the brunt of the court's ire and hatred. He would become the symbol of the entire scandal, even though he bore none of the blame.

Weylind would do whatever it took to protect *all* his siblings. Including Farrendel.

"I know what it is like, shashon." Weylind leaned back, cuddling the infant close. "I lost my macha too."

Weylind was at least old enough to have long years of memories with his macha. And his macha had not wanted to leave them. She had been stolen from them by the trolls.

Farrendel would not even have any memories of his macha. As a baby, he did not understand. He had been crying for his macha, and she was not coming.

"Your macha is gone, but we will take good care of you, shashon." Weylind leaned his head against the wall behind him. "You will never be abandoned again."

The infant gave another shuddering breath, wiggling a bit.

"You are supposed to be sleeping. It is the middle of the night." Weylind kept rocking Farrendel and talking nonsense to pass the time.

He had a brother. That would take some getting used to. There was a time, centuries ago, when he had wanted a brother. Instead, he had gotten two sisters, and he loved them.

But it seemed now that he had no longer believed he would have a brother, suddenly he got one.

RHEVA'S LEGS ached by the time she returned to her and Weylind's room. In a satchel, she had a full pint of fresh goat's milk, several cleansed bottles, and one bottle prepared and warmed, though she would need to add her healing magic to it yet.

What would she find when she stepped inside?

Weylind had not been taking the whole getting-a-surprise-little-brother thing all that well. Understandable. But the scandal was not the babe's fault.

With a deep breath, Rheva eased the door open and tiptoed inside, treading carefully in case Farrendel had fallen asleep.

Weylind was pacing across the room, rocking Farrendel.

The baby was squirming and fussing, his cries building with each moment.

Weylind turned to her, releasing a breath. "Oh, good, you are back. I was wondering what we were going to do if you did not get back in time."

At least Weylind's voice held a note of fondness rather than the anger it had when she left.

She hurried to the countertop and took the items from her bag. She put the pint of goat's milk in the cold cupboard, lined up the clean bottles on the wooden countertop, then tested the warmth in the filled bottle. Still a good temperature. She added a swirl of her magic, judging what Farrendel's stomach would need to help digest the milk. She placed the nipple back on the bottle, then turned to Weylind.

Weylind sat on the bench again and held out a hand. "I can feed him."

Now that was surprising. Rheva handed over the bottle, then curled on the bench next to Weylind, leaning her head against his shoulder.

Weylind held the bottle for Farrendel, and the infant gulped the milk, little fingers grasping at the bottle while his eyes focused up at Weylind so very intently.

Rheva reached over and brushed the back of her fingers over the infant's soft cheek. "He chugs his bottles as if he is afraid he will not see food again."

Weylind took the bottle away as the baby coughed, spitting up some of the milk. "It has been a few years since I held Jalissa, but he seems smaller."

"Yes, he is underweight." Rheva dabbed at the baby's face with a cloth, cleaning up the spit-up.

If she were to guess, the infant had not been eating enough. Likely, his mother had been feeding him goat's milk nearly from birth to make it easier to hand him over to his dacha to raise.

It had made the transition easier, since Farrendel was already used to a bottle. But he had been struggling with spitting up most of his food thanks to his hurting tummy.

"His mother should be punished for neglecting her infant like this." Weylind's jaw worked as he gave the baby the bottle again. It seemed he had gone straight to overprotective older brother, now that he claimed Farrendel as his brother.

"I am sure she did the best she could." Rheva had seen the complicated mix of revulsion and pain when Filauria had been walking away. The woman had been torn by her decisions, and she had done the best she could for Farrendel by giving him to his father to raise. That was a mother's sacrifice, and Rheva would not judge her too harshly for it, even if Weylind and the rest of his family could not see past their own pain to see Filauria's.

They settled into silence for a moment, except for the baby's noises as he gulped the milk.

Weylind rested his head against hers. "You were right."

Rheva gave a slight laugh, tucking herself closer against Weylind. "I generally am."

"Yes." Weylind pressed a light kiss to the top of Rheva's hair.

The kiss sent a flutter through her. But as they

continued in silence, cuddling together, the warmth turned to an ache.

If only they could sit here like this, marveling over their own child. Instead, they were taking care of Weylind's little brother, their own arms empty.

Her throat tightened, and she blinked at the hot tears threatening the corners of her eyes.

Weylind must have sensed something through their elishina for he stilled, then murmured into her hair, "What is it?"

"It is not fair." Rheva hated the way her voice strained past the lump in her throat. "We have been trying for *seventy years* for a child, but your dacha ends up with a fourth child from a brief tryst. It just is not fair."

"I know." Weylind's sigh brushed against her hair. "We will have one of our own someday."

"What if we do not?" Rheva pushed off him so that she could meet his gaze. "Or what if we are like my parents and do not have a child until we are well into our six or seven hundreds?"

"Rheva..." He said her name with that warm helplessness that said he wished he could fix this, but he could not. He could not even promise they would have a child someday.

The idea surged through her, and she gestured from Farrendel to Weylind. "What if we raised him? What if we adopted him ourselves? We could give him a dacha and a macha and—"

But Weylind was already shaking his head. "No. Dacha would not agree to that. He has decided that he will raise Farrendel, and that is what he will do. He is very stubborn like that."

He was correct, of course. But for a moment, Rheva had let herself envision that Farrendel could be theirs.

That she could fill that empty ache in her arms and her heart.

"But we will help Dacha a great deal. He will not be able to raise Farrendel on his own while also running the kingdom." Weylind held Rheva's gaze, something of his own longing glimmering in his dark brown eyes. "I know that is not really what you want."

No, it was not.

But she had no choice but to bite back the ache and keep moving forward.

"No." Rheva rested her head on Weylind's shoulder again, drawing on his strength and warmth. "But you are correct. This little one will need us, even if it is as brother and sister. He is going to have a tough road ahead of him."

Starting with just keeping milk down.

WEYLIND STIRRED at the light rapping sound. He groaned and pushed himself more upright. His neck ached from sleeping upright, leaning against the wall while his shirt and hair were crusted with spit-up.

Rheva lay on the bench, her feet tucked under a blanket and her head on a pillow. She, too, appeared a bit worse for the wear after their long night.

Farrendel had been up every hour, and it seemed that most of the milk he drank simply came right back up all over Weylind and Rheva.

At least he was finally sleeping now, lying on his back in the little cradle Weylind had grown into the wall partway through the night when he and Rheva had finally gotten the infant to sleep for longer than a few minutes.

The light rapping came again, and Weylind hurried to push to his feet. He needed to answer the door before whoever was there woke Rheva. Or, worse, woke Farrendel.

Weylind tiptoed across the room and opened the door.

Dacha stood there, and he met Weylind's gaze tentatively, as if he was not sure how he would be received.

Weylind glanced over his shoulder, then he stepped onto the porch and softly closed the door behind him. "Farrendel is finally sleeping. I do not want to wake him."

Dacha's mouth quirked, but it still held too much weariness to be a true smile. "Thank you for last night."

"You are welcome." Weylind swallowed, his throat a bit thick as he tried to put his late-night muddled thoughts into words. "You were right, Dacha."

Dacha reached, as if to grip Weylind's shoulder, but halted short of the grime-stained fabric. He dropped his hand with a shake of his head. "You are right too, sason. I bear the blame for the mistakes I have made, but all of you will bear the cost." His gaze strayed past Weylind. "Especially Farrendel. I fear I have ruined his life before it has truly begun."

Weylind could not argue with that. Farrendel would be labeled as "tainted" because he was illegitimate, even if he had no say in how and when he was born. There would be those who would whisper that the king should have sent him away or that he was unworthy of even being alive.

"He is my brother. I will look after him." Weylind could not promise that Melantha and Jalissa would do the same. But, for his part, he had made the decision during the night. Farrendel was his brother, and that was that.

"Linshi." Dacha's attempt at a smile seemed more

genuine now, though it faded quickly. "I am calling a meeting of the King's Council later today."

Dacha did not ask if Weylind would come. He would not ask for Weylind's open support.

But Weylind met Dacha's gaze. "I will be there."

He was not sure if Melantha or Jalissa would come, but Weylind would. It would mean that he was openly supporting his dacha through this.

Perhaps if his dacha had been continuing the way he had been, then Weylind would have boycotted the meeting and not supported his dacha.

But Dacha was repentant, and he was willing to bear the consequences of what he had done. He was going to raise Farrendel and give him the love he deserved. Of course Weylind was going to stand by him in that, no matter how much it cost.

WEYLIND HALTED as he was leaving his and Rheva's rooms. What was that noise? Crying?

He turned toward the sound, then followed it along the royal branch to Melantha's rooms. He crept around the porch and found Melantha sitting on the floor, her knees drawn up to her chest, her arms around her knees, as she sobbed.

Weylind dropped down beside her. "What is wrong, isciena?"

It was a bad question. What was not wrong right now? Their macha was gone. Their dacha was currently embroiled in the scandal of having a child outside of marriage. None of them had slept well in a week, thanks to Farrendel's struggles to keep milk down and his howling wails every night. The court was actively snubbing the entire royal family. Several servants had resigned to find positions elsewhere. The servants that remained did not meet their gazes, as if unsure of how to conduct themselves during this scandal.

Melantha stiffened, then said on a wail, "Hatharal called it off."

Weylind bit back his immediate relief. As much as he had never liked Hatharal, Melantha would not appreciate him openly celebrating the dissolution of her betrothal. "Did he say why?"

"It is because of the scandal. He said…he said he did not want to align himself with such a flawed family." Melantha sniffed and sobbed her way through speaking.

Not too surprising. It was clear to everyone but Melantha that the only reason he was marrying her was that he craved the prestige and power of marrying into the royal family. If Weylind and Rheva never had children, Melantha and her children would be next in line.

But now marrying into the royal family held little prestige. Instead, it meant taking on the taint of the scandal, and Hatharal was far too self-absorbed to volunteer for that.

Weylind could not tell that to Melantha right now, as much as he was internally rejoicing. If there was one good thing in this whole scandal—besides gaining a brother—it was that it had saved Melantha from making a huge mistake in marrying Hatharal.

Weylind rested a hand on Melantha's shoulder. "Do you need me to punch him?"

He would gladly do it. After all, he had fantasized about doing just that many times over the years. The only thing that had stopped him had been the fact that such an action would cause a scandal and anger Melantha.

But now what was a little more scandal for the royal family at this point?

Melantha nodded. Paused. Then shook her head. "No."

Bother. Weylind had been looking forward to punching Hatharal finally.

Perhaps he would do it anyway, and give the noble that *stay away from my sister* speech that he had been rehearsing for years.

He let himself toy with the idea for a few more delicious seconds before he sighed and shoved it away.

As tempting as it was, he would have to let Hatharal walk away without any consequences. The last thing the royal family needed right now was a second scandal from Weylind picking a fight with the son of a powerful noble family. Weylind would have to stuff back his true thoughts, take the higher branch, and act like the calm and dignified heir to the throne.

RHEVA HURRIED along the branches of Ellonahshinel, Farrendel in her arms. After a week, it had become very clear that they needed to try to find a wet nurse for him. Rheva had been able to tailor her magic in the goat's milk so that he was not spitting up quite so much and his stomach was not quite as unsettled.

But a wet nurse would be better. Hopefully a mother's milk would settle in his stomach better than the goat's milk.

If Rheva could find one. So far, she had visited the rooms of three different servants who had recently had children, and so far all three had turned her down.

She bounced Farrendel lightly in her arms. If this

servant refused her, she would need to feed Farrendel another bottle soon.

Crossing the branch, she reached the small cluster of servants' quarters and knocked on the maid's door.

The elf female opened the door, a babe in her arms. Her features tightened as she spotted Rheva with Farrendel in her arms, even as she bobbed a bow. "Amirah."

"You likely already know why I am here." Rheva rocked Farrendel as he squirmed again, giving a whimper that would soon build into a cry if he was not fed soon. "The king's son needs a wet nurse."

The servant's mouth curled a bit as she reached for the door. "His illegitimate spawn, you mean."

"Please, just hear me out." Rheva stuck her foot out, preventing the door from closing. "He is just a babe. No matter the king's mistakes, this infant is an innocent. He did nothing wrong."

The woman hesitated, then sighed. "Fine. Give him here. I will feed him as long as my own child still has enough."

"Of course. I would not expect you to starve your own child." Rheva handed over Farrendel. "I have a meeting, but I will be back shortly."

The woman scowled, nodded, then used her foot to slam the door shut in Rheva's face.

Well, then. Rheva stood there for a moment, staring at the door. Why did she have such a churn in her stomach at leaving Farrendel here?

Farrendel would be fine. The servant had not resigned, so she must want the job. She would not mistreat the baby, despite her feelings about the king's actions.

Rheva left and returned to the queen's office. She and

Machasheni Leyleira shared the office at the moment, ever since they had taken over the duties that Queen Vianola had done before her death.

Rheva's meeting with the cook did not take long as they went over the weekly meal plans.

Once done, Rheva hurried back through Ellonahshinel until she reached the higher branches with the servants' quarters.

As soon as she knocked on the door, the servant opened it and all but shoved Farrendel back into Rheva's arms. "Take him. He keeps spitting up everything. I tried, but do not bring him to me again." The servant paused, then bobbed a quick bow as if remembering she was speaking to her future queen. "Amirah."

Rheva propped Farrendel against her shoulder, patting his back. "Linshi."

The servant shut the door in her face once again.

Rheva sighed, rubbing Farrendel's back as he started fussing again. She had tried, but it seemed finding a wet nurse was not going to work either. "It seems we will just have to keep doing what we were doing and try to get some milk into you."

The baby in her arms spit up all over her shoulder.

CHAPTER
SEVEN

90 YEARS BFH

Weylind stepped into his dacha's main rooms. "Dacha, I—"

The giggle from overhead was his only warning. Weylind turned just in time to spot Farrendel dropping from the ceiling, his limbs spread eagled, hair flying, as he cackled.

Weylind might have given a small scream. Certainly one that was dignified and appropriate for the situation of having his little brother drop from the ceiling onto his head.

Then Farrendel hit him, and the force of his small body knocked Weylind onto his butt on the floor. He had enough presence of mind to wrap an arm around Farrendel to keep him from tumbling as he braced himself.

"Sason." Dacha stepped into the room, the tone of his voice sharp enough that Weylind stiffened, almost expecting a rebuke directed at him.

But Farrendel disentangled himself from Weylind, then trudged to stand before Dacha.

Dacha crossed his arms. "What did I tell you about dropping from the ceiling on people?"

"To not to." Farrendel kicked at the floor.

"And why did you do it anyway?" Dacha raised an eyebrow.

"It is fun." Farrendel gave a slight shrug.

"It was less fun for Melantha, Weylind, the two clerks, and the maid you scared so far." Dacha knelt so that he was eye level with Farrendel. "You need to think about how your actions affect others. It is rude to fall onto people, even if you think it is funny. Understand?"

Farrendel nodded, blinking. "Sorry, Dacha."

"I am not the one to whom you need to apologize." Dacha gently turned Farrendel around.

Farrendel flicked a glance at Weylind, his silver-blue eyes big and wet. "Sorry I fell on your head."

"I accept your apology, shashon." Weylind smoothed his shirt, then pushed to his feet. His tailbone throbbed, but he was only bruised. He had also tweaked his wrist. Nothing that Rheva could not fix for him easily enough—once she stopped giggling.

"Sason." Dacha rested his hands on Farrendel's shoulders and turned him to face him again. "You disobeyed my instructions. You are grounded from climbing for two months."

Farrendel stuck his lower lip out in a pout. "Dacha…"

"Do I need to make it three months?"

"No." Farrendel scuffed at the floor with the toe of his boot. "I will not do it again."

"Good." Dacha patted Farrendel's back and stood.

"Weylind, sason. Is it time for the meeting with the generals already?"

They were going to go over the reports from the generals about guarding the border against troll attacks. Attacks that were increasing. Likely, either Dacha or Weylind would have to personally go to the border to aid the warriors there sooner or later.

Fighting at the border was the last thing Weylind wanted to do. Especially now.

Weylind shook his head. "I am early."

"Ah." Dacha crossed the room and reached for a stack of papers left on the table.

Behind him, Farrendel had gone from standing still to bouncing on his toes, unable to stand still for more than a few seconds, even in the wake of a reprimand. Several seconds more, and he was rocking back and forth.

Weylind smiled, taking in the sight of his brother trying so hard to be grown up and still when all he wanted to do was run and play.

Dacha turned, caught sight of Farrendel, and his mouth quirked. "You may still run and play, just stay on the ground."

Farrendel brightened, then raced off. "Catch me, Dacha!"

Dacha made a few feints in Farrendel's direction, and that was all it took to send Farrendel into peals of giggles as he ran in circles around the room.

"Was I this active as a child?" Weylind gestured to Farrendel. Was this the chaos that he and Rheva had to look forward to? After so many years of hoping, Rheva was due with their first child any day. Weylind would soon hold his own son or daughter in his arms.

"No." Dacha shook his head, a wry twist to his mouth.

"You and Melantha were still plenty active. But nothing like this."

Farrendel was racing about the room as if he was half-berserk from energy and giggles. He tripped, ran into one of the cushioned benches, bounced off, then went straight back to running and giggling with barely a break in stride.

"It is said that the more active elf children are, the more powerful their magic." Dacha's gaze followed Farrendel as he bounded around the room. "It is because they have so much magic inside them, but no outlet until they come into their magic."

Weylind nodded but did not say anything. It did not seem like his dacha was looking for a response.

"That certainly held true for all of you so far. You and Melantha were quite active, and you both have powerful magic. Jalissa was a sweet, easy child, and her magic reflects that." Dacha braced himself against his desk. "Your machasheni was telling me about the history books she has been reading. The stories claim that those who have the magic of the ancient kings are downright frenetic as children."

Frenetic would be a good word to describe Farrendel. He would—occasionally—sit still. But he seemed to need an inordinate amount of running around to wear him out.

"I thought the magic of the ancient kings died out with Dachasheni?" Weylind gestured vaguely, not sure what to think. Yes, Farrendel certainly had a great deal of energy. But it still seemed highly unlikely that Farrendel could have inherited the magic of the ancient kings when none of the rest of them had.

"That is what we all thought." Dacha shrugged, then turned back to Weylind. "Perhaps I am simply grasping at impossibilities. It is far more likely that he is simply gifted athletically, even beyond most elves."

Farrendel certainly seemed to be. While most elf children were more agile than human children, despite aging more slowly, Farrendel was especially athletic for his age.

"Time will tell." Weylind headed for the door. They would not know for sure until Farrendel came into his magic somewhere around his eightieth birthday.

WEYLIND all but lunged for the door at the knock, his grin so wide that his face hurt, yet he could not stop smiling. He whipped the door open, finding his dacha and Farrendel standing there. "Come in, come in."

Farrendel raced inside first and dashed to where Rheva sat, skidding to a halt and bouncing on his toes as he tried to get a peek at the bundle she held.

Rheva smiled and leaned over to show him the baby. "Farrendel, this is your nephew Ryfon."

Farrendel peered at Ryfon, his brows furrowing. "He is just a baby."

Weylind laughed and crossed the room, sitting on the floor next to where Farrendel stood. "Yes. What did you expect?"

"I wanted him to play with me, but he is just a baby. Babies are boring." Farrendel sat on the floor, then dramatically flopped onto his back. "No one ever plays with me."

"Is that so?" Weylind crossed his arms, grinning at his brother. "I play with you."

"You are so old." Farrendel flapped his hand at Weylind.

"Really?" Weylind gathered himself, then lunged for Farrendel.

His brother squealed and rolled out of the way before popping to his feet and bounding away.

Weylind pressed his hand to the floor and sent his magic through the room. A branch reached down from the ceiling, snagged Farrendel's ankle, and hoisted him from the floor, dangling him upside down. Farrendel shrieked, then burst into laughter.

Dacha crossed the room, dodged around Farrendel, and sat next to Rheva. "Congratulations, sena, sason."

"Meet your sasonsheni Ryfon." Rheva smiled as she held Ryfon out to Dacha.

Dacha took Ryfon, smiling down at the baby. Ryfon had the black hair that ran strongly in their family; the resemblance to Weylind, and thus Dacha and Machasheni Leyleira remained striking.

Weylind reached up and took one of Rheva's hands. Something inside him ached, missing Macha. She should have been here, smiling and congratulating them and crooning over her first grandson.

Instead the trolls had killed her, stealing her from her family and from all the moments she should have lived.

After a long moment, Dacha looked up from the baby he held, his eyes shimmering with some of the same mix of joy and sorrow that clogged Weylind's throat. "Your macha would have been very happy for you, sason."

Weylind nodded, his throat going tight. How was it possible to be so completely happy, and yet mourn the one who was missing?

Farrendel gave another laugh as he swung himself back and forth, still hanging upside down by his ankle.

Yes, Weylind missed his macha keenly today. Yet it was hard to want to go back, to change the past.

Because if Macha were here, then Farrendel would not be. And as much as Weylind would wish his macha back, he could not bring himself to wish that his brother had never been born. It was a strange dichotomy to sort through.

Perhaps that was why there was no point in wishing for things that were not. Instead, he would have to take life as it was, both with the grief and the joy and the bittersweetness when the two mixed.

WEYLIND PARRIED the warrior's sword thrust, then spun on his heel as he swiped his own sword upward. The warrior danced away, then darted in again.

Sweat trickled down Weylind's back, dampening his hair, as he twisted and parried and swung his sword. Here at the edge of Estyra, the trees grew farther apart, providing an open space for the gathered warriors to practice each day.

The war at the border was escalating, and more and more warriors were being called up and sent north. It was only a matter of time before Dacha or Weylind or both would have to go north and join the fight in person.

Someday soon, Weylind would face his first battle, and he needed to be ready.

The warrior twisted his sword, and the next thing Weylind knew, his sword flew from his hands, landing on the moss several feet away, the other warrior's blade at his throat.

Weylind sighed and held out his palms in surrender. He was getting better, but the warriors who had been training for hundreds of years still had far greater experience and training.

"Weylind!" Melantha's voice carried over the clang of swords and grunts of practicing warriors.

Weylind nodded to his opponent, then hurried to the side of the practice area.

Melantha stood there, holding Farrendel. He had his face pressed against her shoulder, and crusty brown-red splotches stained her dress and his shirt.

"What is wrong? What happened?" Weylind sheathed his sword.

"Some of the noble boys attacked Farrendel. A rock struck his cheek." Melantha's eyes flashed, her jaw tight. "I have healed the wound and sent the boys packing, but I need to talk to Dacha."

Weylind clenched his fists and nodded. "He was drilling with a squad of warriors deeper in the forest last I saw."

Whatever Dacha did, Weylind would back him up. If he wanted to toss entire noble families out of Estyra, Weylind would see that it was done. He would not stand by while his little brother was hurt.

"I WILL SEND reports by courier as often as I can." Dacha took the reins from the servant holding his horse, then swung into the saddle.

"I can handle things here." Weylind would do whatever it took to protect Farrendel. And if retreating to Lethorel to raise Farrendel away from the court was what Dacha needed to do, then Weylind would do what was necessary to make it work. Even if it meant that he had to take on the duties of the de facto king here in Estyra.

He could handle it. He had his own newborn son to

raise, but surely he could handle being a new father and a regent here in Estyra.

"Linshi, sason. I know the burden this decision places on you." Dacha met Weylind's gaze, his grip firm on the reins as his horse shifted, impatient to set out now that its rider was on its back.

"As I said. I can handle it." Weylind would keep telling that to Dacha—and to himself—until they all believed it.

Machasheni Leyleira was finishing up saying farewell to Farrendel, then she nudged Farrendel toward Weylind.

Weylind knelt and gripped Farrendel's shoulders. "Have a good trip, shashon."

"I do not want to go." Farrendel blinked, his silver-blue eyes spilling over with more tears.

"You like Lethorel." Weylind was not sure how to handle the tears.

"But you are not coming. And Melantha is not either. Or Machasheni." Farrendel swiped at his nose.

"We will visit soon. You will have Dacha and Jalissa with you until then." Weylind picked Farrendel up, then handed him up to Dacha.

Dacha settled Farrendel on the saddle in front of him, an arm around him to steady him.

Farrendel sniffed, a few more tears running over the fresh, pink scar on his cheek.

As they moved out, Weylind lifted a hand in farewell, a lump forming in his throat as he watched Dacha, Farrendel, and Jalissa ride away.

CHAPTER
EIGHT

70 YEARS BFH

Rheva cradled her three-month-old daughter in her arms and tried to choke back her tears. Weylind stepped into the room, a pack slung over his back, his sword buckled at his waist. His fighting leathers had already been loaded onto the pack horses.

Weylind knelt and gripped Ryfon's shoulders, talking to him quietly for several minutes. Ryfon nodded through tears.

After a moment, Weylind stood and faced her. Rheva gripped his shoulder. "Stay safe. Come back to me. To our family."

Weylind brushed his fingers along her cheek, then gently cradled the back of her head and kissed her.

She leaned into him, careful not to squash Brina between them. The kiss tasted of tears, and Rheva found herself blinking when Weylind drew back.

He rested his forehead against hers. "I wish I could promise I would come home to you. I wish…"

Rheva squeezed her eyes shut, the hot burn of a tear scalding as it trickled down her cheek and onto her jaw. "I wish you did not have to go either. I wish there was no war."

It was so unfair that he had to leave only a few short months after their daughter had been born. They were starting their family. They were supposed to enjoy life as parents.

Instead, the war was escalating. Tarenhiel's full army was mustering. Including the king and his heir.

Weylind pressed one last, light kiss to Brina's forehead, smoothing back her dark brown fluff of hair.

In their elishina, Rheva's heart ached with the echo of his ache at having to leave them. His fear that he would never come home. That he would not be there to raise his son and daughter.

But the sensations in the elishina were a mere distant flutter. Not strong in the way elishinas were described in stories.

If Weylind were mortally wounded, would Rheva be strong enough—was their elishina strong enough—that she could keep him alive? Especially with the distance between them?

Weylind's father had failed to keep Queen Vianola alive, and from what Rheva had gathered, their elishina had been stronger than hers and Weylind's.

What chance would Rheva have of saving Weylind if it came to that? What choice would she make, in that situation? Try to save Weylind and risk dying with him? Or let him go so that she could be there to raise their children?

Rheva cradled Brina to her and blinked back tears. She was not sure if she was strong enough for this.

Weylind cradled her face and kissed her one last time. Then he picked up his pack and was gone.

WEYLIND ADJUSTED his sword at his waist, trying to ignore the pounding of his heart, the clammy feel of his palms. He reached deep into his chest, searching for that faint sense of Rheva, and clung to the hope and peace she gave him.

He was about to face his first battle.

In front of him, the jagged scar of twisting, ragged gorge cut through the land, dividing Tarenhiel from Kostaria. The Gulmorth River raged at the bottom, frothing white.

In those piles of boulders and stands of spruce trees at the far side, the troll army was camped, if they had not moved in the time since the scouts had spotted them.

Weylind and the rest of the elven army guarding this stretch of the border had climbed through the upper branches of the trees to avoid detection.

Had it been enough? Or would the trolls be alert, ready to spring an ambush of their own?

Weylind swallowed and tensed, waiting for the signal.

A flood of green, forest magic flowed through the trees and down into the Gorge.

The signal.

Weylind added his own magic to the tide, drawing deep inside himself and unleashing his potent magic in a way he had never done before.

The entire forest around them bent, the trees laying themselves over the Gorge.

Silently, the warriors around him raced forward, their balance perfect on the shivering trees.

Weylind joined them, drawing his sword while still shoving wave after wave of his magic before him. The trees on the far side of the Gorge shuddered while roots whispered over the ground, seeking targets.

At the far side of the Gorge, Weylind jumped lightly to the ground, surrounded by warriors.

With a howling yell, troll warriors sprang out from behind the boulders. Their armor gleamed as the stones beneath Weylind's feet surged, grasping at his boots.

Weylind coated the ground with his own magic, trying to shove the raw stone and ice magic away from himself and the warriors around him. Other elf warriors added their magic to his, and the magic twisted and exploded against each other.

Then a troll warrior was before him, and Weylind was swinging his sword as he had been trained.

Blood flowed hot and metallic. Running down Weylind's sword. Spattering his clothes. Flowing onto the ground to pool in the hollows of the rocks.

Warriors—both elf and troll—filled the space around him in a whirling melee of swords and axes. It was all Weylind could do to stay on his feet and keep his sword in his hands, his magic bursting around him.

Then the elven warriors were surging forward, pushing the trolls back. The spruce trees around them lashed out, striking the trolls.

And then Weylind found himself staggering back over the Gorge in company with the victorious elven warriors. He fell to his knees on the mossy, Tarenhieli forest floor, fighting not to hurl his breakfast onto the ground.

He had survived. But he had fought, and he had killed. With the blood on his hands and on his soul, he would never be the same again.

50 Years BFH

"Push them back! Hold the forest!" Weylind stabbed a troll in the chest, ducking the troll's ax as he did so. Around him, his squad of warriors held their ground, fighting back the wave of trolls coming over the stone bridges they had formed over the Gulmorth Gorge.

Those bridges needed to come down.

Weylind pressed a hand to a nearby tree, pushing his magic into the forest. Roots burst from the ground around him, yanking trolls off their feet before curling around their throats. The trolls hacked at the roots with daggers or sliced through them with raw stone or ice magic.

But Weylind kept pouring his magic into the ground until roots as thick as his arms burst from the sides of the Gorge and wrapped around the bridges, squeezing the stone until cracks began to appear.

A new wave of trolls rushed Weylind and his squad of warriors, and for a moment he had to break his focus on his magic to whirl into the warriors, his sword swinging, his steps light on the ground seething with dueling magic.

"Rally to the prince!" The shout came from somewhere behind him, but he only dimly noted it as he wielded both sword and magic, scything into the trolls attacking him.

More elf warriors appeared around him, pushing the trolls back enough that Weylind could pause and press a hand to a tree once again.

Weylind dug deep for his magic, unleashing the power into the trees, the roots, the entire forest around them.

The roots curled more thickly around the bridges.

Cracking. Breaking. A few trolls tried to fight back with their magic, but Weylind gritted his teeth and fought back, the depth of power to his magic resisting any attempt to stop him.

One bridge snapped, falling into the Gorge with a great grinding of stone and screams of those trolls who had been racing across it.

Weylind swung his sword at an oncoming troll, even as he held the magic. Two more bridges cracked and plunged into the depths, disappearing into the tumultuous waters below.

More blood spilled. A sword whispered past his ribs, slicing a line through his leathers into his skin.

The last bridge fell, even as the few remaining trolls on the southern side of the gorge gasped their last breaths.

"Amiriatir!" The cheer rang through the forest, though Weylind was too weary to do more than nod in acknowledgement of the title he had earned in the decades of fighting at the border.

Warrior prince. His kingdom's champion. Where he fought, the elf warriors rallied and won battle after battle.

Soon, his tour here at the border would be over. For now, anyway. He would be able to go home. Spend time with Rheva, Ryfon, and Brina while his dacha took his turn leading the warriors in the seemingly never-ending fight against the trolls.

WEYLIND RODE through the streets of the small town of Arorien, his back, legs, and rear end aching from the long hours on horseback. Around him, his small contingent of guards also slumped slightly in their saddles from the ride they had done.

Perhaps Weylind had pushed too hard to make the ride from the border to Arorien in as few days as possible. But all he could think about was returning to Rheva, holding her in his arms, seeing his children again and letting the warmth of their happy smiles banish the taint of blood and death from his heart, at least for a few moments.

As he halted his horse in front of Arorien's one inn, a shriek pierced the air, and he flinched, his hand flying to his sword.

"Dacha!" Ryfon burst from an upper story window, then clambered down the tree before he jumped lightly to the ground.

Weylind released a breath and his grip on his sword, telling his heart to stop pounding so hard. He was not at the border. He was in a small town deep inside Tarenhiel. There was no reason to be jumpy, looking for enemies in every shadow.

He swung down from his horse, landing on the ground just in time to grip Ryfon's shoulders for a tight hug. "Sason. You have grown."

Ryfon stood nearly to his elbow now, his black hair long down his back and his dark eyes bright as he grinned up at Weylind. "I have been nice to Brina, just like you told me to."

"Good." Weylind straightened as Rheva hurried from the inn, Brina trotting at her side. Brina's face split with a grin as she raced ahead, her brown hair flying.

Weylind stepped forward and gripped her shoulders in a hug, then he wrapped an arm around Rheva's waist and pulled her in close. As soon as they were alone, he would kiss her as he had longed to do. But, for now, he simply leaned his forehead against hers and soaked in her presence.

He was home. He had survived another tour at the border. He was more weary. More burdened. But alive. And home.

WEYLIND RODE around the lake before Lethorel, the tension in his shoulders easing at the sight of the peaceful willow tree trailing leaves in the still waters of the sparkling lake.

Behind him, Rheva, Ryfon, and Brina rode, surrounded by guards.

Here, he would be able to recover from the fighting and remember what it was to be a husband and a father rather than Tarenhiel's warrior prince.

"Weylind!"

His brother's voice rang from somewhere above him as Weylind halted his horse beneath Lethorel. He peered upward and found Farrendel sprawled on a branch twenty feet in the air, a few papers in his hand.

As Weylind watched, Farrendel rolled to a crouch, then hopped down from the branch, landing lightly as if twenty feet was nothing at all. When he straightened, Farrendel was grinning, his silver-blond hair settling around him. "You made it back."

"Yes." Weylind swung down from his horse and clasped his brother's shoulder. "What do you have there?"

Farrendel held up the papers, though he whipped them in front of Weylind too fast for him to actually read anything. "Dacha let me look over the reports on the new inventions our scouts observed in the human kingdoms.

Dacha is especially interested in something called a train. It moves on iron rails and can go really fast over long distances. Our people are already working to create a train for us. Can you imagine how much faster you could travel between Estyra and Lethorel? You could visit so much more."

"I have seen the reports about trains. They do seem quite fascinating." Weylind reached for his pack as a servant hurried forward to take his horse.

Dacha was looking into trains for their military uses more than for pleasure trips between Estyra and Lethorel. A train could transport their army to the border much more quickly and efficiently. That added mobility could turn the tide in this war.

Dacha strode down the last step of Lethorel, something in his gaze both welcoming and somber when he met Weylind's eyes.

Weylind nodded, that gesture communicating both that he was all right and that he would report to Dacha once they had a moment alone.

Dacha would remain here for two more weeks, enjoying their annual summer holiday at Lethorel. Then he would head north for the border and months of war.

Weylind would have to return to Estyra. But Farrendel would remain here with Machasheni Leyleira, still hidden away from the court.

Except for these two weeks at Lethorel, their family was always scattered. Always broken between Estyra, Lethorel, and the ongoing war at the border.

Perhaps it was just as well that Macha was not here to see what their family had become. She would mourn the war her death had caused and the brokenness it had brought to their family.

Weylind forced himself to smile as he helped Ryfon

and Brina down from their horses. Farrendel almost immediately claimed Ryfon, dragging him off amid chatter about trains and human inventions that had Ryfon's eyes widening as if scared he was going to get buried under his uncle's incessant chatter.

With another deep breath, Weylind forced his tight muscles to relax, trying to let go of the months of tension and alertness that had characterized every moment of life at the border.

He was home. He was safe. It was time to set aside the hard, worn part of himself and try to be present for his family.

CHAPTER
NINE

20 YEARS BFH

Weylind dismounted in front of Lethorel, only a small squad of guards coming to a halt around him.

At least the new train that ran the east-west length of Tarenhiel—and happened to have a stop at Arorien—cut the trip from Estyra to a day and a morning instead of a full week of travel.

Dacha hurried down the steps of Lethorel and clasped Weylind's shoulders. "I appreciate you coming so soon after arriving back from the border."

"Of course. Is something wrong?" Weylind glanced around. He did not see Farrendel. Odd. Usually Farrendel hurried to greet any visitors to Lethorel, especially family.

Dacha hesitated, flicking a glance at the trees beyond Lethorel. "Not exactly. But it is something I wished to discuss in person rather than through messages or couriers."

Weylind nodded. Was it the war? Weylind's recent tour at the border? Perhaps the rumors that Dacha was planning to return to Estyra permanently were true. That would certainly be something that Dacha would want to discuss, considering what it would mean for all of them to have Farrendel in Estyra—and in the eye of the court—once again.

Dacha opened his mouth, but a shout interrupted before he spoke.

"Dacha!" Farrendel's yell held a high-pitched, frantic note.

With a muttered word under his breath, Dacha took off, running past Lethorel deeper into the forest.

Weylind sprinted after him, following him past the practice archery range into a denser section of the forest. As they rounded a large oak tree, a blue light filled Weylind's vision.

Farrendel stood there, bolts of blue magic pouring from his fingers and sizzling over the ground.

Weylind stumbled to a halt, his breath catching in his throat. Even as he stood there, frozen, more bolts crawled up Farrendel's arms. His clothing smoked while a nearby sapling disintegrated.

Dacha approached Farrendel slowly, green magic spreading out from his fingers to slowly engulf the forest around Farrendel. "Deep breaths, sason. You can control it."

"It is too much!" Farrendel hunched, more magic crackling around him. "Dacha!"

"Do not panic, sason. Panicking makes it worse." Dacha's voice remained soothing as he crept forward. His black hair rose a bit with the crackle of magic in the air, even as his own magic formed a green shield around Farrendel.

Farrendel's magic sparked against Dacha's shield, and Dacha's jaw flexed as he drew on more of his magic.

"Dacha!" Farrendel curled over his hands, as if physically trying to hold in his magic with his body.

Magic exploded from him. A bolt of it slashed through Dacha's shield, and Dacha gasped, shaking his hand as he stumbled back.

Weylind shook off his paralysis and added his own magic to Dacha's shield.

"Breathe. In and out." Dacha took another step closer, pushing his magic shield tighter around Farrendel's exploding magic. "You can control it."

Farrendel shook, nearly disappearing among the crackling bolts just barely contained by their combined shield.

Then something exploded, and Weylind was thrown backwards. He tumbled to the forest floor, landing hard up against a tree.

For a moment he lay there, struggling to gasp in a breath. He had never felt such power, not even with armies of trolls and elves fighting at the border, their magic clashing and exploding all around him.

Then Weylind pushed himself onto an elbow.

Dacha was sitting up a few yards away, rolling to his feet in a way that said he was sore, but not injured.

Farrendel huddled on the forest floor, his knees drawn up to his chest, his face buried in his arms. But he was no longer surrounded by that crackling, blue lightning.

Dacha crept toward Farrendel, then reached a hand toward him. "Sason."

Farrendel lunged away, scrambling to his feet. "No. Do not touch me. I do not want to hurt you."

"Sason…" Dacha reached again, but Farrendel darted away from him.

With one stricken look from Dacha to Weylind, Farrendel spun on his heel and raced away, disappearing deeper into the forest.

Dacha took a step in that direction, then sighed and halted, turning to Weylind.

Weylind sat upright, then pushed to his feet. "I assume that is what you wanted to discuss."

"Yes." Dacha met his gaze. "Farrendel has the magic of the ancient kings."

That much was obvious. But Weylind still could not wrap his mind around the power he had just seen and felt.

Such a thing seemed impossible. The magic of the ancient kings was said to have died out with Dachasheni Ellarin. Nor had Dachasheni wielded magic with the strength that Farrendel had just demonstrated.

The court would have to accept Farrendel now. Or at least tolerate him. Those with the magic of the ancient kings were revered. They were relics of a greater age, a time when elves ruled an empire and wielded magic the likes of which was rarely seen anymore.

A chill washed through Weylind. They would accept him. But they would also expect much from him. Those with the magic of the ancient kings always became great warriors. Farrendel would be turned into a weapon in a quest to end this war.

He was so young. He was just barely coming into his magic. He should not be forced into the fight for decades, if not centuries yet.

Dacha still stood there, a hand pressed to a burned section of his sleeve, his shoulders slumped. "With the war still raging, I am needed in Estyra when I am not fighting at the border. Yet while Farrendel has gained some measure of control, too often his magic explodes like you just saw. I am not sure Estyra is the best place for him until he gains more control over his power."

Weylind was not sure what to tell Dacha. He desperately needed his dacha at Estyra. There were only so many decisions Weylind could make on his own as the heir without the full authority of the crown.

But Dacha was right to be concerned. With power like that, Farrendel could destroy half of Ellonahshinel if he lost control.

Weylind joined his father standing in the center of the burned patch of ground. "Maybe having more people around to help contain his magic when it does explode out of control would be the best thing."

Dacha nodded, weary lines etching around his eyes. "A valid concern. I do not know how much longer I will be able to contain the explosions by myself. And training him..."

Who would train Farrendel? Normally, elves trained with their closest relative with the same magic.

But there was no one else with Farrendel's magic. At least, no one who had come forward and demonstrated such magic, as they surely would have, considering the war that Tarenhiel had been fighting for over seventy years.

They would all just have to do their best when it came to training Farrendel, especially Dacha.

What would it mean for the war? For the kingdom? How could Dacha train Farrendel and fight the war at the border at the same time?

Worries for another day. For now, Farrendel was out there, scared of his own magic.

Weylind clasped Dacha's shoulder, then stepped past him in the direction Farrendel had gone. "I will talk to him. I think he would rather listen to a brother than a father right now."

Dacha nodded. "Perhaps."

Weylind strode deeper into the forest. He let a little of his magic trail from him, flowing through the trees, grasses, moss, and all growing green things as it sought the disturbance to the forest.

There. Weylind followed the sense until he found Farrendel huddled on a branch thirty feet up in a tree.

Weylind climbed the tree, then settled next to Farrendel.

Farrendel cringed away from him. "Go away. I do not want to hurt you."

"You will not." Weylind placed a hand on the branch, letting a little of his magic flow into the tree so that it glowed and gave a slight shiver. "I remember when I came into my magic. It seemed like every time I tried to do anything my magic just exploded from me."

"Your magic is normal. It is not...this." Farrendel clenched his fists, curling over his hands.

"No. I cannot understand how scary your power is." Weylind trailed a leaf through his fingers. "But I had my own fair share of magical explosions. One time, I woke up to find my entire room was one giant network of roots. I was stuck in my bed until Dacha helped me ungrow everything."

Farrendel blinked up at him, still hunched in a ball where the branch met the tree trunk.

"My point is that coming into your magic is scary for everyone. A few explosions are normal."

"There is nothing normal about my magic." Farrendel flexed his fingers. When a hint of blue sparked at his fingertips, he squeezed his hands into fists, snuffing out the magic.

Weylind was not sure what to tell his brother. There was nothing normal about the magic of the ancient kings.

But that magic would make Farrendel the greatest of them all, once he gained control. He had the magic of which legends were told.

Yet legends rarely resulted in happy lives for those who had to live them. Weylind's heart ached at the thought of what his little brother would face in the future. War. The expectation of becoming a warrior like in the stories of old.

"It will get better, shashon." Weylind rested a hand on Farrendel's shoulder, not pulling away as Farrendel flinched. "You will gain more control over your magic, and then it will not be as frightening. Dacha will teach you how to use it, as he taught Jalissa and me to use our magic."

Farrendel shook his head, as if he did not believe Weylind.

Perhaps Weylind did not entirely believe himself either.

Weylind squeezed Farrendel's shoulder, then jumped down from the branch, landing lightly on the forest floor. "Come. I have had a long ride and would like to eat luncheon."

After another moment's hesitation, Farrendel hopped from the branch, though his shoulders still remained hunched as if he was trying to hide. From whom, Weylind did not know. Perhaps from himself.

As they strolled through the forest, Farrendel remained tense, his fingers twitching, an extra bounce to his step as if he still had far too much energy bottled up inside him.

As they stepped into the cleared space beneath Lethorel's broad branches, Dacha strode toward them, two hardwood sticks in his hands. Without a word, he held them out to Farrendel.

Farrendel snatched them, then sprinted a few steps away before he used a tree to launch himself into a flip, gripping the sticks as if they were swords. He spun into a series of swings and thrusts, as if going through a practice routine with swords.

Weylind raised an eyebrow and glanced at Dacha. Farrendel was young to start training in the ways of a warrior, even if he was only wielding sticks instead of swords.

Dacha gave a slight shrug. "The structure of practice seems to help."

As they watched, Farrendel whirled through another set of complicated flips and swings with the sticks, wielding each independently in a way even many seasoned warriors among the elves could not.

Farrendel had been born to be a warrior. He had the agility, the skills, the hand-eye coordination needed.

And the magic of the ancient kings. It seemed so impossible. Improbable that Farrendel, out of all of them, would inherit that legendary power.

This changed everything, and Weylind was not sure any of them could foresee just how much it might shake the very foundations of Tarenhiel.

CHAPTER

TEN

Weylind leaned against the wall of the king's study, facing Dacha, who was pacing behind his desk. Weylind could not help the slight bite to his words. "He is far too young for war."

"Do you not think I know that?" Dacha whirled toward him, dark eyes flaring. "If you have a better idea, speak up, sason."

Weylind opened his mouth but paused. What else could Dacha do? What could any of them do? They were between a rock and a hard place. One choice would risk Farrendel. The other would risk all of Estyra. One life or many.

"Exactly." Dacha crossed his arms and met Weylind's gaze. "We cannot leave him here when we leave for the war. There is no one else who can contain his magic when he loses control."

Weylind gritted his teeth, refusing to nod to acknowledge the point. Truthfully, he and Dacha combined could barely hold back Farrendel's magic when it broke loose. Even then, they could only contain it because Farrendel had achieved some measure of control over it. If he ever fully lost control…well, Weylind was not sure what they would do. Farrendel could level all of Estyra.

But taking him to war did not seem like the right choice either.

"I do not want to take Farrendel to the front. He is too young. But what else am I supposed to do?" Dacha ran a hand through his hair, slightly tousling the long black strands. "I cannot leave him here. But the war is escalating. You and I cannot stay. We are needed at the front if we are to win this war."

Another valid point. This war had been ongoing for decades. At first, it had just been occasional, large raids across the border. But each year, Tarenhiel and Kostaria mustered more warriors at the border. The battles grew bigger.

Now huge armies were assembled at the border. Instead of occasional skirmishes, the battles were nearly constant. The war had taken a deadlier turn that could only end with victory or defeat. The warriors needed both their king and prince to not only lead them, but also fight with the strength of their magic. They could no longer simply have either Dacha or Weylind there while the other remained in Estyra.

This was full-scale war. There would be no going back until it reached its final, deadly climax, one way or the other.

Weylind sighed and finally nodded. "I do not like it, but I understand."

"I do not like it either." Dacha grimaced. "We will do our best to keep Farrendel away from the fighting. He can remain at the command base while you and I fight with the warriors."

It was the best option they had. Still was not great. If

Farrendel lost control while Dacha and Weylind were both occupied fighting, he could accidentally wipe out a large chunk of their own army. But what else could they do? At least at the front, Farrendel had the chance to direct his power toward the border in the event he could not control it.

Farrendel stepped into the study, glancing between Dacha and Weylind. "You wanted to speak with me, Dacha?"

"Yes." Dacha strode around his desk, then rested his hands on Farrendel's shoulders.

At eighty-five years old, Farrendel stood only slightly shorter than Dacha or Weylind in what was likely his full height. His shoulders remained slim, his limbs gangly, still very much a youth.

Dacha held Farrendel's gaze. "I have decided that when Weylind and I leave for the border in a week, you will be going with us."

"Yes!" Farrendel grinned, his whole face lighting as if he had just been given the best, most exciting news.

And that was the worst part of this. Farrendel had been begging to go for years. He was *excited* to join the warriors at the border.

He was too young to know better. So innocent. All he saw was the glory, the adventure. Not the taint. The death. The savagery. The blood that coated hands and soul.

Weylind would be there to watch as this innocent light was snuffed from his brother's eyes, replaced with the same hard edge that Dacha had. That Weylind had.

"Come, sason. Let us pick out your weapons." Dacha strode to the door, and Farrendel trotted after him with an eager step and even more eager grin.

Weylind trailed after them. What else could he do but

stick close and hope Dacha's plan to keep Farrendel away from the brunt of the fighting worked?

Dacha led the way down the branch until they reached Ellonahshinel's trunk. At a section that was marked with oak leaf ornamentation grown into the bark, Dacha rested his hand on a particular leaf, his fingers glowing with magic.

Some deeper, older magic in the tree answered, flooding into the surrounding wood. It recognized Dacha and his magic, for this door would only open for the king or his heir.

With a creaking of wood, the door parted from the trunk and swung open.

Dacha led the way inside, and Farrendel hurried at his heels, his eyes wide. Despite what was coming, Weylind could not help the slight smile as he stepped inside as well.

A room had been hollowed out of the trunk. Grown that way, rather than rotted out, so it did not harm the great tree.

The walls of the room were covered with weapons, from shining axes to slim swords. Racks at the base of the walls held gleaming daggers and smaller knives.

Dacha swept out an arm, gesturing at the room. "This is the armory of the kings. These are the weapons wielded by many of the great kings and warriors of old."

Farrendel's jaw hung open as he turned in a circle, taking in the gleaming array of weapons.

Weylind turned in a slow circle, taking in the room once again. He had come here a few times over the years, and it never failed to strike him with a sense of awe and solemn duty.

Dacha strode to one wall and took down a matched pair of swords in their sheaths. "I was thinking these would be a good fit for you. They are similar in size to the sticks you have been using to practice."

Farrendel reached out, his eyes still wide, his touch almost reverent on the swords in their sheaths.

Dacha turned and pulled out a leather sword harness. He settled it over Farrendel's thin shoulders, then buckled it in place as Farrendel held still for him. Once it was set, Dacha took the swords and buckled them in place across Farrendel's back.

"We might need to see the leatherworker's shop to have a few more holes punched into the leather." Dacha checked the fit of the harness, and it slopped several inches too loose around Farrendel's slim frame. The harness had been designed for an adult warrior, not a boy still growing into his full frame.

The sight ached deep inside Weylind's chest. Farrendel would be asked to grow into the role of a warrior far too soon.

While Weylind had enjoyed a childhood of peace and safety, all Farrendel had ever known was war.

18 Years *BFH*

"The trolls have moved up units here, here, and here." The general pointed to the places on the map spread out on the table.

Weylind studied the lines of the Gulmorth Gorge, taking in the new positions of the troll encampments, marked with various pebbles. On their side of the Gulmorth, their own troop placements had been marked with wood figurines.

The trolls appeared to be gearing up for a large push over the border near Argar Point. The Gulmorth was particularly narrow there, making an attack across it easier than elsewhere along the Gorge.

They already had a solid presence across from Argar Point for that reason.

Was this attack real? Or was it a feint to distract from another attack in a different spot along the border?

Dacha leaned over the map and discussed the possibilities with the gathered generals and commanders.

Weylind listened, occasionally adding his own thoughts, but mostly staying silent. He did not have the experience of the generals, and his word did not hold the weight of Dacha's. Instead, his job was to learn all he could.

Finally, the meeting broke up with plans to shift a few squads of warriors to combat any attacks across the Point and any of the likely spots if that attack was a feint.

As Weylind stepped from the command shelter, he paused, taking in the bustle of the encampment. Squads of warriors marched across the space while others lounged beneath their treetop shelters, cleaning swords or repairing their fighting leathers.

In the cleared space to one side, the flash and clang of swords rose as warriors fought practice bouts.

At the center of the practice field, Farrendel whirled, his two swords a blur, as he fought five elf warriors. He ducked under a warrior's swing, then sidestepped before parrying a strike.

He must have not been watching the fifth warrior closely enough, for the warrior managed to get behind him and place the flat of his sword against Farrendel's neck.

Farrendel froze, then lowered his swords.

The other warriors withdrew, lowering their swords. The warrior who had gotten behind Farrendel sheathed his sword and said something that had Farrendel grinning.

Weylind took in the sight, not sure if he wanted to smile or grimace.

Strangely enough, Farrendel had taken to army life like a bird to flight. After the isolation of Lethorel and the disdain of the court at Estyra, Farrendel flourished in the acceptance and camaraderie of the warriors. Most did not scorn him for his birth, and his magic and eagerness to learn seemed to endear him to the squads stationed here at the command base. The warriors had all but adopted Farrendel as one of their own. A little brother and pet all in one.

More than that, Farrendel could become one of the warriors in a way Weylind could not. If he were to walk over to that knot of warriors, they would stiffen and bow, always aware that he was their prince and heir.

While Farrendel was a prince, he was illegitimate and far enough down the line of succession that he was unlikely to ever inherit the throne. If anything, Farrendel's illegitimate birth made the common elves embrace him as one of their own. His mother was common, after all.

Dacha halted next to Weylind, his gaze also locked on Farrendel. "He has the makings of a great warrior."

"Yes." Weylind sighed and glanced at Dacha. "I am not sure that is a good thing."

"If he had the time to grow to adulthood and the chance to choose that life for himself, then it would be. Tarenhiel needs a great warrior of old to lead us to peace once again." Dacha heaved a long exhale, giving a slight shake of his head. "But I fear we do not have the time, and Farrendel will be asked to go to war far too young, no matter how much you or I fight it."

Right now, Farrendel would likely jump at the chance to fight alongside them. He begged to be allowed to fight with all the eagerness of a youth.

"Do you think the humans will attack?" Weylind rested a hand on the hilt of his sword, his muscles tensing.

"Yes. Humans are often greedy when it comes to land and power. We have been fortunate that it took them this long to turn their ambitions north toward Tarenhiel." Dacha flexed his fingers on his own sword's hilt. "I fear we will be fighting along two borders before too much longer."

Weylind felt the weight of those words deep in his bones. The elves were surviving their war with the trolls, but if they had to fight on two borders? Who would overrun them first, the humans to the south or the trolls to the north?

Right now, it was the human kingdom of Escarland that was eyeing the resources of Tarenhiel's forests. Tarenhiel could likely hold them off. But if they made an alliance with Mongalia along the sea coast, then they would become formidable. Perhaps too formidable to fight off.

If Tarenhiel were to survive, they would need a great warrior of old.

Even if that warrior was still an adolescent not yet in full control of his magic.

17 Years BFH

Rheva slowly lowered the letter, a silence descending on the room for a long moment.

Ryfon and Brina sat on either side of her as she read

Weylind's latest letter out loud to them.

At least, she read the letter meant for all of them. The other part of the letter—the one meant only for her—remained in her bedchamber, resting in the drawer with all the others from Weylind over the years of war.

It would only get worse, now that the humans of Escarland had declared war. How was Tarenhiel going to survive fighting on two fronts?

She wanted to hug her children close as her heart ached, her throat closed with a squeezing panic. Neither of her children had even come into their magic yet. They were so young. So innocent.

But if Tarenhiel was overrun by either the trolls or the humans, the enemies would not care.

Where would she go? How could she keep her children safe if the worst happened?

"I miss Dacha." Brina swiped at her face and leaned her head against Rheva's shoulder.

Ryfon nodded, but he did not lean into Rheva. He was growing up so fast. He was only a handful of years away from coming into his magic. Would Weylind even be there to witness that momentous occasion in their son's life? If Ryfon inherited Weylind's magic, would Ryfon's training be left to Machasheni Leyleira while Weylind continued to fight at one front or the other?

Rheva dropped the letter onto her lap and wrapped an arm around Brina's shoulders. "So do I."

So very much. Even more than she could ever admit to her children.

While she could faintly feel Weylind through the elishina, he was so very distant, even there. During his brief visits home, he was all hard warrior, never able to relax enough to be the elf she married.

It was not his fault. Of course the war would harden

him. And Rheva did not want to burden him by admitting how much the distance between them hurt.

All Rheva could do was carry on and try to be both father and mother to her children as best she could.

CHAPTER
ELEVEN

15 YEARS BFH

Weylind stared out the windows of the train as it glided through the forests of Tarenhiel, headed for the southern border with Escarland. He had hated leaving Dacha and Farrendel behind at the northern border, but someone needed to check in with the war against Escarland.

The train shuddered its way to a stop—the designers were still refining the train's design—and Weylind gathered his bag and stood.

He disembarked from the train and found himself in a bustling army camp that did not look all that different from the one he had left in the north.

A warrior hurried up to him, bobbing a hasty bow. "Weylind Amir. It is good that you have arrived. The commander would like to speak with you right away."

Weylind nodded, then followed the warrior through

the camp. Now that he was looking, he sensed the extra tension around the camp. What was going on?

Before Weylind had hopped on the train south, he and Dacha had received word that the general here was planning a raid on what the scouts believed was the humans' command base. Had the raid gone poorly?

This was why Weylind was here, after all. While the war against the trolls was the priority—drawing most of Tarenhiel's resources and warriors—the war against the humans could not be entirely ignored.

The warrior led the way up a ladder, then they stepped onto a porch surrounding the command shelter grown into a tree.

When Weylind stepped inside the shelter, the general glanced up, then bowed. "Elontiri, amir. I am glad you have arrived so soon. We have much to discuss."

Weylind approached the table and studied the map laid out there. "Was the raid on the humans' encampment executed as planned?"

"It was. And it was not." The general heaved a long exhale. "We raided the humans' command as planned, and it was more successful than we anticipated. We killed several of their generals." The general paused, then straightened and faced Weylind. "The Escarlish king happened to be visiting at the time of the raid, and he was killed in the confusion."

Weylind stilled, trying to wrap his mind around that. This could be really good...or really bad. Either the humans would escalate the war, wanting revenge for their dead king, or they would seek peace, ready to retreat and lick their wounds.

Peace would be preferable. Tarenhiel was slowly weakening under the strain of two wars. If they could go back to fighting only one war at a time, that might just save their kingdom.

"What has been the humans' response?" Weylind glanced over the map again. The elf encampments were far too sparse along the border, especially compared to the numbers the Escarlish had deployed. The only reason the Escarlish had not overrun them yet was that the Hydalla River proved to be a formidable barrier to cross and the elves' magic could counter the humans' greater numbers.

"They asked for a three-day truce. We, of course, agreed." The general straightened and clasped his hands behind his back. "The truce will soon be over."

"I will prepare a message for the humans, expressing our wish to extend the truce so we can engage in more extensive peace discussions." Weylind pushed away from the table. As the heir, he was authorized to act in his dacha's stead in this matter.

"Very good, amir." The general nodded, then gestured to the door. "I will see that a messenger is alerted to await your missive."

WEYLIND EYED the defenses of the camp critically as the general gave him a tour. If the humans attacked when the truce ended in a few hours, what else would need to be done to strengthen this border?

If they could deploy a few more warriors, that would be a start. But could they spare any reinforcements for this border when the one to the north was far more critical?

"Amir." A warrior jogged up to him and extended a piece of paper. "A message from the humans."

Weylind opened the note, then breathed out a sigh. The humans had requested an extension to the truce for another three weeks and asked to begin peace talks.

Much needed good news. Weylind would have to extend his stay here at this border for a few extra weeks to be on hand for the peace talks, sacrificing his time with Rheva and his children, but it would be worth it if he could end the war with Escarland.

"Amir." Another warrior sprinted to him, thrusting a piece of paper at him. "A message from the king."

Weylind snatched the paper, his fingers already shaking at the white look on the warrior's face.

The message contained only a single line.

Farrendel has been captured.

Dacha did not ask for Weylind to return north. He did not have to.

Weylind faced the warrior who had given him the message. "Ready my train. I will be heading north within the hour." He whirled on the general. "When the humans send their diplomats, do whatever you have to do to get them to end the war."

"Amirisheni?" The general was too composed to gape, but he blinked, giving away his confusion.

Weylind did not bother to explain. The news would filter down to this border soon enough. Forget staying to negotiate the peace with Escarland. Right now, his first priority—his only priority—was rescuing his brother.

WEYLIND JUMPED down from the train, weary after a full day and night of travel. He had tried to sleep while the train had glided through the night, but thoughts of his brother in the hands of the trolls had plagued him too much for sleep.

He shoved his way past the bustle, ignoring the looks the warriors were giving him. While the encampment at the southern border had been tense, this camp held an air of despair and failure.

Marching straight for the command shelter, Weylind pushed past the guards outside. "What happened?"

Dacha straightened from where he had been braced against the table, staring down at the map. "Weylind, sason. I am glad you are here."

Weylind gave only a brief glance to the generals and scouts around the table before he focused on Dacha and repeated, "What happened?"

"We had attacked across the Gulmorth." Dacha's jaw worked, his face etched in grim lines. "But it was a trap. While the trolls lured the bulk of our forces deeper into Kostaria, they attacked our command post here. Farrendel tried to defend the post, but he is unpracticed in using his magic in battle, and he was captured."

This was the reason Dacha had never wanted Farrendel at the front. Yet over the years, Farrendel had taken more and more of an active role in protecting the camp during battle. Of course his magic had drawn the trolls' attention. Of course they would take the opportunity to capture the elf king's younger son while he was vulnerable.

"Where is he? What is the plan to rescue him?" Weylind braced himself against the table, searching the map. But he did not see any markings to indicate Farrendel's location.

Dacha's eyes grew even more dark and grim. "We do not know. Our scouts are still trying to find where they have taken him."

Weylind clenched his fingers against the table, a shudder going through him.

If the trolls were holding him in one of their encampments near the border, they had a chance to rescue him.

But if they had taken him deeper into Kostaria—perhaps all the way to the trolls' fortress of Gror Grar—would Weylind be able to rescue him? The elves had spent decades fighting along the border, unable to get so much as a toe-hold into Kostaria. It would be nearly impossible to fight all the way across Kostaria to reach Gror Grar.

How far could they go to rescue Farrendel? How many lives would be lost in the attempt?

There would be those who would counsel that it would be best simply to leave Farrendel where he was. To give him up as lost to spare the lives it would take to free him.

But Weylind could not imagine giving up on his brother like that.

One way or the other, he would get his brother back, even if he had to tear Kostaria apart with every scrap of magic he possessed. He might not have the magic of the ancient kings like Farrendel did, but he could tear Kostaria up by the roots nonetheless.

"WE HAVE FOUND HIM, DARESHENI." The scout burst into the command shelter, the first breath of hope in the days since Farrendel had been captured.

Weylind blinked at the scout, his head whirling a bit. He could not remember the last time he ate or slept more than a fitful doze. Farrendel had been missing for five days. Five days for the trolls to do who knew what to him.

The scout hurried to the map and pointed. "He is being held here, in a cave in this outcropping of rocks."

Dacha bent over the map, studying the landscape.

Several of the generals leaned over the map as well. One of the generals sighed and gestured. "It is likely a trap. That is the only reason they have not killed the amir already."

A valid point. The trolls had seen Farrendel's magic. They knew the kind of warrior he would become. Killing Farrendel was their best option.

Unless they planned to use him as a trap.

"It does not matter if it is a trap or not. I must rescue my son." Dacha pointed at the map. "Weylind can lead an attack from this direction. You will have the cover of this spruce forest until we are nearly at the encampment."

"They will kill Farrendel before we can get anywhere close." Weylind's teeth ached from how hard he was clenching his jaw at the thought. But it was the truth. The trolls would never let them rescue Farrendel.

"That is why I will lead a small, secondary incursion from this direction." Dacha tapped the map, tracing the route. "While the trolls are distracted with the main attack, I will slip in and rescue Farrendel. You can then cover my retreat. We do not need to fully destroy this troll encampment. Not during this attack, anyway. We just need to get my son safely out of there."

The general's jaw worked. "I do not like having both you and Weylind Amir involved in this attack. It places both of you at too much risk."

"If this is a trap, then you will need both of us there with our strong magic." Dacha met the general's gaze without flinching. "We must rescue my son, whatever it takes."

WEYLIND'S HEART pounded as he crept through the spruce forest in the early, pre-dawn gray. Mist clung thick and heavy around the deep green of the evergreen boughs. Behind him, an army of elf warriors crept through the forest.

A whiff of smoke was the first indication of the camp ahead, though it was still not visible through the shrouding mist and dense trees.

Even though everything in him ached to rush ahead, Weylind slowed his pace, carefully placing his feet to avoid snapping twigs or otherwise making any noise.

After a few more yards, he peered through the dense spruce branches at the sprawling troll encampment. Smooth domes of rock or ice formed the shelters for the troll warriors, lined up in neat rows. Fires burned low at the center of the camp while a larger shelter of stone must be where the commanders were staying.

At the far side of the camp, a heap of rocks and boulders tumbled around an outcropping, a dark hole disappearing inside.

Farrendel was in there. Likely hurt and in pain. Who knew what the trolls had done to him in the past six days.

Weylind scanned the camp one more time, then held up a hand to the warriors. It was time.

He pressed both hands to the spruce trees on either side and poured his magic into the forest in amounts he had rarely unleashed before. A few of the warriors behind him added their own magic to the storm of magic enlivening the forest around them.

The spruces groaned and thrashed. The ground heaved as roots tore upward. Even as the trolls tumbled from their bivouacs, weapons in hand, the roots shot up and wrapped around the shelters. The stone and ice splintered, then cracked, spraying shards into the air.

With a yell, Weylind drew his sword and charged into the encampment, his warriors at his heels.

The troll warriors quickly formed a defensive line. They might have been surprised, but they must have been sleeping at the ready, for most already wore armor, their weapons in hand.

Weylind let anger burn hot and powerful in his chest and down into his magic. His magic lashed out, spreading into a roiling wave ahead of him. Roots burst from the ground, tearing into the troll line. A few trolls tried to hack at the roots or counter with their magic, but Weylind's magic held the intensity of his rage. The ice and stone shattered before him.

Across the way, Dacha and a small group of warriors slipped from the trees and disappeared inside the cave.

Good. Farrendel would be rescued shortly.

Until then, Weylind just needed to keep putting on a show to keep all the trolls distracted.

Not a problem. He had a score to settle.

Weylind sidestepped a troll's sword, then swung his own sword in an arc at the troll's neck. The troll blocked Weylind's sword, but he was not able to block the root that shot out, wrapping around his legs and taking him down.

Weylind leapt over him and kept charging forward. He swiped away rocks and ice with his magic, then stabbed with his sword, until he had nearly reached the very center of the camp. If he was not careful, he would push the trolls all the way back into the path of Dacha's retreat.

What was taking so long? Had Dacha's small team met with resistance?

Finally, elf warriors stepped from the cave, arrows to their bowstrings and swords in hand. After a moment, Dacha strode into the dawn, Farrendel limp and bleeding in his arms. Even though Farrendel was only a few inches shorter than Dacha, their father carried him easily enough.

Weylind released a breath and another wave of his magic. He just needed to keep the trolls busy for another few minutes, then he would call a retreat. This was almost over.

As Dacha took another step from the cave, headed for the safety of the trees, three trolls rose into view, perched on the rock outcropping above the cave mouth. The trolls raised their bows, arrows nocked to the string.

This was a trap.

A trap to kill an elf king.

They had known it would be, but still Weylind had not expected this. Those trolls must have been hiding in the rocks all this time, waiting for Dacha to be vulnerable.

Weylind opened his mouth, gathering the breath for a shout.

Too late. Far, far too late.

The trolls released. Weylind could not shout. Could not blast his magic fast enough, far enough.

Dacha staggered, then fell to his knees, an arrow in his back.

Weylind shouted wordlessly and tore through the camp with his magic, sweeping away the trolls before him. He sprinted forward, heedless of the trolls coming at him.

One of the elf warriors behind him was shouting. An order to rally to the prince. But Weylind barely heard him. Barely paid any attention to anything besides Dacha and Farrendel.

Dacha was sagging over Farrendel, his arms still around him as if he was trying to protect him from the arrows raining down from above. Farrendel was gripping Dacha, shouting something. Blood spread in a pool around them, though how much of it was Dacha's and how much was Farrendel's, Weylind could not tell from this distance.

Two of the other warriors were down, and the others were valiantly trying to shield their king while they launched their own volley of arrows at the much better protected trolls.

Weylind wrapped roots around the trolls on the outcropping, yanking them from their feet, then crushed them with a ruthlessness that might haunt him later. But right now, he could not care about anything but reaching Dacha and Farrendel, no matter how much destruction he left in his wake.

He crashed to his knees next to Dacha and Farrendel, dropping his sword as he reached for them.

Dacha had collapsed all the way to the ground, his face white, blood slick on the stones around him. His gaze —hazy, unfocused—met Weylind's. For a moment, he seemed to be mouthing something. His hand gave a slight twitch, reaching for Farrendel.

The message was clear. Protect Farrendel.

Weylind held his Dacha's gaze and gave a nod, a lump filling his throat.

Dacha's eyes filled for just a moment. Relief. Love. Regret.

Then his body sagged, his eyes blank and staring.

Weylind reached out and pressed his fingers to Dacha's neck. But he already knew, even before the lack of pulse, that Dacha was gone.

Wrapping his arms around Farrendel, Weylind had to all but drag him away, staggering to his feet.

Farrendel struggled, reaching for Dacha, screaming for him, as tears streamed down his face. His movements were odd, stilted, and only then did Weylind notice the pieces of stone sticking out of Farrendel's wrists. Visible through the many rips in Farrendel's shirt, something dark laced just beneath Farrendel's skin. Was that stone? Who tortured a boy like this?

More heat surged through Weylind's chest. Dacha was dead. Farrendel had been tortured. And the only thing Weylind could do was ensure that the trolls paid dearly for what they had done.

Weylind held tight to Farrendel as the elven warriors closed around him. He had to clear his throat to speak, yet his voice still came out choked and rough. "Please see to the king's body and call a retreat."

Vengeance would have to wait for another day. Right now, Weylind had to get his brother to safety.

The warrior nearest him nodded. An elven horn sounded. The warriors around them formed into squads, collecting the wounded and dead as they conducted a fighting retreat.

Weylind gripped Farrendel, trusting the warriors to guard his back.

He had rescued his brother. But the cost…

The cost would be one all of them would be paying for a long, long time.

CHAPTER
TWELVE

B y the time Weylind crossed over the Gulmorth and reached the healing shelters, Farrendel had gone still in his arms. Whether unconscious or simply exhausted, Weylind could not tell.

Weylind swept into the shelter. Unlike many of the sleeping shelters, the healing shelter was grown on the ground, with high upper openings to let in fresh air and light. A large room made up most of the space, filled with rows upon rows of moss pallets. At the back of the space, several rooms had been cordoned off to provide surgery rooms for the healers to work.

As soon as Weylind stepped inside, one of the healers directed him to one of these back rooms. Weylind followed the healer, then laid Farrendel on the surgical table.

Farrendel's chest rose and fell, though his eyes were closed. Away from the chaos of battle, Weylind could fully take in the network of stone lacing beneath Farrendel's skin, from his wrists all the way up his arms, across his chest and stomach, and around his ankles up his legs to his knees.

How dare the trolls treat him like this? Farrendel was just a boy. The trolls could see that. All Farrendel had ever done was protect the elven command base. Yet the trolls had captured him and treated him like...this.

The healers began divesting Farrendel of his tattered clothing and cleaning his wounds as best they could. The head healer, his fingers laced green, reached out and laid his hand on Farrendel's chest.

Almost as soon as the healer touched him, Farrendel cried out. His arms flailed, his magic flaring to life around him.

Weylind jumped forward and shoved the healer out of the way. Something burned across his ribs, but he cast a shield of his own magic in front of him as he reached for Farrendel.

The rest of the healers stumbled back, ducking the flailing fists and bolts of magic.

"It is all right, shashon." Weylind gripped Farrendel's hand, ignoring the way that Farrendel's magic sizzled against Weylind's. Only Farrendel's weakness and disorientation kept his magic from burning Weylind's fingers.

Hands gripped Weylind's shoulders, trying to pull him back. "Daresheni."

Weylind resisted their urgings to step away, shoving aside the pain of hearing that title directed at himself. Grief for Dacha would have to come later.

Farrendel's eyes shot open, and he glanced around, his gaze wild and unseeing.

"It is all right, shashon. You are safe." Weylind reached through the crackle of Farrendel's magic to rest his other hand on Farrendel's shoulder.

Farrendel's gaze focused on him, desperate and searching. "Dacha?"

Weylind hesitated. What could he tell Farrendel? He did not think Farrendel was in a fit state to absorb the news of Dacha's death.

But he hesitated too long. Something pained, then dead filled Farrendel's expression. He slumped back against the table, squeezing his eyes shut.

"Shashon, I need you to get control of your magic so the healers can help you." Weylind tightened his grip on Farrendel's hand and shoulder, as if he could hold his brother together. "Deep breaths, shashon. Please."

Farrendel swallowed, drawing in a shuddering breath. After a moment, the bolts surrounding his hands winked out.

Weylind released a breath, resisting the urge to wince at the burning pain still aching across his ribs. He glanced over his shoulder at the huddled healers, his words coming out more harsh than he intended. "It is safe now. Heal him."

The healers glanced at each other and tiptoed forward.

The head healer approached the table again, his eyes sweeping over Farrendel, though he did not touch him again. After a moment, the head healer met Weylind's gaze. "It would be standard practice to send a patient to sleep for something like this. But for the safety of the healers, I believe he will need to remain awake."

Weylind's stomach churned, but he nodded. "I will keep him calm."

The healer hesitated again, flicking a glance down at Farrendel before looking up at Weylind again. "We will try to numb the pain as much as possible. But between his magic and the troll magic lingering in the stone, I fear the process of removing the stone will be rather painful."

Weylind nodded yet again, and this time he could not bring himself to speak.

He was not sure how much Farrendel had heard of their conversation. He had given little reaction, not even to brace himself or flinch at the discussion of how much this was going to hurt. Was he even conscious? Weylind could not tell.

The head healer waved to the other healers. Two stepped forward and gently rested their hands on Farrendel, holding him down. When he did not react with more than a slight flinch, they eased some of their magic into him, their fingers glowing green.

At that, Farrendel sucked in a breath. He clenched his fists, but his magic did not flare as it had before.

Another elf stepped forward, carrying a tray that contained a small knife.

Weylind swallowed back the bile in the back of his throat. The healers would have to cut out the stone piece by piece.

The healer picked up the knife, then pressed it to Farrendel's wrist above one of the dark lines of stone.

Weylind tightened his grip on Farrendel and focused on Farrendel's face instead of watching the healer. He knew the moment the healer made the first cut for Farrendel cried out and struggled under Weylind's grip.

The healer froze, as if not daring to continue until he was sure Farrendel had his magic under control.

"Deep breaths. Keep control of your magic. I am here, shashon." Weylind tried to keep his voice calm, soothing, when all he wanted to do was yell along with Farrendel.

Farrendel sucked in another breath, and his magic remained dormant.

The healer went back to work. Slicing. Pulling out

stone. Slicing again. The longer he worked, the more Farrendel's breathing grew ragged, his cries louder.

As the healer moved from Farrendel's arm to his stomach, Farrendel flinched, struggling against those pinning him down again. "Weylind...Weylind...make them stop. Please. Stop."

Weylind could have cried. Wanted to break. But he cleared his throat, still pinning his brother down. "They cannot stop, shashon. The stone needs to be removed so you can be healed. I am sorry."

Farrendel arched against the table, screaming between his teeth. But he did not beg again. Tears dribbled from the corners of his eyes, his body shaking beneath Weylind's grip.

Weylind was not sure how long it took. An hour. Two. Forever.

He felt raw, broken, by the time the healer stepped back, sweat beading on his forehead. "Done."

On the table, Farrendel lay still. He did not so much as react as the healers finished filling him with healing magic and bandaging the wounds to keep them clean while they finished healing. Perhaps Farrendel had passed out once again.

Weylind forced himself to release his brother and took a step back. His fingers had long since gone numb.

"We can see him settled, Daresheni." The healer gestured toward Weylind's middle. "Perhaps I can tend to you now?"

Weylind glanced down, taking in the blackened remains of his shirt over his ribs. His skin still burned from where Farrendel's magic had brushed him. He likely had a burn there, but right now, Weylind could not bring himself to look. He could not stand to remain there a moment longer, surrounded by all the death and pain and sympathetic gazes.

He needed to yell. To shout. To let out all the pain building inside his own chest.

"I am fine." Weylind brushed past the healer. He stalked through the shelter, swiping a jar of healing balm as he passed.

As he burst from the shelter, a squad of guards fell into step around him. Four of them, double the number that had trailed after him as a prince.

It was too much. Much too much.

Weylind barely heard the generals and commanders calling him. He ignored the respectful bows as he strode past.

He made for the edge of camp, plunging into the calm of the forest. He only slowed once any sounds of the bustling camp had faded, leaving only the forest cloaked in darkness around him and the four guards trailing after him.

He spun to them. "Wait here."

"Daresheni..." The guard trailed off, as if torn between his duty to protect his king and his duty to obey orders.

"I will not go far." Weylind wheeled again and stalked off before the guard could respond.

After marching into the forest, he reached the edge of the Gulmorth Gorge and halted just inside the tree line. Releasing that tight control on his emotions, he collapsed to his knees, dug his fingers into the moss covering the forest floor, and screamed his pain into the empty forest.

His magic burst from him, howling all around him in a fury he had rarely experienced from his magic before. Roots the size of trees burst from the ground, roiling around him. Great, aged oaks groaned with the force of his magic.

He shoved his magic across the Gulmorth Gorge. A wild tangle of spruce trees and undergrowth burst from the ground.

Weylind pounded his fists into the dirt as tears burned trails down his cheeks. He yelled his pain as it tore through him.

The cliffs of the Gulmorth Gorge cracked with the tearing force of his roots and magic, tumbling boulders into the river below.

He was not sure how long it was before he found himself crouched on the ground, his fists buried in the dirt, roots climbing his arms all the way up to his elbows. He panted for breath, his face damp from his tears.

But his magic was exhausted; his heart was empty and numb.

Freeing his hands from the roots, he opened the jar of healing balm, then lifted his shirt. A line of red and blistered skin marked where Farrendel's magic had burned him.

Weylind spread the balm over the burn, hissing at the pain, though the balm was cool and soothing. He probably should have a healer tend him. But he did not want any risk of Farrendel overhearing that he had hurt Weylind in his panic.

Once he finished, Weylind gathered himself, brushing himself off and drying his face.

As he turned toward the encampment, he was no longer a prince.

He was the elf king.

As he stepped into camp once again, a cry rose above the general hubbub. Weylind flinched. Another elf warrior, in pain after the rescue?

An elf raced up to Weylind, then bowed. "Daresheni, it is your brother."

Farrendel. Had he woken already? Weylind shoved past the elf and sprinted for the healing shelter. He dashed past the rows of pallets and through one of the doors into a private room, following the sounds of the cries.

There, he barely noted the female elf—her arm bandaged—as she knelt across the pallet from Farrendel.

Farrendel huddled against the wall, his knees drawn up, his face buried in his arms. His whole body shook as if he sat in the middle of a snowstorm in nothing but his underclothes.

Weylind knelt on the pallet and gripped Farrendel's shoulders. "Shashon."

Farrendel flinched, a burst of his magic flaring around his fists for a moment before he clenched his fingers, and his magic snuffed out.

"You should rest." Weylind kept his grip firm on Farrendel's shoulders, but he did not try to tug Farrendel to the pallet just yet.

Farrendel seemed a little outside of himself. As if he was still lost somewhere in that cave in Kostaria.

After another few heartbeats of shaking and ragged breaths, Farrendel peeked at Weylind, his silver-blue eyes still wild and aching with desperation. "Dacha? Where is Dacha?"

Weylind did not want to have to tell him. Not yet. But Dacha's absence was far too terribly obvious. "Dacha..." Weylind's voice broke. He had thought he had expelled all the grief in the forest, but it seemed he was not yet as numb as he had hoped. A lump rose in his throat and roughened his voice. "Dacha has passed on. He is gone."

Farrendel made a noise in the back of his throat and

pressed his face back into his arms. "He is dead. Because of me."

"Because of the trolls. Not because of you." Weylind squeezed Farrendel's shoulders, though Farrendel did not look up to meet his gaze. "The trolls captured you. The trolls created that trap. The trolls killed Dacha. None of that is your fault."

Farrendel just mutely shook his head.

Was there anything Weylind could say right now that would make Farrendel hear him? Likely not. Farrendel was too lost in a haze of pain and grief to hear anything Weylind said right now.

After another moment, Weylind was able to convince Farrendel to return to the pallet. One of the healers pressed a hand to Farrendel's forehead, sending him off to sleep once again.

Once Farrendel was resting, Weylind pushed to his feet. He had delayed long enough. But he was now king. He needed to see to his new duties.

Including the arrangements to send his dacha's body back to Estyra for burial.

THIRTEEN

The train glided to a halt at the station in Estyra.

Weylind pushed to his feet, then made his way from the seating car to the first train car.

There, Dacha's body rested on a stretcher, draped with a green flag with its silver tree symbol.

Four guards stood along the walls of the car. They were Dacha's honor guard, escorting the king home.

Farrendel huddled next to the stretcher, his eyes staring off into nothing, the bandages over his still healing wrists visible beyond the ends of his sleeves.

"You were supposed to be resting." Weylind knelt in front of Farrendel, searching his face.

Farrendel gave a slight shrug, his empty expression never changing.

It was all Weylind could do to convince Farrendel to eat. To rise and get dressed. To keep moving. Farrendel seemed to have shut down, only going through the motions of existing.

"We are pulling into Estyra now." Weylind gestured toward the door. As if on cue, the door slid open.

Farrendel tottered to his feet, though he remained standing where he was, staring down at Dacha's body, barely blinking.

The four guards moved almost as one, picking up the poles of the stretcher and hoisting Dacha's body to their shoulders.

Weylind led the way from the train car, and the four guards fell into a solemn pace behind him. Farrendel trailed after them, his shoulders hunched, his eyes still empty.

Their family gathered on the train platform, surrounded by elven warriors. As Weylind stepped from the train, the gathered warriors dropped into low bows.

Jalissa made a noise and pressed a hand over her mouth, hunching as if she had been punched. Melantha stared at Dacha's body, as hard and cold as Weylind had ever seen her, arms wrapped over her stomach as if to protect herself from the pain. Machasheni Leyleira stared at Dacha's body, as if trying to absorb the fact that she had now lost her son.

Rheva took a step forward, her eyes focused on Weylind, conveying her sympathy. She had her arms around Ryfon and Brina, both of them with tears openly trickling down their faces.

There was nothing Weylind could do or say in that moment to mitigate the grief. His own grief threatened to swallow him.

But he was now king. Kings could not break. They could not cry. They did not feel.

Kings led. They were strong for their families and their people.

277

WEYLIND FINISHED his farewells with Rheva, Ryfon, and Brina. He did not want to leave so soon after Dacha's death, but the war with the trolls did not wait for proper mourning periods.

At least the humans had come to their senses and signed a treaty. It was not exactly a peace treaty. It was more a *we agree to stop fighting as long as you stop fighting* kind of treaty. But that was good enough, at least for now. Someday Weylind would likely have to revisit the issue with the humans. Until then, he could focus on holding off the trolls.

As he turned away from his family, he caught sight of Farrendel striding toward him, his two swords strapped across his back, a set look to his jaw and a hard edge to his eyes.

At least that hard determination was an actual emotion in Farrendel's eyes. And he was up and dressed. That was an improvement after the emptiness of the past few weeks.

Farrendel halted in front of him, a travel bag slung over his shoulder. "I am coming."

"You have barely healed." Weylind did not want to take Farrendel back to the front after what had happened to him. "Stay here. Heal. Rest."

Farrendel's jaw worked, and he shook his head, a fire sparking deep in his silver-blue eyes. "No. I am coming. You need me."

Perhaps Tarenhiel needed a warrior with the magic of the ancient kings.

But Farrendel was too young to send into battle. While Dacha had taken Farrendel to the front and allowed him to protect the camp with his magic, he had resisted the generals' urgings to send Farrendel into battle.

Weylind would not go against Dacha's wishes. Nor did he want to send his little brother off to war like that. "No."

"I am getting on that train whether you like it or not." Farrendel brushed past him and strode down the branch, headed for the train. "There is nothing you can do to stop me."

WEYLIND PACED ALONG THE BORDER, as restless as he had been for the past two and a half weeks since Farrendel had disappeared from his shelter at the command base in the middle of the night. He had been tracked to the Gulmorth Gorge before the scouts could go no farther.

What had Farrendel been thinking by sneaking into Kostaria all by himself? He was going to get himself killed, and there was nothing Weylind could do about it.

What if Farrendel was already dead? Would Weylind even learn if Farrendel had been killed or frozen to death somewhere in the mountains of Kostaria?

Weylind should have gone after him, no matter what the generals and his bodyguards had said. Perhaps if he had chased after Farrendel right away, he could have caught up with him. He could have hauled him back to the safety of Tarenhiel. He could have...

Would Farrendel have listened? He had not seemed to hear anything Weylind had said in the weeks since Dacha had been killed, lost in a darkness pressing on his mind and soul in a way Weylind could not banish with mere words.

Now, all Weylind could do was watch the border, hoping Farrendel returned. Perhaps it was foolish, making a target of himself like this to any troll sniper who might be lingering across the gorge. But he struggled to care.

His dacha was dead. His brother was somewhere in Kostaria, all on his own.

The last thing Weylind had promised his dacha was that he would protect Farrendel. Only weeks later, he had already broken that promise.

A flash of blue along the horizon caught Weylind's gaze. A prickling feeling of building magic crawling along his skin. He whirled, searching the skyline to the north. The blue light grew, flashing, crackling.

Weylind spun on the general standing nearby. "Muster the warriors."

"Daresheni?" The general bowed, but the question remained in his eyes and his tone.

Weylind pointed. "That is my brother's magic. I wish to take advantage of the distraction he is providing."

That was not his main reason. No, all he really wanted to do was get to his brother as quickly as possible. But as king, he needed to have a tactical reason for ordering his warriors into battle.

The general's gaze darted to the horizon, then his eyes widened a fraction. "Yes, of course, Daresheni."

As the general hurried away, Weylind increased his pacing, his hand on his sword. If he was not king, if he did not have the weight of the kingdom on his shoulders, then he would grow a bridge over the Gulmorth and attack all on his own.

But getting himself killed would not help Farrendel. The wisest course was to wait for reinforcements and attack in force.

It seemed like hours but was probably only a few

minutes before ranks of warriors marched out of the trees, armed and armored, ready for battle.

Weylind gave only the briefest attention to the orders barked behind him. He knelt on one knee and pressed his hand to the ground, pouring his magic into building a bridge across the Gorge. A few other warriors joined him, creating even more bridges for the warriors.

No troll magic flared on the far side. They must be too busy fighting Farrendel to pay attention to the elves at their back.

Last time he had charged across the Gulmorth, he and Dacha had meticulously planned the attack. And look how that had turned out. Dacha had been killed, and far too many warriors were still healing from wounds they had received in the vicious fighting on that day.

This time, there was no preparation. No plan. Weylind charged across his bridge, sword in his hand.

He probably should be more careful. The elves had already lost one king, and the kingdom could not risk losing another king in such a short span of time. Ryfon was far too young to rule. Rheva would do her best as regent, but she was a healer, not a warrior.

But at that moment, Weylind could think of nothing but getting to Farrendel and making sure he did not lose his brother as he had lost their father.

His bodyguards fell in around him, their own swords drawn and ready. The rest of the warriors charged behind him on silent feet.

They burst through the tree line on the far side, and the troll encampment came into view. All the trolls had mustered on the far side, where their magic swirled against the blue, crackling power that was Farrendel's magic.

There was so very much of it. So much more than

Weylind had ever seen Farrendel unleash before. His brother was not even visible through the burst of blue bolts and swirl of snow.

Weylind shoved his own magic outward. The ground before him rippled, then roots burst from the dirt around the trolls.

A few of the trolls turned to face the charging elves, raising their swords and axes.

Yet even as they turned to face Weylind and the other warriors, Farrendel's magic flashed out. Then Farrendel himself whirled through the magic, his two swords flashing as he carved into the trolls with a fierceness that was so unlike his brother.

But that innocent young boy had died under the trolls' torture and with Dacha's death.

The knot of trolls put up a valiant fight, but they quickly fell under Farrendel's magic and the warriors' swords.

As the last troll collapsed in a pool of blood, the warriors around Weylind cheered, and a few shouted out titles for Farrendel, though the one that quickly spread until they were all shouting the same thing was, "Laesornysh!"

Farrendel halted, his magic crackling, then bursting around him before it dissipated, leaving him standing in a circle of dead trolls, blood spattered and hard-edged. More blood dribbled down the length of his twin blades.

Weylind approached Farrendel slowly. Something about Farrendel's eyes remained both wild and hard in a way that made Weylind wary.

Weylind halted in front of Farrendel, searching his gaze. "Shashon."

Farrendel's gaze snapped to him, but something in

those silver-blue depths remained hard. Almost dead. "The troll king is dead. I killed him."

With that, Farrendel stalked past Weylind, his shoulders set, his face that of a much older elf.

That was the moment Weylind knew he had lost his brother. And he did not know what to do to get him back.

FOURTEEN

FIERCE HEART

After the busyness of planning a royal wedding in a single afternoon, all Rheva wanted to do was close her eyes and fall asleep.

But Weylind was pacing back and forth across their bedchamber, his steps growing more and more heavy with his agitation.

"Weylind, come to bed." Rheva patted the spot beside her without bothering to open her eyes.

"I should go over there. I should check that he is all right." Weylind's steps hitched for a moment, then headed for the door.

Of all the ridiculous notions...Rheva sighed and pushed herself upright. "Do not even think about it. This is their wedding night. They do not need you barging in."

"It is hardly a traditional wedding night." Weylind snorted, then spun back to her. "The human princess is likely a spy. An assassin, for all we know."

"If she is an assassin, then Farrendel can take care of

himself." Rheva did not mean for that to come out sounding so callous, but Weylind was not thinking clearly. Obsessed, actually.

"Yes, but will he? He seems strangely enamored with her." Weylind spun back to the door. "He would probably just let her kill him rather than defend himself and hurt her."

A valid point...if the human princess was an assassin.

Rheva had not spent as much time with Princess Elspeth as Jalissa had, since Rheva had been busy organizing the wedding. But from what she had seen, the princess was exactly what she seemed. An open, joyful person who smiled and laughed readily, even when surrounded by strangers. "She is *not* an assassin. Besides, Machasheni likes her. Have you ever known Machasheni Leyleira to be wrong about such things?"

Weylind halted with his hand on the door handle. "No. But there is always a first time."

Rheva sighed and rolled onto her side, putting her back to Weylind. Over the years, Weylind had grown so very stubborn, especially when it came to Farrendel. "Fine. Go over there. But do not blame me if Farrendel singes your hair off."

"He would not do that." Despite his words, Weylind hesitated, then his footsteps headed across the room toward her. The bed dipped with Weylind's weight as he sat on the edge. "But you are correct that he would be angry with me."

"Of course I am correct." Rheva rolled over so that she could share an attempt at a weary smile with him. "I am also correct that both of us need sleep."

Weylind nodded, then leaned over to tug off his boots.

Rheva settled more comfortably on her pillow and let her eyes fall closed again.

How she missed the way things used to be. Before Weylind became king. Before his dacha died.

Rheva missed the carefree prince she married. She missed her husband. The father he had been to Ryfon and Brina in their younger years.

Now, Weylind gave so much to the kingdom that there was little left for his family. What little attention he had left was usually focused on keeping Farrendel functioning.

Leaving Rheva to quietly carry on alone, raising her children as best she could.

WEYLIND SETTLED onto the bed beside Rheva and stared up at the darkness cloaking the room.

Was Farrendel all right? Yes, Rheva had made a compelling argument that charging over there was not the right course of action. But it still itched at Weylind to lie here, not knowing for sure.

It was Weylind's job to protect Farrendel, and he had done a poor job of it at the diplomatic meeting with the Escarlish king. He should have pushed harder for another option besides an arranged marriage. Anything else. The humans liked wealth, did they not? Surely if Weylind had bribed them with enough gold and silver, they would have let go of the idea of a marriage alliance between their kingdoms.

If Weylind had been given more time, he could have saved Farrendel from this. But the humans' proposed alliance had thrown him. Then Farrendel had latched onto the idea so thoroughly that nothing Weylind said dissuaded him.

What hold did that princess have on him? It was concerning, to say the least.

She would need to be watched. Weylind would not be able to perform such a task himself. He still had a kingdom to run, after all.

But he could assign a guard to keep a watch on the human princess. Iyrinder, perhaps. He got along well with Farrendel and knew how to be discreet.

Yes, that was what Weylind would do. First thing in the morning, he would summon Iyrinder. The peace of mind would be worth Farrendel's ire, if it came to that.

WEYLIND WATCHED as guards carried Farrendel and Elspetha's stretcher onto the royal train for the trip back to Estyra.

A few of the citizens of Arorien paused to watch as well, likely having heard the rumors of what had happened in the forests around Lethorel.

Weylind squeezed his eyes shut, trying to take deep breaths so that he did not break in front of his family and people.

Farrendel had nearly died. Would have died, if not for the elishina he had formed with Elspetha.

That elishina. Weylind still struggled to wrap his mind around it, both hating it and grateful for it all at once.

Thanks to that elishina, his brother was still alive. But due to that same elishina, Farrendel would likely live a shortened life as he shared his years with Elspetha.

Leaving Weylind utterly helpless to save his brother from this choice.

DEATH WIND

Weylind stared at the message, his hands shaking.

Not again. This could not be real.

But the words did not change, no matter how long he stared.

Farrendel had been captured. Again. And all of Weylind's efforts to head off the traitors before they reached the border with Kostaria had failed.

Traitors. Including Melantha.

His family was shattering around him, and he did not know what to do or how to fix it.

No matter what, he was going to rescue Farrendel.

Or die trying, just like Dacha had.

WEYLIND WAS FREEZING.

He huddled in his blankets as a blizzard howled around the shelter he had grown to keep him and the three royal brothers of Escarland warm through the night. His teeth were chattering so loudly he could barely hear the whispers of those same three brothers where they were piled together to keep warm across the shelter from Weylind.

"He sounds cold," one of them whispered.

"He didn't want to huddle with us. Nothing much we can do." That was King Averett's voice.

"Unless we dog pile him." Prince Edmund's voice.

Weylind let out a huff under his breath. Farrendel's one letter from his time in Escarland indicated that he seemed to actually like these annoying new brothers of his. Inconceivable, really.

"You could start an international incident," King

Averett hissed. He was probably trying to stay quiet, but not quiet enough for Weylind's elven hearing.

The two princes snorted. Blankets rustled as Prince Julien spoke. "Not likely. He needs us too much."

"Besides, it would cause more of an incident if he freezes to death during the night." Edmund this time.

"Fine. Let's do it. Farrendel would never forgive us if we let him freeze."

More blankets rustled, then boots scuffed on the wooden branch floor, soft and slow as if trying to be stealthy.

When they were nearly upon him, Weylind rolled to his knees and pressed a hand to the floor. Branches whipped out from the floor and the walls, wrapping around wrists, ankles, and waists, accompanied by grunts and exclamations of surprise. King Averett, Prince Julien, and Prince Edmund struggled against the branches wrapped around their waists, arms pinned to their sides, as they were lifted from the floor.

Prince Edmund rolled his eyes, halting his struggles. "Touchy elf."

"We should have known better. He is Farrendel's brother." Prince Julien wiggled against the slim branches restraining him.

King Averett shook his head. "You've made your point, King Weylind. Perhaps trying to sneak up on you while you slept was not a wise move. But you're freezing. You won't last the night like this."

Weylind gritted his teeth and tried to stop their chattering. He curled and uncurled his fingers, trying to work feeling back into them. Wiggling his toes did not relieve their numbness. Truthfully, he was on the verge of frostbite.

But to accept what these brothers were offering? To

have to huddle with them for warmth? Weylind could barely keep his mouth from curling. It was…undignified.

It had been bad enough agreeing to share his shelter with them when the Kostarian winds made it clear that the flimsy Escarlish tents were no longer a feasible option. All across the camp, the elves had been ordered to create extra shelters or share their own, and Weylind had set the example by sharing his own shelter with the Escarlish royalty. Jalissa had done the same in sharing with Princess Elspetha.

Did he have a choice but to huddle for warmth? He would be in no shape to rescue Farrendel if he lost fingers or toes to frostbite.

"Fine." Weylind brushed his hand against the floor again. The branches snaked back into the wall, releasing the Escarlish brothers. Annoyingly, they all managed to land on their feet.

Weylind settled into his bedroll again, holding his breath as King Averett plopped onto the floor on one side of him, Prince Julien on the other. Prince Edmund flopped onto his bedroll on the other side of King Averett.

It was warmer, but Weylind's back crawled having these humans crowded around him. The things he had to put up with in order to rescue Farrendel.

But if they rescued Farrendel, the help of these humans would be worth it.

WEYLIND WOKE to Prince Julien snoring directly into his ear. An arm that was not his draped over his chest while someone's foot was resting on his shin.

Lip curling, Weylind pinched King Averett's sleeve between two fingers, lifted the human king's arm, and tossed it away from him. King Averett's hand smacked into Prince Edmund's face.

With a snort and a groan, both Prince Edmund and King Averett startled awake in a surge of flailing limbs. Weylind had to lunge out of the way to avoid an elbow to the nose and accidentally knocked into Prince Julien, setting off another round of rolling and thrashing.

Weylind extricated himself from the mayhem as the three human brothers scrambled to disentangle themselves from their blankets and each other, straightening their clothes with little coughs as if trying to regain their dignity.

It did not help. There was little dignity to be regained after they had sprawled across each other during the night.

Still, Weylind had all his fingers and toes. He supposed that was worth putting up with their close proximity.

Besides, he would not complain. Farrendel would be faring much worse as a prisoner of the trolls. No indignity or sacrifice on Weylind's part would compare to what Farrendel was suffering.

Even if...Weylind sniffed at his shirt and allowed himself to grimace. He reeked of the humans. A mix of body odor and gunpowder. A stench that would only get worse as this war progressed without a chance for bathing.

This war had better be short.

Two nights later, after the trolls ambushed the rear lines near the hospital tents and where Jalissa and Elspetha had been sharing a shelter, Weylind assisted King Averett in hanging tent canvas across the shelter since it had been decided Jalissa and Elspetha might as well share this shelter as the rear lines were no safer.

Prince Julien stomped his feet, then stepped inside the shelter, followed by Elspetha. Elspetha's gaze swept over the shelter before latching on the four bedrolls laid out side by side. When she glanced at Weylind, her eyes twinkled, and she smirked.

Weylind glared back. *Do not say anything.*

Jalissa stepped inside next. After her gaze landed on the bedrolls, she turned to Weylind with a raised eyebrow, her own smirk playing at the corners of her mouth.

Weylind raised his eyebrows right back. She could not judge. He assumed she had been huddling with Elspetha just as much as he had with Elspetha's brothers.

Elspetha elbowed Jalissa as she pushed aside the canvas to enter the far side of the shelter. "Told you."

Jalissa's smirk widened, and she shot one last glance in Weylind's direction before the canvas fell back into place behind her.

Weylind would never live this down.

CHAPTER
FIFTEEN

His brother was dying.

Weylind gripped Elspetha's shoulders, holding her upright. On the surgical table, Farrendel lay still, not breathing, as the elven healers and the troll prince worked to remove the stone in him.

Although everything in him was shattering, Weylind knew what Farrendel would ask of him in that moment. He would want Weylind to look after Elspetha.

Weylind might have fought across Kostaria to save Farrendel, but he had been too late. All he could do was stand there and watch Farrendel die.

And make sure Elspetha did not die with him. Her death would be one tragedy too many.

"Let go, isciena. We cannot lose both of you." Weylind swallowed the lump in his throat, hoping Elspetha could not feel the way his hands were shaking as he gripped her shoulders.

He was not sure how he would survive Farrendel's loss. This was all too much like his nightmares after rescuing Farrendel the first time. The dreams where both

Dacha and Farrendel died while Weylind stood by, helpless to move, their blood coating his hands as they bled out.

"No." Elspetha gasped out the word, shaking her head. She pressed her forehead to Farrendel's, holding him with a desperate determination.

"Isciena." Weylind could not force more than that past the squeezing in his throat and chest.

"Essie." Averett joined them, one hand on Elspetha's arm, his other hand coming to rest on Weylind's shoulder, as if the Escarlish king realized that Weylind, too, needed bracing.

Elspetha made a noise that might have been a word. But she did not let go of Farrendel, even though his chest remained far too still.

Across the table, the healer paused, then reached out to rest a hand on Farrendel's chest to check for a heartbeat.

Farrendel's body shuddered, then he gasped in a breath.

Weylind's knees nearly gave out, but only Averett's hand on his shoulder and the need to keep Elspetha upright kept Weylind standing.

The healer turned back to his work, and Weylind forced himself to watch, no matter how much his stomach churned at every cut of the human surgeon's scalpel, every flare of troll magic as Prince Rharreth drew stone out of Farrendel's body.

But Weylind could not risk that Prince Rharreth would take this opportunity to harm Farrendel, despite all the assurances otherwise. Not that Weylind would likely be fast enough to stop Prince Rharreth, if the troll decided to kill Farrendel. But Weylind would surely see to it that Rharreth died moments later.

This time, Farrendel did not scream or fight the healer as he had last time. Instead, he lay almost disconcertingly still, his ragged breathing the only indication that he remained alive.

When it became clear that Elspetha would remain standing on her own, Weylind moved a few feet away and braced himself against the table to assist his own shaking legs.

A buzzing filled Weylind's ears, his head growing light. Somewhere, almost through a fog, he registered Prince Rharreth stepping back, Averett tugging Elspetha away, the nurses stepping in to finish bandaging Farrendel's wounds.

The healer propped himself against a tent pole to remain standing, saying something about having done what they could, and stone remaining in Farrendel, but Weylind could only mutely nod, nothing truly sinking past the shudder coursing through him.

Prince Edmund left after saying something about a tent, and Jalissa eased forward, her words lost in the roaring in Weylind's head. By the look in her eyes, the look she shot toward Farrendel, he guessed she was volunteering to stay with Farrendel until he was settled elsewhere.

Right. He was supposed to meet with Prince Rharreth and begin treaty negotiations. Even now, Averett was talking with Prince Rharreth as the two of them strode toward the tent's exit.

With one last glance at Farrendel—his face still tensed in pain, but his chest rising and falling with even breaths —Weylind pushed away from the table and staggered after Averett and Rharreth.

Outside, he blinked into the sunlight, the beam

glinting off the piles of fresh snow and puddles pooling in the depressions in the stone.

To one side, Averett still spoke with Prince Rharreth, bodyguards standing to the side.

Weylind's own warriors converged on him, but he mutely waved them away. He could not handle this right now. Any of it. Being king. Negotiating peace for a hundred year war. Dealing with the trolls who had so tortured Farrendel.

Instead of joining Averett, Weylind spun on his heel and ducked into the semi-sheltered space between the healing tent and another nearby tent. He sank to the ground, drew up his knees, and gave in to the shuddering, gasping breaths that he had been stuffing down from the moment Farrendel had collapsed in Gror Grar.

Farrendel was alive. But he should have died. Would have died, if not for Elspetha's tenacious hold on him through their elishina.

The horror of the last few minutes rose in his chest, and Weylind gripped his knees, shaking and shattering as silently as he could manage.

After several minutes, Averett's boots crunched in the layer of slushy snow covering the ground before he halted a few feet away. Guarding him while he broke.

Averett spoke, low so that his words would not carry. "You aren't going to throw up, are you?"

"No."

Maybe.

Weylind swallowed back the bile and told himself that he definitely was not going to lose his breakfast with the king of Escarland watching.

Yet something about Averett's joking question helped steady Weylind. A few more gasping breaths, and he squashed the panicky, shaky feeling back to the depths to deal with another day—or never, if he had any say about it.

Rising to his feet, he brushed off the front of his trousers, then reached to brush at his back...only to realize that he must have sat in a snowbank, too consumed with his internal conflict to notice until that moment. The seat of his trousers and the end of his tunic were soaked through.

Averett turned, then a grin twisted his mouth. "Perhaps you should take a moment to change before the treaty negotiations."

Weylind grimaced and nodded. Between the blood spatters and dried gore of battle and now his embarrassingly dirty rear end, he was a dreadful sight. Hardly a dignified elf king prepared for treaty negotiations that would, hopefully, end over a hundred years of warfare.

Drawing in a deep breath, Weylind released a long, steadying exhale. As little as he liked the trolls, he would do his best to be reasonable in this peace treaty. For Farrendel's sake, and the sake of all the elf warriors who had fought, suffered, and died for this cause in the past century.

WEYLIND RESTED his hands on his knees as Farrendel drifted back to sleep. At least Farrendel had awakened and had been alert and aware of his surroundings. That boded well for his recovery.

Especially after they had come so close to losing him that day. If not for Elspetha's determination even when everyone else, including Weylind, had given up hope, Farrendel would have died.

Farrendel still looked mostly dead with his face taut

with pain even in sleep. The hacked ends of his hair stuck to his forehead.

It was not just Elspetha Weylind had to thank for Farrendel's survival. If not for Escarland's army and weapons, Weylind's army alone never could have forged across Kostaria, and certainly not this rapidly. Without Escarlish gunpowder and ingenuity in storing some of Farrendel's magic, it would have been nearly impossible to breach Gror Grar. The small team never could have gotten past the blocked rear entrance into Gror Grar in time to save Farrendel without the humans.

In all his years scorning humans for their lack of magic beyond a few magicians, short lifespans, quarrelsome nature, and undignified ways, he had somehow missed the fact that they had a sheer stubbornness that was almost a magic unto itself.

The tent flap behind him whooshed open with a blast of cold breeze against Weylind's back.

"How is he?" King Averett asked as he approached, his footsteps only somewhat muffled by the rug spread over the ground.

"He was awake a few minutes ago." Weylind studied Farrendel's drawn, haggard face.

"That's good." Averett halted next to Weylind. "Get some sleep. I have the next watch."

Weylind rested a hand on Farrendel's shoulder. He was loath to leave, but he had agreed when Averett had proposed watching Farrendel in shifts through the night. Weylind would need to be alert to deal with the complications that would arise on the morrow. They had to figure out how to hand the conquered Kostaria back to the trolls and work with the soon-to-be-crowned troll king on a plan to allow the Escarlish-Tarenhieli army to peacefully withdraw.

After squeezing Farrendel's shoulder, although his brother was most likely too deeply asleep to feel the gesture, Weylind forced himself to stand. He could trust Averett, Julien, and Edmund to guard Farrendel the rest of the night.

With one last glance over his shoulder, Weylind strode from the tent, nodding to the guards outside, two humans and two elves, as he passed. As he trudged across the camp, a few of the bustling humans and elves greeted him, though none lingered. Even through the night, duties kept many busy.

Finally, Weylind reached the shelter he had grown earlier that day and crawled inside. In the darkness, he found his bedroll and wormed his way between the sleeping Julien and Edmund. He had to elbow Julien to gain more room and lift one of Edmund's arms out of the way. The arm ended up flopping right back onto Weylind's shoulder, but Weylind left it. There was no point in resisting it.

Besides, these humans were not all bad. Weylind might even come to like them. Eventually.

CHAPTER
SIXTEEN

TROLL QUEEN

Weylind stared at the train as it departed from the station in Estyra, heading for Escarland. It took everything in him to watch Farrendel board that train, so wounded and lost. But if Dacha Taranath believed those doctors in Escarland could help, then Weylind would do all in his power to see to it that Farrendel arrived in Escarland in a timely fashion.

Beside him, Machasheni Leyleira lifted her chin and turned, heading back to Ellonahshinel. The two of them were the only ones who had come to the train station to see Farrendel and Elspetha off, since they had not wanted to overwhelm Farrendel right now.

Weylind released a sigh, turned, and fell into step beside Machasheni.

Machasheni glanced at him, her gaze that slightly sharp and assessing one that never failed to make him

300

squirm, even now. "It is high time you released a few of your burdens and let someone else carry the load."

Weylind raised his eyebrows at his machasheni. "I am king. There is no one else who can carry what I do."

Her mouth pressed into a line, her own eyebrow raising in a hint of a reproving quirk. She, of course, knew all about the burdens he carried as king. She had been queen, ruling at his dachasheni's side for hundreds of years. "Perhaps. But you do not have to hold all your burdens so tightly. Farrendel is a grown elf. He is married. He is not your concern the way he was fifteen years ago. You can trust that Elspetha and her brothers will look after him when you cannot."

He did not doubt that. He had seen the way Averett, Julien, and Edmund had rallied all of Escarland to fight to rescue Farrendel. He could trust his brother to their capable care.

But knowing that and actually setting aside his worries were two entirely different things.

"Yes, I know." Weylind released a long breath, trying to ease the tension in his shoulders. It felt like something inside him had been coiled tight and choking for the past fifteen years. He could no longer remember what it was like to relax. Or laugh. Or be at peace.

Machasheni rested a hand on his arm, halting him. "Your siblings have needed you a great deal in the past fifteen years. But do not forget that you also have a wife and children. They need you too."

Weylind nodded again, her words and her gaze tempting him to squirm.

But he shoved that squirming away, not wanting to examine it too closely.

As he and Machasheni reached Ellonahshinel,

Weylind gave another nod. "Linshi, Machasheni. You have given me much to think about."

She pressed her mouth into that line again, as if she knew very well that he was fobbing her off with the right words but his heart was not in it.

Yet, he could not dismiss the words from his head as he strolled through the branches of Ellonahshinel, entered his study, banished his clerks with the instruction that he was to be left alone, and took a seat, staring at the stacks of paperwork that had accumulated in the weeks he had been gone fighting the war.

Rheva and Ryfon had done an admirable job, keeping the kingdom running during a time of war while its king was away. But there were a lot of things they could not do, and all of that had waited for his return.

He reached for his pen and the first sheet of paper. Yet when he had it in front of him, he stared down at it, unseeing.

Over a hundred years ago, he had shattered when he discovered Dacha was not the paragon of virtue he had seemed when Weylind was a child.

But it turned out, Weylind was not a paragon of virtue either. The one thing Dacha had told him on his wedding day was to choose Rheva.

Yet for much of the last few decades, Weylind had chosen the kingdom, Farrendel, the war, pretty much everyone and everything before Rheva. That had to change, starting now. If Weylind could figure out how to go about doing so.

What if Rheva was so distant that she no longer wished to choose him in return? She put on a good show before others, but would she be willing to revive what he had let go so cold?

"Dacha?"

He shook himself and glanced up.

Ryfon stood in the doorway, a clerk hovering just behind him as if unsure if Weylind's orders applied to the heir.

Weylind tilted his head in a hint of a nod, and the clerk's shoulders relaxed before he retreated out of sight.

Ryfon shifted from foot to foot, his gaze flicking from Weylind to the stacks of paperwork, then to the floor. "I was just wondering if the paperwork looks all right. I did the best I could."

A cold chill swept through Weylind as he took in the sight of his son, standing there so uncertain and desperate to please.

Machasheni was right. Weylind had been neglecting his family. Somehow, his son was nearly grown, and he had missed seeing most of it. All too soon, his son would reach adulthood, and Weylind would lose his chance to truly be a father to him the way he should have been all along.

Ryfon's face fell, and he shuffled back a step. "I see you are too busy."

Weylind shook himself. He had been lost too long in his ruminations. He could not let his son leave, thinking that once again Weylind had no time for him. Waving to the chairs across the desk, Weylind met Ryfon's gaze and smiled. "The paperwork was well done, sason. You and your macha did an excellent job with the kingdom while I was away. Come. Let us go through this paperwork together."

The crestfallen lines on Ryfon's face disappeared into a broad, beaming grin. He hurried across the room and perched on one of the chairs, all eagerness.

This was what Weylind should have been doing all along. Spending time with his son. Using that time to train him to be king someday. Being a father the way his father had been.

For the past number of years, Weylind had been a good king and brother, but a horrible father and husband.

That would have to change, starting now. He would have to let Farrendel go and trust someone else to look after him. It was beyond time that Weylind focused on his family.

WEYLIND STROLLED beside Ryfon as they wound their way from the study to the royal branch. The silence that fell between them remained warm and filled with the memories of spending the afternoon looking over reports and discussing politics and policies. The paper-work had been a lot more enjoyable, sorting through it with Ryfon.

As they stepped into the main room, Rheva turned toward them, that same neutral expression on her face that Weylind had seen all too often lately.

When had things become so empty between him and Rheva? They did not fight. They did not argue. But they did not laugh or spend all that much time together. They simply existed in a pleasant but empty neutral.

His fault. He had spared so little time and energy for his family in the past years. Only now was he seeing the damage such neglect had caused.

Was there still time to fix it? Or was he already too late?

Ryfon hurried through, heading for the door to his own room, still grinning.

As soon as Ryfon's door closed behind him, Weylind stepped forward and drew Rheva into his arms.

Her eyes widened, and she peered up at him, as if questioning what had brought this on.

Weylind rested his face against her hair, then pressed a light kiss to her temple. "I am so sorry. I have not devoted the time to you that I should have these past years."

Rheva remained stiff in his arms, her brow furrowed as she leaned back to peer at his face. "Your brother needed you. The kingdom needed you."

"Yes, but you needed me too. Do not deny it." Weylind held her close, meeting her gaze and trying to put all his regrets into his eyes and his tone.

"We managed." Rheva's shrug and the way her eyes dropped away from his sent another shaft of regret through him.

He had not even realized how much he needed to repair until Machasheni had pointed the fractures out to him. He should have seen it sooner.

"You should not have had to merely manage." Weylind stepped back and cradled Rheva's face. "I am sorry for all my neglect and inattention these past years. You have been the oak tree for our family, carrying so."

A tear trickled down Rheva's face, and he swiped it away with his thumb.

He had wounded her. He had wounded his children. And he had not even realized how much he was hurting them until now.

He had tried so hard not to make the same mistakes as his dacha. And yet, he had made his own, just as terrible ones. He might not have neglected the kingdom as Dacha had done, but Weylind had done something worse. He had neglected his family.

Another tear trickled down Rheva's face, then she wrapped her arms around Weylind and pressed her face against his shoulder.

He held her tight, resting his cheek against her hair. He had caused so much hurt.

But, perhaps, with the wars ended and peace at both borders, he could focus on his family and repair the damage.

"Then Dacha filled the tree with his magic, and the whole tree *moved*." Ryfon illustrated the story he was telling with his hands as he leaned forward, his brown eyes animated. "Its roots and everything just slithered through the ground as if the tree was walking. I cannot wait until I have enough control over my magic to make trees move."

Weylind smiled, relaxing into the warmth and eagerness of his children's chatter as his family ate supper together in their room, rather than in the large, formal dining room.

They still had supper twice a week with the rest of the family that was at Ellonahshinel, which was only Jalissa and Machasheni Leyleira at the moment. Jalissa's stewing silence and Machasheni's quiet probing made for rather awkward meals.

But in the months since Weylind had made more of a point to spend more time with Rheva, Ryfon, and Brina, these meals as a family had gotten louder, happier, brighter.

Beneath the table, Rheva's fingers clasped his, and he shared a smile with her. Her deep brown eyes held a warmth and sparkle that had been missing for far too long.

"I cannot wait until I come into my magic." Brina heaved a sigh down into her salad.

"Your magic will come, likely in the next decade or so." Rheva reached out and rested a hand on Brina's arm. "Whatever type of magic you have and however strong it is, it will be beautiful and amazing, as you are."

Brina gave an attempt at a smile, but her shoulders remained hunched.

As the oldest, Weylind had never experienced the frustration of waiting, magicless, while his siblings wielded their magic. But he had seen that frustration in Farrendel, especially, as he counted down the days until he came into his magic, like his siblings.

Only to find himself wielding magic beyond anything that any of them could have imagined.

Brina likely would not find herself in the same situation. Odds were, she would either inherit Weylind's plant magic or Rheva's healing magic. While Weylind would be proud of her no matter which magic she inherited, Weylind hoped she would have Rheva's magic. That particular strain of healing magic was unique in the way it worked, something that would be valuable and would serve Brina well as the second born who would have to find her own place in the world rather than have it mapped out for her the way Ryfon's was.

"Magic gives you another talent, but it does not define who you are. You determine how your magic is used, once you come into it." Weylind glanced between his children, waiting for the light of understanding to brighten their eyes.

The words sank into Weylind's chest, even as his children nodded. He wished he had said this more to Farrendel when Farrendel had been growing up.

And, perhaps, Weylind needed to hear it as well. When he had come into his magic, there had been so much disappointment among the elven court that he had not inherited the magic of the ancient kings. Perhaps he had absorbed more of that disappointment than he had realized. Not that he had ever been jealous of Farrendel and his magic, yet…

Was there a part of Weylind that wished he had inherited the magic of the ancient kings? That he was the one heralded as Tarenhiel's hero and lauded for the strength of his magic?

Weylind was content with his magic. He was strong, and with his plant magic, he could care for the forests of Tarenhiel in a way that he could not have with another type of magic. So what if his magic was not the thing of stories and legends? One did not have to become a legend to live a good life.

"Your dacha is correct." Rheva met Weylind's gaze, squeezing his hand under the table where Ryfon and Brina would not see. After a moment, she turned back to Ryfon. "I am glad you enjoyed the day with your dacha."

Ryfon nodded, that eagerness back to his expression. "It was so cool working with Estyra's maintenance workers, planning out new paths and sculpting the trees to better support walkways and homes. On the north side of Estyra, there are trees that they are infusing with magic so that in a hundred years, the trees will be big enough so Estyra can expand in that direction."

"That sounds like so much fun." Brina stabbed at her salad again. "All Macha and I did today was have various meetings with the cook and the staff for running Ellonahshinel."

Rheva raised her eyebrows at Brina, her mouth pressed into an amused line. "Are you saying the job of queen is boring?"

Brina shifted, wincing. "Well, that part is. Touring the

healing clinics in Estyra and making sure they have what they need was interesting. I liked that part."

"Every job has its boring parts. Just ask your dacha." Rheva flicked another glance at Weylind, her eyes twinkling with suppressed amusement.

"Yes." Ryfon was the one who heaved a weary sigh. "Today was a lot of fun, but the last few days have just been stacks upon stacks of paperwork. And there will be more paperwork because of today."

"That is the job of a king." Weylind could not help his own smile at his son's put-upon weariness. He turned to Brina. "Tomorrow we will switch things up. Brina, you will spend the day with me. King Averett sent me a proposal to make elf and human tourism between Tarenhiel and Escarland feasible. Your uncle Farrendel and aunt Elspetha sent some notes along as well. I would like you to help me go over the notes and brainstorm ideas."

Brina's eyes lit up, her posture straightening. "Really?"

"Yes." Weylind was not sure what he felt about Brina's fascination with Escarland and its culture and people. On the one hand, she was an elven princess who should be concerned with her own kingdom.

On the other hand, this alliance with Escarland was the future. Her generation would grow up interacting with humans far more than Weylind's had. Perhaps an elf princess with a love for human culture was exactly what Tarenhiel needed. It would likely be the younger elves, like Brina, who would be most interested in traveling to Escarland and seeing the sights.

Which was why he wanted Brina's perspective on the tourism question.

Elven tourism to Escarland would not be much of an

issue, besides finding accommodations in wooden buildings.

But Tarenhiel was not prepared to handle waves of human tourists tromping around their pristine forests and creating chaos and noise in the serene elven cities. Weylind did not want to ban tourism entirely. He wanted to encourage humans to come and learn more about the elves and their ways, yet it had to be done in the right way to avoid destroying the very elven culture that Weylind wanted to share.

As Ryfon opened his mouth, a knock sounded on the door. Instantly, the entire family hushed, glancing in that direction.

Weylind pushed away from the table, then strode to the door.

When he opened it, one of his clerks stood there, holding a piece of paper. The clerk would not interrupt a family meal if it was not urgent.

Weylind kept his expression neutral. "Yes?"

The clerk held out a slip of paper. "One of the scouts from Kostaria has reported in."

Weylind took the paper, then quickly read it. As the words sank in, a chill settled into his bones.

There has been a coup. King Rharreth's cousin Drurvas has taken control of Khagniorth Stronghold. King Rharreth and Queen Melantha have disappeared. Word on the street is that they have been killed, but our Escarlish ally doubts this claim. He believes they are in hiding, and he is on his way to attempt to make contact.

Please advise on how we are to proceed.

"Weylind?"

He blinked, realizing that Rheva was now standing next to him, her hand on his arm, her eyes searching his face.

Wordlessly, Weylind handed over the paper.

Melantha was missing.

What if she had been killed in this coup? Weylind should never have agreed to marry her off to the troll king. The marriage had been King Rharreth's demand as part of the peace treaty, and it had seemed the solution at the time. After her betrayal of both Farrendel and the kingdom, Weylind could not simply take Melantha home as if nothing had happened. She had been willing. Farrendel had assured him that Rharreth was not like his brother Charvod.

Had Weylind condemned his sister to death the moment he had left her behind in Kostaria?

Beside him, Rheva stilled, her face paling. "You need to go."

Weylind nodded. Where should he go? Would rushing to the border do any good? None of them knew where Melantha was at the moment, much less if she was still alive.

Our Escarlish ally. That was code for Prince Edmund, who had remained behind in Kostaria with the Tarenhieli scouts to keep an eye on the trolls and give warning if they were about to break the fledgling peace.

If there was a coup in Kostaria, then Tarenhiel would need Escarland's help. At worst, Rharreth and Melantha were dead, this Drurvas was on the throne, and the war would begin again. At best, Tarenhiel and Escarland could send in a team to rescue Melantha and try to salvage the situation with Rharreth.

Either way, Weylind would need Averett's help—and Farrendel's. Whatever Tarenhiel and Escarland did, they would need Farrendel and his magic.

Weylind turned back to his family, a weight settling into his gut. "I am afraid we will have to put our plans on hold. I need to travel to Escarland within the hour." He hesitated, wishing he did not have to tell them the truth. But Ryfon and Brina were nearly adults, and there would be no hiding this from them. "There was a coup in Kostaria. Your aunt Melantha is missing."

CHAPTER
SEVENTEEN

Weylind faced the Escarlish train before him, its stack puffing smoke into the darkness of the midnight sky arching above. Behind Weylind, the Hydalla River rippled in the chill breeze sweeping to the west, the water an inky shimmer in the faint glow of the stars. The soldiers from the Escarlish outpost had assembled, providing an additional honor guard from the dock to the station besides the squadron of elven guards that surrounded Weylind.

This was the farthest Weylind had ever stepped into Escarland. Once he boarded that train, he would travel across Escarland and step foot into the very capital itself. He would be the first elf king to visit Aldon in centuries.

A momentous visit like this normally would call for fanfare and celebrations. Instead, Weylind intended to all but sneak into Aldon. It did not seem right to walk into Escarland amid a celebration while Melantha was missing and their kingdoms were at the brink of another war, if Rharreth and Melantha were indeed dead.

The celebration of the first official visit by the elf king

could wait. Averett had mentioned an official visit for the one-year anniversary of the peace treaty between Escarland and Tarenhiel in the spring. That would be time enough for such things.

Straightening his shoulders, Weylind stepped onto the train. A steward bowed to him, then showed him around the car, mentioning that King Averett's personal royal car had been sent for Weylind's comfort.

The sitting area at the front of the car was plush and sumptuous with well-upholstered couches and chairs in Escarlish red and trimmed in gold. The tables were oak and topped in marble. The sleeping compartment had a large bed. The only thing lacking was the water closet. It had a lavatory and a basin for washing up, but no shower. It seemed the Escarlish had yet to figure out running water on board trains.

Weylind caught a few hours of sleep before he rose with the dawn. The train's steward laid out a breakfast—a hot breakfast as per Escarlish custom, including eggs, sausage, and toast.

Once he finished the meal, Weylind took a seat and stared out the window, taking in the rolling, Escarlish hills, covered in a layer of snow. Occasionally, the train flashed past towns bustling with humans. The larger cities had stacks piercing the sky, puffing black smoke into the air from Escarlish industry.

So foreign compared to the quiet elven towns, clean air, and deep forest of Tarenhiel.

The Escarlish had helped rescue Farrendel. But would they do the same for Melantha?

WEYLIND CLIMBED down the steps of the train, his boots crunching on the gravel of the train station to the side of the ornate stone palace. He struggled to keep his face impassive after seeing the sprawl of the massive human city flash past the windows of the train.

He had heard Jalissa's reports and Farrendel's letters describing the city, but seeing it for himself was something altogether different.

A chill breeze swept over the castle wall, bringing with it the stench of refuse and the choking of coal dust. Barbaric city. Perhaps one part of the tourism initiative between their kingdoms would be a push to clean up Aldon to make it more palatable to elven visitors.

Only a handful of Escarlish guards and the Queen Mother stood there. While Weylind had asked for no fanfare, this was even less than he had been expecting. He had thought King Averett, at least, would be here to greet him.

Dressed in a wool coat, hat, mittens, and scarf, Queen Mother Ariana stepped forward with a smile. "Welcome to Escarland, Your Majesty. My son would have been here to greet you, but it seems the castle pond has frozen solidly enough for ice skating. He chose to join his siblings there."

Weylind tilted his head. That was understandable, especially given the news coming out of Kostaria. "I do not begrudge him. Can you take me to them?"

A casual meeting at the castle pond sounded far better than something stuffy and formal in the palace's foyer. There would be a time for such things, but not on this trip.

"Of course." The Queen Mother smiled, then set off on a path around Winstead Palace. The snow had been shoveled from the bricks while the sun had warmed them enough to melt it clear of any lingering puddles. Snow piled on either side of the path.

As they rounded the corner of the palace, the path turned to gravel and entered the forested parkland, though "forested" was a loose use of that word. The trees here were nothing compared to the trees of Tarenhiel. Most were only a few feet in diameter, with others even smaller.

Voices, lifted in cheery shouts and bursts of laughter, wafted on the breeze between the trees moments before a clearing and a frozen pond came into view.

Farrendel, his hair far longer than it had been the last time Weylind had seen him, whirled and raced across the pond. "Weylind! Shashon!"

Weylind stepped onto the pond, the beginning of a smile on his face at the sight of Farrendel so happy and grinning.

Farrendel partially skidded to a halt in front of him, ice dust thrown up by his skates. Then without warning, Farrendel hugged him. Not a sedate, elven hug. No, this was a full arm, human-style hug.

Weylind stiffened and glared at Elspetha over Farrendel's shoulder. What had these humans done to Farrendel while he was here? This was hardly normal.

Elspetha gave him a grin and a shrug. Utterly unrepentant.

After only a second, Farrendel yanked back, as if realizing what he had done. He gripped Weylind's shoulders instead. "Shashon, what are you—"

A flash of movement behind Farrendel caught Weylind's gaze. Averett and Julien were racing toward them, their backs to them.

"Look out!" Elspetha's shout gave enough warning for Farrendel to release Weylind and partially turn around.

But neither of them had enough time to move before Julien and Averett barreled into them. Someone's elbow slammed into Weylind's gut. Then he was falling, and his back slammed into the ground, barely cushioned by the layer of snow that puffed around him and shoved down the back of his neck. Bodies landed heavily on top of him, further expelling the rest of the air from his lungs.

Clumsy, undignified humans.

Weylind struggled to draw in a breath, but the bodies still piled on him made that difficult. He gasped and inhaled a mouthful of Farrendel's hair. He tried to push the others off him, but they were too heavy.

Then someone started laughing, shaking the whole pile on top of Weylind.

Great. Weylind did not see anything amusing about this situation.

But then Farrendel, too, joined in the laughter. The sound was so startling, so foreign, that Weylind stilled in his attempts to shove the others off him. When was the last time Weylind had heard Farrendel laugh? Not since Dacha had died, that was certain.

Faintly, above them, a voice that might have been Elspetha's, "Are you all right?"

Some of the weight lessened. Averett spoke through his chuckles. "Sorry. We were racing backwards and didn't see you."

More weight rolled off, followed by Julien saying, "Well, I say they shouldn't have been just standing and talking where we were racing."

"Really? Racing backwards?" Elspetha's voice held a laugh.

Finally Farrendel shoved off of Weylind, brushing

snow from the strands of his silver-blond hair. "You did not invite me to race."

"Of course not. You would win too easily." Julien dug a hat out of the snow.

Drawing in his first decent breath in far too long, Weylind sat upright and brushed at the snow coating his clothes, his hair, and trickling down the back of his neck as it melted on his skin.

But the sight of Averett, Julien, and Farrendel equally snow-covered and laughing nearly made Weylind lose his own composure and break into a grin unbecoming of an elf king.

Instead, he worked to keep his expression blank as he stared down his nose at Julien and Averett. "Of course. We elves are far superior."

"Keep telling yourself that." Averett grinned back without missing a beat.

Was this what it felt like to have friends? Weylind had always been the heir, then the king. That left little room for forming friendships. Everyone was always all too aware of his status.

While Farrendel had been scorned by the court, he, at least, had been free to form friendships among the warriors in a way Weylind had not.

But with Averett and Julien, there was no barrier of rank. And, strangely, they seemed to adopt him as part of the family after their experiences crossing Kostaria. He supposed that piling together for warmth would do that.

Farrendel turned to Weylind, his brow scrunching as his grin faded. "Shashon, what are you doing here? Is something amiss in Tarenhiel?"

Weylind pressed his hands into the snow, preparing to push himself to standing. But at Farrendel's words, he froze.

It had been such a relief to see the grinning, laughing Farrendel of a few moments ago. When Farrendel had left, he had been a shell of himself. Now, he was alive and smiling and so much more than he had been in the past fifteen years.

Weylind did not want to destroy this moment, not yet anyway.

Over Farrendel's shoulder, Weylind met Averett's gaze. Averett shook his head, his mouth briefly pressing into a tight line.

The Escarlish king had not received any news while Weylind had been traveling. Melantha was lost, and hurrying to the border was not going to change that fact. Until the scouts found her, until they received word from Escarland's spy prince, there was nothing Weylind nor Farrendel could do.

Besides, the Escarlish train needed more coal and water. It also needed to be taken to the engine house, turned around, and inspected before it could leave again to carry them back north.

There was no reason to rush the telling. Weylind could afford to take a few minutes to set aside the weight he always carried as a king. Perhaps he could remember what it was like to laugh with his brother. "It can wait. For now, there is nothing any of us can do."

Farrendel's jaw flexed as he got that stubborn look, as if he thought Weylind was treating him like a child. "Weylind..."

For once, Weylind was not hiding this because he wanted to smother Farrendel or protect him or anything of the sort. He would tell Farrendel, when it was time. "Truly. There is nothing you can do. We will discuss it later."

Right now, Weylind wanted his brother back, like it

used to be. Before the wars. Before Dacha's death. Before both he and Farrendel had forgotten what it was like to laugh and live rather than merely exist beneath their burdens.

To that end, Weylind began quietly gathering a handful of snow, using his body to hide the movement. "Right now, I do believe you should enjoy the rest of this morning."

Before Farrendel could catch on, Weylind threw the snow right into Farrendel's face. While Farrendel was still blinking, Weylind jumped to his feet and sprinted out of Farrendel's reach.

"No fair!" Farrendel fumbled with his skates, trying to get them off. But a hint of a smile twitched his mouth.

Weylind scooped several more snowballs, tossing them one after the other at Farrendel.

Farrendel shouted through the barrage, his shoulders hunched around his neck as if to protect himself from the snow. "I am still wearing skates!"

Weylind was going to be in trouble once Farrendel got those skates off.

But, for now, he just kept scooping snow and throwing it as fast as he could. How he had missed laughter. Joy. Family.

Life.

WEYLIND PROBABLY SHOULD NOT HAVE INVADED Farrendel's space on top of the train as it glided its way north to the Tarenhieli-Kostarian border.

But the peace he had felt in Escarland had faded as a tightening filled his chest the closer they got to Kostaria. Not even Elspetha's teasing with that horrific mug—elf ears on the side of a mug, utterly dreadful—had been able to banish the worries entirely.

They had yet to receive word about Melantha. To make matters worse, Prince Edmund had also gone missing, something that he and Averett had yet to tell the others.

Then there was Farrendel's shocking announcement that he planned to take classes at that Escarlish university. Such a thing was unheard of.

All of that had created the urge to speak with Farrendel alone. And that meant climbing up here on the train and joining Farrendel's exercises, daring flipping over branches and dodging leaves.

The exercise had loosened Weylind's muscles and the squeezing worry inside his chest.

He ducked under a branch, glancing at Farrendel as he did, his questions about Hanford University still lingering around them.

Farrendel met his gaze, even as the branch whisked over their heads. "I need to do this, Weylind. Not just for me. But for any children Essie and I might have. The odds are high that it is my magic they will inherit."

Now that was the heart of Farrendel's reasoning for going to this Escarlish university. Not just the political reasons. Not just the magical breakthroughs it could make for both Escarland and Tarenhiel.

But for the family he hoped to have someday.

It was a lesson Farrendel had learned well from Dacha. To put his family first and do what was best for them.

A lesson Weylind was in the process of re-learning.

He let himself smirk, raising an eyebrow at Farrendel. "Are you trying to tell me you and Essie will have yet another announcement to make before long?"

Using Elspetha's nickname felt strange but also strangely right. After the snowball fight, and that dreadful mug, Essie was his isciena, as much as the isciena he was rushing to the border to save.

"I..." The tips of Farrendel's ears flushed pink, and his gaze dropped to the train's rooftop. "No...we are not..." A shaky breath, exhaled on a slight laugh. "Maybe someday. But if or when that happens, I do not want my children to be as alone and lost with their magic as I was."

Farrendel's words sliced through him, stealing the mirth of a few moments ago.

Alone and lost. And Weylind had been unable to help his brother.

"I am sorry you ever thought you were alone." Weylind braced himself on one knee and a hand on the rooftop, bowing his head with the weight of the past, his failures. "I failed you. I failed Melantha. Were all my siblings miserable, and I did not notice?"

How had he not noticed? If he had, would he have been able to fix things? Could he have changed the pain his family had endured because of Melantha's betrayal, Farrendel's struggles?

Then again, he had noticed, at least some of it. He had spent the last fifteen years neglecting his own family as he tried to keep his siblings together. It seemed that for all his sacrifices, he had succeeded in nothing but creating more damage.

Farrendel sat cross-legged on top of the train, his hair blowing out behind him, seemingly impervious to the cold wind even though he was shirtless.

Weylind sat as well, the cold breeze tugging through his hair and cutting through his clothes. Perhaps if he sat there long enough, the wind would scour away his guilt.

Farrendel shook his head, the silver puff of his breath

whisked away by the train's passing. "Perhaps you did not notice because you were miserable too."

Those words struck a little too true.

Weylind had to pause, catch his breath, and absorb the pain of the revelations as they tore away his blindness to his own faults.

He, too, had been hurting. He had walled himself off, surviving as best he could. His siblings had suffered. His wife and children had suffered.

Farrendel had worked hard, there in Escarland, to get to the place where he was now. Weylind needed to work equally hard to repair his own relationships. And, perhaps, on his own healing.

"Perhaps." Weylind let the single word flow into him, the truth of it easing some of his guilt and pain. He could not change the past. But he could change going forward.

After a moment, he leaned forward and gripped Farrendel's shoulders, holding his gaze. "No matter the cost, our family would not have been complete without you. Never doubt that, shashon."

Weylind should have said those words to Farrendel a long time ago.

When—and Weylind had to believe it would be when —they found Melantha, he would make sure he said what needed to be said to her as well.

The time for holding back was long past.

CHAPTER
EIGHTEEN

PRETENSE

Weylind lifted his hand, giving a regal wave to the crowds of Escarlish citizens crowding the walks on either side of the street. Thankfully, the moss Weylind had stuffed in his ears prevented the noise of all the cheering people from reaching deafening levels, but even through the moss it was cacophonous.

At his side, Rheva smiled and waved as well, her crown resting on her head in a match to the regal drape of her dark green dress and even darker cape, embroidered with Tarenhiel's silver tree emblem.

On horses ahead of them, Farrendel and Essie rode side by side while Averett and Paige rode in a white, open-topped carriage. Behind Weylind and Rheva, Rharreth and Melantha also waved and smiled for the gathered Escarlish crowds. Marching bands, twirling dancers, elf and troll warriors, squads of Escarlish soldiers, and decorated carriages of all kinds filled out the rest of the parade.

Guards provided a thick, wary cordon around them. With all three kings in this parade through Aldon's streets, they would make for a tempting target for anyone unhappy with the peace treaties.

But so far, the citizens of Aldon had remained pleasant and cheering. It seemed the celebratory mood had swept the crowds up in fervor. The declaration of a national holiday to commemorate the one-year anniversary of the peace treaty might have something to do with the carnival atmosphere.

But Weylind would take welcoming, cheering crowds over the alternative. If that meant putting on a good show to please the crowds, then that was what he would do. Let them jostle for their sight of an elf king, a troll king, a human king, and their queens all riding in a parade together for the first time in living memory.

As she sat on a wooden bench before a crackling fire built in the campsite in the forested parkland, Rheva could not remember the last time she had chatted with someone as easily as she chatted with Paige, Queen of Escarland. Like Rheva, Paige had not come from a noble family, and the Escarlish court, too, subtly never let her forget her humble origins.

It felt so good to talk with someone who knew the same struggles that Rheva did. Since Paige was not an elf, Rheva was free to talk openly with her in a way that she could not with someone who was a subject.

Could Paige become a friend? Weylind had bonded—

rather shockingly—with King Averett. Perhaps Rheva, too, would find a friend with the Escarlish royalty.

Next to Rheva, Weylind stuck and unstuck his fingers together, glaring at them even as he kept up a conversation with Averett, sitting on the far side of Paige.

"I'm glad you and Weylind came for the celebrations." Paige smiled, then gestured at the gathering around the campfire. "You're welcome in Escarland any time."

Rheva smiled in return. "I am sure we will visit Escarland again. You and Averett are, of course, welcome to visit Estyra."

"I would like that. Avie has seen Estyra, and Essie has waxed eloquent about its beauty, making me all the more eager to see it for myself." Paige's smile widened to a grin as she leaned closer. "I'm sure we will visit when Essie and Farrendel's baby is born."

"Yes." Rheva shot a glance to where Farrendel and Essie sat on a bench across the fire. The two of them were tucked closely together, and Essie had her head on Farrendel's shoulder as she blinked a bit sleepily at the gathering.

It would be good to see Farrendel grow into the role of father. Rheva suspected that he and Weylind would bond in a new way once they reached more similar stages in life.

Over the past months, Weylind had stepped back into the role of father in a way he had not in decades. Each time he and Ryfon returned from magic practice with matching smiles or Rheva walked into the king's study to find Brina and Weylind bent over notes on preparing Tarenhiel for Escarlish tourism, she fell just a little bit more in love with her husband.

As Farrendel and Essie stood, voicing their goodnights, Paige sighed, smiled, and pushed to her feet as well. "We ought to get Bertie and Finn to bed. It is way past their bedtime."

Partway around the fire, the little boy Finn had fallen to sleep in Brina's lap while Bertie was sitting next to Ryfon and sporting a marshmallow and chocolate smeared face and equally sticky fingers.

After a round of goodnights and promises to meet up the next day for various fighting bouts or shopping trips, Averett, Paige, their children, Julien, Rharreth, and Melantha headed for Winstead Palace while Essie and Farrendel disappeared into the darkness, wandering toward Buckmore Cottage.

That left Weylind, Rheva, Ryfon, and Brina alone around the campsite, the forest falling quiet for the first time all evening.

Weylind sighed and shot a glance down at his sticky fingers. "I suppose there is no place to wash our hands."

Brina jumped up, hopped over a bench, then knelt by the pile of supplies the Escarlish royal family had left for them. After digging through it, she held up a canteen. "Would this work? There are six canteens in here, so more than enough water for tonight."

Weylind nodded, grimacing down at his fingers. "Yes."

Rheva relaxed onto the bench as Weylind, Ryfon, and Brina poured water over each other's hands to wash away the stickiness of the marshmallows. Ryfon took the longest. No surprise, since he had eaten nearly as many marshmallows as Bertie had.

This was everything she had yearned for in those long years of war and loneliness.

Once his fingers were clean, Weylind returned to the bench beside her. In an uncharacteristic—but not unwelcome—gesture, he put his arm around her shoulders and drew her closer.

If he wanted to snuggle in front of the children, then she was not going to argue.

Brina perched on a bench across from them, opening her palms to the warmth of the fire. "Touring Aldon today was so neat! I hope we will have a chance to see more while we are here."

"Tomorrow, we will visit with everyone at Winstead Palace. But the day after that, Queen Paige invited the two of us to browse the shopping district of Aldon with her." Rheva leaned her head against Weylind's shoulder, soaking in his warmth as the night grew chilly around them. "We can either join your aunts Essie and Melantha on their hot chocolate expedition or branch off on our own if we want to see other things."

It had been a welcome invitation, though slightly daunting. The human city was far more crowded, noisy, and intimidating than Estyra. Thankfully, they would have a day to recuperate quietly here in the sanctuary of Winstead Palace before braving those crowds again.

Brina grinned, bouncing a little in her excitement. "Yes!" She glanced at Weylind. "I will make a note of anything that strikes me as important for our tourism initiatives."

Weylind shook his head. "Do not feel like you need to work, sena. Enjoy the day in Aldon. If you happen to have any insights, then take note. But do not sacrifice your day with your macha and Queen Paige."

Brina nodded, her smile briefly fading into a more solemn expression.

Rheva reached out and took Weylind's hand, squeezing his fingers. He had gained wisdom over the past year.

"What about us?" Ryfon gestured from Weylind to himself. "Are we going into Aldon?"

"If you wish. But first, we will join Prince Julien, your uncle Farrendel, and King Rharreth for morning practice."

"Yes!" Ryfon pumped his fist, grinning as he shared a look with Brina.

Weylind gestured to the stack of supplies. "Sason, would you please grow the shelters for yourself and your sister tonight?"

Ryfon stilled, eyes widening. "By myself?"

"I will help if you need it, but I do not think you will." Weylind's smile dug lines around his mouth, but these lines were so much better than the haggard, deeply etched grooves that had become so permanent before. "Sena, you can help him set up camp."

Shoulders straightening, Ryfon hopped from the bench, facing the forest. He considered the trees for a long moment before he marched over to a tree, his magic flickering green and bright in the darkness.

Brina, too, left the fire, then knelt beside the supplies, sorting through them.

In the quiet and semi-privacy next to the fire, Rheva squeezed Weylind's fingers once again. "We should have done something like this long ago."

"Yes." Weylind leaned his head against hers as they watched their children discuss the best way to fashion a mini shelter and lay out the tarpaulins and bedrolls. "I am sorry I was not present before to think of such things."

"You are present now. That is what matters." Rheva blinked, fighting back the rising emotion squeezing her chest. "This past winter was...it was..."

She could not put it into words. But she did not need

them. Through their elishina, she knew that he knew her heart.

His lips lightly brushed a kiss to her temple before he murmured against her hair. "This past winter was how our family always should have been. I am sorry I did not see that earlier."

Rheva straightened so that she could hold his gaze, their faces inches apart. "No more apologies. You are not the only one at fault. I was so afraid of placing more burdens on you that I did not speak up when I should have. I should have taken a stand instead of staying silent."

"Shh." Weylind leaned his forehead against hers. "Do not take blame that does not lie with you. Perhaps there were things that we both could have done better, but while you were surviving the problem, I *was* the problem. Do not deny it."

She could not help the soft laugh at that. "All right. If you want the blame, I am not going to argue."

"I thought you were supposed to be learning the lesson that you need to be more assertive and argue with me." Weylind's mouth tipped into a smile that held just a hint of the mischief he used to have long ago.

Rheva pulled back from him and raised her eyebrows, wishing she could manage that stern, one-eyebrow look that Machasheni Leyleira wielded with such expertise. "Now you are just being contrary."

"Is contrary better than grumpy?" Weylind leaned a bit closer, as if he was about to kiss her.

"That remains to be seen." Rheva found herself swaying closer as well, her fingers burying themselves in the warmth of Weylind's shirt.

Yet only moments from kissing her, Weylind halted, his gaze flicking to something past her. He sighed, but the smile remained. "Our children are watching. Well, trying very hard not to watch."

Her ears burning, Rheva yanked away from Weylind, then smoothed her hands over her dress. Only once she regained some of her composure did she dare glance at Ryfon and Brina.

They had their backs to the fire, standing in front of two small shelters grown a few feet off the ground and occasionally peeking over their shoulders.

Perhaps it was healthy for them to witness her and Weylind being so affectionate. But Rheva was still uncomfortable with that level of affection in front of others, especially Ryfon and Brina.

Weylind leaned close and murmured, "We will continue this discussion after I build our shelter."

Rheva nodded mutely, her ears still fiery hot despite the cool breeze wafting through the trees.

Yet as Weylind pushed to his feet and joined Ryfon and Brina, Rheva could not help but smile, reveling in the sweetness of this moment.

Her husband and her family had come a long way in the past months. Hopefully this would continue to be their new beginning, even as it was a new beginning for their kingdom.

WEYLIND CLEARED his throat and rested a hand on Ryfon's shoulder. "You did well, sason. These are well designed."

The two shelters both stood about two feet off the ground, balancing on a sturdy array of living saplings. Low walls surrounded the platform while the peaked roof balanced on more poles, leaving most of the sides open to the night air. Ryfon had added a layer of his magic to deter bugs and keep the shelters snug.

Inside of each shelter, the bedrolls had been set up with Ryfon's and Brina's packs set at the end of each of the shelters they had claimed.

"Brina helped. She suggested the open sides and the shape of the roof." Ryfon waved from Brina to the shelters.

"I did not do all that much." Brina shifted, shrugging. But her smile gave away her pleasure.

"You both did well." Weylind rested his other hand on Brina's shoulder, hoping that his pride in them came through in his tone.

His children were growing up, and he could not take much of the credit for the kind, helpful people they had become. That had been all Rheva's doing.

"Perhaps we can camp out like this in Estyra sometime." Brina glanced from Ryfon to Weylind, a glimmer of hope in her eyes.

"That would be fun." Ryfon, too, turned his gaze on Weylind.

Weylind hesitated. If they camped in the forest outside of Estyra, it likely would not be nearly as peaceful as this. His clerks would still know where to track him down to foist more paperwork on him.

If he wanted a true holiday, they would have to venture farther afield.

It would be something to think about. The family trips to Lethorel each summer were supposed to be a time for such relaxation, but with the whole extended family there, the holidays there provided little opportunity to enjoy spending time together as a family.

Perhaps an additional trip to Lethorel with just their family would be the solution. That was what Lethorel was supposed to be. A haven. A place to rest before returning to the duties waiting for the royal family in Ellonahshinel.

Or maybe he should become more creative. It had been many years since Weylind had toured the ocean coast and the western forests of Tarenhiel with his dacha and macha, back when Melantha was still little and Weylind had been barely over a hundred years old. Those regions were long overdue for a visit from their king, and with peace on both borders, Weylind actually had the freedom to travel.

He could picture his family disappearing into the forest between the towns, camping just like this with their guards stationed in a cordon farther out. It would be an experience for all of them, that was for sure.

"A night in the forest outside of Estyra would be a start." Weylind dropped his hands from his children's shoulders. "If we find we enjoy such excursions, perhaps we can take on a larger adventure in a year or two."

"Really?" Brina's grin somehow managed to get even wider.

Ryfon pumped his fist again, his grin matching Brina's.

Weylind nodded, then wished his children goodnight. As Ryfon and Brina clambered into their shelters, he circled the fire and entered the forest on the far side. Here, he pressed his hand to a tree, then willed his magic into growing a similar shelter to the ones Ryfon had formed.

As he finished, he opened his eyes and found Rheva standing there, toting an armload of blankets and bedrolls. She climbed inside and set to work laying out their bed while he fetched their packs. He took the time to scatter the ashes of the fire, then threw dirt on the coals to smother them to prevent any accidental forest fires.

By the time he returned, Rheva had laid out the bedrolls and now lay beneath the blankets.

Weylind set their packs at the foot of the bed, tugged off his boots, then slid beneath the blankets beside her.

Rheva snuggled closer, releasing a sigh. "Tonight was wonderful."

"It was." Weylind wrapped his arms around Rheva, tucking her closer still. Time to return to their discussion from the fire. "Thank you for putting up with me all these years. You stood by me through some hard times the past decade and a half."

"They were hard. But your brother needed you." Rheva clasped his hand, her words soft in the darkness.

Through the open windows of their shelter, a scattering of stars peeked through the foliage overhead, lighting their shelter enough for Weylind to make out the faint outline of Rheva's face.

"Yes. But you needed me too, and I never should have forgotten that." Weylind propped himself on an elbow to face her and brushed a strand of her hair from her cheek. "I know I have not said it nearly enough, but I love you. I have never forgotten that, even while I forgot that love means being present."

Rheva blinked up at him, their faces only inches apart. "I never stopped loving you either."

He did not deserve her. But instead of letting the guilt consume him, he would turn that emotion toward loving her better from now on.

He cradled her face with a hand, then leaned down to kiss her.

But Rheva pressed both hands to his chest, stopping him. "The children," she hissed into the space between them.

Weylind pressed a hand to the wall of the shelter.

Flaps swung down softly, whispering shut and enfolding him and Rheva in nearly complete darkness, lit only by the green of his magic threaded through the branches. "I added a few upgrades to Ryfon's design."

Rheva gave a light laugh. "I see that."

Then, before anything else could interrupt, Weylind kissed her. He looked forward to falling in love with his wife anew, both now and for years to come.

NINETEEN

Weylind strolled into his study, sinking into the chair behind his desk with a sigh. After a long moment of gathering his courage, he reached into the bag and pulled out the elf ear mug that Averett had given him—the mug that Weylind was supposed to display since he had lost the wager he had going with the Escarlish king.

This elf ear mug was even uglier than the one that Essie had gifted Weylind last winter—the one he had promptly passed along to Melantha. Both mugs were sculpted out of ceramic with pointed ears sticking out of either side.

But this mug was a patchy white and silver and garishly veined in both red and green. It appeared to be an attempt to meld the elven colors of green and silver with the Escarlish colors of white and red. The attempt had not yielded a pleasant result.

After seeing this mug, Weylind had no regrets about how scarily ugly the lamp he had fashioned for Averett turned out to be. Now it would be greatly appreciated if Farrendel and Essie had a boy so that Averett would be stuck with that lamp on his desk and Weylind did not have to display this mug longer than absolutely necessary.

With one last sigh, Weylind placed the mug front and center on his desk.

Oh, well. At least every time Weylind caught a glimpse of this mug monstrosity, he would be reminded that it was there because Farrendel and Elspetha were expecting their first child. His brother was happy, healing, pursuing a new interest in magical engineering, and creating a home with Essie and their unborn child.

Reaching into his bag again, Weylind fished out the Escarlish pencils that Rheva and Brina had purchased for him on their shopping trip in Aldon. A few of the pencils were the standard Escarlish pencil, a carved stick of wood filled with graphite and wrapped in red paper. But several of the pencils were knobby sticks, which had been hollowed out for the graphite. Apparently, someone had been selling them as "elven" pencils.

Of all the ridiculous notions. That was entirely a marketing gimmick.

As was becoming increasingly clear from the elf ear mugs and now these elven pencils, the Escarlish people gobbled up gimmicks and knickknacks and such things. Mind-boggling. But it was something he could use to Tarenhiel's advantage.

A soft knock, then his head clerk stepped into the study. "It is good to have you back, Daresheni. I—" The clerk's gaze dropped to the mug. His eyes widened, and his voice cut off.

Weylind stared, daring the clerk to say anything.

The clerk gave a slight cough, then schooled his features again. "Is there anything you need, Daresheni?"

"Not at the moment." Weylind would need a few minutes to sort through the paperwork that had piled up during his absence.

But first...he glanced up and smiled as Brina ducked around the clerk, a pile of papers in her arms. "Sena."

She plunked the papers on his desk next to the mug, plopped into a chair, then grinned. "I have so many ideas. I know you told me not to work on the shopping trip, but I could not help it. I was so inspired with lots of ideas."

"I thought you would be." Weylind took out his own sheet of notes, then claimed one of the Escarlish pencils. He might as well get into the mood of the moment. "What items do you think we should focus on for Escarlish tourists?"

Brina's grin widened, and she flipped to a page where an exhaustive list filled the entire page. "So many things! You should have seen Aldon, Dacha. The humans will buy anything. And I mean anything. One shop was selling fancy seats for Escarlish lavatories that were enameled with ornate patterns. Some were even veined in real gold. I suppose the Escarlish nobles need to show off their wealth even in their lavatory fixtures, but it was still very strange."

Weylind relaxed into his chair, smiling as he listened to his daughter wax eloquent about her ideas.

Shield Band

"You are not going to give me a hint?" Weylind eyed Rheva as they strolled through the network of

Ellonahshinel's branches. At the early hour, the branches were lit with elven lights embedded in the wood while a chilly breeze brushed his hair. Few elves were out and about.

Weylind clasped her first two fingers, the backs of their hands pressed together in a way they rarely did when in public, even if the gesture was acceptable for elves. Usually, they were more aware of being king and queen rather than husband and wife.

But recently, he had found himself more and more willing to throw away such rigid propriety to stroll hand-in-hand with his wife. Perhaps it was Essie and Farrendel's example. Or maybe it was the new closeness he and Rheva shared. At times, it even felt like their elishina had deepened, though he was not sure if that sense was more hope than reality.

Rheva shook her head, her mouth pressed into a line as if she was fighting her smile. "You will see soon enough when we arrive."

"Yes, but it is not fair that you know and I do not."

"We are still the first ones to know. The rest of the family will have to wait for the telegrams. So it is hardly unfair." Rheva's eyes had taken on a decided twinkle now.

He could not argue with that. Even if a part of him anticipated sending that telegram to Averett, either rubbing in his win or assuring him that the mug was now once again on his desk.

They remained quiet as they strolled the rest of the way through the nearly silent treetop palace until they reached Farrendel and Essie's rooms.

Weylind knocked on the door. Would Farrendel and Essie still be awake? They had a long night so far.

But within moments, the door swung open to reveal Farrendel standing there, a bundle topped with a fluff of brilliant red hair in his arms. He did not speak, merely stepped aside in an invitation to enter.

Rheva smiled at Farrendel, gently touched a finger to the baby's cheek, then nodded, as if satisfied with the baby's health check. "Is Essie still resting?"

Farrendel nodded, still mute, his eyes strangely haunted for someone holding his newborn.

Rheva hurried past him, then disappeared up the stairs.

Farrendel retreated across the room and sank onto a cushion, leaning against the wall as he cradled the baby in his arms.

Weylind quietly closed the door, crossed the room, and lowered himself to sit on one of the other cushions a few feet away. He did not say anything but just sat, waiting.

Finally, Farrendel raised his head and met Weylind's gaze. "I have a son."

So much depth of wonder and grief in those words, holding a wealth of memories of their dacha, the decisions he made to protect his sons, the sacrifice of his death.

Weylind reached out and rested a hand on Farrendel's shoulder. "Dacha would have been proud of you today, shashon."

A single tear trickled down Farrendel's cheek, and he reached up and swiped it away before cradling his son in both arms again.

Weylind swallowed, his voice going hoarse. "This is what Dacha wanted for you. It is why he sacrificed himself to rescue you. He wanted you to have a life, to have a wife and children if you so desired. To thrive. You can probably better understand that, now, holding your own son. You would give your life for him, as Dacha gave his life for you."

Farrendel nodded, blinking rapidly though no more tears fell.

Weylind let the silence linger for another moment longer. Then he smiled, banishing his own melancholy thoughts. "May I hold him?"

Farrendel shook himself, then nodded. He leaned forward, carefully transferring the newborn into Weylind's arms. "Keep his head supported."

Weylind gave a soft laugh as the baby's small weight settled into his arms. "I have held babies before, shashon. I did not break you, and I will not break your son."

"Right, yes." Farrendel's smile held a sheepish tilt.

Weylind took in the round, squishy face of the baby boy in his arms. The tips of tiny pointed ears poked through the shock of red hair that topped the baby's head. His first nephew. "What is his name?"

"Fieran." Farrendel gripped his knees, as if it was a struggle to just sit there while his newborn son was in someone else's arms.

He would have to get used to seeing his son passed around. Once the rest of the family descended, everyone would want to hold Fieran, if only for a few minutes. Having a child was certainly going to test Farrendel's anxieties and protective instincts.

Weylind had found himself tested and growing by raising his children. He still was.

Footsteps sounded on the stairs a moment before Essie, followed by Rheva, entered the main room.

Essie smiled, then eased to a seat next to Farrendel. "I see you have met our Fieran."

"Yes. It is quite the appropriate name." Weylind tried

really hard not to smile. Fire hair. It was, indeed, quite the proper elf name for a son born with such vibrant hair.

Weylind would enjoy sending that message to Averett.

EPILOGUE

11 YEARS AFTER FH

Weylind attempted to concentrate on the paperwork on his desk, but it was an impossible feat with the baby fussing and squirming in his arms.

He bounced his knee but that did little to calm the baby's fussing.

Weylind set aside his pen and held out his six-month-old son in both hands, examining him. "You have been fed. Burped. You do not need a change."

Emmyth, being only six months old, did not answer but arched his back and squirmed more.

That was probably answer enough.

The baby was bored and wanted to be set down to play.

"I agree. Paperwork is quite boring." Weylind propped Emmyth against his chest, then pushed to his feet. The kingdom would be just fine if he took the rest of the afternoon off. It was not like the paperwork was going anywhere if he left it for tomorrow.

Today, Rheva was enjoying some child-free time with Jalissa and Essie. Weylind might as well enjoy some rather child-saturated time with Farrendel.

Though *enjoy* might be too strong of a word. Perhaps *survive* would be more appropriate.

Weylind grabbed the bag filled with supplies for Emmyth, then strode from the study.

As he shut the door, he nodded to the clerk that was hurrying his way on the branch. "I will be out of the study the rest of the day."

"Very good, Daresheni." The clerk bowed, then hurried off in the other direction.

The clerk did not ask where Weylind would be, and Weylind did not offer the information. The clerks would think to check Farrendel and Essie's rooms if something urgent developed, though they would likely draw straws for the unfortunate volunteer.

Weylind nodded at several elves as he passed, but he did not stop to speak. Emmyth's wiggling and fussing increased the longer he was held.

Weylind strode past the branch that led to the set of rooms he had helped Jalissa grow for her and Edmund. It was near enough to Farrendel and Essie's rooms that walking between them was convenient, but far enough that neither set of rooms could see or hear each other, giving both families the privacy they wanted by moving onto branches all the way at the edge of Ellonahshinel.

There were times Weylind envied them. As king, he did not have the luxury of living away from the constant scrutiny at the center of Ellonahshinel. At least he found times when he could escape, from afternoons spent hiding in Farrendel and Essie's set of rooms to visiting Escarland.

Even as Weylind stepped onto Farrendel and Essie's porch, the sounds of shrieking rang from inside. He rapped on the door loudly enough that hopefully Farrendel could hear it over the utter chaos of whatever was going on inside.

The noise level rose in pitch as the door swung open. Farrendel stood there, his shirt rumpled and smeared with something wet and sticky. He held his eight-month-old daughter Louise in one arm. She had a fistful of Farrendel's hair, alternating between tugging it and stuffing it in her mouth. Farrendel did not even bother to disentangle her fingers and just wearily tilted his head to minimize the tugging.

Behind Farrendel, the two older children Fieran and Adry screamed like little terrors as they chased each other around the room, occasionally climbing up the walls before jumping down, landing as if a drop of ten feet was nothing.

For a long moment Farrendel just stood there, bracing himself against the door frame and blinking.

"Shashon." Weylind adjusted his grip on Emmyth, who was wiggling in earnest now, eager to get down and play with his cousin. "I had forgotten how much work babies are. I blame you."

"Me? I had nothing to do with..." Farrendel trailed off, wearily gesturing at Emmyth.

"There you were with all your babies and young children and Rheva got baby fever again and, well..." Weylind shrugged. "A third child seemed like a good idea at the time."

A high-pitched shriek came from directly over Farrendel's head. Without even looking, much less flinching, Farrendel reached out and snagged Fieran from the air as the boy plunged downward.

Farrendel did not break eye contact with Weylind as he set a laughing Fieran on his feet. "*This* looked like a good idea?"

"I see we were mistaken." Even as he said it, Weylind could not help the twitch of a smile. Despite their weary joking, he knew neither he nor Farrendel regretted parenthood in the least.

Weylind braced himself as Fieran turned to him, as if just realizing he was there.

"Uncle Weylind!" Fieran raced to him and hugged his leg.

"Uncle Weylind?" More thumping came from inside, then Adry burst past Farrendel, her red-blonde hair flying, her green eyes gleaming. She scurried halfway up Weylind's leg before she clung there, grinning up at him. "Do the magic!"

Weylind pressed his hand to the wall. Branches shot from the walls and the ceiling, quickly forming branches that filled the whole space near the ceiling, turning it into a jungle for children to climb and explore.

Just below these branches, he formed a net of thin but sturdy roots just above head height as a safety feature, just in case either of the children should fall. Though considering Farrendel's childhood antics, the safety part was more for any adults who might get squashed by falling children rather than for the children themselves.

Fieran launched himself off Weylind's leg, darting for the door. Adry raced in his wake.

Farrendel snagged the back of Fieran's shirt, then stuck out a foot to halt Adry. "What do you say to your uncle?"

Fieran twisted around, giving a slight wave. "Linshi!"

Adry beamed a beatific smile up at Weylind. "Linshi, Uncle Weylind!"

"You are welcome." Weylind did not smother his grin.

Farrendel released Fieran and Adry, and the two of them surged away, quickly disappearing among the tangle near the ceiling, the shrieks and laughter even louder than before.

"May we come in?" Weylind juggled Emmyth in his grip.

"Yes. If you are sure you wish to brave...this." A hint of a smile playing across his face, Farrendel stepped out of the way.

He was sure. The chaos was better than paperwork.

Weylind entered, closing the door after him. He set Emmyth down in a corner, which was corralled off with a low railing. Toys filled the space, and Emmyth picked one of the stone animals, giving a drool-filled grin.

Farrendel set Louise in the corner as well, then sprawled on the floor, resting his head on one of the cushions that lay scattered around the room.

Weylind set his bag of supplies on the countertop, shoving aside the miscellaneous detritus that had accumulated since the last time this room had been picked up. He dug out the bottles of milk and added them to the cold cupboard until they were needed.

Then he, too, sprawled on the floor. After a moment, he dug through his pockets and found a clump of moss, which he quickly formed into two small balls and stuffed into his ears.

There. That cut some of the noise, at least. He and Farrendel would have to raise their voices if they wished to talk, but they would likely have to do so either way. Farrendel was likely already wearing earplugs of his own.

With a sigh, Farrendel scrubbed a hand over his face.

"Are elven children always this energetic? I know I had a lot of energy when I was young, but I do not remember our home being this...chaotic." With his free hand, he gestured upward, where Fieran and Adry were screeching as they chased each other through the tangle like a pair of incredibly loud squirrels.

"Most elven children are not born with such... frequency." Weylind raised an eyebrow as he glanced at Farrendel. "Most of the time, the older siblings have a chance to grow out of the excessively exuberant stage before the next child comes along."

Granted, Weylind had not exactly followed this either. The twenty years between Ryfon and Brina was a startlingly small gap between elf children. But even at their wildest, Ryfon and Brina had never been quite as riotous as Farrendel and Essie's children.

Farrendel gave a little shrug and lift of his hand, as if to acknowledge that point. Then he flopped one arm over his eyes. "Essie and I want a big family. We do. But I think three...three is enough."

Weylind nodded, taking a moment to glance at Emmyth. He and Louise appeared quite content to wave toys at each other and giggle uproariously.

Overhead, Fieran and Adry raced through the branches, vibrations traveling through the walls and floor with the force of their movements.

So much energy. Just like Farrendel had when he was their age. Back then, Dacha had begun to suspect what magic Farrendel would have, once he was grown.

Weylind waved at the ceiling. "You know the saying, that the more energy elven children have, the stronger their magic. It is said that those with the magic of the ancient kings are especially wild as children."

"It will hardly be a surprise if my children inherit my

magic." Farrendel lifted his arm long enough to peer at Weylind. "It would be more surprising if they did not."

"Perhaps. But this would confirm it." Weylind rested his hand on the floor next to him once again, sending a hint more magic into the treehouse to check that it remained structurally sound. "Your children show all the signs of great magic."

Farrendel and Essie would have their hands full when their children started to come into their magic. Three children, all with the magic of the ancient kings, all coming into their magic within a decade or so of each other, and not a one of them with an ounce of control right at first.

And they thought this was chaotic. Estyra would be fortunate to survive.

A knock sounded on the door before it opened, and Edmund stuck his head inside, his one-year-old daughter gripped in his arms. "May I join the fun?"

Farrendel gave a *Well, another child is not going to add to the chaos* gesture. "You might as well."

Edmund grinned, stepped inside, and closed the door behind him. After crossing the room, he set his daughter down in the corner with Louise and Emmyth. Jayna's rich dark brown hair was the same color as Jalissa's, but her ears were only barely tipped while her facial features were more round and human than elven.

She plopped herself down next to Emmyth, eyed the stone wolf he held, then picked up a different toy, waving it about as if playing.

With a sigh, Edmund sprawled on the floor on the other side of Farrendel. "I should have realized this was where you would be holed up."

"Emmyth wanted the distraction." Weylind eyed Emmyth and Jayna. Emmyth seemed fascinated by the toy Jayna was waving about, following it with his eyes as his grip loosened on his own toy.

"There are plenty of distractions to be had here." Edmund grinned up at the ceiling.

Farrendel just made a noise that was somewhere between a sigh and a groan.

Emmyth's grip slipped on the toy, and he reached for the toy Jayna held. Instead of whining that Emmyth was taking her toy, Jayna relinquished it, then snatched up the toy Emmyth had dropped. Then she toddled across the corner, sitting down well away from the other two.

Weylind scowled, then glared at Edmund. "I do believe your daughter just conned my son out of a toy."

Edmund just sighed and shrugged. "Probably."

"Of all of them, I find your child the most frightening." Weylind kept his expression almost too stern, though Edmund would hear the underlying humor no matter how much he disguised it. "At least Farrendel's children are merely feral."

Farrendel just made another one of those sigh-groans, his arm flopped over his eyes again.

Edmund shrugged, as if he could not really argue the point. Then he nudged Farrendel with an elbow. "I might have a lead on an estate for you."

"An estate?" Weylind glanced between Farrendel and Edmund. This was the first he was hearing of this. "Do not you and Essie already have an Escarlish estate?"

"Yes, but we turned it into a place for warriors from all three kingdoms to heal and find work in a community that understands them." Farrendel pointed upward to his children, running rampant. "My children are not compatible with the goal of a restful sanctuary."

As another peal of cackling rang from above, Weylind could only nod.

"While spacious, Buckmore Cottage was never designed to hold two families trying to share a living space." Farrendel gestured from himself to Edmund.

Edmund shared a look with Farrendel, then glanced past him to Weylind. "With my continued work in Winstead Palace, it made more sense for Jalissa and me to stay. Not to mention that we do not mind hosting elven dignitaries."

"The real reason is that our children were becoming far too destructive in a home that still belongs to the Escarlish royal family, even if it had been temporarily granted to us." Farrendel gave another wave toward the ceiling, his mouth twisting in an expression somewhere between a wry smile and a grimace. "The Escarlish officials were growing concerned about damage to the property."

Weylind raised his eyebrows, though it really should not surprise him. Not with the way Fieran and Adry were currently bouncing about like raccoons that had raided the cookie jar.

"Well, yes, there is that. There are a few rooms that will need re-plastering once you and Essie move out." Edmund folded his hands behind his head. "Nothing that can't be fixed easily enough."

"We have tried to remind Fieran and Adry to be careful but, well..." Farrendel shook his head, heaving another sigh. "As you said, they likely have the magic of the ancient kings running in their veins. They cannot help but run a little wild, and they need the space to do so."

"You will always be welcome here in Ellonahshinel, shashon." Weylind gestured around them, unable to help the smile that twitched his mouth. "It has withstood thousands of years of elf children growing into adulthood and coming into their magic. I do not think even your brood is capable of damaging it."

Edmund gave a snort. "I wouldn't say that too loudly if I were you. They might take it as a challenge."

"Perhaps. But they will not be the first children with the magic of the ancient kings to scramble over these branches. Nor will they be the last." Weylind felt the certainty of that deep in his bones.

Far from dying out, the magic of the ancient kings was reviving, thanks to Essie and Farrendel. Their line would provide a new strength for elves and humans alike.

"Essie and I will continue to split our time between Tarenhiel and Escarland." Farrendel shrugged, then hesitated, his nose wrinkling.

After another moment, Weylind smelled it as well. A whiff of something foul drifted from the area where the three youngest children played. He grimaced. "I changed Emmyth shortly before we came."

"I also recently changed Louise." Farrendel glanced at Edmund.

Edmund sighed and rolled upright. "Probably my child then."

He stepped over the baby barrier, picked up Jayna, then sniffed. His grimace said it all as he held Jayna out, heading for the corner where he had set his bag of baby supplies.

Weylind shifted on the floor, trying to find a more comfortable spot, as he met Farrendel's gaze, lowering his voice. "Are you all right with the move, shashon? I know you do not always enjoy change."

Farrendel stared up at the ceiling for a moment, though his eyes were unfocused rather than following his scrambling, playing children. "I will mourn leaving Buckmore Cottage. Essie and I shared a great deal there.

But Buckmore Cottage was always going to be temporary. We knew we would have to move out eventually."

Once Averett died, though Farrendel did not say that out loud.

Weylind squashed his own pang at the thought. He would dearly miss his friendship with Averett when the Escarlish king passed on.

But that would not be for many years yet. For a human, Averett seemed to be aging remarkably well.

"As lonely as my childhood in Lethorel was, it was the best Dacha could do for me." Farrendel's voice lowered, though it was likely more due to the weight of his memories rather than a wish to keep Edmund from overhearing. "I was free to play all through Lethorel and around the lake without the restrictions that would have been placed on me in Ellonahshinel. I want that for my children."

Weylind nodded, not trusting himself to speak. He had missed a great deal of Farrendel's childhood because of Dacha's decisions. But having seen Farrendel's children —wild with the excess of magical energy inside them—he could not disagree.

"Space will only become more important once they come into their magic. We will need a place for training and practice." Farrendel's mouth quirked. "Both Essie and I can help contain any uncontrolled magic, but there will still be a few explosions. Especially when all three of them are still learning control at the same time."

"Another reason elf children rarely come with such frequency." Weylind tried, but he could not manage to fully stuff his smile behind a glower.

"I am hoping there will be efficiency in training three at once." Farrendel gave a shrug, a wry tilt to his mouth. After a moment's pause, he continued, "Lance and Illyna are also discussing moving farther out of the city for raising their children, and of course Iyrinder and Patience will go wherever Essie and I do. It made sense to look for a large estate that we can divide between us with plenty of space for all the children to run freely."

Now Weylind was picturing a horde of screaming children running back and forth across the Escarlish hills.

Yes, perhaps Escarland would be the most appropriate place for raising a pack of half-elf, half-human children.

Edmund flopped back to the floor on the other side of Farrendel. "All clean. Now as I was saying about the estate…" He trailed off, as if to build suspense.

Farrendel raised his eyebrows. Weylind, too, gave a small huff. Edmund just could not help himself sometimes when it came to his flare for the dramatic.

Edmund grinned at both of them, utterly unrepentant. "I have it on good authority that a very large estate is going to be seized by the crown shortly. Tax evasion. I'm sure the crown would readily sell it at a reasonable price in order to recoup the lost tax revenue as quickly as possible. Even better, it is only a short train ride outside of Aldon but the local village is very quaint at the moment. Exactly what you've been looking for."

Farrendel opened his mouth, then hesitated, as if realizing it would be foolish to ask how Edmund had come by such information. All of them, including Weylind, had learned long ago that it was best not to ask too many questions where Edmund was concerned. Or Jalissa, now that she had taken up her husband's slightly sneaky ways.

A piercing shriek came from above, this one filled more with anger than the laughter of before.

"Dacha! Adry hit me!"

"Fieran hit me first!"

"Did not!"

"Did too!"

"I accidentally bumped you. I didn't hit you."

"Dacha!"

Farrendel sighed, then rolled to a sitting position. "I had better sort out my children."

Edmund gave that *I am so glad the problem is not my child this time* grin and clasped his hands behind his head once again.

Weylind settled more comfortably on the floor. Life was so much easier when he was the uncle, and the children were not his to deal with.

As if on cue, Emmyth bonked himself in the face with his toy and started wailing.

So much for having the quietest child there. Weylind rolled to his feet and went to fetch his son.

FREE BOOK!

Thanks so much for reading *Elf King*! I hope this book didn't completely destroy you or, if it did, that it put you back together again with warm fuzzies in the end! If you loved the book, please consider leaving a review. Reviews help your fellow readers find books that they will love.

A downloadable map and a downloadable list of characters and elvish are available on the Extras page of my website.

If you ever find typos in my books, feel free to message me on social media or send me an email through the Contact Me page of my website.

If you want to learn about all my upcoming releases, get great book recommendations, and see a behind-the-scenes glimpse into the writing process, follow my blog at www.taragrayce.com.

Did you know that if you sign up for my newsletter, you'll receive lots of free goodies? You will receive the free novella *Steal a Swordmaiden's Heart*, which is set in the same world as *Stolen Midsummer Bride* and *Bluebeard and the Outlaw*! This novella is a prequel to *Stolen Midsummer Bride*, and tells the story of how King Theseus of the Court of

Knowledge won the hand of Hippolyta, Queen of the Swordmaidens.

You will also receive the free novellas *The Wild Fae Primrose* (prequel to *Forest of Scarlet*) and *Torn Curtains*, a fantasy Regency Beauty and the Beast retelling.

Sign up for my newsletter now

IN THE MOOD FOR FAE FANTASY?

FOREST OF SCARLET

The fae snatch humans as playthings to torment. The Primrose steals them back.

Vowing that no other family would endure the same fear and pain she felt when her older sister was snatched by the fae, Brigid puts on an empty-headed façade while she rescues humans in the shadowy guise of the Primrose, hero to humans, bane to the fae. Her only regret is that she can't tell the truth to Munch, the young man in the human realm who she's trying very hard not to fall in love with.

Munch has a horrible nickname, an even more terrible full name, and the shadow of his heroic sister and five older brothers to overcome. It's rough being the little brother of the notorious Robin Hood and her merry band. The highlights of his life are the brief visits by Brigid, the messenger girl for the dashing fae hero the Primrose.

When an entire village of humans is snatched by the fae in a single night, Munch jumps at the chance to go to the Fae Realm, pass a message to Brigid and through her to the Primrose, and finally get his chance to be a hero just like all his older siblings.

But the Fae Realm is a dangerous place, especially for a human unbound to a fae or court like Munch. One wrong decision could spell disaster for Munch, Brigid, and the Primrose.

Will this stolen bride's sister and Robin Hood's brother reveal the truth of their hearts before the Fae Realm snatches hope away from them forever?

Loosely inspired by *The Scarlet Pimpernel*, *Forest of Scarlet* is book one in a new fantasy romance / fantasy romantic comedy series of standalones featuring magic libraries, a whimsical and deadly fae realm, and crazy fae hijinks by bestselling author Tara Grayce!

Find the Book on Amazon Today!

ACKNOWLEDGMENTS

Here we are at the final (for real this time!) book in the Elven Alliance series!

I can't thank everyone enough who has made these books possible! My dad, who reads my books and gives me insights so that I don't accidentally incite my readers. My mom, who asks how the writing is going each and every day. My brothers, who inspire Essie's fictional brothers. My sisters-in-law, who are the absolutely BEST sisters! My friends Jill, Paula, and Bri, who celebrate every writing milestone with me! To my writer friends, especially Molly, Morgan, Addy, Savannah, Hannah, and Sierra for all your fangirling and encouragement and support. To Deborah and Mindy for lending your proofreading skills to polishing up my books.

Thanks once again to all of you, the readers, who picked up these books and stuck with this series as it has continued to grow! I hope you enjoyed this final book!

ALSO BY TARA GRAYCE

ELVEN ALLIANCE

Fierce Heart

War Bound

Death Wind

Troll Queen

Pretense

Shield Band

Elf Prince

Heart Bond

Elf King

COURT OF MIDSUMMER MAYHEM

Stolen Midsummer Bride (Prequel)

Forest of Scarlet

Night of Secrets

A VILLAIN'S EVER AFTER

Bluebeard and the Outlaw

PRINCESS BY NIGHT

Lost in Averell

Printed in the USA
CPSIA information can be obtained
at www.ICGtesting.com
LVHW051513110923
757848LV00026B/312/J